CARRY YOU

Beth has always loved to write, a trait probably inherited from her uncle who is a very successful children's author. Languages were her forte at school, but she decided not to go to university after her A levels as she had had enough of education by then. Also she had met her future husband and had started making plans. Her desire to be a writer was put on hold for a decade while she got married and had her two children, but when they were safely at school, or tucked up at night, she started again.

One day a friend suggested that they challenge themselves to do the MoonWalk, and it changed her life. The experience was not just the training and the event itself; it became a pivotal moment in her life that has inspired her over and over again to do more, to achieve more. She realised at the finish line that she could accomplish anything she set out to accomplish, and it gave her renewed belief in herself. She wrote *Carry You* partly in the midst of training (some of it dictated onto her phone while she was actually out walking) and partly a year after the event, by which time she had completed her second MoonWalk.

She now sets herself a new challenge every year. This year she has already faced her paralysing fear of heights and climbed Mount Snowdon. Working full time and writing every spare moment whilst giving her two teenagers the attention they deserve, and distance walking in between is a challenge in itself, but she needs something for next year. Ideas anyone?

BETH THOMAS

Carry You

AVON

This novel is entirely a work of fiction.
The names, characters and incidents portrayed in it are
the work of the author's imagination. Any resemblance to
actual persons, living or dead, events or localities is
entirely coincidental.

AVON

A division of HarperCollins*Publishers*
77–85 Fulham Palace Road,
London W6 8JB

www.harpercollins.co.uk

A Paperback Original 2014

1

Copyright © Beth Thomas 2014

Beth Thomas asserts the moral right to
be identified as the author of this work

A catalogue record for this book is
available from the British Library

ISBN-13: 978-0-00-754481-3

Set in Sabon LT Std by Palimpsest Book Production Ltd, Falkirk, Stirlingshire

Printed and bound in Great Britain by Clays Ltd, St Ives plc

All rights reserved. No part of this publication may be
reproduced, stored in a retrieval system, or transmitted,
in any form or by any means, electronic, mechanical,
photocopying, recording or otherwise, without the prior
permission of the publishers.

MIX
Paper from
responsible sources
FSC
www.fsc.org FSC® C007454

FSC™ is a non-profit international organisation established to promote
the responsible management of the world's forests. Products carrying the
FSC label are independently certified to assure consumers that they come
from forests that are managed to meet the social, economic and
ecological needs of present and future generations,
and other controlled sources.

Find out more about HarperCollins and the environment at
www.harpercollins.co.uk/green

Acknowledgements

There are so many people who deserve a mention here because of their courageous and moving battles with cancer. I won't name anyone, but two incredible ladies in particular recently have filled me with awe and admiration. To have that much dignity and cheer whilst fighting for your life is a lesson to anyone who complains about traffic. You know who you are.

I need to say a huge thank you to the numerous people who walked with me during the writing of this book, in particular Sandie Hines, Lynne Sheridan and Richard Carbin, who covered the most miles.

Many many thanks also to Jason Danger Mckeen for the detailed information about sharks and marathons. Interesting hobbies . . .

Thank you to everyone who read this story and gave me feedback and encouragement as it came along, most notably my fab sister Annika Dann; and Suzanne Allen and Tracey Owen. You are truly the best sister and friends a woman who wrote a book about walking could ask for.

And finally thanks must go to the lovely Laura Morris and Lydia Newhouse, for sticking with me. I am so very grateful to both of you.

For my Beano. Are you still doing all your walking?

ONE

Daisy Mack
is reclining on the sofa eating Jaffa Cakes watching Hugh Grant punch Colin Firth. Could life get any better?

> **Jenny Martin**   Ever thought about going out occasionally? Life can get a LOT better.
>
> **Daisy Mack**   Thanks Jen. Great tip.
>
> **Nat 'Wiggy' Nicholson**   Aw Daze that sounds miserable. Want me to come over?
>
> **Daisy Mack**   Thanks Nat, but it's OK. Gonna get an early night. ☺
>
> **Georgia Ling**   Hope your ok hun xx

Ah, the fight scene in *Bridget Jones's Diary*. This calls for another cake, to maximise the enjoyment. I pull the edges of my dressing gown round me a bit more tightly and snuggle down further into my duvet. Doesn't matter how many times I've seen this, it always cheers me up. Well, it makes me smile, anyway, which in my life is as close as I'm going to get to actual cheer. It's not the sight of two inept men fighting like nine-year-old girls

1

who don't know how to fight that makes me smile. It's the fact that there are two men left in the world to fight over one woman. I know, I know, it's not real, it's just fiction. But that's the thing with fiction – anything can happen. Boys turn out to be wizards; vampires fall in love with human schoolgirls; husbands travel through time; men hit each other with dustbin lids.

I dunk my Jaffa Cake into my hot chocolate as I work hard on suspending my disbelief for a bit longer. It's an effort but so worthwhile. The disbelief thing, I mean. Not the dunking; that's no effort at all. Dunking these delightful spongy confections in hot chocolate is one of God's best and yet simplest ideas. If you get it right, the cakey bit soaks up hot chocolate without falling apart, and the chocolate and orange bit on the top goes all warm and soft, so they just melt in your mouth. Too long in the heat, though, and it's gooey mush at the bottom of the mug. Timing is everything; it's a lot like life. Ooh, that sounds good.

Daisy Mack
is dunking Jaffa Cakes in hot chocolate. The timing is everything: it's a lot like life.

My laptop makes an electronic popping sound, and I glance down. It's an instant message from my best friend Abby.

Abby Marcus   Hey, what you doing?

Oh God. Quickly I grab my mobile phone on the sofa next to me and switch it off, dropping it back on the cushion. But I'm still not safe. I reach up to the landline on the wall next to me and break through the dust and cobwebs on the handset. Abby is the only actual human dogged enough to ring it, and she will when she finds my mobile switched off. I press the 'Call' button so the dialling tone is audible. Colin lays Hugh out on the road with one good punch. Colin and Hugh really aren't very good names for two drop-dead-gorgeous, Hollywood A-list actors, are they? They sound more like a pair of nerdy IT geeks in specs. It's not exactly Brad and Matt.

My laptop pops again.

Abby Marcus   Just tried to ring you but mobile on voicemail and landline engaged. Are you actually talking to another human being???????
Daisy Mack   Hey! Yeah, on phone. Speak later x
Abby Marcus   No, speak now. Wanna go out?
Daisy Mack   Can't. Am tucked up in PJs, and on phone. X

The landline phone is starting to make that multi-tonal alarm noise that lets you know when you've accidentally left it off the hook. I've heard it so many times these past few weeks, nee-nawing away in the background like an emergency siren, it's become the sound track to my life. I end the 'call', then start another one immediately. Better actually make a call now, I suppose; guilt is

3

encroaching. I press 4 on the memory list and it connects me through to Oxfam, where I make a ten-pound donation. Immediately I feel better. I genuinely am in my PJs, and on the phone, so I have not lied to my best friend; and now I've made a donation to charity. I'm a saint.

Pop.

Abby Marcus It's half past two in the afternoon.

I love Abby. I do. She doesn't take any crap. Sometimes I wish she would. Just once or twice. Actually, I don't think there's anything wrong with being in your PJs on a Sunday afternoon, enjoying a film with a Jaffa Cake or two. And if I stare hard enough at the telly and maintain the suspension of my disbelief – and move my head so the armchair is blocking the view – I can't even see the three empty McVitie's boxes on the floor. If no one saw me eat them, no one will ever know.

Abby Marcus Are you eating Jaffa Cakes?
Daisy Mack Just a couple. Watching a film. See you tomorrow. X
Abby Marcus No, now. Come on, come out for a walk.

Oh God. A walk. I so don't want to go out for a walk. It's bloody miserable weather today, which is exactly why I'm bundled up on my sofa with Col and Hugh, and the world's best ever dressing gown, instead of tramping the streets in freezing fog.

Daisy Mack Too cold. X

I, on the other hand, am toasty warm, and very snuggly.
I'm staying put.

Abby Marcus Get your arse off your sofa and
look out the window.
Daisy Mack OK, OK, I'm up.
Abby Marcus No you're not you're still typing.
Come on Daze, do it.

Abby really is a fantastic friend. She's the best. So
caring, so thoughtful. So . . . tenacious. Bridget is embarrassing herself at a party now. Not so keen on this bit.

Daisy Mack OK, horrid winter's afternoon.
Definitely not walking weather. What's your
point?
Abby Marcus It's the 11th of April.

Oh, God, yes, of course it is. How did I forget that?
I was still stuck in November for some reason. Well,
not for *some* reason. I know the reason. Everything
stopped for me in November, and I often forget that for
other people time has carried on ticking, events have kept
occurring, and everyone else has continued to experience
things.

I suppose I'd better actually look out of the window
then. She'll never shut up otherwise. She does love to
talk, Abby. She's a driving instructor and her life is one
long hilarious series of adventures, with dual control

pedals. They should make a film about it. It could be called, I don't know, *Driving Games*, or *Driving Down*, or, no, no, wait: *Drive Hard*. Brilliant.

I move the laptop off my lap and put it carefully down on the sofa next to my mobile phone, then push the duvet back, pull my feet up and roll unsteadily sideways onto my knees. I let my face drop into the fabric of the back of the sofa. Feel a bit dizzy suddenly. I grip the back of the sofa for a few seconds until I'm steady, then turn myself round slowly so my back is to the telly and I am facing the closed curtains behind the sofa. I wonder why Abby is so desperate to get me to look outside. I reach out and pull the curtain back a crack and am instantly blinded by the bright sunshine streaming in. My pupils practically scream out in agony and immediately shrink to the size of single atoms, which is still not small enough to stop the searing white-hot rays from burning into my retinas, leaving a trail of blackened, scorched tissue and permanent damage. I squint a bit and shield my eyes with my hand. That's better.

'Open the bloody door, you numpty!' a cheerful voice shouts, and I make out at last that it's Abby herself, waving on the lawn.

'Oh my God, Daisy, look at the state of this place!' she says as she strides purposefully in a few seconds later. She glances quickly around, then throws me a sidelong look. 'Daze, it's very smelly in here.' I'm retreating to the comfort of the sofa and my duvet, while Abby moves around my darkened living room, scooping up the McVitie's boxes, as well as one or two Twix wrappers, dirty coffee cups, tissues and, embarrassingly, a half-eaten cheesecake with hardened edges that I think was from yesterday.

'One or two Jaffa Cakes you said,' she's muttering as she cleans. 'God, have you been on that sofa all weekend? Have you actually had any nutrition at all since Friday lunch time?'

I'm not answering. It's all rhetorical anyway. She knows what I'm like. Plus at this moment Bridget is running through the streets in her underpants and cardigan, about to snog Colin. I snogged someone called Colin once. Not a very enjoyable experience. We both had braces at the time and some kind of unpleasant electromagnetic force was caused by the presence of all the steel.

'Are you even listening to me?' Abby's voice breaks into my thoughts and I make my eyeballs rotate towards her blurry shape. She's standing in the middle of the floor, hands on hips, frowning hard.

'Oh, yeah, course I am. I'm sorry, Abs.'

She cocks her head. 'So what are you sorry for?'

I shake my head and shrug. 'You know. All this.' I move my hand generally in the direction of the world. 'I'm so hopeless.'

A small beam of sunshine breaks through the thunder clouds on Abby's face, and she moves over to where I'm huddled. 'No, Daze, you're not hopeless. You're depressed, disorganised, lost, confused and . . . well, a bit malodorous.' She sits down on the sofa by my feet, picks them both up by the socks and lays them gently in her own lap. 'But you're not hopeless. You have hope. We always have hope, don't we?' She rubs my shin affectionately.

7

'And you've got me. I mean seriously, what more could you possibly need?'

Ah, she really is great. I make my face smile because I know it's what she's hoping to see, but I'm still not feeling the smile brewing up from inside me. I'm not sure if I'll ever get that back. 'Abby, you're the best friend a girl in this mess could possibly want. Or be lucky enough to have. I don't deserve you.'

'You're so right. Now get upstairs, get your teeth cleaned and get some trainers on. We are going for that walk. You've got ten minutes.'

I haven't always been one of life's smelly, shambling drop-outs. As I trudge reluctantly upstairs, my knuckles practically dragging on the carpet, one of the framed photos on the wall catches my eye, and for a moment the image there expands and brightens and fills every molecule of my mind and all the spaces in between. It's me and my sister, Naomi, shoulder to shoulder, laughing hysterically at my graduation party. I can almost hear us, screaming drunkenly, the sounds of chatter and music from the party loud in the background, a crowd of friends and family mingling, enjoying themselves, having a fantastic night. Our heads are tilted towards each other, foreheads almost touching. I must have been twenty-one, Naomi about twenty-three, and we had our whole lives ahead of us, with nothing but fun, success and joy to look forward to. Abruptly the image greys out and shrinks back, the party noises fade away, and once again I am left floundering in silent desolation, the contrast of me then and me now almost knocking me to the floor.

It takes a bit longer than ten minutes for me to get

ready. More like forty in the end, mostly because I didn't have any clean clothes. Or partly because of that, anyway. It was an issue for a while. But also I was moving pretty slowly because I'm so not motivated to get myself ready for a walk, or a drive, or a skip – or any kind of inter-action with the outside.

'Come *on*, Daisy!' Abby shouts up from the hallway. I pretend I can't hear, and continue listlessly kicking the piles of clothes heaped around my bedroom floor. Eventually I manage to disinter a reasonably clean yellow tee shirt with a big round smiley on the front and match it with some old tracksuit bottoms that were screwed up on the floor of my wardrobe. They've got a couple of lilac paint splashes on them. Probably from when I was painting in here, all those months ago.

'*Beckham's arse, Daisy, what the hell are you doing up there?*'

Oop. Right. 'OK, OK, I'm coming now.'

When I come back down the stairs, Abs is standing in my hallway holding out a pair of old trainers she's unearthed from the hall cupboard. She's holding them out to me with both hands and with the light behind her she reminds me so powerfully of my mum, impatiently urging me to get my shoes on when I was about five, that it takes my breath away. Then she moves and her face comes back into the light. I carry on slowly down the stairs.

'Here you go,' she says, thrusting the shoes at me. 'Get them on.'

The trainers don't look familiar at all. They're white with a very nice metallic lilac stripe down the side, and close up it's obvious that they're not an old pair that Abby has unearthed. They look brand new. I must say it's a relief to see that, although I'm currently failing at life, I've still had the presence of mind at some point to go out and buy myself a pair of good trainers. I'm picturing myself, making a mental list of what I needed in town: bread, milk, Jaffa Cakes, nice trainers, toilet roll, soap. Odd that I don't remember doing it, but it wouldn't be the first thing I've forgotten doing. Or forgotten to do. Or just plain forgotten. I take the trainers and sit on the bottom stair to put them on. Apparently I have very good taste in trainers. They're incredibly light and spongy, and so comfortable that when I stand up I feel like I've forgotten to put anything on my feet. I glance down quickly but no, there they are, gleaming away at the bottom of my legs.

Abby is peering at me a bit oddly, her eyebrows lifted expectantly. It makes me think I've forgotten something else, so I check discreetly from my neck down, but it seems every item of clothing is in place. 'I'm ready,' I say, just in case she's thinking I'm about to go and get some leg warmers on.

'Don't you want to, I don't know, put some make-up on, or something?' She peers at me from her flawless face and Barbie eyes.

'Oh.' I think about that for a moment. She's obviously worried that I might scare children and old people as I tramp round the neighbourhood, arms swinging, in my baggy, paint-spattered outfit, glowing trainers and pasty face. I shrug. 'Nah.'

'Ohhh-kaaay.' She opens the front door and the

10

whiteness of the outside makes me blink rapidly. Good job I didn't bother to get all mascara-ed up. 'Let's do this,' she says, in an exaggeratedly dramatic American accent, then ushers me outside like a primary school teacher.

As we walk up the path to the pavement, I accidentally catch a glimpse of the 'For Sale' sign that's still stuck in the front lawn, and quickly avert my eyes. Doesn't matter how hard I try not to see it, it still punches me in the face every time I walk past. Maybe it's because it's bright blue, white and yellow and the size of Mum's dining table. And now there's red on it too, of course, with the arrival of the little 'Sold' sign that has been slapped on at what no doubt someone thought was a jaunty angle over the original wording. I catch sight of Abby glancing at it, then looking at me, but I'm making no comment. She knows what's what already.

After we've been walking for about seventy-five seconds, we've completely filled each other in on what we've been doing over the weekend. That is, Abs has told me about the club she was in last night and the sleazy fifty-year-old guy who was there rocking his corduroy trousers and bushy sideburns. Why, I wonder, does brown corduroy appeal only to those over fifty? On second thoughts, why does it appeal to anyone at all, ever? It must be the single most drab, unattractive substance known to man.

She's glancing at me repeatedly. I mean, more frequently than someone just out for a stroll with someone. It's as if she's worried I'm going to spontaneously combust in

11

a minute. 'What is it?' I say eventually, after discreetly patting myself down.

'Well, aren't you even going to ask about the trainers?'

I glance down at the glowing trainers. 'Um, yeah,' I say, nodding vaguely, 'I was kind of thinking about them. I didn't even know I had any like these.'

'No, you haven't. They're mine.'

I nod. That explains it then. It did seem a bit weird that I'm pretty much unable to function on any level except the most basic – foraging for chocolate cake, keeping myself sheltered, selecting DVDs – but still managing to buy trainers. 'Right. I thought it was odd that I'd bought them.'

'Odd? When you haven't been out of the house for more than a few minutes for weeks?'

'Yeah. Exactly.'

'Daze, how could you have thought they were yours, when you have no memory of buying them?'

'Um, yeah, that is odd too. I suppose I thought I'd just forgotten buying them.'

Her eyes widen further. 'Oh dear,' she says, in exactly the same way as Mrs Matthews did, when I was eight and had a childish accident in the toy cupboard.

'What does that mean?'

She stops walking, turns to face me and takes both my arms. 'Daze, come on. You're in a state. No, don't shrug, we both know it's true and we both also know that it does matter, even though you're trying to convince yourself that it doesn't. I'm worried about you. Seriously, I am.'

'Ah, Abs. You don't need to. I'm fine.'

She nods, exaggeratedly. 'Oh, yeah, sure you are. Spending days on the sofa? Living on Jaffa Cakes? This whole "trainer" thing, for God's sake?'

'The orangey bit makes one of my five a day.'

Her chest jerks with a tiny laugh. 'No, Daze, it doesn't. You . . .' She stops and shakes her head. 'You're . . . You're killing yourself.'

'Oh what crap.'

'All right, maybe it's a bit of an exaggeration. But if you carry on like this, you *will* get rickets. Or scurvy.' She pauses. 'Or you know, zits. At the very least.'

I'm smiling again, making my lips curve up. 'Zits are the least of my worries, Abs.'

'I know that, but you need to start somewhere. Your appearance seems like a good place. I've been talking to Suzanne on Facebook, and when I told her what's been going on, she was as worried as I am. And she's come up with a really good idea. She suggested that . . .'

Wow, Suzanne Allen. I haven't heard from her for a while. Suze and I used to work together, years ago when I first left school. It was some kind of terrible call centre, selling pet and home insurance. We had to make disastrous phone call after disastrous phone call, being roundly abused and insulted by virtually everyone. Hard to imagine really how we managed to forge any kind of friendship, as there was absolutely no conversation permitted during call hours. Or tea breaks. Even toilet breaks were closely monitored.

'. . . so I've signed us up. What do you think?'

Abby looks excited. She's grinning at me with her whole face, waiting for me to react to something she's just said. Quickly I cast my mind back a few seconds and try to re-hear whatever it was. Oh, there's a lovely thick band of daffodils all the way along the grass verge at the side of the road, waving gently in the breeze, their little yellow bells knocking together. Of course, it's April already. I keep forgetting.

'Daze?'

'Yeah, sorry, Abs, I was just thinking about . . .' She raises her eyebrows. 'Doesn't matter. Can you just say it again, please?'

She stares at me a moment, lips pressed together. Then she says something that completely changes my life. 'Daze,' she says, grinning in spite of herself, 'I've signed us up to do a MoonWalk.'

TWO

Daisy Mack
is feeling a little perturbed. Is this a good sign?

   Lou Stephens   Depends what it's about!

   Jenny Martin   Can perturbation ever be good?

   Suzanne Allen   Yes, that is definitely good. Perturb away – it will help.

   Daisy Mack   Great, thanks Suze. Now I know it's good to be perturbed, I am less perturbed. Is this a paradox?

   Georgia Ling   Everything ok hun? xx

Five months ago, my mum died. It was her second outing into breast cancer, and unfortunately it didn't go as well as the first. But isn't that always the way with sequels – never as good as the original, are they? Look at *Bridget Jones: The Edge of Reason*. Still a great film, don't get me wrong. Col and Hugh are still geeky sex gods, they still fight like inept girls and Bridge gets to snog both of them again. But . . . We've seen it before, haven't we? We know she's hopeless, and can't stop smoking and wishes she was thinner. And as much as we love her, in the end we'd have preferred to watch the first film again. It had a much better ending.

I'm watching *Love Actually* in my silky dressing gown now. Second time today. I'm supposed to be cleaning. Better get on with it, I suppose.

Daisy Mack
Gloves, actually.

> **Suzanne Allen** OK, I'm deciphering that to mean you're cleaning.
> **Daisy Mack** Wow, you're good!
> **Suzanne Allen** Elementary. It's spring so they're not woollen gloves. You don't own a motorbike. You don't like gardening. You don't work with radioactive material or infectious diseases. Oh, and puppets scare you. Ergo, cleaning. Well done! X
> **Daisy Mack** Mind = blown.

There, that's that done. Abby's coming round in about half an hour so I may have to finish the film off later. She wants to talk about the MoonWalk. When she told me she'd signed me up for that, I have to say I panicked.

'Shit, Abby, you haven't!' I yelled. 'I can't do it! I failed science, remember? And I hate heights, and fast things. Remember Alton Towers? I nearly passed out on that Nemesis thing. And that's only, like, a hundred feet off the ground. I can't go ten million miles up, I'll die! And look at me – I'm so unfit, you said so yourself. I'll never get through the training programme . . .'

I stopped there because she was already laughing. I mean really, really laughing. She actually bent over and put her hands on her knees. Then she stood up, took a deep breath, looked at my face and started laughing all over again.

Turns out she didn't actually mean a walk on the moon. Apparently they don't offer that to members of the public. Well, how was I supposed to know?

'It's a night-time walk, Daze,' she said, wiping her eyes.

'Huh?'

'It's called the MoonWalk because it's at night. It's a twenty-six-mile walk round London, starting at midnight, for charity. Nothing to do with Michael Jackson, and we don't have to walk backwards.' Her face calmed at this point and her smile faded. 'It's for breast cancer.'

Which meant of course that I couldn't say no. I don't think Abs would have let me say no even if it had been for Homeless Llama relief, or something. Anyway, how hard can it be? It's only walking.

Back on the sofa now, my instant messenger pops.

Abby Marcus All right you, I'm leaving now. Get off your computer and clean up a bit. This is important.

How did she know I was on my computer? I might have been doing the hoovering.

Abby Marcus Don't try and convince yourself that you might not have got that message. I can see your name on my screen and it says you're online. You're always online. Get offline NOW.
Daisy Mack OK, I'm going . . .

17

She wants to talk to me about training today. Apparently she's got a plan. No doubt it will involve a lot of walking. I'm thinking, the walk itself is just under two months away, on May 30th, so we should get a couple of good walks in a week or so beforehand. No need to go mad. I've been walking for years – piece of cake. I can do it almost without thinking now. I glance at the film. Hugh has just seen Billy Bob Thornton trying to kiss Nathalie. Ooh, he's mad about that.

Abby Marcus *Get offline, numpty!*

I close my laptop and put it down on the sofa, then pause the film on Liam Neeson's face. Abby's right, I don't really have time for this any more. Time is running out.

I have already picked up all the rubbish and dirty crockery from the living room floor, so it looks a lot better than when Abby arrived yesterday. And I'm dressed, in jeans and a clean-ish hoodie, so she won't hassle me. Not that she judges me, I know she doesn't. She's been so fantastic since Mum died, I don't know what I would have done without her. For the first couple of days I just lay on the sofa under a blanket and Abs stayed, rubbing my back, bringing me food and drink, stroking my head. Nagging, eventually. It's what she does best, love her. Get out of bed, change your clothes, clean your teeth, all that. Of course, I didn't really have the luxury of lying prostrate with grief for very long. Mum's husband, Graham, my stepdad, ill with emphysema, still relied on me then to look after him, which

Abby knew. He of course was grieving too and didn't come out of his room for a week, so could have starved or shrivelled up to a dry old husk in there for all I knew. I was so consumed by my own wretchedness, I didn't even think about him. I was unbelievably selfish, and Abby let me be. She took over the job of looking after Graham until I felt up to it again. And then two months ago, three months after Mum, Graham died too. As if he'd looked at living without her, given it a try, but didn't like it. Nah, it's not for me, he thought, and jacked it all in.

Oh, she's here.

'Well, this looks a lot better,' she says when I let her in. She walks around the room like Mary Poppins, checking the floor for wrappers, looking between the chairs for tell-tale socks or plates. Then she gives a Poppins-esque nod. 'Well done.'

'Do I get a treat?'

'Shut up.'

'Right.'

'OK. Sit down.' I do. It's like a kind of mind control thing she's got. She says sit, I sit. She says clean up, I clean up. She says we're walking twenty-six miles round London during the night, I'll even do that. I am powerless against her penetrating stare and firmly set jaw. I think she can speak to snakes too. She's rummaging through her bag now, and eventually pulls out a piece of folded-up paper, which she spreads out on her lap. 'Daze, we have got our work cut out for us.'

I nod. 'Right. Uh-huh. Yes. Sure. What do you mean?'

'I mean the guidance says that to walk a marathon it

19

takes at least twelve weeks' training. We have seven. It's going to be tough, but it's do-able.'

Twelve weeks' training! For *walking*? Who writes these guidance things? Some eighty-year-old granny with arthritic ankles? No, no, actually I bet it's the trainer manufacturers. Of course. They're onto a winner there. Put it out that walking twenty-six miles will require three months' training, national panic ensues, trainer sales hit the roof. Classic herd mentality at play. They must think we're such brainless idiots who can't think for ourselves, while they rub their hands together and count their ill-gotten gains. They didn't reckon on me though: I see straight through their wicked plans.

'OK,' I say, nodding.

Abs looks up from the sheet of paper on her lap and eyes me seriously. 'But before we start training,' she says ominously, 'there's something else we need to tackle.' She raises her eyebrows, apparently waiting for me to fill in the missing blank. I don't want to though. I'd quite like that particular blank to stay missing. I look away quickly before her eyes compel me to do her bidding, but I'm just a fraction of a second too late. 'Daisy,' she says, as if she's trying to get me to own up to smashing something. 'You know what I'm talking about.'

I do. She's right. Of course. As if to reinforce the message – as if it needed reinforcing – I catch a brief glimpse of the 'For Sale' sign through the window, the small 'Sold' panel in its centre drawing the eye like a blood stain. The house is sold. I have to move out by Friday. It's Monday.

'Yes,' I say quietly.

'Yes,' she agrees, more forcefully.

But that's easy for her to say. It's not her that's got to do it. And it's a complicated business. She doesn't understand that you can't simply pack all your belongings away and move out; there are things that need to be done first. I mean, I haven't got any of the stuff I'll need – cardboard boxes, marker pens, tape . . .

'I've got a load of boxes, pens and tape in the car,' she says helpfully.

'Oh that's helpful. Thanks.'

'Right. Let's do this.' She slaps her hands on her thighs and stands up. 'I'll get the bits from the car, you get upstairs and start sorting out your stuff.' She performs an elaborate comedy 'I'm-about-to-dash-off' move, swinging one arm and leg backwards across herself, holds it, then trudges off slowly.

I raise myself off the sofa, feeling as if there are suddenly a million tons of air pressing down on me. It makes moving around unimaginably difficult.

'What the hell are you still doing standing there?'

Ah, she's back already, staggering into the room under a giant stack of flat cardboard boxes. She's peering at me round the side of them, and even though more than half her face is obscured by 'Young's Frozen Fish', she still manages to look disapproving.

'Get upstairs and start getting your clothes out.'

'OK.'

When Mum and Graham both got so ill at the same time, Naomi and I decided that I would move back in with them, to help care for them both. Of course it should be me; Naomi was living in domestic bliss with Russell,

21

I was sharing a rented house with three other girls. It made sense. I packed my stuff up into boxes then and made myself at home in my mum's spare room. It was only ever a temporary set-up, but it was horrific knowing it was only temporary. Knowing why it was only temporary.

Upstairs in my room I start pulling all my clothes out of the drawers and wardrobe, but most of them are on the floor so I just scoop them up and dump them on the bed. Then I stare at them. Then I sink down onto the edge of the bed. There isn't much there, not really, not for three years of my life. Tee shirts, jeans, socks, pants. Swimming costume. Not that the length of time you live somewhere should have any bearing on how many clothes you have. But three years I've been here, and all I'm taking with me are a couple of boxes of clothes and some toiletries.

That's not to say I wouldn't like to take more. Right here on the dressing table is a gorgeous photo of the whole family – Mum and Graham and all of their combined children – on their wedding day. I'd love to take that with me, but I can't. I'm not allowed. I pick it up and move it reverentially towards the pile of clothes on the bed, holding it as if it were a photo of Elvis reading *The Times* on the tube in 2001. Perhaps I could just squeeze it in, between my knickers? Who would ever know? But then the thought of my stepbrother Darren's face in between my knickers makes my lip curl and I replace the picture on the dresser. It's just not worth it.

A few minutes later Abs appears with a newly three-dimensional box in each hand and we spend the next hour or so filling them with my things and carrying them out to her car, then starting again. There are a few things downstairs too that are mine – laptop, some CDs, all my DVDs – and once they're in, and the bathroom is cleared, we're done.

'That was quick,' I say, as we stand together in the hallway. She squeezes my arm, and I look at her gratefully. Then I realise that she's not squeezing my arm to say, 'I know, this is really hard, but I'm here for you, my friend, and I will help you get through it.' This particular arm-squeeze means

'We're not done yet, Daze.'

Turns out she thinks we need to clean the entire place, really thoroughly, before I quit it forever. She says it will put me in a good light. She says I owe it to my mum. She says I can't ever let anyone find out what a complete and utter disgusting slob I've been for the past few months.

'Oh my God, Daze, that girl is such a terrible slob,' Naomi's scandalised voice comes back to me, in a conversation we had about a girl called Heidi who flat-shared with her for a while a few years ago. 'There's always at least two pairs of shoes left in the hallway, letters on the bread bin, a knife in the washing-up bowl, and she never puts her jacket away in the cupboard. Always leaves it on the sofa!'

'Oh for fuck's sake.' I was as appalled as her at these disgusting character flaws. 'What does she expect to happen to it there? The cleaning fairy will put it away?'

'Huh, yeah, no doubt. I'm not sure how much more I can stand. May have to burn it.'

'Bring it on!'

Somewhere along the road, my exacting standards for cleanliness have taken a bit of a nosedive. 'You're not a disgusting slob,' Abs says now, 'but people will think you are when they see . . .' she indicates the entire house with a wide sweep of her arm '. . . this.'

Twenty minutes later I know she's right when I find what once was either a chocolate Hobnob or lasagne in a mottled beige arc by the dining room door. I glance over at Abs, currently positioned rump-end towards me as she scrubs at some other disgusting bit of filth on the carpet, and I feel glad that she can't see the disgusting bit of filth over here. Because I'm definitely going to keep my dignity as long as she doesn't see this particular stain. The fact that she's already seen the mouldy coffee cups, the stale pizza crusts, the coffee spills and the unopened post will have no bearing on her opinion of me.

Actually, knowing Abs, it won't.

I met Abby just over four years ago in a queue in Tesco. It's an electrifying story. I only had a basketful of items, although I might have had one or two more than ten items in there. It's a possibility; they were all small. They all fitted in the basket, so I definitely qualified to go down the basket queue. I was perfectly justified. Abs was behind me with a carton of orange juice and a bottle of tequila and some limes. Goodness knows what she was up to with that strange combination. Anyway, it was all going very well – the person in front of the person in front of me had paid and left; the person in front of me put his basket on the little shelf thing to unload it; and the rest of us all shuffled forward silently without

24

making eye contact with anyone or actually looking at anything. Eventually the man in front of me took his dog biscuits and meal for one and left, and I moved forward and unloaded my basket onto the conveyor belt. Then suddenly, it all kicked off. Quick as a flash, the bespectacled boy behind the till anxiously eyed my line of shopping and didn't start swiping it.

'Um, sorry, I think you've got, um, got more than, er, ten, yeah, ten items there,' he nervously stammered out.

I raised my eyebrows and he flinched. His name was Spencer, I remember that. I hadn't had a good day so far – I'd had to take Mum to the hospital that morning for some reason, can't remember what it was that day – and I think Spencer could tell in my eyebrows that things for him had suddenly taken a downward turn. 'And?' I said, not moving.

A smile appeared on his face the way you sometimes catch a fleeting flash of sun reflected on someone's glasses across the street. Then it disappeared. 'Well, um, this is the ten items queue . . .'

His voice tailed off as I started shaking my head. 'No it isn't,' I said confidently. Actually I said it a lot more confidently than I really felt. I was *fairly* sure the sign said 'Baskets Only', but at this point I suddenly experienced a lurch of fear dropping in my belly. The queue behind me was starting to shift its weight from foot to foot and heft baskets of shopping around needlessly. I sensed that it wouldn't be long before they were dropping their baguettes in favour of pitchforks and lanterns and driving me out of town. Mentally I picked up a cudgel, squared my shoulders and turned round slowly and threateningly to face the restless villagers. In actual fact I was hunching a bit while checking behind me nervously. 'I think you'll find,' I cringed, 'that this is the "Basket Only" queue.'

Spencer gave the fleeting glimpse of teeth again, only this time with less conviction. 'Noooo . . .' he started, but then there was a rustling sound and a low, menacing voice behind me said,

'Some time today.'

The queue shuffled its feet in agreement and the hairs on the back of my neck stood up. My animal instincts were sensing approaching danger, and I felt trapped, like cornered prey. I glanced around me nervously, assessing my exit possibilities, but there wasn't much choice. Walk slowly and with dignity, head high, towards the exit; or leg it? Oh but I really didn't want to do that. Maybe I had another option. Maybe I could stand my ground, have the courage of my convictions, like Mum had always told me. 'Have the courage of your convictions, Daisy Duck,' she said. 'Stand up for what you believe in, be strong, no matter what anyone else thinks.' I know, it's incredible isn't it? Still calling me Daisy Duck well into my adulthood.

'I will, Mum,' I thought to myself fervently now, pressing my lips together. 'I'll do it for you.'

'Pardon?' said Spencer.

'Huh? Oh, no, nothing. Um . . .'

I was stalling and he knew it. One of us was going to have to concede, and we were both starting to believe that it was going to be me.

'You'll have to . . . move your things,' he said very quietly, avoiding eye contact at all costs. 'You need to use the trolley tills.'

I lowered my head towards him. He visibly flinched. 'Spencer,' I said, using my mum's voice that was in my head, 'you don't honestly think it's going to take less time for me to pack all these things back into this basket, than it would for you to run them quickly through the till, do you?'

'Um,' Spencer began helplessly, doing an 'I-don't-make-the-rules' face, 'actually . . .'

'I'll take half the items,' the girl behind me – Abby, it turned out – piped up suddenly at this point. Spencer and I exchanged a glance, then turned in unison to look at her. She was dark haired – it was almost blue-black – and wearing a denim mini skirt, stripey footless tights and flip-flops. As we stared at her, she scooped roughly half of my things back down the conveyor towards her, then stuck the 'Next customer please' sign in the middle. 'Pay me back later,' she said to me, and winked. Actually winked, perfectly, without accidentally closing both eyes or screwing up her mouth or grimacing in some other gauche way. I thought that was so incredibly cool.

'Christ, it was like a stand-off between the country's two biggest jessies,' she said in the car park a few minutes later. 'Not so much which one of you was going to hold out the longest, more like a race to see who was going to cry first. I couldn't stand to watch it continue for another second.'

And we've been friends ever since.

OK, so maybe it's not a very good story. No actual violence and mayhem. No bloodshed. Not even a raised voice. But the potential was there. Simmering.

Daisy Mack

On my knees like Cinderella. Literally and figuratively.

    Georgia Ling OMG that's a big clean lol! xoxo

    Nat 'Wiggy' Nicholson come and do mine after xx

'Right,' Abs says now, and levers herself back onto her feet. She puts her hands on her hips and raises her eyebrows. I know exactly what that means. It's a gesture I've seen Abby do countless times in the last four years, usually when she's trying to get me to do something I'm not one hundred percent keen on. Or focused on. One or the other. Basically it means 'Come on, Daisy, sort yourself out, now is the time to face the thing you've got to do and there's no point trying to argue with me because I won't stand for any nonsense.' Whenever I see her hands go to her hips, I get a resigned feeling, like Pavlov's dog getting hungry when the bell rings. Or was it ringing the bell when it was hungry? No, that wasn't it. That was probably rats, wasn't it? Going round exciting mazes and over ramps to get a treat. I got lost in a maze once. Naomi told me to keep on turning left every time I came to a junction but it didn't work. I went round and round in circles for over half an hour before Mum shouted to me over the fences to stop being such an idiot and walk towards her.

'Daze,' Abs says, using the particular tone of voice that goes with the gesture.

'Yeah, yeah, I know.' I push myself up and stand, ready to move on to the next dirty mark or pile of crap, but when I look round I see that there aren't any more dirty marks, or piles of crap to be dealt with. While I've been listlessly rubbing away at the chocolate Hobnob/lasagne mark, Abs has done all the rest of the cleaning. Which means . . .

'Time to go,' she says softly.

So. This is it. We take our cloths and the bowl of warm water solemnly back to the kitchen and dump everything in the sink. The kitchen looks amazing – all the sides are clear and wiped and the floor is spotless. I can't remember the last time I saw it looking this good. Some time in the early part of last year, I expect. I'm walking around it slowly, running my hand along the sides, touching the knobs on the hob, stroking the dent on the fridge door where Mum threw a tin of custard powder at Graham one Christmas. This is the spot where I was standing when she told everyone about the cancer coming back. Over there on the windowsill was the plant I bought her for Mother's Day a couple of years ago. I think it's died now. Actually I have no idea where it is. One minute it was there, dropping brown leaves and generally shrivelling up; next minute it was gone. When was that? Must be at least a week ago. I can't believe I let that plant die. I watched it, every day, curling up, needing my attention, crying out for help to relieve its suffering, and yet I did nothing. I didn't even try. Maybe there was something I could have done. Maybe I could have saved it, if I'd only been a bit more . . . a bit more . . . careful.

Inexplicably, I'm starting to cry, standing there in Mum's kitchen, staring at the empty spot where a dying plant used to stand. It starts with an ache in my throat and heat in my eyes which quickly spills over into hot tears and choking cries, and before long I'm sobbing so

29

hard I'm bent over, one hand pressed on the counter top, the other clutching my stomach, shaking, and little drops of salt water are splashing onto the tiled floor by my feet. On some level far removed from where I am I feel hands go around me and I'm vaguely aware of the warmth of a person nearby. We move together, jerking, through the kitchen, down the hallway and out of the front door, and then I look up and find that we are standing outside. I rub my face and see that Abs is there, her hand on the door, which is still open. She looks at me intently as she gently pulls the door closed. I heave in a breath. Is that it? Is that really it? All the years of my life lived in this house, all the happy moments, all the sad ones, the laughter, the tears, over and done with, just like that? Ended by the closing of a door? It can't be that final, can it? It can't be so . . . complete?

But Abby isn't moving, and is still looking at me meaningfully. I raise my hand and drag it across my sniffly nose, and as I do I realise that I'm still holding the front door key. Abby's eyes focus on that, and she raises her eyebrows again. I move the key from my palm to my fingertips and stare at it for a moment. I press my lips to it once. Then I step forward, open the letter box with my other hand, and drop the key inside.

THREE

Daisy Mack
is making a multidimensional cosmological model using superstring theory, entanglement theory, and papier mache.

> **Jenny Martin** Wtf???
>
> **Suzanne Allen** Sounds like you have way too much time on your hands, my friend. I'm sure you must have something else you could be doing????
>
> **Daisy Mack** Suze, yes I have, but this is metasystems modelling, it can't be done quickly.
>
> **Georgia Ling** Give me a call, hun? Xx

I'm not really doing that. Failed science, remember? I'm on Abby's sofa, under my duvet, watching *Notting Hill* on Abby's DVD player. How cool is Hugh in this one? Not geeky at all. Supersmooth, even when he meets a superstar. Makes me fall in love with him all over again. And that makes me feel guilty about Colin, which means I'll have to watch a couple of episodes of *Pride and Prejudice* afterwards. That's OK, I've got loads of time before Abs or Tom get home from work.

Tom is Abby's lovely boyfriend. He's some kind of regional manager for a brand of sportswear I think. I know it's sportswear, and I know he's quite high up, but that's about all I do know. Oh, no, I also know that he feels it's his duty, being in the sportswear line, to keep himself incredibly fit and well-toned; and I know he walks around the flat without a shirt on sometimes. But it's OK. I'm so flabby, white and spotty at the moment that his being here, looking like that, doesn't do anything to me. It's a bit like what it would be like to be a little pebble looking up at a daffodil. Or a lump of mud looking at the Taj Mahal. The Taj Mahal is not in a million years ever going to look back, so the lump of mud doesn't pay much attention to the Taj Mahal either. At this point in its life, it's not even looking at other lumps of mud to be honest, let alone stunning white marble Indian temples.

When I first got here a week ago, with my cardboard boxes full of stuff and my blotchy tear-stained face, Tom was amazing. I mean, you know, in a Taj-Mahal-ish kind of way. He's got that sort of face that makes you think of churches. I don't mean *literally* churches. Not the actual building. That would be ridiculous, if he had a face like a church. What I mean is, his face makes me think about the pictures you see in churches. Those blokes with shiny light round their heads. Saints and holy people. And when we got to the flat and Abs opened the door, he came out into the hallway with his hands clasped, as if he was just about to deliver a blessing, or marry us, or something. He gave a sad smile to the air somewhere near my head, pressed his lips together, then helped us carry the boxes from the car and into the spare room. Then he made us both a hot chocolate with a generous splash of Baileys in it, and cleared off. He did give another sympathetic smile to the room I was in, and touch my shoulder, but he could have been touching a rack of tracksuit tops for all we both cared. Lovely guy, though. How many boyfriends would happily let their girlfriend's slobby, depressive friend move into their spare room indefinitely? Abs is so lucky. They're always kissing, or just touching each other's hands or arms when they pass each other. He's so affectionate and sensitive. It's very moving.

Ooh, this is the bit where Julia Roberts turns up at Hugh's place looking for a haven. That's where I would go if I could. Not that I'm not grateful to Abby and Tom for providing a roof over my head in my hour of need, but there's no way Hugh would have dragged me reluctantly round a load of shops the day after moving in like Abs did. He would have doubtless brought me some croissants in bed, with orange juice and coffee, kissed my head really tenderly, then left me alone to wallow in my misery. Or made energetic love to me all afternoon. Either one would have been good. Frankly, all I wanted to do at that point was lie in bed under a duvet, with or without a naked Hugh, but Abby wasn't having any of it.

'Get up,' she said, yanking the curtains back at something like five a.m. 'I've made a plan.'

I pulled the duvet up over my head. 'Jesus, Abs,' I whined. Yes, I know I was whiney, but I was dog-tired,

I couldn't help it. 'It's the middle of the night. You know I'm not sleeping well at the moment, seriously. I didn't get off until gone two, and five or six hours' sleep just isn't enough. I can't get up yet. Call me in a couple more hours.'

'It's midday.'

I didn't move for a second or two, then took hold of the edge of the duvet and dragged it slowly down, gradually exposing my entire pale face. 'What?'

She nodded. 'Yeah, for someone who's not sleeping well at the moment, you sure do sleep a lot.'

I stared at her a moment, making the extremely rookie mistake of engaging in direct eye contact with her almost straight away. She raised her eyebrows and put her hands on her hips, and I felt that oh-so-familiar feeling of resignation.

'Come on, Daze, you need to get up. We've got things to do.'

I knew resistance was futile, but I gave it one more try anyway. She would not have respected me if I hadn't. 'Yes, I know I've got things to do. It starts with "s" and ends with "leep". Or "ob". Or maybe "igh". All three of which require that I remain horizontal, right here.'

'Oh no you don't, young lady,' she said, snatching the duvet off my cold miserable body, leaving me curled up in the foetal position, trembling. 'Come on, get up.' She strategically positioned herself two millimetres from my face. 'We're going shopping.'

'Abby, I don't want to go shopping. You know I don't. There's no point anyway. I've put all this weight on and I'm not buying anything until I've lost it all.'

'I don't care about that. Come on, get up, we're going out like it or not. You've got half an hour.'

I have no idea how it is that Abby manages to make me do things I absolutely do not want to do. When she starts talking, I have that feeling in my head, that absolute granite determination, that no matter what she says, I will not do it. I am in charge of me, not her; I can simply refuse. Like those people who go to presentation evenings for the free champagne, sniggering to each other about the poor saps who get taken in by it all; and then come away with two weeks a year in a flat in Beirut. They're scratching their heads, thinking 'How the fuck did that happen?' No one else in my life has ever managed it with me. Not Mum; not Naomi; not even my dad, when I saw him (and, being less familiar with him, he was always more scary). Naomi once tried so hard to get me to do something – lend her my denim jacket for a date, I think – that she lost her temper and kicked a hole in her bedroom wall. But I didn't relent. Actually, that just made me more determined. I didn't need the jacket that night, wasn't going out and never wore it much anyway. But if she thought she could get me to do what she wanted, just because she went red in the face and performed an impressive karate kick, she was wrong.

I felt instantly sorry for her of course. As soon as she'd done it, she froze, clapped her hand to her mouth, then sank to the floor and started sobbing. I got down there on the floor with her and cuddled her for ten minutes until she'd calmed down. Didn't loan her the jacket though.

It took me just over an hour to get ready for Abby's

shopping trip, which is probably my personal best for extremely slow and reluctant preparation for an outing I have no interest in and don't want to be a part of. Twenty minutes after that, we were walking across the car park in town, heading towards the main shopping precinct.

'Trainers?' I was saying, trailing a good four or five feet behind her.

'Yes.' She turned her head to the side as she spoke to me, in recognition of the fact that I was behind her, but she refused to turn all the way round to face me. 'You liked those trainers of mine, didn't you? The ones you wore last week when we went out for that short walk?'

I shrugged. She couldn't see me. 'Mnyer,' I said – the audio equivalent of a shrug.

'Good,' she said decisively, interpreting – no doubt deliberately – my indeterminate sound as a positive. 'You need some proper trainers for the MoonWalk, and you need them straight away so that you can train in them. Tom's told me what to look for, and where to go, so it won't take long.'

'Oh.' Insanely, I actually felt a bit disappointed. Then I realised I was insane, and cheered up.

We found my perfect pair of trainers in the first sportswear shop we went in. Thank God. I had never been in a sportswear shop before then, and I felt about as comfortable in there as a flabby, spotty lamb in a slaughterhouse full of fit, attractive lambs. The salesman – Martin – made me get up on a treadmill right there in the middle of the shop, in front of absolutely everyone, then turned it on and made me walk on it while he filmed me. I felt like I was somehow starring in my very own porn film. No doubt the footage will find its way onto YouTube eventually. Truly horrific. I actually lost the ability to walk sensibly. I'm twenty-eight, for God's sake, and have been able to walk competently on and off for the past twenty-six years; but when that rubber surface started to move, I was Bambi on ice. My feet went behind me before I had even worked out what was happening and my body stretched out until I was almost horizontal. 'Move your feet, Daisy,' Martin said helpfully, nodding to encourage me. 'Try to walk normally.' Abby clapped her hand to her mouth at this point, and said nothing.

'How fast *is* this?' I panted, desperately dragging my feet forwards in a pseudo-run as fast as I could to bring my body back upright.

'Four K,' Martin said. 'About two and a half miles an hour. Get your balance, then we'll speed things up a bit.'

I panicked. I must have done. There's no other explanation. One minute I was upright, walking confidently and calmly, even starting to enjoy it in some insane way, then Martin leaned over and pushed a button and everything went wrong. The ground whizzed away beneath me and my feet went sideways instead of forwards and hit the non-moving edge of the platform briefly. I lost my balance and had to grab the handrails to steady myself, but didn't manage to get a proper grip in my panic. My shoes scuffed the walking surface repeatedly and I kept staggering forwards, my arms flailing in the air. Eventually I managed to grab the handrails again and lifted my entire body weight off the platform, but my elbow gave out and I collapsed suddenly back down onto the walking surface, and fell onto my knees.

'YAAH! HELP ME!' I yelled out as I was gently and smoothly transported to the end of the conveyor and deposited into the insoles display.

'Christ alive!' Martin yelped, and leaped into the air in a rare moment of abandon, as the entire rack of insoles teetered for a few seconds, then finally tilted forwards and showered me soundlessly with weightless packets of feet-shaped foam. 'Jesus tonight, are you all right?' He touched down lightly by my side and bent over to look at my humiliation more closely.

I nodded. 'I'm fine. But I need to put my bruised ego in your accident book.'

He blinked, then frowned a little. 'Oh, right.' He straightened up and glanced quickly at Abs, who was by now folded in half with one hand over her mouth and the other wrapped round her belly. He looked back at me, then craned his neck anxiously towards a door marked 'Staff Only'. 'Well then, I'd better just go and get . . . the . . .' It was obvious he was struggling to understand whether I was serious, so I let him off.

'No, it's fine, I'm fine, don't worry.' I stood up and picked boxes of feet out of my hair. 'See? No harm done.'

Martin visibly brightened. The thought of paperwork was clearly bringing him down. Obviously one of those types who excelled at sport at school. 'Oh, great! Well . . . I think we probably got enough footage there, so . . .'

I was frankly astounded by that statement. As far as I could work out, the only footage he'd have captured featured me upside down in the air, which wouldn't have told him an awful lot about my walking technique. Oh, except for the fact that I wasn't very good at it. But I had no intention of having another go, so I didn't argue.

Abs – red-faced and still amazingly silent – and I followed Martin over to the wall of trainers and he talked us through which pair he thought would be most suitable.

'Now Daisy,' he began earnestly, 'the interesting thing about the way that you walk is . . .' But it wasn't interesting at all. My attention immediately wandered over to some movement behind the demon treadmill. Two boys in hoodies, both around fourteen or fifteen, were glancing furtively around the room, then focusing back towards the in-store pharmacy. They were obviously about to start shoplifting things. I wondered vaguely whether to mention it to Martin, but it was far more interesting to see what happened. They moved closer together so their hoodies met up and formed a kind of hoodie tunnel for them to talk in. They conversed for a few seconds, re-emerged and looked around again, then edged nearer to the display. After one more quick scan of the room they were satisfied that no one was watching, so advanced finally to the display and, in a lightning-fast and clearly well-practised manoeuvre, seized a small, familiar-looking purple box each. The boxes flashed briefly in the air between them before being instantly concealed somewhere about their person and they moved off quickly. I turned back to Martin to alert him, but then noticed that the boys were slouching über-casually

39

over to the tills. Of course. They weren't shop-lifting; they were buying their first condoms. Romance isn't dead.

Eventually I had to tear my eyes away and pay the million pounds Martin wanted for the space-age trainers he'd selected. Apparently they were made with some kind of new technology, involving a recently developed innovative substance probably derived from something that fell to earth from a galaxy far, far away, and would improve my balance, increase my fitness and tighten up the overall tone of my buttocks and thighs as I walked.

'Wow,' I nodded, exaggeratedly impressed. 'Are they bringing an end to suffering and world poverty too?' I handed over a thick wad of cash.

Martin looked from side to side, a tiny frown confusing his face. 'Er, well . . . no. I don't think so. Not really. I'm not sure that's . . . You know, because they're not made in the . . .'

I sagged with disappointment. 'Oh. What a shame.' Then I brightened. 'Well, never mind. It's certainly a relief to hear that the scientists are all keeping themselves busy.'

Martin glanced at Abs, then back at me. 'Erm, I'm not sure that I . . .' He trailed off.

I smiled and nodded. 'Yeah, you know, after that whole cure-for-cancer fiasco.'

'Right, OK, well, thank you very much,' Abby said suddenly, grabbing my arm and dragging me towards the exit. 'Bye!'

So I had the magic trainers. In a cardboard box, in a carrier bag, on the back seat of Abby's car. As we drove, the bag jangled softly, and little gold and rainbow-coloured sparks erupted from it then evaporated in the air. Abby kept up an excited monologue all the way back to her place, about how great it all was, and how I could now finally start my proper training, and get out on the streets every day, starting tomorrow, even if it was just for twenty minutes to begin with, and then I could build up to an hour by increasing by ten minutes every day. And she would join me at weekends, and some evenings. And we would both get fit and toned and healthy and then complete the MoonWalk next month really easily and feel fantastic and a huge sense of achievement as well as raising a bucketful of cash for the cancer that killed my mum, which would in turn contribute towards improving research and treatment and could in the end help save someone else's mum or daughter or sister or grandmother or auntie. I said nothing. I wasn't feeling it. One step at a time, I thought. No need to get carried away.

OK. Julia Roberts has just told Hugh that she's just a girl, standing in front of a boy, asking him to love her. I adore this bit. Internationally worshipped multi-millionaire A-list movie star falls for witty and diffident but obscure small bookshop owner, and propositions him. It makes you believe that anything is possible. Like maybe one day I'll be standing in Tesco by the hair removal cream and Matt Damon will happen to have popped in for cotton buds and a travel iron, and he'll see me and tell me he's actually just a simple man who's fallen in love with a simple girl or something, and all he can offer me is his heart, no more, no less. And unlike Hugh I'll snatch his

41

bloody hand off and jet off with him straight to his Beverly Hills mansion for a life of parties and extravagance.

Hugh has turned her down though. Big mistake. Huge. But it all works out in the end. Of course it does, it's a film. I'm a bit distracted this afternoon, actually. Can't concentrate properly on the story. Well, I do know the story already, but that doesn't mean that I don't get something new out of it each time I watch it. The problem now is that it's already half past three, and Abs is likely to get in from work anywhere between four and five, without warning. Being her own boss, she can finish work as soon as she's had enough. No, all right, probably not as *soon* as she's had enough. Not that exact second. She probably has to finish the lesson she's giving before packing up for the day. Be a bit much if she just leaned over on the bypass, opened the driver's door and gave her current pupil a good shove to send them tumbling out, then drove home. But she's a professional, I'm sure she doesn't do that. She probably pulls over first. Anyway I have no way of knowing what time she'll get in, which means I have to be ready. I wait for a good shot of Hugh's face, then pause the film. I can come back to that. I need to shut my computer down, put my quilt back on my bed and get the magic trainers on before she gets home. Then I can tell her I've just got back from a twenty-five-minute walk.

My messenger makes the popping noise just as I'm about to close the web page I'm on. I have to move quickly now. That message is bound to be Abby checking up on me.

Daisy Mack

Is alternating contact with the ground of the lowest append-
ages of my body for 30 sweeps of the long hand. It's more
difficult than it sounds, people.

OK, that's that done. Hey, no one ever said that what
goes on to Facebook has to be truthful.

I click on the message and find that it is from Abby
and my body floods with relief. I've still got plenty of
time to get sorted before she gets home. I relax down
into the sofa again.

Abby Marcus   What you doing?
Daisy Mack   Hi Abs! Just got back from a walk.
What are you doing?

I'm pretty pleased with myself there. Straight away
I've given her the impression that I've been out walking,
no hesitation. Add that to my status when she reads it
later and she'll have to believe me. No, wait. Maybe I
should have not answered her for ten minutes or so, *then*
I could have said I'd just got back. Would have been
much more believable. Never mind, never mind, it's too
late now. Anyway, I can save that one for tomorrow. Yes.

Abby Marcus   You've been online a long time.
Are you sure you've been out??

Shit shit shit. Of course. Facebook always tells you
the other members known to you who are online at the
same time as you, so you can instant message them if

43

you want. Which is clearly what she's just done. Why didn't I realise that? I've been on here for hours.

Daisy Mack Yes, definitely. Twenty-five minutes, to the park and back, just like you said. Must be some kind of error on your computer. Have you refreshed the page recently?

Yeah, I know, pretty lame. But Abs is so trusting, bless her, she's bound not to even question it. Or maybe she just assumes that no one would ever dare to do anything other than what she's told them to do. That's probably more likely.

Abby Marcus How odd. I just assumed you'd left your computer logged on when you went out for your walk.

Bugger it. Bugger bugger bugger. What the hell is the matter with me? God, if I'd thought it through properly and not panicked, I'd have realised that of course I would have left the laptop logged onto Facebook while I was out walking. Because I was only going to be out for twenty-five minutes max, so I could simply pick up where I left off when I got back.

Abby Marcus You didn't really go out, did you? Be honest, Daze.

Shit.

Daisy Mack Course I did, Abs. Do you really think I would be lying about it? What would be the point of that??
Abby Marcus Yes I do. And the point would be to get me off your back.
Daisy Mack

Actually, I don't really know what to say here. She's completely and utterly, absolutely, one hundred percent right. And I am exactly the same amount in the wrong. She's my best friend, she's really been there for me since Mum died, kind and supportive, helping me out with all the hideous arrangements, checking up on me all the time; and now she's taken me in and let me have her spare room while I pull myself together and sort myself out somewhere to live. And she's only making me do this MoonWalk thing for my own good. Everything she's doing right now is for my own good. I absolutely cannot lie to her any more.

Daisy Mack Well actually, Abby, to be totally honest, I'm pretty upset that you're even questioning me about it. Of course I have been out walking. I said I would, didn't I? And I didn't want to tell you that I'd left the laptop on while I was out because I was a bit ashamed that I was wasting your electricity. But don't worry, I'll make sure you're recompensed for that.

Don't look at me, OK? I'm only lying to her for her own good. I want to make her happy, that's all.

Abby Marcus *pokes out bottom lip* I'm so sorry Daze. I do believe you, of course I do. Well done for getting out there, I'm proud of you. Hey, shall we get a take-away and watch Notting Hill tonight? I haven't seen that one for ages!

Daisy Mack Brilliant idea. I love that film. What time are you getting home?

Abby Marcus Finishing in about half an hour. Will get food on the way home. Fire up the DVD player!! Xx

Daisy Mack I'm warming it up even as we speak!

Don't look at me, I said. I've been through a tough time. I need empathy and understanding.

FOUR

Daisy Mack
is thinking that maybe the time has come to get her act into gear. Or at least, to have a browse through the gear and try and pick something her act might like.

Suzanne Allen   Dare I say that it's about time?

Daisy Mack   Apparently you do.

Georgia Ling   Luv ya hunni <3 X o X <3

Jenny Martin   Your wierd.

Is there anything more gorgeous than the park on a warm spring morning, with daffs and crocuses clustered in colourful clumps around every shrub and tree, sun filtering in golden patches through the thick greenery, a gentle breeze with a delicious sea tang whispering through the leaves, and all the kids at school? Well, yes, possibly a walk by the actual beach would be just as nice. The rush and pull of waves lapping, shouts of children, gulls calling and the air sharp with that strong sea smell. The south-east coast is only four miles away from here, but that means to walk beside the seaside would add eight

47

miles onto my journey. I'm finding that a walk in the park is much more pleasant anyway.

I'm taking a breather on the grass – don't see why not, I'm in no rush – and the only other people here are dogwalkers (inevitably with their dogs, unfortunately), a few mums with toddlers on leads, and elderly couples sitting silently together on the benches. They've been married so long, they don't even need to speak to each other any more. They're just staring straight ahead, enjoying the tranquillity and comfortable companionship of their golden age. Either that or each is wondering how much it will cost to put a plaque on the bench when the other one dies.

Ah but that doesn't matter: it's an idyllic scene. They could be plotting to kill each other with a faulty electrical connection for all I care. I stretch my legs out in front of me a bit more and tilt my face up to the sun, resting the weight of my body behind me on my hands. Abby said nothing about taking a breather when I got here, so this is definitely allowed. And this is all new for me; I need to be careful.

Sitting here on the grass in the park, surrounded by daisies and dogs, I'm feeling pretty proud of myself. I have been propelled out of my bed, into my trainers and onto the road – pausing only long enough to put on the rest of my clothes – by my deep commitment to the challenge before me, and my passionate, altruistic desire to help anyone who might be suffering. Oh, plus Abby was on to me.

I say she was on to me, which makes it sound like she'd caught me out being deceitful; but all I was doing was pretending to be out walking when I was actually reclining on the sofa. And believing I was out walking every day was making her happy, so I went to a lot of effort to keep the illusion up. Well, Abs is my best friend in the world – I'd do anything for her.

'I'm so proud of you,' she said every day when she got in from work and saw all the effort that I'd gone to. She came over to me and rubbed my arm. 'I know it's not easy, Daze, but it will be worth it.' She was absolutely right; it wasn't easy at all. I had to rub my new trainers in the flower borders to get them dirty, and then rake over the earth afterwards to hide the shoe prints. Then I had to clean the rake. Putting it back in the shed was always a bit tricky. I had to make sure I put it back exactly where it came from, without disturbing any of the other tools. I started off trying to memorise how everything went, then after the third day I realised that was stupid and just took a photo of all the tools with my phone. But she was also right about the effort being worthwhile. She started to transform from pale and worried to glowing and happy. Which made me feel all warm inside.

I've taken my trainers and socks off now and am rolling over onto my stomach. The sun on the backs of my legs is delicious. I rest my head on my arms and close my eyes. I love this park. My mum used to bring me here when I was little. Well, not here exactly. Not this actual park. But one similar. One park's pretty much just like the next really, isn't it? Especially when you're five or something. I can't really remember it, but there was definitely grass, and some trees. Probably dogs with

Frisbees in their mouths. Old people: they're everywhere. I was forever wandering off back then, foraging, exploring, discovering new territories or previously unknown species of things. I remember I once found an uncharted island in a park that was exactly like this one – except it had two very important things that this one lacks: a gigantic lake in the middle; and my mum. I spotted the landmass from the shore, and went straight into the water in my daisy-spotted wellies (needless to say, I adored all things daisy) so I could study its flora and fauna and make a detailed record in my log at home. By the time I got to the island in the middle of the lake, (OK, it was probably more of a pond than an actual lake, but I was only five or something), thick muddy water was sloshing over the top of my wellies and filling them up, forming a new habitat for several different types of algae and a couple of lizards. But I barely noticed. Why would I, when I was about to make a significant geological discovery? I climbed onto the landmass and turned back triumphantly, shielding my eyes and peering through the haze to view the distant shore.

'Daisy Macintyre, what in God's name do you think you're doing?' Mum said, four feet away from me. Maybe it was more of a large, deep puddle than an actual pond. But to me it was an ocean, with new terrain to be charted and an indigenous population to be encountered and studied. 'Come back here, please.'

'I found an island!' I yelled, as if she were a speck on a far-away horizon. 'Look at me – I'm the conker!' I punched the air with a grubby fist.

'Conqueror,' Mum automatically corrected. 'Daisy,

look at the state of you. You're absolutely filthy.' She put her hands on her hips and pressed her lips together. 'I am *furious* with you. You will come back here straight away, or there will be consequences.' Slowly she moved her gaze down my mucky self. 'Do you want me to march right over there and get you?'

'You can't *march* across the sea. And anyway, you haven't got an army.'

'I don't need one. Are you coming back, or am I coming there?'

I glanced around me quickly, looking for potential weapons or allies. A large duck was standing on the mud next to me, calmly observing the hostilities escalating. I pointed at it. 'I've got a terrible froshus beast on my side,' I called across the channel. 'It's gonna eat you.'

'It's a herbivore,' Mum countered, 'everyone knows that. Anyway, ducks are impartial. They don't take sides.'

'What does that mean?'

'It means it doesn't take sides. Do you, Impartial Duck?'

We both looked at the duck. It said nothing.

Mum turned back to me. 'See?' she said.

Like the duck, I didn't move.

'So are you going to surrender peacefully, or do I have to storm your battlements?'

'Storm!'

Mum stared at me for a few moments, then took her hands off her hips and rolled up her sleeves. Then she bent down and took off her trainers and socks and rolled up the bottom of her jeans. She straightened up and looked at me. 'You can't win, Daisy Duck,' she said calmly. Her hands went back to her hips. 'If I have to

51

come over there and get you, we will both be filthy and disgusting, which will not make me happy; or you can surrender peacefully and we have a chance to negotiate the terms of your defeat.' She raised her eyebrows and I started to experience a resigned feeling, although I don't think I recognised it at that point. 'Either way, the outcome is the same.'

'What's the outcome?'

'It's what's left at the end. And in this case, it will be you coming back here, either willingly, or' – she slitted her eyes – '*under my power*.' Her expression at that point went with the word 'power' so well, I still remember it now. It was like Voldemort. 'Which is it to be, Queen Daisy of the Ducks?'

I knew she had power. I had always known it. She was the mummy, after all. I had no choice but to surrender peacefully, and I was on the verge of doing it when a high, cold voice called out sweetly from somewhere behind her, 'Oh Daisy, why are you always such a problem child?'

It was my sister Naomi. She was sitting on a blanket next to where Mum was standing, eating a slice of Battenberg, sunlight bouncing off her long shiny hair. Wearing a yellow dress. What happened next was thoroughly deserved, I thought. Well, I was already holding handfuls of mud and filth. I barely had to go to any effort at all.

My phone quacks in my pocket so I lift one hip off the ground and reach down to wrestle the phone to the surface. It's telling me I've got a message on Facebook, and I think I know exactly what that's about. I touch the screen and open up the web page.

Abby Marcus Daisy Quackintyre, what are you doing?

Daisy Mack It's OK Abs, I'm in the park right now, as we speak. Or, you know, type.

Abby Marcus Oh good. That's more like it.

Daisy Mack Yeah – I do still remember every-thing you said on Sunday, believe me.

That's true, because most of what she said on Sunday were swear words.

Abby Marcus Excellent. Keep it up, Daze. I'm proud of you ☺

Right. Time for me to go, I think. Abby is a truly great friend, and a good person, with the soul of an angel and the heart of a giant. She is kind and thoughtful and considerate and gentle, and when she gets annoyed fire comes out of her nostrils and her voice can split atoms.

'You haven't been fucking walking at all this past week, have you?' was her opening gambit on Sunday afternoon. I almost didn't understand her because her jaw was clenched together and she barely moved her lips as she spoke.

You know that feeling you get when you've been found out doing something? Or not doing something? Or some-thing you've done, and shouldn't have, has been discovered? Well that's exactly the feeling I got at that moment. It was like something solid and heavy plunging down through my abdomen, making me curl inwards and grasp my tummy.

I frowned. 'Abs,' I started to say, but I didn't have anything else.

She raised her eyebrows and put her hands on her hips. Then tilted her head a little and gave a teeny smile. 'Ah Daze,' she said, her voice much less like a nuclear missile than I had been expecting, 'I understand that you're down. I really do. I know that it's making you not want to do anything. I even get why you lied to me. No, don't deny it. It's undeniable, isn't it? I mean, if you really had been walking down to the park and back every day this week, I'm fairly sure you would have learned how to get there by now.'

She's incredible, isn't she? I mean, stand aside, Columbo. Take your beige mac and your wonky eye and get out of here. Of course, I did make it easy for her with that idiotic blunder. Completely ridiculous when you consider the lengths I went to to cover my tracks – or lack of them. But then I never expected to be tested on my knowledge of 'Parks Near Abby's Flat and How to Get There'. Abs suggested that morning that the three of us go out after lunch for a nice long walk, starting off at the park and from there to the seafront. It sounded like an awfully long way to me but I couldn't let Abby see me thinking that.

'Sure,' I'd said nonchalantly. 'Should be a piece of cake.' I hadn't done the walking I'd said I'd been doing, but I figured it wouldn't be too challenging. It was only walking after all. How hard could it be?

As it turned out, of course, the distance wasn't the relevant factor. It all ground to a halt long before the distance became an issue. There was a bit of preamble when Tom and Abby had some kind of disagreement about whether or not he was coming with us. I'm not sure who was arguing for which angle, but the whole thing ended with a lot of 'Fine', 'Fine', 'Suit yourself', 'I will', and he didn't come. I was glad, actually. He's about as easy to talk to as a marble statue. And I'm always just as surprised when he responds.

'Everything all right?' I said to Abs as we went out of the gate of her building. I didn't want to pry but felt I had to say something. Bit weird if you witness a horrible row between two people and then calmly start a conversation about *Hollyoaks*.

She was frowning and blinking a lot, which I guessed meant she was trying not to cry. I was a bit taken aback by that, as she's not usually one to cry. It's something we both feel the same about. Crying is a blatant demonstration – on your face, of all places, to make sure absolutely everyone sees it – of self-pity. It is self-indulgent, attention-seeking and achieves literally nothing. Normally I can't bear it, particularly from women. All those weepy heroines in the forties have given us a lot of ground to make up in the crying stakes. Small wonder we are generally despised as a gender for our tap-like qualities. But lately, of course, I've been doing crying enough for me *and* Abby. And, let's face it, all those weepy heroines from the forties. I can picture all their black and white expressions, smiling at me winsomely every morning as my face leaks sickeningly from every orifice. 'Chin up, old gal,' they'll be saying, in soft oblique lighting, 'you look tarribly queeah.'

'Fine,' Abby'd said, nodding vigorously. 'It's all fine.'

We walked on to the end of her road in silence, turned left, and Abby stopped abruptly – violently, even, if it's possible to do that – put her hands on her hips and spoke that memorable and immortal phrase, 'Daisy Macintyre, you haven't been fucking walking at all this past week, have you?' Enter Columbo.

That was the day before yesterday. Today is Tuesday, April 21st. My magic trainers are officially a week old today. Happy Birthday trainers. I roll back over onto my bottom and stand up, brushing grass and dirt off me. It should take me about half an hour to get back now, provided I don't get lost, which is actually quite likely, even though this is my third visit here. I don't have the best sense of direction in the world – got lost in a maze, remember?

A movement at the periphery of my vision attracts my attention and I turn sharply to focus on it. It's a woman jauntily walking away from me, crossing the arc of my vision from right to left. I stare at her, noting the thick brown ponytail, the boot-cut jeans with trainers, the navy blue fleece jacket. The way she's walking, almost bouncing along, arms swinging, is achingly, heart-breakingly familiar. I hold my breath, gazing after her as she moves further and further away from me, receding from my sight. I blink and start moving. The logical part of my brain knows it isn't her, knows it can't be her, knows that – even if it is her – there are so many hurtful questions that would have more hurtful answers that I almost couldn't bear for it actually to be her, but her gait and her hair and her clothes are so right, so distinctive, so *exact* that I set off after her across the park anyway.

'Mum?' The word comes out of me in a whisper but I hardly notice as I try to reach her. But she turns, she moves, she disappears, she reappears, all the time out of my grasp, each time getting further away, smaller and smaller until I'm breathless and panting with the effort of getting to her. 'Mum, Mum, Mum,' I puff rhythmically, not really noticing the harsh rasp of desperation creeping in as I turn the final corner, look up the street and see that she's gone. I stop and stand for a few moments, eyes fixed on the empty horizon.

''Scuse me?'

The voice behind me interrupts my thoughts and I snap back to where I am. Disconcertingly, I find I am outside the park boundary, on a pavement somewhere, with no recollection of how I got here. Oh shit. This is how it starts. I feel the first faint, familiar stirrings of panic as I accept that I am probably lost. Again. I scan my surroundings quickly to try and find something that looks familiar, but it's just a load of nondescript semi-detached houses, with black or blue cars parked on the driveways. One of them has a tree in the front lawn. It's lovely – covered in pink blossom, like candyfloss on a stick.

'Er, excuse me? Again.'

I turn round to look, partly to see who's speaking but mostly to see if there is any way I can work out which direction the park is from here. Surely I've just come out of a gate or something and it will be directly behind me? I can't have gone far. But there's nothing there; just the same bland street stretching away into the distance. Well, as far as the T-junction at the end, anyway. A motorbike goes past, right to left, and disappears. Where in God's name is the park?

A man's face inserts itself into the frame, blocking out the left-hand side of the picture. He's smiling broadly, but his eyebrows are pulled together slightly, as if he's looking at a ninety-year-old woman in a nightie trying to buy a ticket to Afghanistan.

I meet his gaze and raise my eyebrows. 'Yes?' I say, in a tone that lets him know without a doubt that I don't need help of any kind. 'What is it?'

He's quite scruffy in a dirty grey tee shirt and denim cut-offs, with messy brown hair pushed away from his face and damp with sweat. His forehead and top lip are beaded with it, although rather annoyingly my attention is drawn to the cute dimples that are showing in his cheeks as he grins. Attractively boyish for someone who's probably in his early thirties. I look away hurriedly and at this point I notice that he's holding the handles of a huge wheelbarrow, which is full of masonry or bricks or something else that is firmly lodged in a world I don't go into. Immediately to my left is a wide driveway that appears to be in the middle of having block paving laid down on it. Half of it is finished, in a clean, herring-bone pattern (which I have to say looks so lovely, really picks up the whole front appearance of the house) while the other half, nearest the pavement – nearest to me – is still a shallow layer of sand. I glance back at the man with the wheelbarrow. A single drop of sweat is trickling down the side of his head and over his cheek-bone.

'Just wondered, would you mind giving me a hand

with this?' he says now, grinning and chewing gum. 'It's bloody heavy.'

My eyes widen and my chin jerks forward. 'You want me to help you? Carry that? In these clothes? And *trainers*?' I glance down overtly at his feet and note that they are clad in huge, heavy-duty, probably steel-toe-capped, Magnum builders' boots in a gorgeous tan nubuck. 'Hm. This could result in a lawsuit for you, you know. I take it you are being paid to do this? I mean, this is your job, right? You will be getting actual money from someone for moving these bricks around? So tell me just exactly why you think this is something I should help you with, for no money, and risking painful injury?'

He shrugs – the wheelbarrow full of bricks goes up a little, then down again. I try not to be impressed that he was able to do that. I certainly don't sneak a peek at the massive muscles in his arms and shoulders. 'Hey, you might want to lighten up a bit, lady. It was only a little joke.' He winks at me, and makes a clicking sound with his mouth as he does so.

'A joke? Really? No, it can't have been. Surely not. I know about jokes. They're funny. They're to make people laugh.'

He grins even more broadly and inclines his head a little. 'Duly noted. Thanks for the feedback. I am off right now to go and write some more material.' He moves as if to put the wheelbarrow down, then picks it up again and jerks his head. 'Ah, damn it, I can't do it now, I've got to finish this first. Tell you what, you move out of the way and I'll promise to work on some funnier material as soon as I get home tonight. Deal?'

I stare at him, and realise at that moment that I am standing on the pavement, midway along the entrance to the driveway, essentially blocking it to all cars, vans and anyone with a large, heavy wheelbarrow. I feel that solid thing dropping in my belly again. When he said 'Excuse me' the first time, he literally meant, excuse me, you're in my way, please move. It wasn't the sort of 'Excuse me' that you say to someone to get their attention before you ask them something. I glance down at the unfinished driveway, wishing it was still a big hole so that I could jump into it. Then I look back up at the man. A sheen of sweat is covering the huge muscles now. I look away quickly and give a decisive nod.

'OK, that sounds fair.' I turn round and start to walk away, then half turn and speak over my shoulder. 'Twenty-four hours it is. I'll be back tomorrow with a clapometer.'

'A clap . . .?' I hear him snort. I hope it's laughter. I suspect not. 'Excellent,' he says. 'I'll look forward to that.'

Thankfully he can't see my red face as I march as fast as I can up the street and into uncharted territory.

FIVE

Daisy Mack
is so used to getting lost, you'd think I'd be better at it by now.

> **Daisy Mack**   Actually, getting lost I can do. It's what I'm good at. If you ever need to get lost, come and see me. Oh, if you can find me, that is.
>
> **Jenny Martin**   What the hell is going on with you, Dozy-Doo?
>
> **Georgia Ling**   Lol! xx
>
> **Suzanne Allen**   Where are you now? What can you see?
>
> **Abby Marcus**   Pay no attention Suze, she's on the sofa, watching Rotting Hell.

I don't know why Abby's put that. She likes *Notting Hill* as much as I do.

No she doesn't. What am I thinking of? Of course she doesn't. No one does. Richard Curtis doesn't like *Notting Hill* as much as I do.

Anyway, I think I deserve this relaxing little interlude. It's been a very strenuous few days since I marched rapidly away from Wheelbarrow Man on Tuesday and got myself instantly and completely lost. I've been out walking every day since then, and that was five days ago. I must have covered at least ten miles every day, which is fifty miles all together. Bloody hell, I could actually have walked to Bluewater shopping centre. Could have had a Subway of the Day. Tried on shoes. Bought tights.

Julia Roberts is arguing for the last brownie. I pause the film at this point because Abby has just come and sat down near my feet and is staring at me pointedly. She looks like she wants to have a serious talk with me about something. I wonder what on earth it could be. Any ideas anyone? Answers on a postcard . . .

'Daze, we need to have a serious talk about your training plan.'

Ding ding ding – correct answer, you're a winner!

I smile and nod. 'Yeah, I know.'

'Do you? Because I'm still not convinced you're completely aware of how much work there is left to do.'

She's entirely wrong there. Why on earth else does she think I've been walking so much? I've been like a walking demon this week, out every day, marching down to the park, marching around the park, marching backwards and forwards across the park, marching around the park again, becoming so familiar with the park and all its entrances and exits and all the housing estates that border it that I'll never ever get lost again. It's quite surprising really that, in all that marching down to, and through, and round and round the park and its environs, I never bumped into that man again. Or actually, I suppose I could have seen him again, I really wouldn't know. I can barely remember what he looked like, except that he was holding something, I think. What was that again? Some kind of statue, was it? Or a bicycle? I can't remember, it's all gone.

I've also never seen that woman with the ponytail again, the one who walked like her and moved like her and looked like her. It doesn't matter. It's not as if I was looking for her.

Anyway, the point is that I have done some pretty substantial walking this week, whatever Abs might think, and I'm proud of myself. I'd like to see *her* cover ten miles a day. On foot, obviously – she does far more than ten miles every day in her car of course. I know that for a fact. She gave me a lift into town once when my car was off the road, and the only problem was I had to sit in the back while she gave a lesson first. It was only an hour, and it probably would have taken me that long to get the bus anyway, so I went with it. I had never seen her with a client before, and I was really surprised at how flirty she was with him, a lad of about nineteen or twenty. There was a lot of, 'Oh hi there, Justin, OK, first gear to pull away, you look good today, braking carefully towards the junction, don't you smell nice, what is that, Calvin Klein? Red light, Justin, *red light*.' I sat in the back and rolled my eyes, and they kept on rolling for the entire sixty minutes. I felt a bit sick by the end of it.

'What the hell was all that about?' I asked her, once Justin had parallel parked (badly) to gushing praise from Abs ('Oh well done, Justin, I've never seen such a beginner do it as well as that, you're a natural' – forget the fact he needed to get the bus to the kerb) and got out.

'All what?' she said easily, flipping down the sun visor and checking her appearance in the little mirror. She didn't do anything to her face, like touch up her lipgloss or rub away mascara smudges like the rest of us have to, she just looked, scrutinised, turned slightly left, slightly right, once more in the centre, and was satisfied.

'Yeah, don't pretend you don't know what I'm talking about. You know *exactly* what I'm talking about.' I affected a high breathy voice. '"Ooh, Justin, look at your bulging muscles; ooh, Justin, you smell so delicious I could just eat you all up." You were blatantly flirting with him, Abs! It's outrageous! He must be all of eighteen!'

'He's twenty, Daze – in a couple of months – and stop looking so scandalised. This is me you're talking to. I know you're not that innocent, remember?'

She was right about that. Before I moved back in with Mum and Graham three years ago, I used to work in an office, processing food orders for restaurants and cafés. I gave that job up in the end, when being a carer became full time. But I used to be a real flirt-hound, when I had nothing less trivial on my mind. It was something of a hobby for Abby and me. We used to compare notes and swap tips over a glass of wine in the evenings. That is until Tom hove alongside and Abby was forced to give it up. It was like a habit she was trying to quit after that, with the occasional cute nineteen-year-old relapses. But she was with me when I flirted my way into Jamie Powell's Spider-Man boxer shorts four years earlier. Oh calm down, he was twenty-one, it was all above board. He just had a bit of an obsession with superheroes, it turned out. Well, no, not superheroes. I would have liked that.

He could have rescued me from things. Burning buildings, spiders, that kind of affair. What Jamie loved was comics. And action figures. Wanted to peer at me using Superman's x-ray eyes, which basically consisted of a tiny red dot of light travelling up and down across every inch of my body. It took nearly forty minutes. That one was over before it started.

'Oh yes, bring that up again. You haven't mentioned it for at least two weeks, so we were well overdue. But the point is that this lad is your client, which makes it slightly different from me getting it on with the photo-copier repair man, I think you'll agree.'

She inhaled deeply, and sighed. 'All right, yes, fine, I was flirting with him. So what? I flirt with all of them. It makes them feel strong and confident, so they're more relaxed about driving. It's perfect sense.'

I stared at her. She stared back. I raised my eyebrows. She raised hers. I folded my arms. She folded hers. Then unfolded them. Then fiddled with the bottom of her jumper. 'Plus I get lots more business,' she said quietly. 'Word gets around.'

'Uh-huh.' I continued to stare at her.

She ran her hands lightly around the steering wheel, and focused intently on the cube of air that was sitting on the bonnet. 'And he was really fit.'

'There we go.'

'Oh so what, Daze? It's harmless, it doesn't mean anything, does it? And Tom doesn't know, and wouldn't care even if he did ever find out, which he won't, will he?'

I pressed my lips together and shook my head. Of course I wasn't going to tell him. My loyalty was, and is, to Abby. Not the Monosyllabic Monolith she lives with. And anyway, she was absolutely right, there was nothing wrong with a bit of harmless flirting. It was harmless.

'Training plan, Daze,' Abs says now on the sofa, slapping my shin. I think she meant to pat it affectionately, but my leg muscles are feeling rather tender at the moment, so an ant crawling across my skin feels like someone dropping a chimney on me.

'Owwww! Be careful, Abs. It all hurts, remember?'

'Oh, yeah, sorry.' She removes her hand as if my leg is a sleeping lion. 'I'm so pleased with what you've done this week, you know,' she goes on, although the tone of her voice suggests that she's got more to say on the subject.

'Thanks.'

She nods slowly, staring at the hairs on my knees. It makes me wish I'd shaved them today. They really do need to be shaved at least twice a week, and the last time I did it was November.

'But I think you need to increase your distance now,' Abs is saying, still nodding slowly at my knees. She looks up at me and smiles. Ah. It was a joke.

'Yeah. Ha!' I grin back at her. Like ten miles a day isn't enough at this stage!

A small frown appears between her immaculately groomed eyebrows. 'What's funny?'

'You are. Telling me I need to increase my distance.'

The frown deepens. 'I'm serious, Daze. Three or four miles a day is good, great actually, to go from nothing to that, but you have got to do more. Longer. Maybe spend next week doing seven or eight miles every day – something like that?'

I stare at her. My mouth falls open a little. My eyes widen and start to dry out. I am forced to blink. My head jerks once to the left. 'Nuh . . .' I say, to convey my disbelief at her massive confusion and misunderstanding while explaining to her exactly where she's mistaken.

She smiles at the same time as continuing to frown. 'Daze, it's not that bad, honestly. Seven or eight miles should only take you about two and a half or three hours. Less as you get fitter and faster. And until you get a job of some description, you've got all day anyway, haven't you? We are going to be walking twenty-six miles in five weeks, remember?'

'Nuh-uh.'

'You're being silly . . .'

'No, Abs. I'm not. You've got it wrong. I'm totally on top of this already. I've been doing about ten miles every day this week.'

Her frown disappears at this point and her face takes on the expression of a mum looking at a four-year-old's appalling attempt at a self-portrait. 'Ah Daze. No you haven't. Nothing like it.'

'Yes I have. I haven't just been going to the park and back, you know. I've been walking round it a couple of times and round all the estates near it, which must have been at least another two or three miles. So when you add that to the going all the way down there and back, which must be at least four miles each way . . .'

'Mile and a half.'

'What?'

'It's a mile and a half down to the park. And a mile and a half back. That's three miles.'

I blink again. It's because of all the incredulous staring at Abby I'm doing. This is utter nonsense. I look back at her and shake my head. 'I don't believe it. You're just trying to get me to do more by telling me I've done less.'

She shakes her head. 'I'm not. I'm serious. I mean, come on, Daze, Tom works in sports equipment, for Nike's sake. He owns a pedometer.'

An image pops into my head at this point of Tom's placid, immobile face, with its closed-mouth half-smile and immaculate blond hair, wobbling backwards and forwards on top of one of those bikes with only one wheel you see clowns on. I start grinning, wondering if he rides round the warehouse on it to save time. I mean, it's the ideal form of transport for that kind of thing. Both hands are free at all times for holding clipboards and ticking things off lists. Or is it just a hobby of his? Goes out on it at weekends? Maybe there's a club or something where they can all meet up and wobble about together. Race each other. Oh no, wait. I don't think that's a pedometer, actually, is it? Isn't it called a mono-bike or something. No. What is it? Unicycle. Yes. So what's a pedometer then?

'It measures the distance you've walked,' Abby says at this point, surprising me not at all with her mind-reading capability. Yeah, I know, it is very impressive that she can actually read minds – or maybe just my mind – and leave exactly the right sized gap of silence for me to think about what she said before answering my unspoken question. But I have seen it before. She looks at me sometimes and somehow just *knows* what I'm thinking. Unless maybe I show every single thought and idea on my face, and she just reads that. It's possible, I suppose. Then again, I don't really see how she could pick up that I was wondering what a pedometer is just from, I don't know, the way my eyebrows are, or what my mouth is doing.

'DAISY!'

I jump in my seat with a little yelp. 'Oh my God, Abby. What?'

'Pay attention! Seriously, you've got to start focusing on what's going on around you.'

'I *am*.'

'No you're not. You're on some kind of constant internal monologue, incessantly debating with yourself about stuff that's trivial and unrelated to what is actually occurring.' Her voice softens and she touches her hand to my arm. 'God, I know you've been through a terrible time lately, Daze, and I know you're drifting and finding it incredibly hard to focus on your life again and connect with the world around you. You're like a . . . a delicate little blossom flower that's dropped from a tree and is now being tossed around in a fast-flowing stream, unable to find your way. It's . . .' She smiles at me sweetly and tips her head on one side. 'It's pissing me right off.'

I flinch. 'Oh.'

'Yeah.' She inhales deeply with closed eyes, then lets all the breath out again. 'I'm telling you for your own good, you know. Because I care about you so much. You *do* know that, don't you?' She pauses while I sit up a

69

bit straighter and open my eyes wider. 'OK. Now. I know it's only three miles to the park and back because Tom and I have walked it plenty of times and we've measured it. Which means that what you've been doing this past week is no more than four miles a day. So you have got to increase the distance.' She unfolds a piece of paper that I hadn't noticed she was holding and spreads it out on the sofa. 'So I've worked out this route for you. It's about eight miles all together, and I want you to do it at least four times next week. Or every day, preferably. I will walk it with you for as long as it takes for you to learn it, OK? Then there's no danger of you getting lost again.'

Unfair, to say the least. Makes me sound like some kind of child. Or idiot. I smile and nod, but I'm a bit put out, to be honest. And not because she's patronising me. I'm put out because this week I have actually managed to sustain my first ever sports injury. It's a massive achievement, and something I never thought I would be capable of, and I'm really proud of myself. It's been making me feel like a proper athlete – pushing myself too hard, stretching myself to my absolute limits, and beyond, in order to reach my goal. If I had spoken to anyone other than Abby and Tom, they might have said, 'Why hello there, Daisy, why are you limping?' And I'd have said, 'It's a sports injury. I've walked fifty miles over five days.' And they'd have nodded and said, 'Wow, a sports injury, you say? You must have been pushing yourself far too hard. And you could have walked to Bluewater from here!' But of course I haven't spoken to anyone outside of this flat since I got here. Apart from Wheelbarrow

70

Man, and he doesn't count. Speaking of which, I have a bit of a confession to make. All this walking I've been doing this past week hasn't entirely been down to the burning desire inside of me to get out there and train my bum off. There has been an ulterior motive. You may have spotted it, actually. I have been marching every which way around the park and its environs the past five days in a desperate attempt to try to avoid seeing that man again. When I finally got back to Abby's flat the day I saw him, I was horrified when I looked in the bathroom mirror. I was an absolute fright. I had been lost for so long, my hair was a tangled mess, I was caked in mud and leaves, my clothes were torn and ragged, and I had virtually lost the power of speech. I was reduced to communicating in grunts and hand signals. I shudder now when I think about what Wheelbarrow Man must have thought when he saw me. He's not quite so Taj-Mahal-ish as Tom is; more Machu Picchu, maybe – older and not so gleaming, but interesting to look at and very precisely sculpted – but I'm definitely still just a lump of mud. And on that occasion I was a gauche, incompetent lump of mud that all the other lumps of mud were looking down on and smirking at.

Anyway, in a determined attempt to avoid bumping into him again, I found myself walking until my feet hurt. Which would have been good, except it turns out that my feet start hurting after a total of only about fifteen or twenty miles, spread over five days. It's humiliating, actually, considering Abby took me back to the sportswear shop where we bought the trainers and made a complaint.

'Fifty miles, you say?' Martin had said, holding one of the trainers delicately in his fingers, as if it were made of glass.

I nodded vigorously. 'Yes. And now my foot is hurting. Quite badly.'

He turned the shoe over in his hands a few times, then gave it back to me with a strange smile that I didn't get at the time. I just assumed he had a sudden wind pain or something. Now of course I realise that he thought I was lying about the number of miles I'd walked. Probably to impress him. Oh God.

'There's nothing wrong with these,' he'd said, and his tone of voice was different suddenly. Deeper, more manly. As if he'd just stepped out of a 1960s public information film about safety in the kitchen. 'You just need to build up your muscles and stamina more.' And in the event of a pan fire, call a big strong man to sort it out for you.

'So? What do you think?' Abs says now. She means the training plan.

I nod. 'Yes, OK, fine. I'll do it.'

She grins and pats my leg. 'Of course you will. We start tomorrow.' She slaps her hands onto her own thighs and starts to get up, then notices my hands flapping and my head shaking. She sits back down again. 'What?'

'Tomorrow? Really? But my muscles are all aching and my foot hurts.'

She pulls one of those really sad faces you see people do when they're generally pretending to be playing a violin. 'Oh, Daze, of course, I forgot about that. Well don't worry, you must take it easy for a while. We can start in a week or two, OK?'

I smile gratefully. 'That would be a lot better. Thanks, Abs.'

'No problem, sweetheart. You take all the time you need. I'm sure all the people dying of breast cancer will understand totally.'

'Tomorrow is perfect.'

'I know.' She gets up abruptly, then turns to face me. 'Have you been eating Jaffa Cakes, by the way?'

I shrug nonchalantly and shake my head. 'What makes you say that?'

'Well, they're all gone. I only had two, and Tom says he hasn't had any since last Wednesday.' This surprises me. I didn't think Tom could say that many words all at once.

'Well, I may have had one or two but I don't think . . .'

'Plus I can see that flattened empty box stuffed under the sofa cushion.'

Shit. 'Ah. Yes. You're right. Sorry about that.'

She steps nearer and pulls the flat carton out from under me. 'Daze, if you finish them up, can you at least get some more? It's the same with the milk. Tom and I would like to enjoy some of our food and drink from time to time, you know.'

'Yes, yes, I know, I'm sorry. It won't happen again.'

She nods. 'OK,' and walks to the door as if she's leaving the room. Then at the last minute she turns, Columbo-style, and says, 'Oh, there's just one more thing.' She reaches behind her and pulls out an envelope that was tucked in her jeans back pocket. 'The estate agent brought this round yesterday.' She hands me the envelope – thick and white, with my name and Mum's address on the

73

front. And then she hits me with something far more devastating than a heavy glass paperweight. 'It's from Owen and Lake.'

Mum's solicitor.

SIX

Daisy Mack
Sometimes, acceptance is just easier. In fact, all the time. Every day, at every possible opportunity. Accept, and find happiness.

    Abby Marcus Stop complaining, it looks lovely.

    Georgia Ling Aww bless yah un xxx

    Jenny Martin You had a marriage proposal, Daisy??? xxx

Abby thinks I'm talking about my super-duper new haircut. She's right, annoyingly. I wanted to sound intriguing and deep, so that people would think I was, you know, intriguing and deep, while actually I was just talking about a haircut. Although there are one or two more things it applies to of course. My life in general, to be more specific.

After Abby inadvertently rubbed the hairs on my legs up the wrong way two days ago then frowned at me with her perfectly sculptured eyebrows, I secretly decided it was high time I gave my whole body a bit of a de-fuzz.

The local paper had already started running stories about glimpsed sightings of an escaped bear, complete with close-up photos of residents looking concerned, so I knew it was time to dust off the razor and tweezers and put everyone's minds at ease.

It's amazing really how smooth legs and shaped eyebrows can make you feel kind of invigorated. I actually felt a bit like I was on the periphery of the human race, rather than out in the field miles from anywhere. I wasn't back in, but I was approaching the steps to the porch. Maybe it was the fresh air finally touching my bald skin after all these weeks.

After it was done, I took another long look at myself in the mirror in the bathroom and decided that my head hair would also have to go. Or the ends of it would, anyway – this was only about grooming, not aero-dynamics. It was generally up in a ponytail these days, but when down had started to look like a frayed rug: fairly smooth and straight three-quarters of the way down, then the final quarter exploding outwards in an indistinguishable blur of light brown fluff. That part was no longer welcome at the Daisy Macintyre establishment.

'Just take off the ends, please,' I said to the hairdresser. Stacy, I think she was called. She had the most ruthless eyebrows I've ever seen, plucked to a line no wider than a centipede. I couldn't take my eyes off them in the mirror as she examined my head.

'Ooh isn't your hair lovely, hun,' she said, trying to jerk her fingers through the tangle at the end. She leaned forward and put her mouth right next to my ear. 'Just sooo gorgeous.'

'Oh, really? Thanks.'

'Oh yeah, it's really stunning, so silky and lovely.' In the mirror, a snarl appeared on Stacy's face as the brush got stuck again. 'You're very lucky, I'm so envious actually.'

'She's patronising you,' Mum's voice said in my head. 'Look at her hair, thick, smooth and glossy. It's insulting, Daisy. Tell her to stop.'

I opened my mouth to speak, but a sudden searing pain from the back of my head told me that clumps of my hair were being torn from my scalp by their roots. 'YOW!'

'Oopsie daisy, sorry, sweetpea, my fault.'

'Of course it's her fault,' Mum whispered furiously. 'She's yanking your hair with the brush, you're not yanking her brush with your hair. Say something!'

'Oh, er, heh heh, that's OK. Made me jump a bit, that's all.'

'Yeah, it will do m'darling. Just a teensy weensy little knot or two, all riii-iight?' By now, the muscles were standing out on Stacy's jaw and a vein was pulsing in her neck. A collection of metal bangles on her wrist were crashing repeatedly into my head and ears and her enormous tanned cleavage was squishing hard into my back. She worked the brush roughly through to the ends, then gave up on it and picked up a comb. I eyed it nervously, then gripped the arm-rests of my chair and braced.

'So how's life treating you, sweet?'

My head was being yanked back then pushed forwards repeatedly in a kind of giant exaggerated nod. I tried to relax my muscles and go floppy to avoid whiplash. 'Life is shit, actually, Stace. My mum died, then my stepdad, my real dad's in America, my sister and stepbrothers hate me and I've got nowhere to live and no job, thanks. You?'

I didn't say that. No one ever wants to hear it. I said, 'Fine, thanks. How about you?' Mum tutted loudly in my head.

'Aw, I'm good thanks, sweet. Off to Tenerife next week, can't wait actually!'

'Oh really? That sounds nice.'

'Yeah. One week all inclusive, sun, sea and sangria, three stars. Really really looking forward to it.'

'Wonderful, lucky you.'

'Yeah, I know. We go back there every year, me and Steve. They absolutely love us there 'cause we're always so up for it, ja know what I mean?'

'I think I do . . .'

'We really go for it, me and Steve. We're always messing around, having a laugh, life and soul of the party, it's a proper giggle. Last year I won the Loveliest Jubblies competition and Steve glassed the judge.'

'Shit!'

'Oh my God it was soooo funny. People shouting, tables going over, Miguel running around waving his arms, total carnage! We were in complete stitches, actually.'

'Jesus . . .'

'I laughed so much, well, everyone did, afterwards, you know, once we knew he wasn't really hurt. Hysterical.'

'Sure.'

'Yeah, holidays are brilliant. You got anything booked then?'

78

'Um, no, not yet.' Absolutely no need for her to know I was currently unemployed.

'Aw, bless. You gotta have something to look forward to, sweetie.'

At that moment, I was looking forward to gently stroking my head with my hands and telling it everything was going to be OK.

Twenty-five minutes later, she held a mirror up behind me while I examined the damage in the one in front. It was a hideous disaster. She'd taken at least three inches off the length, cut some layers in around the sides and shortened the fringe. The lack of weight from the shortened length was making the whole thing more curly and little tendrils of hair were sticking up randomly at the sides and bobbing under. The overall effect had taken fifteen years off me. I was now thirteen.

'Is that all riii-iight?' Stacy asked, although she wasn't really asking it, she was reciting lines. Her attention was fixed on an elderly lady wrapped in a towel who was being brought over from the sinks. 'Be with you in a minute, Ada, all riii-iight?' She made reflected eye contact with me again and smiled encouragingly as she picked up random sections of my hair and pulled it through her fingers. 'I've just put a couple of long layers in there, to give it some softness and definition.'

'How can it give softness *and* definition?' Mum demanded, but I was mute.

'Is it okaaa-aaay for you?'

'*Say something!*'

I nodded. 'Yes, yes, it's lovely. Thank you.'

Stacy smiled and put the hand mirror back down on

the counter. 'Fantastic. If you'd like to go and see Debra at the desk, she'll sort you out.'

I paid Debra at the desk, added a tip for Stacy, then slowly walked the three miles back to Abby's flat. It's OK, I kept telling myself, I'll wash it when I get in and dry it myself, that'll make all the difference. As if washing it would help it grow the three inches back that were gone. It didn't.

'Oh my God,' Abby said when she saw me later that day. She walked up to me, her eyes wide and stared at my face. 'Your eyebrows! Oh my God, your hair! Wait . . .' She flicked her eyes down once. 'Have you . . .?'

'Bugger off!' I stepped back away from her.

'Ooh, all right, chill. Well your hair looks lovely, anyway. It really suits you.' She examined my head critically, peering all the way round the back, then nodded approvingly. 'It's lovely. Excellent.'

I'm on the canal bank now. It's not going terribly well. I think I need some moral support.

Daisy Mack
Not approaching my nemesis. Not slowing my steps with mounting terror. Not about to die a violent and horrible death. Everything's fine.

    Suzanne Allen   Good God Daisy, what on earth is going on?

    Daisy Mack   Nothing Suze, told you. None of that is happening. Everything's fine.

    Georgia Ling   Luv it lol xxx

    Susan Pimms   What you up too?

    Abby Marcus   Brad's balls, Daisy. Get on with it.

Immediately after I post that, my instant messenger pops. I click on the message with relief: this will be the moral support I need, thank God.

Abby Marcus   Where are you?
Daisy Mack   Approaching footbridge. Stop distracting me.
Abby Marcus   OK. You can do it! Just keep going.
Daisy Mack   Ohhhh, I never thought of it like that. Thanks Abs.
Abby Marcus   Ah. Sarcasm. This is good. Things really are starting to get back to normal. xxx

When Mum was in what turned out to be her final month of life, she started to obsess about trivia. I don't mean she was desperate to spend the last of her precious time on this earth swotting up on which country has the largest temperature range in the world, or how many drops make a dash. As if she was expecting to have to pass some kind of general knowledge quiz to get . . . where she was going. What I mean is she was intensely and constantly worried about what was going to happen to us all, and all her things, after she died. Which may not seem trivial, but compared to dying in a hospice it seemed pretty irrelevant to me. She talked endlessly about the things in the house that she wanted us to have: a glass punch bowl; a china set; some silk scarves.

'Daisy, I want you to have the scarves,' she said, trying to squeeze my hand. Her hand in mine didn't feel real.

81

It felt more like a collection of twigs than anything else, but I held it anyway. I held it for as long as I could stand it.

'Mum, it's fine,' I said, smiling very widely. 'Please don't worry about it. We'll sort it all out.'

'No, no, you've got to listen. I want you to have the scarves because Naomi doesn't suit a scarf. She's too serious. But you mustn't be upset if I give her the Wedgwood set. I just think it will be better for her because she's got Russell and the house and everything.'

'Mum . . .'

'And then if she's having that, you must have the jewellery box. It needs looking after, though, Daisy Duck. It's over sixty years old so you've got to take care of it. My dad gave it to my mum on their wedding day, you know.'

'Really?' I did know. She'd told me months earlier. But she was on morphine by then and wasn't always clear about what she'd already said.

'And I need to sort out my jewellery. I need you to help me, sweetheart. I can't ask Graham because he gave me most of it and it will only upset him to know I'm giving it away.' She smiled sadly. 'I don't think he wants to face what's happening here until he absolutely has to. Do you understand?'

I nodded. Of course I understood. He didn't want to be reminded of the fact that she was dying. I totally got that. 'Yes, I understand.'

'So . . . will you do it for me?'

'Of course I will, Mum. Anything. Just tell me what you want me to do.'

It turned out she had a folder in the house with photographs and a description of every item of jewellery she owned, for the insurance, and she asked me to bring it into the hospice, with Naomi, so we could leaf through it and choose what we wanted. I used my door key to visit the house when Graham wasn't there, sneaking in and opening Mum's bedroom cabinet. I felt like I was violating her. She lost her dignity in so many ways.

Naomi went first, while I sat on the bed with an aching throat.

'I love this ring,' Naomi said excitedly, pointing to a page in the folder. 'Can I have it?' She looked at me. 'Daze? You don't want it, do you?'

I shook my head. I didn't want it. I didn't want any of it. I just wanted Mum to keep on wearing it for the next forty years.

'Excellent.' Naomi pulled the sheet of paper out of its plastic sleeve and wrote a large black 'N' on the page next to the photograph. 'Lovely.' She slid it back in and continued turning the pages until eventually she had labelled about ten things. 'Here you go, Daze,' she said, handing the folder to me. 'You choose ten, and then we'll fight over the rest.'

I took the folder but didn't open it. Mum had gone to sleep and I stared at her for a few moments, watching her chest rising and falling, willing it to keep going. I started counting the seconds that elapsed between the end of an exhale and the start of the next inhale, and as it grew from three seconds to four, then five, I began wondering if today was going to be the day.

'Wakey wakey,' Naomi said suddenly, and I jumped a

83

bit and turned to look at her. She wasn't talking to Mum, though; she was talking to me. 'Get a move on, Dozy, I've got to get going in a minute. We're going to Ikea.'

So I picked my ten, and then Naomi divided the rest out between us. By the time Mum woke up again twenty minutes later, Naomi had gone and each item had either an 'N' or a 'D' next to it.

'Oh, hi, Daisy Duck,' Mum said, smiling at me. 'When did you get here?'

I'm glad she did it now. It gave me a chance to wear some of it when I went to visit her, which she loved. She was so thin by this time that she hadn't been able to wear any of it for ages, so she was happy to see it again.

'Just don't let Graham see you wearing it,' she said, fingering a gorgeous aquamarine and diamond ring I had just taken off. She slid it onto her own pathetically thin finger and it dangled there loosely like a curtain ring, the heavy gem immediately sliding round to the underside. She laughed and slid it off again. 'Here you go, it looks a lot better on you. But don't forget, poor Graham would be devastated if he knew you had it already, before . . . anything has happened. Don't let him see, sweetheart. Promise me.'

'I promise, Mum.' I slid the ring back on my finger, not realising how devastating that promise would turn out to be.

Of course, because she was so organised about all that, it meant she didn't have to put any of those things in her will. Which meant the letter from Owen and Lake was about the house and whatever liquid assets Graham left. I knew that as I took it from Abby last Sunday.

'Aren't you going to open it?' Abby asked me, while I ran my fingers over the heavy paper.

'Yeah, course I am.' I folded the envelope in half and tucked it in my own jeans pocket. 'Just not right now.'

'Might be important.'

I shrugged. It would wait. Nothing was all that important any more.

This route that Abby and Tom have worked out for me isn't too bad actually. It's a circuit, which means I just have to keep walking until I get back again, minimal orienteering required. I start off along the road and go down to the park – one and a half miles. I skirt around the edge of the park and go through a little gap in the fence at the top end, which leads to a footpath – half a mile. I follow the footpath alongside the canal, then cross over the dual carriageway and keep on the same path all the way to the next town – four miles. Then I come back along the road for a bit, use the underpass to get back to the other side of the bypass and cut through a housing estate back to Abby's – three miles. In total, it's about nine miles. I know this because I have a brand new pedometer in my pocket, which counts my steps, multiplies that number by the length of my average pace, which I had to input in advance, and converts that figure to a measurement of how far I've walked. Also because Abby told me.

Daisy Mack
Clothed in cobwebs; feasting on flies.
  Suzanne Allen Jesus, Daisy, do some shopping for the love of Gucci.

Georgia Ling LMAO! xxx

Nat 'Wiggy' Nicholson You sound like you need a make-over, hunni.x

I'm on the approach to the footbridge over the motorway now. I'm not happy about this part of the walk, for two principal reasons. Firstly, the path is a bit overgrown and I keep swallowing insects. They stay in your throat for ages and I never know whether to swallow them to get rid of them, or try to spit them out. I'm also finding this part of the canal path is permanently festooned with cobwebs, which of course are completely invisible to the naked eye. It's not until you walk through one and find yourself trying to pull swathes of sticky strands off your face that you even know they're there. And of course, as you're trying to free yourself from their deadly little silken traps, you know that the eight-legged architect is no doubt now somewhere about your person.

Not that I'm scared of spiders. I'm not. Why would I be? They're wonderful because they don't live on left-overs, like some insects do, they set traps and hunt and provide for themselves without involving anyone else. OK, so they've got eight eyes and eight hairy legs, and let themselves down out of nowhere into your hair, and sometimes move really fast just when you're least expecting it, but –

Shit. What was that? I think there's one on me. I just felt something tickling the back of my arm. I swat at myself a few times, then rub my arm roughly, to make sure. Then I have to rub the other arm, just as roughly,

86

then both my legs, the back of my neck and finally my hair, all while hopping about madly on the spot and yelping.

I think I inherited my casual indifference to spiders from Mum. 'Spiders are fantastic,' she used to say, letting one she'd rescued from the bath run across her hand. 'They hunt and kill their own food. And you know what that food is? Flies. Flies eat poo and rubbish and give birth to maggots. The fewer of them on the planet, the better, as far as I'm concerned.' She never used to hoover up cobwebs from the corners of the rooms at home either. 'Cobwebs are nature's own flypaper,' she would say to anyone who questioned it. Although no one ever did, really. Only Graham. And only once.

Mum was pretty cool with just about everything. She could complain about bad service in shops. She could *not* tip taxi drivers. She could send food back in restaurants. She could even say she wasn't happy with a haircut. But she was paralysingly terrified of one thing. Which brings me to the second reason why I don't like this part of the walk. The footbridge. Mum was petrified of heights. And so am I.

When I was about eight and Naomi was eleven, the three of us went on a weekend away to London. I'm not entirely sure why – it may have been Mum's birthday or something like that. On the first day, we checked into our hotel, before going out for dinner and a show. We had a family room, which turned out to be a quad. Mum was not happy about that at all, I remember.

'It's a quad room,' she said to the receptionist half an

hour after we'd arrived, 'presumably because that is what this hotel thinks of as a typical family: mum, dad, little John and little Jane. But we are a family, and there are only three of us. Sadly our fourth member decided three years ago to follow his dream, and his colleague's arse, to Peterborough in search of clichés.' She smiled sweetly. 'Do you know what that means?'

The receptionist smiled. 'Well,' she started to say, then realised very quickly that she didn't need to.

'It means,' Mum went on calmly, 'that we only have one income. I am supporting myself and my two children here on only one lot of pay. So probably roughly half as much as the standard family that this hotel would usually put in the quad room.'

'Madam,' the receptionist tried, but got nowhere.

'So although I have half as much money as the people you would normally put in that room, you still want to make me pay exactly the same amount of money as they pay, by charging me a supplement for the empty bed.' She smiled at this point, and tilted her head on one side a little, as if she was watching a chimpanzee juggle oranges. 'It's hardly fair, is it, Kirsty?'

We had a slap up meal that night. They must have refunded the supplement. 'Don't let hotel bastards wear you down,' Mum said to us over dinner. 'You fight for what is right, girls, and you keep on fighting, no matter what.' She leaned towards us across the table and whispered behind her hand, 'I've never lost one yet.'

She did lose one eventually. It was her final fight, last November.

Anyway during that London trip, the three of us got

stuck on a bridge somewhere. I don't know what bridge it was, but I remember it was over water, so it didn't feel dangerous to me. Not at first, anyway. But apparently it did for Mum. Naomi and I hadn't noticed that she'd slowed her steps quite a lot as we set out on it, and scampered off ahead. By the time we heard her faint voice calling our names and turned round to see what she wanted, she was motionless, white and crouching. I stared at her in horror as she moved one arm about two inches away from her body and pulled her fingers very slowly towards herself twice. I looked up at Naomi, not understanding what was going on.

'Oh for goodness' sake,' Naomi said, taking hold of my arm. 'Come on, we gotta go back.'

'What's happened, Nomes?'

She didn't answer, just marched me back across the bridge to Mum's side. When we got there, I could see that Mum's left hand was wrapped around the lower part of the railing so tightly that not just the knuckles had gone white, her whole hand had. And, oddly enough, her face. I looked at her and was horrified by the terror in her eyes.

'Mummy?'

'It's OK, Daisy Duck,' she croaked, skinning her thin lips back from her teeth. I recoiled, and I remember wondering if this was really my mum squatting there or some other being inhabiting her body. A frightened, weak other being.

'What's the matter?' I asked tremulously.

'I'm OK,' she said, trying to smile again. I didn't like it when she did that. I wished she'd stop.

89

'Mum, you've got to move,' Naomi said at this point. She put her hand on Mum's white fingers and tried to unwind them from the railing, but Mum started shaking her head and moved her other hand on top of the first one.

'Can't,' she whispered, probably hoping I wouldn't hear her. She was very fond of telling me there was no such word.

Naomi sighed and let go, then sat down on the ground next to Mum. 'Might as well sit down, Dozy,' she said. 'We're likely to be here for a while.'

'Why? What's going on? Why won't you tell me?'

'May I be of assistance, ladies?' a male voice broke in at this point. The three of us all turned and looked up at a man in jeans and gleaming white trainers, standing above us. I remember that his jeans had a crisp crease running down the centre of each leg.

'We're fine, thanks,' Mum half-whispered immediately, trying to give the impression of strength and capability. She was pretty convincing, in spite of a bloodless face and tremors in her voice.

'You don't look fine,' he said, crouching down to mirror her pose. 'Seriously, won't you let me help you? You can't live here – the council won't allow it.'

'Thank you,' Naomi said at this point, standing up. 'My name is Naomi, that's my sister Dozy, and this is our mum, Anne.'

'Nice to meet you all,' he said, glancing briefly at me, then focusing back intently on Mum. 'My name is Graham.' He extended his hand to her. 'Take hold of my arm; I'll help you get across.'

Daisy Mack
Getting high. Not good.

> **Suzanne Allen** Certainly sounds good. Although, of course, I would have absolutely no idea whether it's good or not. It's all a complete mystery to me. Unknown territory as it were.

> **Jenny Martin** Suzy you're protesting far too much lol!

I'm at the footbridge now. Actually I've already been standing here for a few minutes, trying to get up the courage to go over it. My stomach is churning and my heart is thudding as if I've just bumped into Hugh Grant. I don't know how Mum even *began* to cross that bridge in London back then, when she had two children with her. I feel nervous enough carrying my iPod across. For some reason it feels like everything I'm holding is in danger of going over the side.

OK, there's nothing to be done other than put one foot in front of the other until I reach the other side. I've discovered that if I sing that old song 'Help', it really does help.

'Why don't you close your eyes?' Abby said to me, the first time she walked over it with me.

'How will that help?'

'Well, you won't be able to see how high up you are.'

'Again, how will that help?'

Right, I'm on the bridge. I am not going to look anywhere except straight ahead. I am not paying any attention to the cars and lorries speeding past below me.

'Afternoon,' says a voice unexpectedly, and I suddenly realise that under the whoosh of the blood rushing in

91

my ears I've just heard some light footsteps approach behind me.

'Hi,' I say weakly, as a man in tight black Lycra shorts and a clingy vest top jogs easily past me. As he passes, he turns slightly, makes eye contact and gives a little smile. His blond hair is falling beautifully across his forehead in a floppy curl, and the eyes that meet mine are clear and crystal blue. My knees, already dangerously weak, practically give out at this point. 'Come on then,' he says, and makes a forward sweeping gesture with his arm, as if he's moving over to allow me to go past.

I shake my head. 'N'th'nks,' I manage to croak out, the combination of the footbridge and his thighs making me virtually unintelligible. Oh God, I used to be good at this. And I don't mean walking.

'Come *on*!' he repeats, turning again and grinning more broadly. Then, to my utter horror, he actually runs backwards on the bridge for a few steps and I almost vomit. I have to look away as my heart stops dead in my chest and even though I've turned away, I squeeze my eyes shut too. He's going over, he's so going over, he's definitely going over. I cringe and tense, clenching my fists and my jaw, my whole body a taut muscle waiting for the trip, the shout of terror, the scream; and after two or three seconds of heavy anxious breathing, I don't hear it. I crack one eye open. Sunny day; bridge; man jogging lightly away. Now I'm just a very tense woman watching a fit man jogging. With effort I relax my shoulders and loosen my fists, turning to face forwards again and straightening up a little. Thank God he didn't see that.

He's almost at the other end of the bridge now. If I'd

been jogging like him, I might have reached the other side too. I might also have caused a deep, ancient fault in the concrete finally to splinter under the thud of my feet, and have tumbled to my death in a sickening avalanche of twisted metal and rock. I shake my head and accidentally catch sight of a couple of cars and a lorry speeding past below me, which makes me gasp and wobble. I have to stop and grab hold of the handrail quickly and bend my knees. Somehow getting my centre of gravity six inches nearer the ground seems to help, even a million feet up in the air.

'See you again!' the runner calls back to me from the safety of the path on the other side. I'm frozen here, thanks to him, and I realise as his beautiful buttocks bounce out of sight that I had been kind of hoping he would come back and rescue me, like Graham did for Mum more than twenty years ago.

'I don't need any help.' Her voice between gritted teeth sounds in my head, and I remember that once Graham offered to help her, she managed to stand up and get moving without once taking his arm. She was such an inspiration to me: so incredibly strong and capable. Even when sheer, undiluted terror had her in its grip and reduced her to a gibbering jelly, she was still able to make herself get up and get moving because she had had to learn to rely on no one but herself.

I'm nothing like that. It is totally unnatural for this bridge and this path to be up here in the air. It defies gravity and surely can't hold out much longer. I feel so exposed and unstable up here, as if the whole thing is about to disintegrate beneath my feet and send me plummeting the two hundred thousand feet to the motorway below, where I will be smashed and broken before being pulped under the wheels of a ninety-ton lorry, five cars and a camper van. I curl my fingers more tightly around the railing and lower my body further towards the path. I'm rigid with fear now, completely unable to think about moving, or think at all, and there's only one thing I can do. I reach round behind me very slowly and pull my phone out of my pocket; then, keeping my entire body absolutely still apart from my left hand, I write a text.

Abs, I need help

Seconds later, the phone vibrates in my hand as the reply arrives.

Daze, I'm wrking. Client in 15. You gotta get yrself across on yr own.

I can't.

NO SUCH WRD. Just do it.

Am paralysed. There is no 'just do it'.

Nikes sake, stfu. NOT paralysed. Get on with it. It'll mak you strnger.

What a great friend she is.
Ten minutes later I reach the other side of the bridge, and stand up. Fortunately no one walked past me as I

crossed, and after I've brushed the dirt off my hands and knees, you can't even tell what I was doing.

When I get back to Abby's flat half an hour later, I hear raised voices in the kitchen as I let myself in. It's a man and a woman, although Abs said she had another client so she shouldn't be home yet. I stand in the hallway and take my magic trainers off as quietly as possible. So that the two people arguing aren't embarrassed about being overheard, of course; nothing to do with wanting to hear what they're saying.

'That's not what I mean,' the man's voice says and I realise that it's Tom. He was the obvious choice of course, this being his home, but I was thrown by the quantity of words being said.

'Well, what *do* you mean?' says a woman's voice. This one I don't recognise. Definitely not Abs. The kitchen door bangs suddenly and I jump as a woman, presumably the owner of the voice, marches through it and towards me. She stares at me oddly and I realise that I am standing completely stationary with one shoe on and the other one in my hand, half bent over. I drop the shoe quickly and lift my other foot to start undoing the laces.

'Don't leave it like that,' Tom says, coming through the door. 'Sally, for God's sake.' He reaches an arm towards the woman, then sees me and drops it abruptly back to his side. His alabaster face has a very faint pinkish tinge to it, and three or four of his hairs have become displaced. The man's a mess. 'Daisy,' he says, glancing awkwardly at me, then looking away. 'I didn't hear you come in.'

I'm not used to talking to him directly and I'm not sure how to go about it. In the end I just smile and say, 'Oh.'

'I'll see you soon, Tom,' Sally says, then pulls the front door open and marches at top speed through it. 'Nice to meet you,' she says to the street, presumably meaning me, then disappears and slams the door.

In the ensuing silence, Tom and I stare at each other for a second or two. His face looks different somehow and it takes me a moment to realise what it is. His eyebrows have moved. They're fractionally closer together than usual, which changes his entire appearance. He looks . . . pained. Distraught, almost. He stares at me with those eyebrows – there's even a faint crease in the skin between them – and he looks like he's pleading with me.

'Daisy,' he says, his voice one semitone higher than normal, unrecognisable from his usual monotone. It's practically cracking with emotion.

'Erm, I gotta have a shower,' I say quickly, before he has a chance to ask me not to tell Abby what I heard. I limp past him on one trainer towards the bathroom, trying not to add it up, trying not to put the two twos together. But each time I think about it, no matter how hard I try not to, I just keep on coming up with four.

SEVEN

Daisy Mack
Is facing a bit of a dilemma . . .
    Suzanne Allen Anything I can help with?
    Daisy Mack Not really. Thanks anyway.
    Abby Marcus Whatever it is, forget it. It's not important.

She's wrong. It is important. Very much so. It's so important it has been occupying my mind constantly for the past ten minutes. And it affects her directly. The question is this: should I buy Jaffa Cakes, milk, or both?

I'm in Sainsbury's. I've walked here. This means of course that I will have to walk back, and anything I buy will have to be carried. This will make the walk home fairly hard work and pretty uncomfortable, unless I only buy small, light things. Round things. Spongy things covered in dark chocolate. They will fit nicely in my rucksack and I won't even know they're there.

That is my dilemma. Abby has asked me to get both while I'm out today, milk and Jaffa Cakes, but I so don't want to carry the milk home.

Were you thinking that my dilemma was whether or not I should tell my beautiful, kind and generous best friend Abby about the strange goings-on I witnessed in the hallway of her home two days ago, involving her statuesque yet stilted boyfriend, and a mysterious and (if I'm not mistaken) slightly older, other woman?

No. Nothing to do with me.

'Aha,' a voice says suddenly behind me and I look round to find a tall, scruffy-looking bloke with messy dark hair, wearing an old grey tee shirt, frayed jeans and dusty, scuffed work boots. I don't know him so I turn back. Maybe I could get one very small carton. They don't weigh much at all. Ooh, wait, they've got chocolate flavour . . .

'That's cold,' the voice says behind me, blatantly stating the obvious. I glance quickly to my left and right but can't see anyone else nearby. He must be one of those losers who feels the need to commentate on everything around him, as if the rest of the world is permanently gripped by his mundane and totally apparent observations. My Aunt Hazel does that. 'Phone's ringing,' she'll say. Or 'Car won't start.' When she hears a siren approaching on the street, she'll either announce 'ambulance', 'police car', or 'fire engine', depending on the type of siren. I don't really care what's coming as I'm always far too busy panicking and trying to drive my car off the road and into a parallel dimension to make sure I'm well out of the way.

I carefully ignore the man behind me, to make it clear that he's wasting his time with me. And everyone else, in fact.

'You don't recognise me, do you?' he goes on, relentlessly. 'Perhaps if I was holding a wheelbarrow . . .?' And suddenly, it clicks. This is Wheelbarrow Man from last week, the man I have been frantically trying to avoid meeting again by walking, literally, all round the houses. And now here he is, by the milk in Sainsbury's. At exactly the same moment I am. Don't you just love irony?

I turn slightly, not fully round this time, just enough to catch sight of him and let him know that I'm acknowledging him, and give a half-smile. 'Oh, yeah, sorry. Hi.' I turn back to the impossible milk choices before me.

'I thought you were coming back with a clapometer,' he says now, and I can hear that he's grinning. 'I worked so hard on some new material; never got a chance to test it out.'

What the hell is he going on about? I have no idea, so I give a meaningless 'huh' noise and shrug without turning. Hopefully he'll realise that I need all my concentration to decide on the milk.

A hand reaches into the picture and closes around a four-pinter of skimmed. I only get a view of it for a couple of seconds before it retreats with its prize, but in that time I can see that it's generally grimy all over, and there is black filth under all the fingernails. My lip curls. Right here is the reason why I'm not buying milk today.

'See you on the tour then,' he says to my back. I give a minimal nod without turning, and wait for a couple of seconds until he moves away. Thank God for that. Filthy people always give me the creeps. Or maybe it was just him.

On the way home, I have to walk through the housing

estate. I love this bit of the walk, for two principal reasons. Firstly, it's all good solid pavement, so no mud, loose shingle, scary bridges or eight-legged freaks. The going is good to firm, with no elevation or dangerous foliage. There are lots of large hydrangea and lavender bushes bursting out of gardens, some of which overhang badly over the pavement which is a little bit annoying, but they're easy enough to avoid. The homeowners shouldn't really let them get into the sort of state that affects pedestrians, but at least if they do brush me as I pass, I don't get stung or scratched. I frown in the general direction of the house windows when this occurs, hoping someone might some day see the inconvenience they're causing and do something about it. It hasn't worked yet.

The second reason I like this part is that it's so inter-esting to look into the gardens and un-becurtained windows of the houses and observe a snapshot of the lives playing out behind them. It's a bit like watching a soap, except less murder and brawling and more hoovering. For me, it's a little tether to normality, at a time when I'm feeling adrift and directionless.

'It seems so weird that life is just going on as normal,' I said to Abby once when we walked past here. 'Everyone carries on buying milk and hanging out the washing and paying the leccy bill and arguing and loving, as if every-thing's fine and nothing devastating has happened.'

'Yes, I know,' she said, looking at me pointedly. 'It's hard to believe sometimes that thousands of people have died or lost their homes in floods and earthquakes in some parts of the world, isn't it?'

There's one particular house along here that I'm

looking forward to passing today. It's got such a beautiful front lawn, very green and smooth, no weeds, it's plainly obvious that someone lives here who really cares about it, and has got the time to spend on it. The edges are really crisp, too, where it meets the flower borders. It pleases me, the sharpness of the earth there. It looks like the inside of a slice of mud cake, with grass icing.

The houses along here remind me very much of Mum and Graham's house. Well, technically it was Graham's house, but when they got married Mum sold our old place and put all the money she got for it into extending Graham's, so there was enough room for all of us. I think a lot was spent on updating it too. He'd lived there on his own for years, so it was in a terrible state. Really gruesome. He had wallpaper in the kitchen that featured pictures of cutlery; an avocado bathroom suite; and bright red swirly patterned carpet everywhere. There were only three bedrooms, so they had a huge two-storey extension built at the side which made a bedroom each for me and Naomi, and a second bathroom for us to share. Darren and Lee – Graham's two boys – didn't live there, but he wanted them to have a room each anyway, for when they visited.

Ah, there's a woman standing on the driveway of the house with the lovely lawn. Is she tending it? I'd love to know how she gets her edges so crisp. I turn the music off but leave the earphones in, as a kind of disguise. It's a great way to look like you're deaf to your surroundings, while straining every nerve to hear what's going on, just in case something interesting happens. Also it tends to stop weird strangers from talking to you. Having said

101

that, wearing earphones has on at least one occasion actually encouraged one of the weirdos out there to approach me. It was while I was walking along the canal bank a couple of days ago, and there was no one else around. This particular weirdo was shirtless and carrying a lager can in one hand, two factors that immediately made me feel apprehensive. I dropped my gaze and moved quickly to the extreme edge of the path, employing my standard tactic for avoiding any kind of contact with weirdos: the old classic 'if I don't see them, they can't see me' manoeuvre. In my peripheral vision I could see that he was lurching towards me, looking directly at me, and that his mouth was moving. He was clearly slurring something to me. There was absolutely no way I wanted to engage in any kind of interaction with this grinning freak, so it was crucial to make not the slightest eye contact, even accidentally, and to maintain the stance of being completely oblivious to his presence in front of me by shunning him in every way possible.

'Pardon?' I said politely, stopping and taking one earphone out of my ear. Oh damn, shit, bugger and balls! My good manners, bred into me relentlessly by my mum, had kicked in automatically – testament to her top notch parenting. Thanks to her, I was completely unable to ignore another human being when he was clearly addressing me, even though he was half naked and wholly drunk – exactly the sort of stranger Mum would have wanted me to avoid at all costs. Great. Now I had engaged him in conversation. Thanks, Mum.

'I said, can I press my cheek against yours and listen to your music with you?' he repeated, coming even nearer and smiling still more broadly. He swigged from his can enthusiastically. For one alarming moment I thought he was going to embrace me.

'Um, no,' I said, stopping myself at the last minute from adding 'thanks'. I don't have to be polite to this one, I kept telling myself. You can ignore him, just get away from him as quickly as possible. I resumed walking and plugged my earphone back in as I did so. But not before I heard him call after me, 'Will you have an affair with me?'

'No thanks, I'm all set,' I called back, then kicked myself again for responding. What was the matter with me? Why couldn't I just be rude?

'Good manners at all times,' Mum's voice said in my head. 'Remember, girls, it's what sets us apart from the ill-mannered.'

Yes, well, my involuntary good manners could end up being my undoing one day.

Abs is waiting in the kitchen when I get home, kettle boiled and two mugs on the side with tea bags in them. 'Thank God,' she says, coming towards me. 'You've been gone ages. I'm gasping for a cuppa. Where's the milk?' I say nothing. She jerks her head forward and raises her eyebrows. 'Daze?' She grabs my rucksack and pulls it off my shoulders. 'You did get milk, didn't you?' Still I say nothing. She's rummaging through the bag now and pulls out the carrier bag with the Jaffa Cakes in it. It's clearly far too light and cardboardy to contain a large carton of milk. Or a small one. She opens it anyway and peers inside, then looks up at me accusingly. 'You didn't get any, did you? Oh for fuck's sake, Daisy.' She dumps the carrier bag on the counter, snatches up her handbag and marches to the hallway.

'Abs . . .'

'Save it. I'll get it myself.'

So she goes and gets the milk, while I make myself comfy on the sofa once more.

Daisy Mack

On the sofa, feet up, relaxing after walking 500 miles. And soon I'll have tea to dunk the Jaffa Cakes in. Couldn't ask for much more.

>   **Sarah White**   Wow, youre so lucky, wish I could, I gotta take mum shopping, gonna be such a joy lol xxx
>
>   **Suzanne Allen**   I thought you'd finished doing the whole tea and Jaffa Cake adventure by now Daisy???
>
>   **Georgia Ling**   PJ day for me to lol xxx
>
>   **Sarah White**   omg daisy I'm sooooo sorry, didn't mean that to be so insensitive, I'm such a dick just ignore me xxxxxx.

When Abs comes back fifteen minutes later she bustles around in the kitchen for a few minutes then comes through to the living room with the two mugs of tea. She hands one to me, hesitates by the sofa for a second, looking at me, then moves to one of the arm-chairs and sits down. It's totally obvious she's got something to say to me, almost definitely something bad, but apparently I am going to have to coax my reprimand out of her. It's almost overwhelmingly tempting not to bother.

'Nice tea,' I say casually, by way of an opener.

'Mmm,' she says, giving me nothing. She's produced

a magazine from somewhere and is leafing through it lethargically.

'Sorry about the milk,' I attempt, fairly confident that this is why she's annoyed with me and that it will prompt the looming lecture.

She shrugs. 'Forget it,' she says without looking up. 'Doesn't matter.'

Hm. Now I'm stumped. Didn't think I'd have to work this hard for a telling off. Right, I've got two choices here. I can give up, offer to make dinner, watch a bit of telly and get an early night; or I can ask her outright what's bothering her. One of these two options will give me a peaceful and relaxed evening over a nice meal; one of them will probably result in an argument, but in doing so will get to the bottom of Abby's mood and hopefully make amends for whatever I've done wrong and resolve it once and for all.

'Want me to make dinner tonight?' I venture.

She shakes her head. 'Nah, it's OK. Tom's getting Chinese.'

'Oh. Great.' Damn. I sip my tea, knowing that I've got no choice now but to tackle option two. I put the mug down on the floor, look up at her and say, 'Abs.'

At this moment her pocket plays the opening bars of McFly's 'Star Girl' and she slaps her hand to her hip and jumps to her feet. I think it means she's got a text message. She pulls out her phone and reads the new message, a small frown flickering across her face.

'Right,' she says, still staring at her phone. 'Apparently he's not getting the Chinese now.'

'Oh. Why not?'

She shrugs and drops her phone carelessly onto the sofa. 'Who knows? Or cares. Come on, let's sort something out ourselves.'

So we go into the kitchen and make spaghetti bolognaise together. Tom doesn't turn up and Abs doesn't mention him again. The strange woman from the hallway two days ago flickers at the periphery of my memory, but then Abby asks me to open a tin of tomatoes and she's gone.

As the evening moves on, I realise that her strange mood is probably more to do with Tom's non-appearance than anything else. Which I have to say is a bit of a relief for me as it means I'm off the hook lecture-wise. I didn't realise how tense my shoulders were until they start to loosen up a bit. We eat our spag bol on trays in front of *America's Next Top Model*, and I finally relax in the contented togetherness of good friends sharing a meal. There's no taciturn Tom to bring us all down, and the sermon I was anticipating is obviously not now going to materialise. I beam over at Abs affectionately as she drops her fork onto her empty plate. What a wonderful, generous and sweet friend she really is.

'Stop gawping and get on with your food,' she says. 'You know we've only got about a month left before the MoonWalk?'

'Bloody hell, I'd better eat up.' I bend low over the plate and spade quantities of food rapidly into my mouth repeatedly. Abs rolls her eyes. I chew and swallow exaggeratedly quickly before loading my fork up again, ready to go. 'Anyway, it's at least two months, Abs. Honestly, you're panicking over nothing.'

She leans forward and fixes me with her voodoo stare. My fork freezes mid-air between plate and mouth, but I am powerless to do anything. My mouth is open, waiting to receive the food, but I can't even close it to preserve a milligram of dignity. It's like looking at Medusa. Except, of course, Abs really has got the most gorgeous hair. Very thick and lustrous, and at the moment a beautiful shiny mink colour. I think this might actually be her natural shade, but I could be wrong – I haven't known her long enough.

'One,' she says, in a voice that reminds me of cudgels with bits of broken glass sticking out of them, 'I am *not* panicking. This is not me panicking, Daisy, believe me. If I was panicking, you would most definitely not be relaxing comfortably on the sofa in front of a giant plate of pasta, watching some trashy crap on my telly.'

'Wh— ?' is all I manage to say with locked jaw muscles. My mouth is filling with saliva in anticipation of the forkful of food that is tantalisingly close, but it might as well be a million miles away. I wish it was – I probably wouldn't be able to smell it.

'You would be out there right now, pounding the pavement. You would have been out there for four hours already. And you would have covered fifteen miles in that time. At least.'

I manage to nod my head a millimetre, to demonstrate my understanding. 'Uh-huh.' That at least is easy to say with an open mouth.

'But I'm not panicking, so here you are, stationary and peaceful.' She stops and eyes me thoughtfully for a moment. 'Thinking about it, maybe I should be panicking.

I mean, your walk today, all nine miles of it, took you almost four hours.'

'Uh . . .' I interject, to remind her succinctly that I did have to detour into Sainsbury's for the milk today, which must have added at least half an hour onto my time, if not more.

'Fifteen minutes tops,' she says, 'and you didn't even get the milk so it was a wasted journey anyway. But that's not what I want to talk to you about now.' She glances abruptly at her watch and stands up, collecting the empty plate. 'OK, secondly,' she says, turning to face me, 'the walk is not two months away, it is exactly four weeks. It's the second of May today, and the walk is the thirtieth. Four weeks, Daze. You're doing well, but we need to intensify your training now. You're going to have to step up the pace, otherwise we'll still be trudging round London at eleven o'clock in the morning, hours after everyone else has finished.'

'What?'

She rolls her eyes. 'God, don't you ever listen? The MoonWalk starts at midnight, remember? When I put our names forward, I said that we would complete it in between six and seven hours. That means we have to finish by seven a.m. At the latest.'

At last she releases her mental hold on me and I am able to lower my fork back down to my plate. I don't though. I drop it. It clatters noisily and spectacularly on the china, and bolognaise and spaghetti fly off it in little orange splatters on the plate, my lap, the sofa and, in one case, the floor. There's a second's hiatus as Abby and I stare at it all, then we both start talking at once.

108

'What are you *doing* . . .?'

'What were you *thinking* . . .?'

'That's so careless of you, look at the mess . . .'

'That's so rash of you, look at me . . .'

'It'll never come out . . .'

'I'll never be ready . . .'

'So get practising then!' she shouts finally, before storming out of the room dramatically and slamming the door. I have time to draw breath once before she bursts back in, damp cloth in hand, and drops to her knees, where she starts rubbing at the orange stain on the carpet and the sofa cushion next to me. For a few moments the only sounds in the room are the desperate friction noise of J-cloth against velour, and her own angry grunting. I watch her as she works, not really knowing what to do. I feel I should help in some way, but it's a one-person job and she seems to have it covered. Eventually she sits back on her haunches and puts her hand on her forehead.

'Shit,' she says, which I do think is a bit of an over-reaction. The stains are gone, there's no harm done. She's got her eyes closed and is frowning really hard and shaking her head. 'Oh shit it all, shit to everything, it's all just complete shit.'

'Oh Abs, I'm really sorry . . .'

She opens her eyes. As she looks at me her frown smooths out and she gives me a weak smile. 'Oh, no, it's not you, Daisy, don't worry. It's fine.'

'But I feel awful, Abs. I didn't get the milk, I've dropped food everywhere, I'm not training hard enough . . .'

'No, honestly, don't worry. Seriously. It's really and truly not you.' She reaches up and gives my knee a little squeeze. 'You're great, Daze. I mean it. Sometimes I just don't know what I would do without you.'

She smiles weakly again, then gets up and goes back to the kitchen. And suddenly I wonder, somewhat belatedly, if she's a bit more upset about Tom's whereabouts than I first realised.

EIGHT

Daisy Mack
has got plenty of other things to be getting on with. Like slumping. Why doesn't anyone ever slump any more?

> **Jadeyy-Jo Armitage**   Heyyy Daizy, jus got bak from LA! Met Robbie williams – fan-fuckin-tastic! Looool! Hows everytin wit yu?

> **Daisy Mack**   Much the same as you actually Jade.

> **Georgia Ling**   Love yu babes x

The next day is Sunday but there's no rest for me. Or for anyone, apparently. Abby bangs on my bedroom door at half past eight with the affectionate and time-honoured greeting 'Get up, you lamo.' An hour later we're tramping along the misty canal bank together. That's slumber to saunter in sixty minutes – my personal best. I'm really pleased.

Abby doesn't seem impressed, though. She's unusually quiet for the first fifteen minutes of our walk, no doubt dwelling over something to do with the late arrival of her lover last night. I'm not even sure that he came home at all, but then again, I wasn't lying awake in my bed all night waiting for him.

'Do you know what time Tom came in last night?' Abs says suddenly, not slowing her pace at all. I'm distinctly out of breath and my calf muscles feel like they're about to explode in a ball of fire out of my skin, but I'm determined to keep up with her. Tom's very fit, of course – he has to be, in his line of work (whatever it is) – and they're always off doing something together. Playing squash, riding bikes, jogging, that kind of thing. Although come to think of it, I haven't seen much of that since I've been living with them. Wonder why that is. But Abs is still pretty fit, so she's confident she doesn't need to do all that much training for this simple little walk we're planning. Looking at her now, striding along like a furious teacher, I have to say I agree. She's not panting, her face isn't red, she hasn't even broken into a sweat. Miss Chambers, my old art teacher, was more out of breath after a short march back to the staff room from the art block. Mind you, she may have been breathless with fear at the time; Stewart Dawson had just threatened her with a craft knife.

Abs has turned her head and is looking at me expectantly. She's waiting for an answer. I was hoping her question was rhetorical. 'No,' I gasp. Luckily I can get away with just the one syllable.

'Two o'clock,' she spits, flaring her nostrils. 'I'm surprised you didn't hear him. He made the most godawful noise coming in. Tripped over something, let the door slam, didn't even bother to lower his voice.'

'Uh-huh.'

'He was pissed, of course. Completely shit-faced. Fell into bed and breathed alcohol fumes all over me. Just as well there were no naked flames in the room – we would all have gone up.'

'Ah.'

'Are you all right?' she says, finally noticing how near to death I am. I shake my head and stop at last, then bend over and put my hands on my thighs. 'Oh, sorry, Daze,' she says, walking over to me. 'I was forgetting you're not as fit as Tom.'

'S'OK.'

We stand together for a few moments while I claw my way back to life. Abs has her hands on her hips and is looking at me the way my granny used to look at her dog Tina while she waited for her to 'do her duty'. When I'm no longer in cardiac arrhythmia we set off again.

'You really should be able to handle this pace a bit better than that by now,' Abby says as we approach The Footbridge. My heart starts quivering again.

'I'm absolutely fine,' I pronounce, in a feeble, shaky voice.

'What's up?' She turns to look at me full on and I can just about make out in my peripherals that her eyebrows have shot up. 'Oh my God, no way! Daisy come on! You're not still scared of this tiny little bridge, are you?' I look up. I'm certain I can see the remains of a crashed aeroplane caught up among the bridge's topmost cables. Abs folds her arms. 'Seriously, how many times have you been over it these past few days?'

I try to answer but there's a mysterious boulder in my throat making all speech impossible. Abs isn't really

113

interested in the answer anyway. Any number more than one would mean I was being pathetic.

'Morning, ladies,' a voice says suddenly behind me and I jerk up to see a man jogging lightly towards us, turning as he reaches us to smile. As he makes eye contact with me I realise with a start that I recognise him – it's the same runner that came past me on Thursday, in this exact same spot. When I was looking like a pale, pathetic, terrified, wobbly jellyfish, crossed with a sweaty hippo. A jell-ippo. Either way, I wasn't at my best. God, what must he have thought of me? But Abs is with me today, and I'm not quite as terrified with her here as I was alone, which means I probably look quite different. Quick mental rundown of how I look now: pale, pathetic, terrified, wobbly jellyfish. Great. Well OK, maybe not pale. The pace Abby has had us at this morning has at least made me red in the face, so I've got some colour in my cheeks other than grey. It's a start. With a conscious effort I stand up straighter and smile calmly, assuming the appearance of someone who is totally fine with walking across footbridges over motorways. I even take one hand off the railing and lean a bit. I look right at home. To see me there now, you would probably think I've just got back from a bridge holiday in Nepal, crossing gaping chasms on a rickety rope bridge every day like Indiana Jones. I'm strong, confident and relaxed. There's absolutely no way he'll recognise me.

'Oh, hello again,' he says. Bugger. 'How's it going? Good to see you upright today.' He glances at my strong, confident stance. 'Or almost!' Today he's in black Lycra shorts and black top with neon pink side panels. It's a very becoming outfit – sets off his blond hair and chiselled jaw perfectly.

I ignore Abs's scandalised expression next to me and find myself automatically performing the next move in the dance: a winning smile back to show that I have received his initial advance, found it agreeable, and am open to more. It's like muscle memory. He's turned right round now and is jogging backwards, grinning, the distance between us already extending. I can see the glutes moving beneath the skin of his thighs. 'I'm much better today, thanks. Just pausing before we cross the bridge.'

'What's the problem with the bridge?'

'She's–' Abby starts, but this is definitely my conversation.

'I don't like heights,' I cut in. I see in my periphery that she's put her hands on her hips.

'Ah, is that all? Nothing to fear there, you know. This bridge has been here for over fifty years.' He's having to shout now, and keeps glancing over his shoulder to make sure he's not about to crash into something.

'All the more likely to crumble away then,' I call back.

'Ha ha!' he says, not actually laughing. 'See you again.' He waves, then turns back to face front.

'Only if I survive!' I shout. Without turning he raises his arm again in acknowledgement, then disappears round the corner.

Abby has been staring at me open-mouthed the entire time. 'What the fuck was that?' she says now. 'Were you . . . *flirting*? Come on, let's not cross the bridge today, I want to hear about this. Walk and talk.'

We continue past the bridge and I relax with relief. Then I frown. 'Oh, God, I wasn't flirting was I? Looking like this? He'll be in the pub tonight telling all his mates, "Hey, guess who flirted with me today? Only Nanny bloody McPhee."'

'He'll probably keep that to himself, to be honest . . .'

'Yeah, OK, thanks. Anyway, it wasn't a proper inter-action, I just saw him here a couple of days ago. He said hello, I said hello. No hidden meaning, just standard greetings.' Abby knows as well as I do – better, probably – that the secret of successful flirting is hidden meaning. So if I'd said, 'Ooh, what an absolutely *gorgeous* pair of shorts, where did you get *those*?' the meaning would have been something else entirely and all three of us would have known exactly what was going on.

Oh bloody hell, why didn't I say *that*?

'Ooh-ooh. Well, nice work, Miss M. Almost seemed a bit more like your old self for a second there.' I look at her for a few moments and can see that she's reflecting on what just happened and seems pleased. She looks up and catches me staring.

'Hey, don't get carried away, Miss M, it was just a vague hello to a passing stranger. The MoonWalk litera-ture advises to do that to reduce the risk of attack. Or something.'

She shrugs. 'Fair enough. I'll say no more.' She grins at me. 'He was pretty fit though, wasn't he?'

I turn to her with a serious expression. 'That, Madame, is a *woefully* gross understatement.' We grin at each other, and as we walk, our shoulders knock together.

When we get home later she pours us a lemonade each and we drink it standing in the kitchen. Or at least she

116

does. I daren't drink for a few moments as my body is still completely occupied pulling in large volumes of oxygen as fast as it can. Introducing lemonade into the mix could result in disaster.

'I've got a plan, Daze,' Abby says suddenly.

'Uh?'

'Yeah. You know what I was saying about you needing to speed up? How about if someone goes walking with you?'

I shake my head emphatically. 'No need.'

She juts her chin towards me. 'Seriously, Daze. I know what you're like. It's not as if you're physically incapable of walking faster, because you aren't. You've improved so much these past three weeks. But I think you get so distracted, your steps slow down without you even realising it.'

'Nah, I don't think so.'

'Yes, I know you don't think so. That's my point. The clue's in the "without even realising it" part. No, just listen a minute. We started out at a good pace, you kept up with me all right. But then for some reason you slowed right down before we even got to the canal bank, and when I looked at you, you had that kind of glazed faraway look in your eyes.'

This lemonade is quite delicious. I've taken a tentative sip and have successfully managed to get it down my throat to my stomach, completely bypassing my windpipe and lungs, even though they are still sucking in air hard. I sip again. It's luscious. Sweet, with a strong tartness, making the glands in my jaw throb. Which surprises me because Abby and Tom usually go for the value stuff, with the white label, which is always a bit tasteless. But this stuff is completely different. I hold up the glass and notice for the first time that it's cloudy and greenish-yellow, and actually seems to have bits of lemon floating around in it. If I didn't know better I'd have said this was home-made lemonade. It's not even fizzy. I look up at Abby and try to imagine her squeezing lemons, mixing in the sugar, adding it to all the other mysterious ingredients, whatever they are, and producing this yummy concoction like some kind of domestic goddess. Today she's in extremely short shorts made of black spandex, a very tight pink crop top and long pink fingernails. She's wearing full make-up – mascara, lipstick, eyeliner – even for walking, and her hair is, as always, immaculate. Her idea of home-made is to use one of her fingernails to slit the cellophane on a microwave meal. No way did she make this.

'Yeah, that's the one, right there,' she says now, incomprehensibly. She puts her hands on her hips and nods at me.

'What?'

'Doesn't matter. The point is, I want you to walk with someone during the week. It can't be me, I've got work. So I've got this friend who has agreed to walk with you. To speed you up and help you focus. It will be . . . What? What's the matter?'

I'm already shaking my head. 'No, no, no, I do not need to walk with any of your lame, nerdy driving school mates, thank you very much.'

'I wasn't talking about them . . .'

I put my hand up. 'No. Seriously, Abs. I won't walk with some stranger. Oh my God, that would be so unbelievably

118

embarrassing. I'm not a child, I don't need a supervising adult with me to hold my hand when I cross the road.'

'I'm not talking about the Green Cross Code man. I just mean someone to keep you on track. Literally. Not doddering off blithely into the path of an oncoming post office van without looking.'

I roll my eyes. I don't know how many times over the next fifty years she's likely to bring this up, but I bet it's more than fifty. She's mentioned it at least twice a day for the past week already. It's not even as if I was in any real danger. The van managed to swerve and skid into the hedgerow behind me in plenty of time. 'Can't you let that go now? It must be at least a week ago.'

She glares at me for a moment, then relaxes. 'OK, yeah, you're right, sorry, Daze. I don't know why I got so worked up really. It wasn't anything major, was it, just one element of our walk last weekend.'

'Exactly.'

'It was a good walk, wasn't it? Really lovely.' She holds out her hand and extends the fingers one at a time. 'That sweet dog on the canal bank; the ducks on the lake in the park; a yummy ice cream; standing helpless at the roadside screaming my best friend's name repeatedly while she totters into the road straight in front of a giant, red, *fast* approaching vehicle.' She nods thoughtfully. 'Yep. That walk had it all.'

I don't remember it being like that at all. I reckon she's over-reacting. Probably having one of those adrenalin rush things that makes you see everything in slow motion or bigger or yellow or whatever it is.

'All right, you've made your point. Several times. So I was stupid that one time . . .'

'No, I'm not saying you were stupid, Daze. You're just a bit . . . unaware at the moment. No, that's not the right word. You're not unaware. You're more . . . off the fucking planet. Come on, face it. You've got horribly lost a couple of times. You nearly got killed on the road. You got propositioned by a weirdo. You've been scratched, stung, bitten, burnt . . .'

'Burnt?'

'All right, that was an exaggeration. But all the others are true and I worry about you.'

'You don't need to . . .'

'Yes I do, you witless fathead, because if I don't you *will* get stabbed, or abducted, or fall off a bridge, or drown in the canal, or go under the wheels of a bus and *die*.' She glowers at me a moment. 'Or, you know, get a nasty shock.'

Isn't Abby just the best friend ever? Looking at her now, standing across the kitchen from me holding her drink, I notice that her face is a little bit pinched and grey. I don't mean she's pinched and grey. I mean she's moved one notch towards being pinched and grey. There are still hundreds of notches ahead of her. She'll probably never be pinched, or grey, even when she's a hundred and four. But she's obviously genuinely worried about me, which surprises me. No, it doesn't surprise me. That's not what I mean. Of course she's worried about me. I'm a mess. I would worry about me, if I were her. What surprises me is not that she's worried, but that I've never really noticed it there before. I've been aware of her worrying, and taking care of me, and sorting out aspects of my life for me, but I've never seen it on her face before. Now her expression looks like she's in actual physical pain. Not excruciating torture. Not searing, white hot agony. Just pain. An ache. A chronic, depressing, exhausting ache that she just wants to be free of.

'Oh Abby. I'm sorry.' I feel a huge surge of affection for her at this moment, and cross the kitchen to give her a hug. 'I'm so, so sorry.'

She hugs me tightly and we stand together like that for a few seconds before she pulls back and looks into my face. Her eyes are shiny and she blinks a couple of times and rubs them. Well, she does the mascara-ed up version of rubbing her eyes, which is to very carefully push the side of her index finger up along her lower eyeline on each eye in turn.

'So, this friend of mine has agreed to walk with you, to watch out for you when you zone out, and to help you keep your speed up. Like a . . . I don't know what the correct expression is. Someone who sets the pace. You know?'

'A pacemaker,' Tom says now, walking suddenly into the kitchen. He strides easily over to where Abs is standing and embraces her tightly, then they pull apart a little and kiss.

'Isn't that something that controls your heart?' Abs says softly, gazing up into his face. Looks like everything is fine between them now. The hallway woman flashes briefly into my mind, but whoever she was, it seems she was nothing to do with Tom and Abby's relationship. Some kind of sweat band crisis, I expect. They probably all fell off the display onto the floor, and she couldn't be bothered to pick them up. 'Don't leave it like that,' Tom would have said. Which explains everything perfectly. Time for me to make myself scarce, I think. And I'm more than happy to leave the subject of a walking companion unresolved.

When I get into my room, the first thing I see, as I always do, is the letter from Owen and Lake, Mum's solicitors, that arrived last weekend. Well, actually it's the second thing I see. The first thing is always the giant poster-sized note that Abby has stuck to the wall directly opposite the door, with a 'TO DO' list on it in giant, poster-sized thick black marker pen letters. I know things like 'Call Naomi', 'Get a job', 'Find a flat' are all on there, as well as one or two others (mostly relating to smiling and being more positive), but I've decided not to look at it just yet. I've got enough on my plate at the moment with my rigorous training programme. I am intensely focused, like a top athlete before an event, using visualisation techniques, deep breathing, yoga and meditation to prepare myself physically and mentally for the challenge ahead. If I allow myself no distractions at all and concentrate one hundred percent on my training, I will have a much better chance of succeeding.

I fling myself down onto my bed and flick onto Facebook on my phone.

Abby Marcus
is wondering if anything ever stays the same. Answers on a postcard . . .
   Suzanne Allen Hey Abs. Wanna give me a call?

Ha. Maybe subconsciously she actually wants me to stay here in her flat forever. No, that can't be right. I'm pretty sure that 'Find a flat' is actually the first thing on the giant 'TO DO' list that she's created for me.

Daisy Mack You're right, Abs, it doesn't. Which means, on the plus side, that I won't be in your spare room forever.
Suzanne Allen Does this mean that you've found a flat, Daisy?

After reading – and not deigning to respond to – Suze's comment, my gaze is inexorably drawn to the 'TO DO' list again, so I quickly avert my eyes. Unfortunately they land automatically on the letter from Owen and Lake, which is propped up against the mirror on the dressing table. To start with I left it folded in half and stuffed it in my underwear drawer (no one ever looks in there, ha ha), but after a couple of days of trying not to think about it and failing, I faced up to the fact that I couldn't ignore it forever and forced myself to deal with it. I yanked open the drawer, pulled out the letter and propped it up on the dressing table. Now my eyes land on it every time I look away from Abby's list. I could avert my eyes from it quickly now, but they'd only end up looking at the 'TO DO' list again, and I could potentially end up stuck here forever, like a ball bearing in a pinball machine. Instead I get up, move slowly over to the dressing table and pick the letter up, holding it lightly at arm's length, just with my fingertips. It's a kind of desensitisation process, to bring me nearer and nearer to the moment when I'll actually have to open it. Like that girl who had to get nearer and nearer to a box with a spider in it, until eventually she was able to let the spider crawl over her hand. I'm not quite ready to do that, yet, but I'm getting nearer. The spider's still in the box but I can hold the box now. No need to open it anyway; I know it's a spider in there. My eyes sting a little and my throat aches, but it's better than the first time I held it. As I eye it nervously, I can't help but be reminded of a certain other letter I received recently, containing similar information to what I know is going to be in this one. I had no idea at all what was going to be in that first one, though.

It was about two weeks after Graham died, back in February. I was on the sofa, of course, and Hugh was on the telly. I think it was 'Two Weeks Notice' – that one with Sandra Bullock. I'm fairly sure it's not a Richard Curtis, but still good. Although she's annoying, as usual. I can never decide whether it's the writer or the director that makes her so annoying, or whether it's just her. It's probably just her.

Anyway, Abs arrived. She was by my side practically all day, every day then. She had her own key to the house. She let herself in, scooped up the post that was lying on the mat, then waded through the McVitie's-box sea that surrounded my sofa island, and sat down next to me. I quickly pressed 'pause'.

'Post,' she said, by way of a greeting. We'd established a routine by this time. She didn't move out of my view of the television screen until after I'd opened and read all the post. 'Only two things, Daze. Come on.'

I wriggled myself into a semi-upright position and opened the first one. It was a sympathy card from

124

someone or other. I handed it back to Abs and she stood it up on the mantelshelf with the others. The second envelope contained a letter, but it may as well have been a giant, eight-hairy-legged spider jumping suddenly onto my hand. It was a single sheet of paper with handwriting in black biro on one side. I looked immediately at the bottom to see who it was from and, finding it was Darren, my stepbrother, I felt momentarily relieved. Nothing bad was likely to be here, I thought. I was wrong.

Daisy,

It will come as no surprise to you I'm sure to learn that my late father's wishes regarding the proceeds from the estate do not include you. I remember only too clearly the distress and upset you caused your mother over the years, something my father never forgot for the rest of his life.

The house is already on the market and we will expect you to move out before it's sold. You are not permitted to take anything with you other than your own belongings that you brought with you. We also expect you to leave it in a clean and presentable condition. God knows what sort of state it's in now. I suggest you make a start on the cleaning straight away.

They say that if you wait long enough people will get what they deserve. My father waited a long time for this but finally his wishes will be executed and you will get what you deserve.

Regards,
Darren

'Everything OK?' Abs had said, peering at my face.

I had nodded and forced a smile. 'Yeah, fine.' I waved the letter feebly. 'Darren.'

'Oh. What's he want?'

'House is on the market. Gotta move out.'

Abs nodded slowly, then rubbed the back of my hand and smiled kindly. 'Well, we knew this would be coming, didn't we? It's good news in a way – it means you'll get the money your mum was so desperate for you to have. That'll make her happy, wherever she is.'

My eyes had filled with tears at this point, but that was OK, I was tearful nearly all the time anyway. Abby leaned forward and gave me a cuddle, not realising I had just been told my mum's wishes were going to be ignored, which felt like losing her all over again. I knew she had taken some comfort from the fact that her death would ultimately result in Naomi and me inheriting quite a large amount of money. 'You're both going to be quite well off,' she had said, over and over, during her final weeks. 'You'll be set up for life.' It was the only good thing to come out of her illness. I would gladly have given it all up to have one more day with her. Looks like I was giving it all up anyway.

'When the cheque comes through,' Abby said gently, rubbing my arms, 'we'll go flat-hunting together. Don't worry, Daze. I'm going to help you.'

I couldn't tell her the rest of what Darren had said. He was absolutely right, of course; I didn't deserve anything. But I couldn't bear for Abby to know that. She didn't know what I had done all those years ago, and I never wanted her to find out.

126

There's a single bang on the door now and it opens immediately to reveal Abby standing there grinning happily. 'We're going out for dinner,' she says. 'And when we get back, we *are* going to talk about your training partner.'

'OK, pardner.'

She'd turned to walk away, but now stops dead, then turns, shoulders first, very slowly round again. She slits her eyes and jerks her chin up once. 'Hey. Are you talking to *me*?' Her voice is deep and gravelly, and faintly Americanised. She sounds like Don Corleone, only more dangerous.

I slide off the bed onto my feet and stand to face her. 'So whhhut if ah ayum?' I've gone a bit Scarlett O'Hara, which is about as intimidating as Snow White.

Abby's mouth twitches as she struggles to maintain killer menace. 'I'll see you . . . later.' She's trying – quite successfully actually – to sound like she has a mouth full of cotton wool balls. 'And don't leave the country.'

'Ah won't.'

She turns, very slowly, staring at me the entire time with narrowed eyes, and only breaks eye contact at the last minute. Then she swings round again, grinning cheerfully. 'D'you wanna come with?'

'What, and play gooseberry all evening? No thanks.' No need to mention that I can't afford it. 'Don't worry, I'm going to have some toast and watch *About a Boy*.

NINE

Daisy Mack
Chilling in the garden with a glass of wine on a rare day off.
This is the life.
  Abby Marcus WTF????
  Daisy Mack Facebook rules apply, Abs, remember?
  Abby Marcus Ah, yes, now I understand. You go for it
  then!
  Sarah White Sounds like my kinda day! xx
  Georgia Ling Me to! <3<3

The next morning finds me out again, sitting in the sunshine on a park bench with my eyes closed. It's all right, calm down, I'm not idling the day away. Even if my brain, my conscience and my best friend would let me do that, my feet and legs certainly wouldn't. They start to get a bit twitchy if I don't take them out for a good walk every day. I swear when the magic trainers come out of the cupboard, they spring into life and start quivering with excitement.

Today I'm here for a good, solid, conscience-free

reason. Abby has asked me to wait here to meet her friend Joanna who is to be my brand new walking companion. Turns out the whole walking companion issue wasn't unresolved at all, which I discovered as soon as Abby and Tom got back from their meal last night.

'Walking companion,' she said, taking off her coat. 'Let's do this.' She plopped herself down on the sofa next to me, leaped back up again immediately, moved the toast plate I'd left there, then sat back down again with a muted sigh. 'My friend Joanna has said she's happy to walk with you, starting tomorrow. She's absolutely lovely, I've known her for years, I'm sure you'll get on really well. What do you think?'

She'd unfolded a sheet of paper at that moment and for a second I thought I was going to see Joanna's CV, and what she thought she could bring to the role.

'I don't know her, do I, so how can I think anything?'

'Well, you know she's a friend of mine, which is surely a good recommendation?'

I'd shrugged. 'I suppose so.'

'And she's run marathons and stuff, so she's definitely fit.'

Oh God. She sounded awful. 'I bet she's vegetarian, isn't she?'

'What's that got to do with anything?'

'I knew it. She's not going to try and get me to run, is she?'

'No no, definitely not. I've explained this is for the MoonWalk, no running allowed. She's fine with it.' She handed me the paper. 'Joanna's mobile number and home address.' I glanced at it, noticing as I did that there were another couple of names underneath Joanna's.

'Wh— ?'

'If Joanna can't make it any time, you ring the next person on the list. They're in order of desirability, so you work your way down until you get someone. OK?'

All hope left me then. Even if – God willing – something ghastly happened to Joanna to prevent her getting to me, like a broken toe or tonsillitis, I still had other options open to me before I could return to the desired state of solitude.

So here I am, and here, I believe, comes the amazing Joanna. She's in hot pink leggings and a microscopic crop top which reveals a row of abs like quorn sausages. Her hair is up in a very long swingy ponytail and she's jogging energetically towards me, a giant grin plastered across her face. As she gets nearer I notice that her face, chest and arms are all shiny with sweat already, and she's slightly out of breath. Something tells me she may have started without me.

'Hiya! Are you Daisy? Yeah, you must be, it's so funny seeing you sitting there, it's exactly, *exactly* what Abby said you'd be like, sitting on the bench, closed eyes, sleepy expression, so funny. I'm Joanna, by the way, ha ha, you probably worked that out already, or you're wondering what the hell some random stranger is doing introducing themselves to you for no apparent reason!'

I'm exhausted already. The entire time she's speaking, she's jogging on the spot and the enormous ponytail is swinging jauntily backwards and forwards behind her. It's like a little pet that's desperate to see what's going on.

I stand up and hold out my hand. 'Hi, Joanna. Yes, I'm Daisy. Nice to meet you.'

'Lovely to meet you too, Daisy. Sorry to hear about your mum and everything, Abby told me all about it, it's so horrible. Shall we go then?'

She turns back round to face the way she's just come and looks at me pointedly. Still jogging.

'Um, Joanna, did Abby tell you I'm training for a walk, not a run? Running's strictly not allowed on the walk, actually, so I won't be . . .'

'Oh, no, no, that's fine, yes, she did say, don't worry, it's not a problem.' She shakes her head, then nods, then shakes again, and the whole time the ponytail is peeping in and out of view. 'If you don't mind, I'm going to jog anyway, but I'll stay with you the whole time, I'll just jog really slowly, if that's OK with you?'

'Oh, right, OK then.'

'Excellent.'

We set off and Joanna immediately sprints to the edge of the park, goes through the gap in the hedge and disappears from view. I walk on as usual for two and a half hours without seeing her again.

'Bloody hell!' Abby explodes later on when I tell her what happened. 'She's fucking awful, that girl.'

'You said she was lovely . . .'

'Did I? Well she fucking isn't. Never mind.' She glances around the room briefly and, after failing to spot a pen, she deftly scores through Joanna's name on the sheet with a fingernail. 'Forget her, useless cow. Let's move on. Malcolm.'

Malcolm is a fellow driving instructor of hers, so I'm

reserving my excitement. Driving instructors as a race are generally quite nerdy and they all labour under the misapprehension that the Highway Code is good fodder for comedy. They drive Nissan Micras and Honda Accords for God's sake! Abby told me once that they're such dullards that they all use complete words and correct punctuation in their texts. Full stops, commas, even semi-colons on occasion. I mean, who does that? And *why*? Texting is like the fast-food of communication. It's not a beautifully crafted *pièce de résistance*, it's not always exactly as it should be, but it does the job it's meant to do, and it does it quickly. Why would you spend valuable seconds of your life saying 'Oh my God, that's a bit strange, isn't it?' when you could say 'WTF?!'

We're meeting in the town, near the bank. Abby has done the arranging for me by text. No doubt Malcolm's reply went something like this:

> Dear Abby, Thank you for your message. Please would you ask your friend Daisy to meet me outside the bank at ten o'clock tomorrow morning? Many thanks. Kind regards, Malcolm.

In fact 'OK, tmrw 10, o/side bank' would have done just as well. Actually 'tmrw o/s bank 10.*30*' would have been preferable as he keeps me waiting for almost half an hour. Which leaves me loitering here by the cashpoint for thirty minutes, trying not to look like I'm memorising people's PIN numbers. What a waste of my time – I could've been half-way round the canal path by now. I'd

132

be annoyed if I was waiting here for half an hour to meet Hugh Grant, let alone some tedious stranger who probably looks like Mr Bean. Actually no I wouldn't. I'd wait weeks for Hugh.

'Oh, hello there,' a voice booms behind me suddenly and I spin to see a shortish man in his forties in a navy blue velour leisure suit and loafers. I blink, hard, but he's still there. 'You must be Daisy. I'm Malcolm Rivers. Nice to meet you.' He holds out a hand so I take it and instantly regret it, as his fingers are covered with little hard lumps of dead skin. It reminds me of the hull of a boat below the waterline.

'Shall we go, then?' he says, and turns to face down the sloping precinct, towards the centre of town. 'Straight ahead here, Daisy, down towards Waterstones, watching closely for pedestrians.' In silence we walk briskly for about two minutes as we head down the slope. OK, this is acceptable, as long as there are no interruptions or attempts at conversation. 'Just pausing here a moment,' he says suddenly, looking behind him quickly before stepping over to the side of the path. 'Hope you don't mind, just need to pop in for a sec. Won't be long.'

Eight minutes later, he emerges, blinking in the sunlight, carrying a huge Waterstones bag with what looks like The Book of the Dead or something in it. It's enormous.

'OK, are you ready? Then off we go.' He glances up the precinct behind us quickly, then steps out and down the slope. 'Child on a bike there, Daisy, just so you're aware.'

'Yes, thank you, I saw him. Um, Malcolm?' I begin, but he puts up a hand.

133

'Just slowing down a little here, Daisy, OK? Watching the lady with the pram, she might just stop suddenly.'

'Yes, but even if she does, it doesn't . . . Look, Malcolm, I don't need . . .'

'Hope you don't mind if we make another stop here, Daisy? Just got a couple of errands to run while we're in town.'

The next stop is Boots, for razor blades. Then the library – taking back some CDs which apparently he had concealed somewhere about his person. I'm stunned when he produces them – that leisure suit is pretty unforgiving. Finally we arrive at a white building on the corner of a residential road, just outside the town centre.

'Lovely. Right, just a little break here, if that's OK. Doctor's appointment.' And infuriatingly he marches into the building and closes the door behind him. We've walked about five hundred metres through the precinct, and have taken over an hour to do it. It reminds me of a very bad blind date I went on when I was about seventeen. I stood in Gamestation for forty-five minutes while he played on the Xbox. Then he bought himself a burger and made me hold his rucksack while he ate it.

When Malcolm comes out of the doctor's surgery some considerable time later, he finds me long gone.

'The *doctor*?' Abby erupts later that evening. 'You're kidding.'

'Sadly not. Actually, I was glad to get rid of him. God knows how long it would have taken us to cover any meaningful distance.'

I catch Abs glancing at me sideways and smiling to herself. 'What?' I demand.

'What, what?'

'What's with that secret little smile? I know you, Abby Marcus. You've got something planned, haven't you?'

She frowns fleetingly, then shakes her head. 'No, no, I haven't. I was just thinking about you getting impatient that you couldn't cover any meaningful distance.' She smiles warmly at me now. 'I'm just pleased to see how motivated you are now. Bit different from when you started, isn't it?'

I think back to only a matter of weeks ago, when I went to quite extreme lengths to hide my absence of training from Abs: tramping around in the garden in my trainers to get them dirty, then disguising the footprints in the mud by raking it all back afterwards. A little heat comes into my face, but thankfully Abs doesn't notice.

'Right,' she says, spreading out the well-creased list of names again, 'who's next? Aha. Marianne.'

'Look, Abs, is this really necessary? I mean, we've tried the top two on your list and they've been disastrous. Joanna was almost entirely absent, and Malcolm actually slowed me down. You said day before yesterday they're in order of desirability, so the next few are likely to be even worse.' I point at the next names on the list. 'Marianne is probably going to turn up pissed or something . . .'

'She wouldn't!'

'. . . and then Felix after her will be scoffing a Big Mac and fries while I carry his rucksack.'

'What . .?'

'Doesn't matter. The point is that there will be something that caused you to rank him and Marianne lower than jogging Joanna and Leisure-Suit Malcolm. Can't we just forget about the others and get back to letting me go on my own?'

She's already nodding before I've got to the end. 'You're absolutely right, Daze. Those first two were appalling. I'm pretty pissed off with them, to be honest, although of course I can't say that to them because they were doing me a favour to begin with.'

'So let's not risk it with Marianne, and let me get back to going on my own.'

She considers it. She actually does. I can see the thought process on her face: will Daisy keep it up? Yes, probably. Will she speed up? Hmm, maybe. Will she totter off the path and get eaten by a wolf dressed as an old woman? Definitely.

'Don't say that,' I cut in, as she opens her mouth to speak. 'I'm not a child.'

'I know, Daze, but you can be forgiven for not being one hundred percent focused at the moment. That's why I want someone with you.'

'Then let me find someone myself. No more Marianne. Lose jogging Joanna. Ditch Malcolm X.'

She narrows her eyes and peers at me, clearly thinking: if I agree to this, Daisy will never, ever be able to find a walking partner herself. She has no friends except me and Tom. It will not happen. And when she fails, she will have to accept my choice of partner anyway, and she will be more amenable because I agreed.

'OK,' she says. 'But the walk is getting nearer. You'll need to find someone quickly so that you can really start stretching yourself.'

'I know.'

'Good. You've got a week.'

'OK.' I've also got a plan.

Well, it's more of an idea, really. I'm three drawing boards away from an actual plan.

Daisy Mack
Something needs to be done. So I'm doing something.
   Abby Marcus   Brilliant Daze. Keep it up.
   Nat 'Wiggy' Nicholson Girl Powerrrrr!
   Abby Marcus   You do mean walking, don't you?
   Daisy Mack   Course I do Abs. Now let me get on with it.
   Georgia Ling   Good 4 u babes x

So the following morning I'm up early and marching up the canal bank at a rate of knots. I'm determined to show Abs that I don't need a walking partner at all, but if that part of my non-plan fails, I'm going to find someone myself. Yes, I know, as plans go, it's Wile E Coyote balancing a boulder on a strategic see-saw in the faint hope that Road Runner comes past. But it's the best I can do so I'm sticking with it.

My speedy progress alongside the canal this morning has two main aims: 1) get to the bridge at a certain specific time – I glance at my watch: I've got just over ten minutes; and 2) get my speed up myself and get round the circuit in record time all on my own. Of course there's also the side issue of 3) training for the MoonWalk; but my first two reasons are much more pressing at the moment.

Almost before I realise it, I'm back at the bridge. I

check my watch and am stunned to find that it's four minutes past ten. By total coincidence (and military precision timing) I have arrived here at exactly the same time as Abs and I did on Sunday. I pause and rummage in my back-pack for a moment but completely fail to find either a professional make-up artist or a sexy black evening dress. It's ridiculous, I don't know why I'm even bothering, I look an absolute wreck all the time at the moment. But it's an excuse to stop for a minute or two and glance up and down the path. I won't stop for longer than two minutes though. Five at most. I'm determined to get my lap time down, and by a significant amount, so that Abby realises I'm not as lame as she seems to think I am.

Twenty minutes later, my patience pays off and I spot someone in the distance jogging towards me. He's a bit far away to see properly so I jut my head forward to bring my eyes two inches nearer. It works, and I can now make out that, sure enough, it's the same runner from Sunday and last week. He obviously spots me too as he approaches and waves, so I wave back. We then have to endure fifteen seconds of awkwardness – waiting for me, jogging for him. Do we look at each other as he approaches? Do we wave again? At what point do we smile? I resort to rummaging in my bag until he's almost here, then look up and we smile together.

'Hello again,' he says, and stops, although he continues jogging on the spot.

'Hi. We must stop meeting like this.'

He frowns fleetingly. 'I don't see why. Do you always pause here?'

I nod. 'Yeah, I have to. Steeling myself to get over the bridge.'

He glances across the bridge, then looks back at me. 'Steeling yourself? Why?'

'It makes me nervous. It's my fear of high places. I know it's irrational . . .'

'Oh yes, I remember now. You did mention that the other day. So even this little one frightens you?'

'There's nothing little about it. Haven't you noticed how much thinner the air is? You have to breathe at twice the normal rate on that thing.'

He chuckles. Dimples appear in his cheeks. 'I'm sure you're exaggerating.'

I shake my head. The fat on my cheeks wobbles. 'Uh-uh. It should have lights on it to warn aircraft.'

He chuckles again. Those dimples are kind of addictive. 'Surely not.'

'Oh yes. You could seriously kill Godzilla with that thing.' His grin falters a little and that fleeting frown makes a brief appearance again. He obviously hasn't seen the film. 'Um, I'm Daisy, by the way.' I put my hand out and he takes it.

'Nice to meet you, Daisy. I'm Danny.' Danny. My favourite name. He squeezes my hand gently, then lets go immediately. My hand feels cold and exposed now.

'Likewise.'

He smiles at me, then glances across the bridge again. 'Would it help at all if you came across it with me?'

There's a loud DING DING DING in my head, but I can't dance and leap around ecstatically, I'm far too close to the steep slope down to the motorway. So I raise my eyebrows and try to look as though this thought has never occurred to me. 'Oh, wow. Um, I honestly don't know.'

'Ah. OK . . .'

'But it's worth a try. At this point, I'll try anything. And I do have to get across it.'

He grins broadly and nods once. 'OK then.'

For one horrible moment I think he's going to jog along next to me, incredibly slowly, while I walk, but he doesn't. Then I think he's going to want me to run with him, but he doesn't do that either. He stops jogging, stands and waits for me to be ready, then escorts me at my own pace across the bridge. My own pace being mostly stationary, with the occasional shuffle forwards now and then. I just about manage to resist the urge to grab his arm as we go over, and it's got nothing to do with his muscles. Halfway across, I'm so dizzy and terrified, I actually have to stop.

'Why have you stopped?' Danny says, coming round to the front and looking into my face. His clear blue eyes almost send me over the side.

'Can't . . .'

He frowns. 'You do know you're halfway across already?'

Being halfway across is not a good thing. It just means that the drop below my feet is at its greatest, and safety is as far away as it can ever get. The concrete I'm on feels as sturdy as pastry and I know it is going to break up and crumble beneath me as soon as I change the pressure of my feet. I'm frozen. My breath is speeding up and my heart with it until there is a terrible roaring in my ears and blackness starts to creep in at the edge of my vision.

Suddenly I feel a warm hand take hold of mine and my arm extends as my hand is pulled away from me. At the end of a long tunnel I can just about hear a voice saying, 'Come on, Daisy, come on, just move one foot,' and some part of me knows that this is cute Danny with the blue eyes and the dimples and he thinks I'm a total lamo by now, so tentatively I push one foot along the shortcrust bridge, trying to do as little damage to the surface as I possibly can. 'Great, now do the other one.' So I do, hyperventilating, trembling and out of my mind with fear, but I do it. 'And again,' the voice says, and little by little, three inches at a time, we move over the bridge.

Three weeks later, we emerge on the other side, like plane crash survivors stumbling out of the jungle. We're malnourished, dehydrated and physically and emotionally exhausted – well, I am – but we did it. We fucking did it. It's the first time I have ever crossed that bridge upright, on my feet, and I'm struggling to control an intense sense of elation that is swelling inside me like a shaken Coke bottle. Eventually I give up, grab Danny's arm, squeal 'Yay!' and fling my arms round his neck. At this point I'm not sure if I'm celebrating the fact that I'm still alive; ecstatic that I've conquered my fear for the first time; or have momentarily lost control of my hormones in the face of Danny's obvious charms. Either way, I'm sure I'll think about this moment later on when I'm lying in bed and will want to curl myself into a tiny ball and scream quietly into my pillow while banging my legs on the mattress. Or I might just shoot myself in the face.

'Wow,' he says now, 'you are pleased, aren't you?'

Fortunately I haven't lost all sense of propriety – just about ninety percent of it – and I pull away. I'm grinning broadly and fidgeting on my feet, and I nod emphatically. To add to my delight, I see that Danny is also grinning, not glancing nervously around looking for a policeman. 'Thank you so much for helping me,' I gasp, still a little breathless from all the panic. 'That's the first time I've *ever* walked across that bridge.'

He frowns briefly again. 'Really? But I've seen you here before – don't you usually go across it?'

I nod again. 'Yes I do, but on my hands and knees. Or . . . stomach. Kind of commando style. Except with my eyes closed.'

'Really?'

I press my lips together and close my eyes briefly. 'It was a low point. But you think that took a long time today – it usually takes me three times as long. You helped me so much.'

He looks genuinely delighted at this. I'm not surprised. My theory is that, deep down, all men want to be superheroes or cavemen so they can rescue damsels or protect their women from rampaging dinosaurs. They'd also like to throw spears given half a chance. It's a primal need that is no longer satisfied in the modern world, which is why they have to race fast cars round and round a track, or go on roller coasters. You have to feel sorry for them really. All testosteroned-up and nowhere to go.

'It was my pleasure, Daisy,' he says now, clearly fulfilled as a man. His chest puffs out a bit and for a second I think he's going to pound it. 'So why are you walking along here exactly?'

'I'm in training. For the MoonWalk.' He looks immediately massively impressed, so I clarify quickly. 'It's on Earth. Not in space. Twenty-six miles power walking around London, in aid of breast cancer research. It's called the MoonWalk because it's overnight.'

He's nodding already. 'Yeah, I know. A few of my friends did it last year. That's very impressive, Daisy.'

I am filled with little bubbles of pleasure that make my face go red. 'Thanks.'

'I'm training for a marathon too. What's your expected time?'

I'm flummoxed. What does that mean? I plan to start when they fire the starting pistol, or whatever they do. I pretend to be thinking about it for a moment.

'I'm hoping for sub four,' he goes on, incomprehensibly.

I nod. 'Oh really? Great.'

'So? How about you? How long do you think it will take you?'

Ohhh. 'Um, I haven't really thought about it. I suppose, as it's twenty-six miles and we're walking, which is usually between three and four miles an hour, it should take . . . um . . .'

'About seven or eight hours?'

'Exactly.' I smile. 'Unless we have to cross any bridges.'

'Oh yes.'

'In which case, more like three days.'

He smiles. 'You do actually have to cross quite a few, you know.'

'Oh.'

'But it won't matter because by then you'll have crossed this one so many times, it won't make you nervous any more.'

'Maybe . . .'

'Definitely. Do you walk this way every day?'

'Yes. Most days.'

'So what are you going to do next time you're here?'

I shrug. 'Hands and knees again, I expect. Although my friend Abby is threatening to arrange a walking companion for me, for this very reason.'

'Ah. Well that's good then.'

'Oh no it isn't. It's likely to be some dull nerd who will take great delight in explaining to me the hilarious benefits of a Keep Left sign versus a Road Narrows. A few days of that, I'll be wanting to hurl myself off it, not cross it.'

He frowns, for a bit longer this time. 'Really?'

'Yeah. Suffice to say that in two weeks' time you might jog past here and see my poor broken body at the bottom of the ravine down there, being picked over by coyotes and buzzards.'

He looks genuinely horrified now. 'Good God.'

'I know, right?'

He looks thoughtful for a moment and I have to stop myself from saying any more. So much better if he reaches the conclusion himself. I don't watch him as he thinks it through, but I'm praying he's remembering how great it made him feel to rescue me, how manly he was, how strong and capable and how much the weak, helpless female needed him. Wouldn't it be great to get that feeling again? Like, maybe, every day?

Eventually he jerks his head a little, as if a brilliant idea has just slammed into it, and I look up at him. He's smiling and there's an expression of beatific generosity on it. I raise my eyebrows and smile.

'Daisy,' he says, 'I think I might have come up with a great solution.'

Daisy Mack Hi Abs! Guess what?. I've got it all sorted myself. Without help.
Abby Marcus Whaaat??
Daisy Mack Got myself a walking companion. A volunteer. Worth two pressed men, remember.
Abby Marcus *pauses; scratches head* OMG. Is it a *man*?
Daisy Mack Tell ya later! Xx
Abby Marcus *falls backwards off chair* Fuck me! It is!

Danny and I part company somewhere in the housing estate. He's walked with me all the way from the bridge, and amazingly we chatted easily the entire time, while I was pulling some long-remembered flirting techniques without even thinking about it.

'Ooh, I think I've just been bitten by something, right here – can you see anything?'

'Wow, I love your shirt, where did you get it?'

'I can't wait to soap myself off in a long hot shower when I get home.'

145

Didn't even realise I was doing it.

We arrange to meet up tomorrow at ten at the start of the canal path, and as he jogs away and I watch him go I can't help but marvel that someone like that would offer to assist me with my training. I made it quite clear that I wouldn't be running, and he definitely accepted it, so he's actually prepared potentially to sacrifice his own training regime to help me with mine. What a thoroughly decent, upright citizen. What a paragon. What a bum.

Not that that matters. Of course not. Yes, I am prepared to admit that he looks amazing in Lycra, but that's just decoration. Wrapping. Lovely to look at but the inside is still going to be the same. I could tell he was a good guy as soon as I looked into his beautiful blue eyes.

The Lovely Lawn lady is nowhere to be seen as I pass her house today, so I have a good stare in through her front window. Judging by her smooth lawn I want to see pristine perfection everywhere, and I'm not disappointed. Even the china dogs in the display cabinet are all gleaming in quiet satisfaction.

'Hey, heads up there!'

I snap up and find that I'm about to walk straight into a ladder that is propped up against the side of a house, obstructing nearly the entire pavement. The voice has come from above and I screech to a halt and look up like a saint having a vision. The sunlight is shining from behind the person speaking, making him just a silhouette with a halo of fire, and I raise my hand to shield my eyes from the burning brightness.

'Christ alive, you nearly sent me flying then!' the voice goes on. 'I might have had to sue you!'

'I don't think . . .'

'No, seriously, I'd have had no choice.' The tone is dead serious now. 'You must've seen that public information film on the telly? Where there's a blame, there's a claim. If you fall, make the call. Hurt your foot? File a suit.' There's a momentary pause. 'No, I've lost it now. Never mind.'

'OK. Well, thanks for the info. And thanks for the warning just now. I might have had to file a counter-suit on you if I'd walked into your ladder and hurt myself. Which I could have done. Quite seriously, actually.'

'Yes, that's true. Especially if I landed on you.'

Something about the way he's speaking to me feels irritatingly familiar. I feel like he's laughing at me, and it certainly would not have been funny if he had landed on me. I could have been killed. Crushed to death by a falling window cleaner. You read about that sort of thing in the papers all the time.

'Probably would have saved my life though,' he mutters now.

'*Pardon?*'

'I said, if I'd landed on you, it probably would have saved my life.'

'Is that meant to be funny? Or are you just unbeliev-ably rude?'

There's a brief pause. The top part of the shadow moves a little, as if he's looking around while he considers his answer. 'Um, well it certainly wasn't meant to be rude. So, I suppose I'd have to go for "funny". Yep. Funny. Final answer.'

'You're *kidding*? You actually think it's acceptable to make jokes based on a person's size, in this century?'

There's a brief moment's pause, then, 'Wh-a-a-t?'

'I mean, it's never been acceptable to poke fun at someone just because they're large, but for some reason people do seem to have got away with it in the past. Disgusting. But now there's probably some law against it. It's harassment, or bullying or something. It might even class as assault. I could probably have you arrested.'

Back in my other life, before I gave up everything to be Mum and Graham's carer, I really enjoyed my time at the food place, mostly because of the great people I worked with. Steph, Ahmed, Georgia, Mark, Khatira and Tracey. And of course Jamie Powell, the photocopier repair man, of the Spider Man boxer shorts. I worked there straight from school – Mum helped me fill in the application form pretty much as soon as I'd got home from my final exam. She put the pen in my hand as I stepped off the bus.

'Earn your own money,' she was always saying. 'Don't ever let yourself get dependent on anyone.'

Steph was my age and started the same day as me, and Tracey was a few years older and had shown us round the office and trained us up. As part of our induction, she gave us a ten-minute lecture over a ciggie in the ladies' loos about the company's policy on bullying and harassment. This was ten years ago so admittedly things have changed a bit since then. You could still have an illicit ciggie in the loos in those days. As long as you wafted the smoke away from the smoke detectors.

'Basically, you can't take the piss out of anyone any more,' Trace said, with a sad shake of the head. 'It's criminal.'

'Is it really?' Steph asked, her face going white with worry.

'Yeah. Totally. I'll give you an example. OK. There's this bloke who works in the post room – Alistair. Killer B.O. and breath that will slay you where you stand if you get within six feet of it. But you can't call him Allie-tosis or your feet won't touch the ground. I'm serious. I mean, a name like Allie, with bad breath, it's a gift, but you just can't do it. Criminal.'

Steph widened her eyes at me. 'I'm gonna try and stay out of the post room, then,' she whispered, obviously beside herself with worry that she might forget herself one day and accidentally say the word 'Allie-tosis' out loud.

'Oh, everyone still does it,' Tracey said, stubbing her ciggie out in the sink and dropping the end into the waste paper basket. 'Christ, no one can pass up an opportunity like that. I'm just saying don't get *caught* saying it.'

I had quite a nice life, back then.

So I feel like I have a pretty good understanding of what's allowed and what isn't. And to imply that someone is so fat they would provide a nice comfy landing for someone falling off a ladder is most definitely not.

'Arrested?' the voice from the ladder says now. 'For pointing out that falling onto a human body would be a darn sight more comfortable and enjoyable than falling onto concrete? I don't have a law degree so don't quote me, but I'm pretty sure that's not an arrestable offence.'

149

At this moment my phone quacks, rather loudly, and the shadow on the ladder jerks in surprise. I could retort but it's a message from Facebook, so I tut loudly, to make sure he knows I am not happy and am still considering making a formal complaint, then walk on, pulling my phone out of my pocket.

'Are you carrying a duck in your pocket?' the voice calls out after me, but I don't stop, I want to read the message. 'Coz I'm pretty sure that *is* illegal,' I hear as I click onto Facebook. There's a pause. 'Or, you know, it's frowned upon, anyway.'

The message is from Abby. And it fills me with dread.

Abby Marcus   What are you doing? Where are you?

Daisy Mack   Duh. You can have one guess and not a single guess more.

Abby Marcus   OK, I'm absolutely sure you haven't forgotten that we're going to my neighbour's barbecue this afternoon, have you?

Daisy Mack   Of course I haven't. Been looking forward to it for ages. Can't wait!

Abby Marcus   Well luckily for you, you won't have to. We have to be there in twenty minutes.

TEN

Daisy Mack

It seems barbecue season has finally arrived.

👍 Nat 'Wiggy' Nicholson likes this.

Suzanne Allen   Yum yum, sausages, salad and sunshine. And pavlova afterwards. Lucky you!

Daisy Mack   Oh yes Suze. There really is nothing finer, is there?

Abby Marcus   Get off your phone and get your arse in here.

Georgia Ling   PMSL!!!

I hate barbecues. They're such a farce, aren't they? It's taken thousands upon thousands of years of evolutionary struggle for the human race to haul itself out of caves and into purpose-built mud huts, invent the house brick, install central heating, double glazing and a state-of-the-art dual hob range with fan-assisted oven. But every May, without fail, with the arrival of the first warm afternoon of the year, man likes to remember the old ways. He squats barefoot (or in flip-flops) over an open flame and cooks meat for the family using only the fuel that nature provided (unless it doesn't catch, then he'll pour petrol from the lawnmower on it), then eats it – partially raw – using only his fingers and teeth to rend flesh from bone, on a purpose-built block paved patio that his brother's mate did for him at cost.

It compounds my theory that inside all men just want to be cavemen or superheroes. There's something so essentially masculine about charring patties of meat over coals, and handing out blackened chicken wings drenched in a honey glaze. It makes them feel macho, I guess.

I'm lying on my bed in Abby's spare room. She thinks I'm frantically choosing something nice to wear and sorting out my hair and make-up, but I'm ready. My hair's still a bit damp from the shower, but it looks OK, loose on my shoulders; and the only make-up I'm wearing is pink-tinted Vaseline on my lips. Clothes are by Tesco – jeans, blue and grey stripey tee shirt. Shoes: magic trainers. Might as well get as much use out of them as I can, they cost enough.

I have absolutely no memory of Abby telling me about this barbecue. In fact, I'm fairly sure she didn't mention it, just so she could spring it on me at the last minute, knowing I'd think I'd forgotten about it but would have to pretend I hadn't, and therefore would have no time to come up with an excuse or be out training all afternoon. I've told her enough times that I don't like barbecues, so she's using subterfuge to get me to one. Either that, or I really have forgotten it.

'Is that what you're wearing?' she says to me, standing up as I enter the living room a minute later.

I look down at myself, just to make sure I haven't accidentally put on a clown's outfit. Nope, stripey tee shirt, jeans, just as I remember. I raise my eyebrows and nod. 'Yeah?' The interrogative comes out accidentally and I instantly regret it. We both know that it represents a chink in my Tesco armour, and I drop my head back in resigned defeat.

Abby just looks at me for a moment from a pair of gorgeous white linen trousers and floaty pink top with spaghetti straps and glitter on the front. She closes her eyes. Some sort of internal battle goes on for a few seconds. Then she opens them again. 'OK. Fine. Whatever. Let's go.' I blink. It seems my defeat was short-lived.

I had been wondering which neighbour was hosting this barbecue because Abby and Tom live in a purpose built block of flats, with no garden, and therefore so do all her neighbours. But when we reach the street it all becomes clear as we cross over the road and head for the row of semi-detached houses a little way up.

'How do you know people who live here?' I ask her, as we push open the front gate. There is an A3-sized piece of paper Sellotaped to the front door that says 'Barbie – round the back please!' It seems to have been written in blue crayon.

Abs stops and turns to look at me. 'I'll allow you no more than one guess.'

I press my lips together exaggeratedly. 'Um, pony-trekking holiday in Tuscany?'

153

She rolls her eyes, then grins and shakes her head. 'Yeah, got it in one, Sherlock. Nothing to do with the fact that we live on the same street and see each other on the pavement, in the corner shop, putting the recycling out. We went all the way to Italy to meet.' She hesitates. 'It *is* Italy, right?' I nod silently. 'Great. Thought so. Now come on.' We dutifully follow the wobbly blue arrow at the bottom of the sign towards a gate to the side of the house, from behind which a sprinkle of classic barbecue sounds is coming: the sizzle of saturated fat dripping onto hot coal; the crack-fizz of a beer being opened; a ripple of laughter; a faint whimper of distress . . .

Abs stops at the gate and turns to me. 'You OK?'

I realise at this point that the whimpering is coming from me. 'Yeah, sorry.'

She puts her hand on my arm. 'Seriously, Daze. Are you OK with this? I mean, you don't have to come with me if you really don't want to.'

I like how she gives me this option now, standing at the gate to the garden where we're already expected. Earlier on it was all, 'Get your arse in here NOW!' and 'I *know* you haven't forgotten about this barbecue.'

I smile and heave a deep sigh of relief. Now I can bow out gracefully and spend the afternoon with Hugh instead. I open my mouth to say it, but then the expression on Abby's face suddenly registers on my conscience. She's got her eyebrows up in an interrogative, but at the same time those cursed eyebrows are imploring me to stay, damn them. She really wants me to come to this barbecue with her. With a sinking feeling of dread, I realise that I owe it to her to be there, and I shake my head. 'No, no, of course I want to come. Looking forward to a change of scene, actually.'

She visibly relaxes, and smiles. 'Oh that's great, Daze. I'm so pleased. I really want you to stay, but I didn't want to have to blackmail you.' She turns and pushes the gate open.

'Just don't leave me alone,' I whisper to her back as we march up the shadowy side of the house towards the sunny garden.

'Don't worry,' she says, glancing briefly over her shoulder. 'I won't.'

'Promise?' The white glare of the garden is getting bigger and brighter ahead. Abs doesn't answer.

Ten minutes later I'm sitting on a chair on the lawn, trying to make conversation with a woman who looks like she ordered her dress from 1985. Not that I've got anything against 1985. It was an excellent year if, like me and that dress, you were born then.

'I've never really liked scuba,' my new friend is saying. 'Never really feel safe do you? I mean, it's not a natural environment, is it, underwater? Not for us air breathers.' She's just got back from the Maldives, which is lucky for me as it means I don't have to say much, just look like I'm listening intently. I nod occasionally and throw in the occasional 'Uh-huh', and it seems to suffice. When I begged Abs not to leave me alone, I actually meant not to leave me *at all*. She glances over at me now, satisfied that I'm not alone, and goes back contentedly to her conversation on the patio.

'But the snorkelling was incredible . . .'

155

'Uh-huh.' I wonder idly what the time is, but it seems rude to look at my watch while someone is talking to me. I can see my new friend's watch easily, but it's too far away to make out the face properly. Plus of course it's upside down. She pauses to lift a chicken leg off her plate and a blob of potato salad falls onto her lap.

'Oh bugger,' she says unexpectedly. 'Bugger bugger bugger.' She stands up. 'Back in a mo, just gonna go and sponge this off. Help yourself to food, love.' And she scurries off towards the back door. I watch her go and wonder why she would bother. That dress is truly awful. A little potato salad on it is definitely an enhancement.

While she's gone I glance around the garden and feel suddenly self-conscious in my very drab outfit. Most of my nice clothes from pre-November are too small for me now, although these jeans went on pretty easily today, now I come to think of it. They must be a pair I bought more recently, after the Jaffa Cake diet had taken its toll. I don't remember buying any clothes recently, but that doesn't mean that I didn't. Or does it? Either way, I need to get out at some point and get myself one or two nice things, even though I'm not sure at this point when I'd wear them. Unbidden, an image of Danny pops into my head, smiling at me with the sun behind him as he brushes a stray strand of hair off my face. Even from here, it's obvious to me that I'm not wearing Tesco jeans, trainers and a grey tee shirt. I will definitely need a floaty floral skirt and spaghetti strap top for that one . . .

'Wow, it's the ladder police,' a voice says beside me suddenly, and my beautiful vision of Danny on a beach breaks up to reveal a familiar-looking man standing next to me. It takes me a second but then it hits me that it's the man I saw holding the heavy wheelbarrow when I got lost near the park that time. And his reference to the ladder police makes complete sense as it dawns on me that it was him I was talking to about law suits up the ladder earlier on. Oh no. He looks rumpled and cheerful in a pale blue linen shirt but, if I'm honest, he also looks pretty sexy, and I'm cringing as I think back to my stroppiness earlier on. Why didn't my flirt muscle kick in automatically, like it did with Danny? God knows what sort of impression I've made on him. And I have absolutely no chance to retrieve the situation from a grey crew-neck tee shirt. 'Got the afternoon off?' he goes on. 'Or are you here in an official capacity, to ensure all ladders and wheelbarrows are the regulation distance away from walkways?'

I smile up at him politely. 'No, no ladder violations here.' I leave the smile there for a second more, then turn away. Hopefully he'll get the message.

'Well that's a relief.' Apparently he doesn't. 'Nothing like a ladder violation to ruin a perfectly good barbecue.'

'I don't think the words "perfectly good" and "barbecue" can be used in the same sentence, can they?'

'Oh ho ho! I'm sensing something here. Would I be right in thinking that you are one of that strange, shadowy band of individuals who find sitting outside on a summer's afternoon enjoying food and drink in a social setting disagreeable?' He puts a hand up, palm out. 'No, wait, don't answer for a minute. Hang on.' He glances around him quickly, then strides away towards the big table on

157

the patio, grabs a chair and returns with it. 'I need to be sitting down to hear this,' he says, plonking the chair on the grass next to me and sitting on it. He leans forward and clasps his hands between his knees. 'OK. Go on. I'm ready.'

'Go on what?'

'Go on, explain to me why you find . . .' he waves an arm vaguely in the direction of the rest of the world '. . . *this* so unpleasant.'

'This? You mean the barbecue?'

'Ha, good point. It probably does apply to the whole world. But let's start small, shall we? What is it about barbecues – and this barbecue in particular – that you find so unpleasant?'

'I didn't say I found it unpleasant.'

He turns his head a little so that he's looking at me sideways. 'Oh but you did. Maybe not in words, but everything about you is shouting it. You're over here on the grass on your own, you've been staring into the same empty glass for the past twenty minutes, you're dressed like you're going to a funeral.' He grins and shakes his head. 'Actually, if you don't mind me saying so, you look like you've dressed up in your mum's clothes. Your mum's funeral clothes. This is a party, you know. Not a wake. It's meant to be fun.'

I frown. 'I am having fun, thank you. And I'm only on my own for a moment while . . . um . . .' oh crap, what was her name? '. . . the lady I was talking to has popped inside.'

'Hmm. "The lady you were talking to". No name? No sign of her? Only popped in for a moment?' He looks pointedly around the garden, then leans forward and squints up at me. 'She doesn't really exist, does she? Come on, own up. You've just invented her, haven't you?'

Defensive outrage flares up in me suddenly. 'No, I have not. She was right here.' I glance around too, feeling like I'm in a Hitchcock movie, trying to find evidence of scuba-lady's existence. My eyes land on a blob of potato salad on the ground. 'Look at that, see? She dropped that. I'm not eating anything, so it obviously wasn't me.' I fold my arms self-assuredly. 'QED.'

'Hey, OK,' he laughs as he puts both hands up in a 'stop' gesture, 'fair enough. The old lady really was here.' He winks theatrically. 'I believe you, Miss.'

'She was!'

'No, no, I know, I'm not doubting you, I'm merely making an observation. No, maybe observation is the wrong word. I'm lodging a query. I'm interested. You're interesting.'

'Yes, you're right, I am. But not in the way you think.'

He nods vigorously. 'Oh but you are. Vanished lady notwithstanding, you are cutting a bit of a sad figure over here on your own. It's a lovely sunny day, friendly people are here, there's food and alcohol. But still you're miserable. That is interesting.'

I shake my head. 'I'm not miserable, I'm just feeling a bit . . .' I stop. Oh my God, why was I even going to say that to him? He's looking at me very intently, his eyebrows up as if he's fully expecting me to spill my most private thoughts to him right here in this sunny garden. Well I'm not. 'Actually very little about this situation is interesting. I'm just here because my friend made me come.' Dammit, didn't mean to say that.

'Hmm. That's an interesting statement.'

'I mean, my friend brought me.'

He laughs. 'Interestinger and interestinger. So, which one is the selfish, inconsiderate friend?'

I nod towards Abby, who is currently looking curiously my way. 'That's her. But she's not selfish or inconsiderate. She's amazing and wonderful. Which you would find out if you weren't so busy making snap judgements about people, and actually spent some time to get to know them.'

'Hi Felix,' Abby says now, walking over to us. 'Great to see you. How's things?' My jaw practically hits the floor and I find myself gawping from one to the other.

'Hi Abs,' he says, standing up. He embraces her lightly and kisses her cheek. 'I'm pretty well thanks. Wow, you look beautiful.' He stares openly at her for a moment, then glances around with exaggerated nervousness. 'Is Tom here?' For some reason this makes me furious. Abby is *my* friend! He's not allowed to assume some kind of relationship with her. And I'm the one who calls her Abs!

She smiles broadly. 'Don't worry, he's at work. Probably going to join us later, when he finishes.'

'Hang on,' I cut in, putting my hand on her arm. 'You two know each other? How?'

They both nod, both with identical pleased grins. 'I guess it's just that kind of neighbourhood,' Abby says.

'Hey,' he says, 'don't say that. People will think something untoward has been going on.'

160

As they laugh together easily, I can't help but think how I wouldn't mind being part of a neighbourhood where someone like this could just happen along at any moment.

'So, Daisy,' Abby says, turning back to me, 'this is Felix Bryson. He lives two houses up. Felix, this is my very best friend, Daisy Macintyre.'

'The pleasure is all mine,' he says, bowing very slightly. 'Now, can I get either of you two ladies a drink?' He makes a quarter turn towards the back door of the house, his head still turned to face us.

Abs shakes her head. 'I'm fine thanks, got one over there.'

Felix turns to look at me. I regard him coolly through my fringe for a moment, and as I do his eyebrows bounce up and down a couple of times. A small laugh escapes me involuntarily.

'Aha!' he bursts out suddenly. 'She smiles! And there was I thinking she was absolutely determined to be cheerless today.'

I frown. 'Don't get used to it,' I say darkly.

He frowns back. 'Good God no. That would be a mistake. So, Madam. Can I bring you something delicious to imbibe?'

'OK. Your eyebrows have convinced me. Thank you.'

'Marvellous.' Quickly he pats his eyebrows. 'Nice work, boys.' Then he rubs his hands together excitedly, all of which makes me have to actively stop a smile from creeping out. 'What is Madam's pleasure?'

'Surprise me.'

He narrows his eyes and turns his head slightly as he

looks at me. 'Ooh, you are interesting. A surprise it is then. BRB.' He winks at me, then strolls off whistling towards the door. We both watch him go, then Abby turns to grin.

'Isn't he great?'

I shrug. 'I barely know him . . .'

'Oh, look, there's Eva,' she says suddenly, and strides away. Now I really am on my own. At a barbecue full of strangers, in a grey tee shirt. Seriously wishing now I had put some mascara on, and a slightly more flattering top. And maybe done my hair a bit more . . . stylishly. Self-consciously I reach up to touch it and am surprised yet again with the shorter length. It feels OK actually; kind of silky.

Felix returns carrying two tall, pink, creamy-looking drinks and sits back down next to me.

'It's called a Pink Panther,' he says delightedly, handing me a glass.

'Oh? Why's that?'

'I guess because of the . . .' He trails off. 'Ah. Are you teasing me now?'

I keep my face bland. 'Maybe.' I take a tentative sip of the drink and realise, too late, that it's alcoholic. It's sweet and creamy and delicious, but definitely alcoholic. I look up at Felix to find him staring at me expectantly, like a dad watching his kid open a present. 'What's in this?'

'Um, frozen pink lemonade, Malibu and cream. If I remember right. What do you think?'

'Oh.' I lower the glass back down to my lap.

His face falls a little. 'You don't like it?'

I shake my head. 'No, no, I do. Thank you. The thing is . . . I just . . . I haven't been drinking alcohol for . . . quite a long time, and sitting here in the sun, hot day, not having had any for so long . . .'

'You're worried you might get trollied and lose control of your inhibitions? Striptease on the lawn? Air guitar "The Power of Love"? Slow dance with a stranger?'

Embarrassing myself while tipsy is not something I've been worrying about. Getting mind-shatteringly wasted every day is. It's been such a colossal temptation the past few months, I decided from the outset to avoid alcohol completely if I could. Otherwise who knew where it could end? Absolutely no need for Felix to hear about that, though.

'I might get a headache, is more what I was worried about. My air guitar is in the attic.'

He smiles. 'Ah, right. Well, if it's any consolation, it's only a very small amount of alcohol. Just to give it that coconutty flavour. But I'll get you something else, if you'd rather?'

I take another sip. It really is absolutely gorgeous. 'No, it's OK, don't worry. I'll risk it.' I'm fairly sure that at this point in my life, the slopes are much less slippery than they used to be.

He grins. 'Excellent.' He takes a slug of his own drink and smacks his lips exaggeratedly. 'Bloody lovely. Now. Where were we?' he says, leaning forward conspiratorially. 'Oh yes. You were telling me how selfish and inconsiderate Abby is.'

'No I wasn't!'

He chuckles and puts both his hands up again. 'Joke.'

163

'Oh, right. I see. Good. So, how long have you known her?' I'm trying very hard not to sound competitive.

'We're not doing that now, that's fodder for a different day. I want to know about you. Tell me, Miss Daisy, what has happened to you to make you hate life so much?'

I stare at him for a second, feeling tears heating up in my eyes. I blink them away quickly. 'I don't hate life,' I say quietly. 'I just hate barbecues.'

'Hey, just observing. Didn't mean any offence.'

'You know what else I hate? Nosey people.'

He nods. 'Oh yeah, me too. Dreadful, aren't they? Act like nothing's sacred or private, like they have the right to know even the deepest most painful secrets about someone.'

I nod pointedly. 'Exactly.'

'Although if you think about it, maybe they're not really nosey at all. Maybe they're genuinely interested. Maybe they see a sad, lost soul now and then and wonder if that soul needs some company.'

I glance at him. He seems to have inched forward on his seat a bit and is getting fractionally nearer to me.

'Maybe,' he says, his voice low, 'they see someone who looks like they've been through a tough time recently, and they feel a need to help in some way. If they can.'

I've got goosebumps on my arms, and it's not because of the breeze.

'Maybe.' I clear my throat. 'Although mostly I reckon they're just busybodies. So tell me, are you a window cleaner or a driveway builder?'

He nods slowly. 'Nice deflection.'

'Thanks.'

'You're welcome. OK, well, in actual fact, I'm neither, and I'm both. I'm just doing a bit of handyman stuff at the moment while I . . .' He breaks eye contact and studies his pink glass for a moment. 'While I decide what else I could do.'

Ah. Unemployed. Like me.

'So, what do *you* do?'

This is awkward. How do I answer that one without giving away my entire life history? Or at least, the past five months of it. I shrug. 'Same as you, actually.'

'Really?'

'Yeah. Not the handyman part. Just the deciding part.'

'Oh.' He's staring at me very intently and it makes me feel very peculiar. 'You really are extraordinarily interesting, Miss Daisy.'

At this moment there's a kerfuffle from the lawn and we both look up to see a giant game of Jenga being set up.

'Ooh,' he says, putting his glass down on the ground. 'Unfeasibly Large Jenga. Do you?' He inclines his head towards the game.

'Um, no. I don't. Do you?'

He grins. 'I do now. Excuse me.' And he gets up and walks over to the activities, rubbing his hands together.

The game is actually quite entertaining. To watch, that is. It looks downright dangerous to play. Toes are crushed under falling blocks, nails are broken, fingers are pinched. I start to wonder whether a paramedic should have been parked out the front, like they do at Wimbledon and the Grand National.

'You enjoying yourself?' Abby says, coming over to sit in Felix's empty chair.

I think about it. 'I wouldn't say enjoying, exactly.'

'Oh . . .'

'But I'm not hating it.'

She brightens. 'Oh.'

I nod and rub her arm. 'It's better than I was expecting.'

She smiles at me. 'Good.'

'Thanks for making me come.'

'Thanks for coming, Daze. I'm really glad you did.'

'Me too.'

She squeezes my hand on her arm and we watch a small child of about seven on his tiptoes trying to pull a block out of the middle of the tower. It looks like a disaster movie waiting to happen.

'This game is pretty funny, isn't it?'

She nods. 'You don't fancy playing?'

'You're kidding?! It looks lethal!'

At this moment there's a shout and a rumble and the child gets buried beneath an avalanche of falling blocks. I stand up in horror. 'Oh my God . . . !'

There's a second's hiatus as everyone stares at the mound of rubble; then a hand bursts through the top in a triumphant clenched fist, and the crowd erupts into cheers and clapping.

After Jenga, there's a game of Giant Dominoes, followed by Colossal Connect Four and then Enormous Snakes and Ladders.

'I'm sensing a theme here,' I say to no one, as Abby and Felix are both playing by this time.

'Come on,' Abs calls over, a foam die the size of a

small chair in her hands, but I shake my head. I'm out, I'm in a garden, I've spoken to two new people and still feeling OK. Why spoil it?

After another hour, I'm ready to go. The sun's dropped down behind the neighbouring houses and the temperature has dropped with it, so a few cardigans and sports jackets are being pulled on. I don't have a cardigan with me. Actually I'm glad to say I don't own one. Scuba-lady never re-appeared so I've had to suffer comedy 'Where *is* she?' gestures from Felix from across the garden every time someone comes out of the back door. Once it was actually a woman in a ghastly dress, and I felt vindicated, but it wasn't her. At least, it wasn't the same dress. Felix wasn't looking anyway.

'Do you mind if I leave now?' I say quietly to Abby, as she spoons coleslaw over a black sausage on her plate – trying to hide it apparently. 'I'm getting a bit cold.'

She stands up straight and focuses on me. 'You OK?'

I nod, but inexplicably my eyes start to feel hot again. I've been thinking this spontaneous weeping was behind me now. 'God, this is ridiculous. Sorry, it's nothing. Just tired I think.' A single tear squeezes out and runs down my cheek. I look at Abby and see that her eyes are filling up too, which makes me love her even more.

'Don't cry, Daisy,' she says and puts her arms round me. I rest my forehead on her shoulder. 'I'll come home too. Hang on there, I'll just say goodbye to everyone.'

I pull back and shake my head. 'No, no, you stay. I don't want to ruin your evening.'

'No, I'll come.'

167

'No, seriously, Abs. I'll be all right. I'm only going to go and have a little lie down anyway. No point you coming with me.'

'I don't mind . . .'

I shake my head. 'No, please. Don't come. It sounds stupid but . . . I think I'd rather be on my own for a bit.'

She searches my face for a few seconds, then comes to a decision. 'All right then. I've got my mobile – ring me if you need me.'

'I will. But I won't.'

She smiles weakly. 'OK. See you later then.'

I nod, we hug, and finally I am free to go back through the gate to the world beyond.

As I walk – well, I say walk, it's more like a trudge – home – well, I say 'home', it's actually Abby's home – my mind is filled with thoughts of Felix, which is odd. I was expecting to dwell on Danny's beautiful eyes for the next few years at least, but it's a laughing brown pair that feature now. I can't decide whether he's infuriating, funny, kind, or all three. He certainly made me smile once or twice, which was a wonderful feeling after so long. But he has absolutely no social skills whatsoever. To talk to a complete stranger like that, enquiring about private and intimate details of my life, commenting on my clothing and personal habits . . . Assuming that I hated life . . .

Oh God. Why did I wear this hideous tee shirt?

By the time I reach the flat, I feel tears threatening again and I head straight for my room. How dare he call Abs Abs? How dare he call me Miss Daisy?

He doesn't even know me! I fling myself face down on my bed without even taking off my magic trainers, wrap my arms around my pillow and sob hard into it, knowing that I'm going to cry myself to sleep yet again, and this time it's all that man's fault.

After about fifteen seconds, though, I realise I'm stopping. In fact, I didn't even get going. I open my eyes and sit up, then try an experimental sob, but no, nothing comes. I'm definitely not crying. Huh. I swing my legs over the side of the bed and find myself face to face with Abby's giant 'TO DO' list. Automatically I glance away and am instantly looking at the letter from Mum's solicitors again. I look away from that, too, and focus down at myself instead. At my shabby jeans, which aren't new at all but are apparently far too big for me. At my magic trainers, gleaming white and ridiculous for barbecues. At my reflection, with my unstyled hair and my pale face looking even paler next to the grey of my tee shirt. I get off the bed and kneel on the floor by the dressing table, peering into the mirror. I don't hate life. Of course I don't. I love life. It's death I hate. I peer closer, heroically avoiding seeing the letter propped up in front of me. I grab hold of the flesh of one of my cheeks and pull it roughly, then do the same with the other side. Then pummel myself in the face with my fingertips a couple of times. I don't hate life, not any more. But maybe I do hate myself a bit. Abruptly I stand up, grab my purse, pick up the flat keys and go out.

The next morning I'm on the canal path at ten minutes to ten, waiting for gorgeous Danny, who would never intrude into my personal life and make assumptions without knowing a thing about me. I'm early and I'm pacing, ready to go, feeling full of energy for the first time in months. I feel like an athlete today, powerful and sporty, and I'm enjoying the sensation as I pace up and down. I'm even bouncing a bit. Admittedly some of my new found athleticism is down to my newly purchased tracksuit I got in Pineapple yesterday. My legs being encased in tight black Lycra with pink piping down the sides is making me feel incredibly vital and fit. I feel like I could run a marathon right now.

'Mmm, that's a great outfit,' Danny says appreciatively ten minutes later. Ten o'clock on the dot. He looks me up and down, nodding. 'Wow. You look more than ready to go. Shall we?'

'Oh absolutely,' I say, nodding enthusiastically. 'Try and stop me.'

'Ha ha! Well that would be a bit counter-productive, wouldn't it? But,' he adds as I set off down the path, 'you might want to pace yourself to start with.'

'I'll be fine,' I call back over my shoulder. 'It's only walking – how hard can it be? I've been doing it for years.'

In two powerful strides he's at my side again. 'Yes, you're right, but this is a bit different. We'll be going much faster than most other people, and we'll be covering more ground today than they do in a week. It's not the same as strolling round the shops, Daisy.'

I nod again, energetically, to show him how committed I am. 'Absolutely.'

'*Ex*cellent.' He grins at me and I almost stumble. 'Seems

to me that you're a bit more clued in than most. That's really good, well done.'

'Thanks.' I beam and swell a bit under his praise, like someone who's completely clued in. Which I am. I'm a serious athlete, a proper sportswoman, inside the magic circle with Danny. We're in this together, separate from everyone else who isn't clued in.

'I'm thinking eight to ten miles today, how does that sound? Just say if you think it's too much.'

'No, no, that sounds perfect.' Of course it's not too much for a serious athlete like me.

'*Ex*cellent.' He nods approvingly. 'This is going to be fun.'

'Oh yes, definitely.' He's right, it is fun. He's fast, too.

'So. Where did you get this sexy new outfit?'

'Oh, this? It's not new, had it for ages.' Absolutely no need for him to know that I've only just become a serious athlete today.

'Really? Oh. Well, it looks like . . .' He peers closely at the leggings. 'I'm going to say . . . Pineapple. Am I right?'

I'm stupefied. 'Wow. You are right. How did you do that?'

He narrows his eyes with a little smile while he ponders some more. 'And you've had it for ages? How long would you say? Roughly?'

'Oh, um . . . probably about . . . a few months, maybe?'

'Oh. Well that's interesting. Because that particular style – the black capri track and field pant with double pink side banding and seventy-five percent Lycra content is definitely this season. Only came out about, ooh, three weeks ago. So. I reckon I'm totally onto you. You've got a little secret, haven't you?'

Shit. 'Oh, er, well, you know, when I said I'd had it, er, a few months, what I actually meant, in fact, was . . .'

He nudges my arm playfully. 'Hey, don't worry about it, I'm only winding you up. It doesn't bother me at all. It's only a little bit illegal, isn't it? Although,' and he leans in conspiratorially and lowers his voice, causing an electric thrill to rush up my spine, 'if you could put me in touch with your supplier, I'd be incredibly grateful.'

I blink. 'Oh. Well, you know, I'm not really sure . . .'

'Hey, no problem. I totally get it.' He taps the side of his nose and winks. 'Just, you know, bear it in mind. OK?'

I nod. 'OK.'

'*Ex*cellent.'

Shortly after this, I have to stop talking. Even one syllable is too much. But luckily Danny keeps us both entertained for the whole walk, chatting away about all the marathons that he's done in the past, the other people who ran it with him, what it feels like to run for that length of time; all while I try not to sound like I'm dying of emphysema.

'You've heard of The Wall, no doubt? Well it literally exists, Daisy. I mean, *literally*. One minute you're running along nice and smoothly, like a locomotive, you know, that's the image I keep in my head. Pistons pumping, all greased up and slick, raw power in my legs, my muscles like iron, driving me on, keeping me moving. Then BOOM! Suddenly you hit this wall. Face on. Thud! Straight into the brickwork, whack.' He turns to look at me. 'Can you even imagine what that feels like? It's

172

awful, that's what. Terrible.' He talks about sportswear and the different types of trainers you can get. I had no idea there were so many, all offering different levels of support for your feet. 'It's your single most important purchase if you're into sports,' he says. 'And if you get the wrong kind, it can actually do you more harm than good.'

I am amazed and show it by nodding vigorously.

'I do hope your trainers are the right kind, Daisy,' he says. 'Support isn't just important in your bra.'

I shake my head. 'No . . .'

'The lay person just doesn't get it,' he goes on, bouncing up and down energetically as we walk. 'If you're going to be serious about sports, you need to be serious about sportswear.'

I nod interestedly. This is probably what Tom would be like to talk to, if he was interesting and agreeable. And, you know, talked.

After two hours and fifty minutes, I arrive back at the flat. Danny watches me from the pavement as I jog energetically up the path and in through the front door, but the second the door shuts behind me, I collapse with a groan onto the floor. I lie there, face down and unmoving. Well, apart from my chest heaving in and out. I might never rise from this position. There's absolutely no way my legs will ever support my weight again, I know that. The muscles in them are so tight they feel like they'll snap like guitar strings if I bend my knee even slightly, and both hip joints are throbbing with a hot, dull ache. For the final half an hour of the walk, it felt

173

like all the cushioning between the ball and the socket had been worn away, and the bones were grinding together with every step, no doubt producing a very fine white powder. What a fantastic walk.

I can probably survive here for quite a long time. I've spotted a Twix wrapper under the sideboard, and I think there might be one finger left inside. I could nibble on that very very slowly, eke it out for ages. I could most likely make it until Abs gets home this afternoon.

But after a few more minutes, my phone quacks, so I have to stretch an arm down to reach my pocket. It's a message from Facebook. No doubt Abs is checking up on me. She always messages me this way because she only gets three hundred texts a month on her contract, and she saves them for . . . well, for Tom, I suppose.

Abby Marcus   Are you back yet? How's it going?
Daisy Mack   been bak ten mins was v gd now dying bye x

I'm only using one hand so can't make capital letters or punctuation. She'll get the message though. Maybe she'll realise from that message that I'm in excruciating pain and will cancel the rest of her lessons for the day and rush home to look after me. That's the kind of wonderful, selfless person she is.

Abby Marcus   Bloody hell, Daze. Man up.

Maybe not.

Abby Marcus *Get yourself into the bath. Quick. Extra hot. That way, your muscles will be all right for tomorrow.*

Tomorrow. Oh God. I close my eyes and drop my phone in despair. I'll definitely be dead by tomorrow.

ELEVEN

Daisy Mack
is not only not dead today, but wasn't dead yesterday either. At this point, though, I can't vouch for tomorrow.

   Suzanne Allen Wow. That's deep.

   Georgia Ling Glad your OK hunni xxxx

   Nat 'Wiggy' Nicholson Daze, that so doesn't make sense.

You might be surprised to find me skulking round the flat this morning at ten thirty, and not out on a brisk power march with the delectable Danny. It's Friday, 8th of May, the day after my first high speed walk and subsequent brush with death, and three weeks until the MoonWalk. I genuinely can't afford to waste a single day not training, but don't worry, I'm not going to. I'm meeting Danny at twelve today, since he's got something else to do this morning. Not sure what, though. I dropped some subtle hints yesterday, when he told me it would have to be later today, but he was a bit tight-lipped on the subject.

   Danny: Is it OK to meet a bit later tomorrow? Say, twelve?

Me: Yeah, sure, no problem. Why's that?

Danny: Got something to do in the morning.

Me: What?

Yeah, subtle right? He didn't let on though. Just said he had an errand to run. The word errand always makes me think of ten-year-old boys in flat caps carrying bits of paper to the grocery store. Anyway, the late start today gives me plenty of time beforehand for a bit of skulking.

Actually, don't look too closely. I'm not really skulking. I'm in Abby's room, and I'm rooting around in the bottom of her wardrobe. It doesn't look good, I know, but there is a genuine, well-intentioned reason for it.

Graham started smoking when he was eight years old, which has always struck me as a little bit odd. I mean, why would someone of that age need the crutch of nicotine to help him get through the day? Was the stress of learning to tie his shoelaces just too much to handle? Did he suffer anxiety over conker matches? Maybe being called Speccy Four-Eyes really got to him, and he relieved the tension by doing the only thing an eight-year-old kid in those difficult circumstances can do: light up at lunch time.

I think he tried to quit when he was ten. He never told us an awful lot about that time, but the idea of a ten-year-old going cold turkey always intrigued me. I imagined him fretfully stirring his Sugar Puffs in the morning; nervously picking at a loose thread on his Action Man jumper; snapping at his friend Jack who wanted to know if he was coming out to climb trees; dropping his head back onto his Transformers pillow in despair when he woke up to another day without cigarettes. OK, maybe this was before the time of Transformers, but I don't know what else a ten-year-old kid might have on his pillow in 1956. Something about Marlboro country, maybe?

There were no nicotine patches or ashtray-flavoured chewing gum in those days, I think, so I guess it was just too hard and Graham fell back into it. When he was twelve he realised that all his paper-round money was going on cigarettes, not sticker books, so he moved onto roll-ups. He very quickly discovered that a fifty-gram pouch of rolling tobacco was less than half the cost of twenty ciggies, and lasted him virtually all week, instead of one day. In his twenties, on a health kick, he started to roll filters into his fags, telling himself that it wouldn't kill him with a filter to protect him. And there he stayed until he died of emphysema at the age of sixty-three.

I think he must have tried to quit several more times as Naomi and I were growing up, but of course we weren't really aware of it. Only that he was often very changeable and moody, favouring one of us over the other, then reversing.

'Jesus Christ, Daisy, can't you ever move your sodding shoes from the hallway?' he shouted regularly, when he came in from work. My shoes were lying in a pile of general debris, male and female, that accumulated over days. I scuttled downstairs and grabbed my shoes, noticing Darren's trainers and Naomi's strappy sandals also left there. As well as several items of post on the floor by the letter box, Darren's leather jacket draped over the chair, a comb, a cardigan, a bunch of keys and a crash helmet. All not mine.

'Why are you only having a go at me?' I whined. I was about fourteen, so it's allowed. 'There's everyone's stuff here . . .'

'Just move your crap,' he'd seethed. 'I'm sick to the back teeth of seeing it. Christ, Daisy, you're nearly an adult, don't you think it's about time you started acting like one?'

'Um, no, actually. Not for four more years.'

Of course my smart retort had the desired effect of illuminating for him very clearly just exactly how unfair and unreasonable he was being, and he calmed right down. Ha ha.

A couple of weeks later, he would be on Naomi's back, moaning about her mess – coffee cups in the living room, clothes in the kitchen, handbags, jackets, crumbs, washing up. And I would be able to get away with anything. I loved it that way round. Left my coats and shoes all over the place, just for fun, as a kind of experiment. Once I deliberately put my school bag with books and folders and pencil shavings spilling out of it in the middle of the dining table, after it had been set for dinner. Graham came in, saw it, and walked straight past it towards a peanut butter jar with the lid off that he knew Naomi had left there that morning. I found her crying in her room once, when she was about eighteen and I was sixteen. She'd just endured a prolonged rant about how she treated the place like a hotel, coming back for meals then going out again, parking her car where she liked without regard for anyone else, leaving her shit lying around in every room. She was well into week three of being on the receiving end by this time, so it was quite likely to switch fairly soon. Of course, later on that year, the unpleasantness switched to me more or less permanently. But this was before that, before everything turned so nightmarish.

'He's so horrible,' she'd sobbed, while I sat with her on her bed. 'No wonder I don't ever want to be here.'

'Oh come on, that's not true,' I'd said, rubbing her shin. 'He's lovely sometimes.' That was true. He'd been smuggling me cigarettes for months. I'd sometimes find a pack of twenty in my bed when I got into it.

'No he isn't,' she'd sniffed. 'He's just nasty, all the time. You know it Daisy, you must have seen it. You're only saying that because he's not getting at you. If he ever treated you like this, you'd feel the same as me.'

'What?! He does treat me like this! What are you talking about?'

She regarded me coolly. 'No he doesn't. He goes easy on you because you're the baby. They both do.'

'They do not!'

'Yeah, well, I knew you'd say that. You don't know how horrible Graham is to me sometimes. And it's even worse when I see him being really lovely to you.'

'Oh my God, Nomes, that's so not true! Haven't you noticed that he favours one of us, then switches?'

'No.'

'You're kidding? Are you honestly telling me that you think he's nice to me all the time?'

'He is.'

'No he isn't. God, I can't believe this! Just wait a

180

couple of weeks. Actually, it's more likely to be a couple of days, then you'll notice. He'll start doing nice things for you again, and start coming down on me like falling masonry again. Just wait.'

'I don't believe you . . .'

'OK, so you don't remember him picking you up from that club at two in the morning last month? And, oh, who gave you the money to get in? And didn't he make sure he kept a dinner warm for you that night you got held up at work? And he set that programme about army recruitment up to record for you, because you said six months ago that you were thinking about it.'

She was thoughtful, then shook her head. 'Those were isolated incidents. It's obvious to everyone that you're the favourite. All my friends have noticed it, you know. I reckon it's just you who thinks it's OK.' She'd wiped her face at this point and sat up. 'And why the fuck wouldn't you? You've got it easy.'

She was wrong, and realised it eventually. Graham had been fairly pleasant to both of us for some time – no doubt in smoking phase – but then he must have had another go at quitting and the smokeless dragon was unleashed yet again. That's when Nomes and I made our pact. We rendezvoused in her room, having both fled there after a particularly brutal and unfair tongue lashing directed for a change at both of us at once. Our miserable faces met in silence and stared at each other for several moments as Graham's cruel words echoed in our minds. It was Naomi who spoke first.

'You're right,' she said, wide eyed. 'I've been paying attention and you're right.'

181

'About what?'

She jerked her head towards the door. 'Graham. He's horrible to you too.'

I nodded slowly.

'I've thought for years that you were the favourite. But . . .' She tailed off, shaking her head. 'You're right. He varies his favourite, from week to week.'

'Or day to day.'

'Yeah. God. So unpredictable.'

'I know.'

We both stood in silence for a few moments, then, out of the blue, Naomi said, 'Whichever one of us is out of favour when he dies will probably get disinherited.'

I frowned. 'Fucksticks, Naomi! Where on earth did that come from?'

'It's obvious.'

'No it isn't.'

'It is! Daze, I'm serious. One day, one of us will be cut off. I can see it coming.'

'No. No way. He wouldn't do that.'

'Reckon he would. Bearing in mind what he's like at the moment. What he's been like these past few weeks. What he's always been like.'

I thought about it for a minute, but I really couldn't see it ever happening. Naomi was adamant.

'We have to prepare for it, Daisy. It's gonna happen, and we need to make a pact, right now. Let's agree that if one of us is left out, the other one will split their share exactly fifty-fifty, so that we both get an equal amount. Even though it will mean the one not left out will only end up with half as much as they would have done. But the one who is left out won't get nothing. What do you think? Fair?'

I felt a huge rush of affection for her then as I looked at her anxious face. And I agreed, in a heartbeat. It was a lovely sisterly thing to agree to, and it meant we were both protected. Plus I was sure it would never come to it anyway. Mum was going to live forever so Graham would obviously die first. Plus he would never *ever* do something so terrible. We grinned at each other, and hugged tightly, united more completely in that moment than ever before or since. Our sisterhood had never been stronger.

Graham's emphysema really started to take a hold of him about four or five years before he actually died from it. Shouting about shoes in the hallway or coffee cups left on the floor would cause a desperate coughing fit that left him either leaning against the wall or slumped into an armchair, red in the face, so he stopped doing it. Those final years of his life, while my mum was fighting for hers, he was in and out of hospital experiencing periods of extreme shortness of breath, coughing, wheezing and difficulty exhaling that left him weak and frightened. He stopped smoking then, of course. It would have been madness to continue in those circumstances. Like losing a leg to a crocodile, then hopping back to ask it if it wanted to have another go. The symptoms of emphysema are irreversible, but all his doctors said that he could prolong what time he had left by stopping smoking immediately.

'I'll never smoke again,' he promised my mum as she sat by his hospital bed. He promised the same thing again

183

a year later as he sat by hers. Maybe the stress of trying to cope with a wife dying from breast cancer was too much for him, though, because I knew that, against the wishes of all his doctors, all the nurses that visited him and helped him at home, all his friends, his family, his children, and his stepdaughters, he was smoking again.

I can't blame him really. I found dealing with my mum dying incredibly stressful too. I dealt with it in a Jaffa Cake frenzy, and by being increasingly unpleasant to everybody around me. We all have our little vices. I found a snippy word to the checkout girl, or a sarcastic comment in the post office queue to be just as satisfying as a quick Benson & Hedges out the bedroom window.

You'd think that spending years of my childhood listening to someone wheezing and rasping every time he went up and down the stairs or got up from the sofa, and coughing until he retched and his eyes watered every morning when he got out of bed, would be the ultimate deterrent to ever taking up smoking. But I found that it held a kind of fascination for me. Graham seemed to suffer so much for his art. What could possibly be so good that someone would go through all *that*, just to keep doing it?

By the time I was fifteen, I was already caught in the stranglehold of a full-blown nicotine addiction. It had taken me several months to get there, but I persevered. The nausea and sweating, not to mention explosive coughing, dizziness and near-vomiting I experienced on the first try could not possibly be what Graham loved so much. Why would he want to keep doing it if it just made you feel like throwing up? There had to be something more. So I kept trying, and trying, and trying, until eventually, inevitably, I found out.

Naively I thought that no one knew about it, because I sucked Polos immediately after every cigarette; and if I smoked at the bus stop or on the walk home, I went very slowly, and often took a detour, the better to allow the fresh air to wipe out any lingering odours. At home, I only smoked out of my bedroom window, when I was sure I would not be disturbed. I found out years later that when Mum cleared the gutter in the autumn of the year I turned sixteen, thinking it was clogged with leaves, she found instead that it was clogged with fag butts. She didn't say anything. She wasn't even surprised. She'd known the entire time, of course, that I had been smoking. The smell isn't just on your breath; it's in your hair, your clothes, your fingertips, under your nails, and probably seeps out of your pores the same way that garlic does the morning after a chicken balti. But the only time she ever spoke to me about it was after discovering my cigarettes and a lighter in a Sainsbury's carrier bag rolled up and tucked away safely – I thought – inside the Tampax box under my bed, a few months after my seventeenth birthday. She'd gone in there to borrow a tampon. It seems ridiculous to me now that I hadn't predicted that this might happen. Hadn't even considered it. What, a woman in her forties, needing sanitary protection? As far as I was concerned, she'd had her children, she was old and didn't need that kind of thing any more. Never had, actually. Never had sex, either.

'Oh my Daisy Duck,' she said to me that evening, 'don't smoke, sweetheart. Please don't smoke.'

'I don't, Mum,' I replied, not quite meeting her eye.

She just looked at me without saying anything for a few seconds. 'All right, well, that's good,' she said eventually. 'But don't start, my darling girl. Don't ever start. Don't be dependent on anything, or anyone, to make you happy. Be strong. Be stronger than that. You can exist in the world with only you to rely on, only you, yourself. Find other ways to be happy.'

'Don't worry, Mum,' I said, meeting her eyes now and finding real anxiety there, 'I won't ever smoke. I've seen what it's doing to Graham. I don't want to go through that. No way.'

She narrowed her eyes at me, just to let me know that she knew the truth. She didn't need to do more than that. She knew. And I knew that she knew. Then she nodded. 'I'm glad to hear it,' she said. 'You're better than that.' She didn't mention Graham, who even at that moment could be heard coughing fruitily in the next room. But she didn't need to. He'd effectively brought himself into the conversation as a warning all on his own. 'You must be a slave to nothing,' she added darkly. 'To nothing, and to no one. That will weaken you. Have you got any homework?'

I gave up the next day.

When Graham started again, she was already very seriously ill for the second time. Except this time we knew she wasn't going to get better. He tried to keep his habit secret from us all but she was probably aware. I certainly was. He was quiet and tolerant so much more of the time for starters. And on top of that dead giveaway were all the tell-tale signs of a secret smoker, which I was very familiar with, of course. After every meal, he'd find some excuse to pop outside for ten minutes. Getting something out of the car; checking the padlock on the shed; calling in on Elsie at number 10. Then when he came back in, he was always eating a Polo or sucking on a mint humbug. He'd lock himself in the bathroom for half an hour at a time, then leave all the windows open afterwards, even in mid-winter. 'I wouldn't go in the bathroom for a while,' he'd say with a grin, coming back downstairs. 'I lit a match in there, but it's still a bit poisonous.'

'I can't understand why anyone would ever smoke,' Abby would say to me whenever I talked about it. 'It's like committing suicide really really slowly. I mean, you might as well put a stick of dynamite between your teeth and light the end. Or put a gun in your mouth and pull the trigger. I just don't get it.' She didn't mention it after Graham had died, though. The silence of his gravestone spoke loudly enough for anyone.

I've found some fairly interesting things in this wardrobe, including a shiny pink wig and a hideous devil mask with bloody teeth that I'm hoping is more to do with Halloween than something she and Tom might have used in this room. Truthfully, I've got no memory of either of them ever wearing this mask, but I have to believe it was worn to a party I didn't go to. The alternative is making me feel even more uncomfortable than I was already. I handle it and the wig as little as possible, using only my fingertips to put them back where I found them. They're not what I'm looking for.

I pull my phone out of my back pocket and click open

the photos folder. The most recent picture is one I took about five minutes ago and features the inside of Abby's wardrobe, before I started rummaging through it. Quickly I rearrange all the clothes and boxes in the wardrobe so that they match the photo exactly, then carefully close the door. I've learned from experience here.

My next stop is under the bed and thankfully I find what I'm looking for fairly quickly. I was dreading having to look in the bedside drawer. I say thankfully, but actually I'm not at all happy with what I've found. It's an open packet of Silk Cut cigarettes and a box of matches, wrapped up in a carrier bag inside the Tampax box she keeps here. Evidently she remembered me telling her about my childhood hiding place and decided it was as good as any. I sit back on my heels and stare at the booty in my hand. This is not good. Abby has always been so completely against smoking of any kind, I'm pretty surprised to have my suspicions confirmed. The signs were so easy to spot: always eating Polos; rushing up for a shower as soon as she came in from work; constantly washing her hands. I'd seen it, and done it, all before. But what is Abby doing smoking at all? What on earth could have prompted her to start? At twenty-eight? No one starts smoking at twenty-eight; that's when everyone is giving up. She can't be bowing to peer pressure at this age, surely? Or wanting to look more grown up? Trying to look cool? Turning eight?

My phone quacks suddenly and I fling the cigarette packet away from me in panic, as if the person on the other end can see me illicitly rooting around under my best friend's bed. Not that there's an un-illicit way of doing it. A licit way. No, that's not right. What is the word? Legal? No, that doesn't seem right either. What I'm doing isn't illegal, it's just grotesquely immoral. Or is it amoral? Hell, this is a minefield.

My phone quacks again, jerking me back to my surroundings, so I pull it out of my pocket with one hand, while retrieving the thrown packet of cigarettes with the other.

Abby Marcus Daisy Doo! What you doing? I'm sooooo boooooored!!!

Daisy Mack Hi Abs. Well guess what? Right now, I'm kneeling on the floor in your and Tom's bedroom, having just been rummaging through all your private things, only to find exactly what I was expecting and dreading to find, in a carrier bag, inside your box of Tampax under your bed. Have you got anything to say for yourself? Because quite frankly, given my current circumstances and the reasons for them, I'm disgusted in you.

I don't say that. Of course I don't. I'm not going to judge Abby, whatever she does. She never judges me, and God knows she's had reason to lately. But now that I've got this little piece of information, I have no idea what to do with it. I don't even know why I was so desperate to find out in the first place. It was probably just to know if I'd sussed it right or not. Yay, well done, Daisy, give yourself a pat on the back.

Quickly I re-roll the cigarette packet up in the carrier

bag and shove it back in the tampon box under the bed, before tiptoeing out of the room and closing the door.

Back in my own room I sit on the bed and decide what to reply to Abby. I can't think of what to tell her, so I fudge it a bit.

Daisy Mack Hi Abs! Why are you sooooooo booooooored?

Hopefully that will engross her in telling me about her day and she'll forget all about wondering what I'm doing.

Abby Marcus Aha. I sense a deliberate avoidance manoeuvre. Why aren't you answering me, my young friend? Something to hide? Hmm?

Shit. Why do I so often forget about Abby's amazing psychic ability to look into the depths of my soul and see my darkest thoughts?

Abby Marcus I'm just fucking about!

I'm not convinced. I once read an article in a magazine that said the things people say as a joke are actually what they're really thinking. Because obviously they've had that thought, haven't they? It was in their head, and accidentally came out when perhaps they didn't mean it to, and the only way they could think of taking it back was by pretending it was a joke. Or was it people who are drunk? I can't remember. The point is that I've now got to tell Abby in great detail what I was doing that will also

190

explain why I initially tried to avoid the question. After a moment's thought, I come up with the ideal solution.

Daisy Mack OK, sorceress, you've looked into my mind again. The truth is, I was just about to open the letter from Owen and Lake. I've got it here in my hand.

Quickly I leap the one step to the dressing table and seize the letter that's propped there. I can't bear lying to Abs.

Daisy Mack Feeling a bit tense about it, but I've got to do it sooner or later, haven't I?
Abby Marcus Wow, are you really? Well good for you, Daze. I'm really proud of you. You know that don't you?
Daisy Mack Yeah, I know. Thanks Abs.
Abby Marcus Good. Xxx So let me know what it says, then, yeah?

Which means, of course, that I am actually going to have to open it now.

Daisy Mack Will do. Later on, OK? When you get home. Xx
Abby Marcus Of course, fathead. I wouldn't expect you to reveal all on bloody Facebook. *Glances nervously upwards* I meant no offence, Gods of Facebook.
Daisy Mack I think I know what it's going to say anyway.

191

And that's actually true. My stepbrother Darren has already taken great delight in telling me that Graham has left me out of the will, so I'm sure this is just a letter from Mum's solicitors confirming it. Which means I have nothing to fear from it. In fact, once I get it open and read, it will cease to have any power over me and I can move on with my life. My fingers run over the stuck-down flap on the back of the envelope, and as they do I glance up at the giant 'TO DO' list on the wall. Opening this letter is on there, but it's right at the bottom, in slightly smaller letters. Abby had to add it on to the end because it arrived after she'd already made the list. This time, my eyes don't bounce straight off the list, like two matching poles of a magnet. They linger there a moment – long enough for me to read the item immediately above. It's 'Call Naomi'. Yeah, I knew that was on there. But for the first time now, I notice that there are some smaller letters squashed underneath, that say: 'She lost her mum too'. And then there's a smiley face. How strange. I've never noticed that before. Has it been there all the time? I stare at that smiley until my eyeballs start to dry out, as the realisation sinks in for the first time that Naomi is also grieving.

No, no, that's ridiculous. I never thought she wasn't grieving. Of course she's grieving: her mum died, followed swiftly by the stepfather she adored. Who wouldn't grieve, in those circumstances? Christ, even Norman Bates didn't cope too well when his mum died. No doubt Naomi is in a mess, just like me.

Except she's not in a mess, just like me. She didn't give up her job, or her home, and is not now homeless and unemployed. Not that I blame her for that. Of course it should be me who did that – I'm unmarried and had no mortgage. It made sense. But each time I've seen her or had any contact with her since November, she's seemed remarkably together. Her grief was conspicuous by its absence, I have to say, although I didn't really give it a conscious thought at the time. I suppose I just dismissed the possibility that she might be grieving. No, not even that. The thought that she might be grieving didn't even enter my head. It was me who was grieving, me who had lost my mum, me who was swallowed whole by a blackness I couldn't even lift my head out of. Naomi just got on with going to Tesco and voting on *X Factor*.

Now, staring at that smiley next to Abby's words, it hits me for the first time that Naomi's grief may not have been visible – least of all to me, a person who couldn't even see that it wasn't winter any more – but that didn't mean it wasn't there. Whatever she's like, she did love our mum, and was pretty distraught the day it all happened.

That's it. My mind is made up now. Naomi is my sister, she's in a mess – not like me, but a mess nonetheless – and she needs me. I'm going to stop prevaricating and ring her. After I've opened this letter. I drop my eyes to the envelope in my hand and after only a second's more pause, I push my finger under the flap and force it open.

When Abby arrives home from work in the evening, I've got dinner ready on the table. It's only sausages and mash, and the sausages are a bit black on one side – the outside – but she stares at the plates on the table as if they've been enchanted by a beautiful sorceress and are now dishing the food out onto themselves. Perhaps that's easier for her to believe than me doing it.

'Wow!' she says, circling the table in wonder. 'You've made food for us.'

'It's not that amazing, Abs. I have done it before.'

She nods at me with a warm smile. 'I know that, Daze. It's just been a while.' She pulls out a chair. 'Which one's mine?'

'Shouldn't we wait for Tom?'

She shrugs. 'Nah, let's have it now. God knows what time he's getting in.'

'OK.'

She cuts into a sausage enthusiastically. 'So. You finally opened the letter today. What did it say?'

God. Not even five minutes have passed since she walked through the door, and already the moment I've been dreading most of the day is here. How can I tell her what the letter said, when doing that will involve me explaining to her why it said what it said? And doing *that* will inform her finally of the sort of person I really am, which is bound to lower her opinion of me. The entire time I was out walking with Danny this afternoon, I was pondering how I would explain this to her. I was so preoccupied, I barely noticed anything he said or did.

'Try to pull your buttocks and abs in really tight as you walk – it will harden you up.'

OK, one or two things filtered through. But I didn't enjoy the walk as much as usual, even though Danny's

194

incredible buttocks and abs were right there next to me, within reaching distance.

The letter, as I anticipated, is simply a confirmation from Mum's solicitor that Graham has left me out of the will. Well, I say left me out. What he's actually done is leave me a 'very generous' legacy of five thousand pounds. Which is five thousand pounds more than I was expecting to get, so the letter should have been a pleasant surprise. A nice little windfall that will help me get a flat and some furniture to put in it. But it wasn't. It was more like being hit in the face by a wrecking ball. The fact that you've seen it coming from a great distance, slowly getting larger, its shadow increasing steadily and covering you in darkness, doesn't lessen the impact when it finally does hit. Not one bit. After I'd opened the envelope and unfolded the letter this morning, I didn't read the words immediately but spent a few moments steeling myself for what I thought they would say. Graham had reason to want to hurt me, he would do it, I knew he would. Darren had already made that clear. But you can't prepare for the impact of a wrecking ball. No amount of armour will protect you from that. Eventually my eyes moved onto the words on the paper and *WHAM!* It flattened me. I fell sideways from the blow and curled around myself, clutching my stomach with both hands, the letter forgotten on the bed next to me. My mum's face, her poor, wretched, skeletal face came into my mind, trying to smile at me with thin lips as she proudly told me that I would be well off when she died, the feelings she had about that plainly visible. It wasn't joy; that was impossible. But it was the nearest she could get to joy in the final days of her life. She couldn't stop what was happening to her. But she knew her two girls would be secure forever because of it, and it gave her some peace.

That peace was an illusion. Her own husband had other plans.

'Daze?' Abs says now. I look up at her and find her staring at me worriedly, the food forgotten. I'm guessing from her expression that my face is telling her all is not well. 'What was it, Daze? What did it say?' Her voice is so soft, so gentle, it brings tears to my eyes again. In an instant Abby is up and round the table to kneel at my side, wrapping her arms around me, cradling my head on her shoulder. 'God, Daze, tell me – what the hell has happened?'

TWELVE

Abby Marcus

Sometimes you just gotta wonder at the fucking nerve of some of the fucking arseholes in this fucking world. Unbe-fucking-lievable!

👍 Wendy Harber likes this.

Wendy Harber   You crack me up!

Suzanne Allen   ☹ What's this all about Abs? PM me. xx

Tom Wilson   Try to stay calm sweetheart. x

Beth Sheri   Whatever it is, Abigail, forget about it. Be happy! ☺

I'm a little bit worried about Abby. Since I told her about Graham's will, she's been a little bit . . . I don't want to say 'odd'. That's not really right. Let's say fucking insane. Let's say unhinged. Let's say that she looks like she spent the first twenty-eight years of her life *pretending*. She was beyond furious when I told her what was in the letter, and went from kneeling by my chair, cuddling me and stroking my hair to full-on mushroom cloud in less than half a second. She practically exploded in front of me, leaping to her feet so forcefully it was as if the ground had expelled her. She started stomping around the kitchen, clenching her fists, lowering her body weight, thinning her lips.

'I don't fucking believe it!' she started saying. 'Unbe-fucking-lievable!' She turned on the spot and glared at me. 'Can you believe it, Daze? Because I can't. I seriously fucking can't. Your mum's money? Not going to you? Her own *daughter*?! It's unbelievable! It's unbe-fucking-lievable!' She didn't really stop saying that for the next couple of days. At least, every time she saw my face she said it. She may not have been going on like that with all her driving clients, or when she was in Sainsbury's. But whenever we were together, she seized me and shook her head with her lips pressed together.

I've decided to give her a couple of hours' peace by keeping my face out of her line of sight for a while, so I crept out of the house nice and early this morning for a walk with Danny. It's Saturday, so Abs would normally come with me, but as well as her needing this break, I also don't want to let Danny down. After all the effort he's gone to to help me out and get me going, it would just be rude if I suddenly said, 'Oh, no, sorry, I don't need you today, I've got someone else.' Wouldn't it?

The sky is a gorgeous clear blue today and as I make my way to the canal bank the air is full of Saturday summer noises: lawnmowers whining, radios playing, shouts of children, the odd extraordinarily loud bee bumbling suddenly past my head. Life going on as normal as it always seems to, regardless of what else is happening. My mind is a seething confused mess, so I put my magic trainers onto automatic pilot and sort through what's in there as I walk.

Obviously engulfing everything is black, wretched misery; also, no surprises, anxiety and purposelessness. Then new from yesterday, a large portion of betrayal and shock, mixed with disbelief and, oddly, resignation. (How can I not believe the thing I'm resigned to?) But just breaking in at the side is a thin streak of silver, gleaming in the otherwise murky darkness. For all its tiny size, it's nonetheless making its presence felt and it gives me a little boost as I acknowledge its existence. It's called Danny, and as I arrive at the sunshiney canal bank, I can admit to myself that I am looking forward to seeing him.

He jogs into sight now and I'm immediately embarrassed to be seen wearing the same new Pineapple leggings as yesterday, while Danny has turned up in matching yellow shorts and top with neon yellow piping that I've not seen him wear before. Even his black and yellow trainers tone in nicely, and his sunglasses are attached to a neon yellow cord that goes around the back of his head. Oh God, why didn't I buy more than one outfit? Serious athletes like us have to have a new outfit for every day of the week. Because they train every day of the week. Obviously.

'Morning,' Danny says, arriving at my side with a lovely smile. 'How are you today?' His face looks tanned and healthy, obviously from being out in the sunshine so much. He even seems to have got more tanned since

I saw him yesterday. It makes his teeth and eyes seem whiter and more brilliant than ever.

'I'm great, thanks,' I say, with a gauche grin. Danny is jogging comfortably by my side as he looks at me and for some reason it makes me start swinging my arms. I feel about eleven.

'*Ex*cellent,' he says, finally coming to a stop. 'Shall we get going then?' He starts up again.

I adopt an overly dramatic American accent and say, 'Let's do this thing.'

Danny gives me an odd smile and squints a bit at me. 'Yes. Let's.'

As we walk, I notice that he's aggressively blowing the air out of his mouth and pumping his arms in time with each step. It's very impressive and makes him look even more powerful and sexy. I wonder if I should do it, and discreetly have a go, but it makes me feel a bit dizzy. And a bit of a dick to be honest, so I stop. My normal inhale/exhale technique has always been quite sufficient, so maybe I'm not quite as serious an athlete as he is.

'So, how long is it now until your big challenge?' he asks between puffs.

'Um, let me think. What's the date today?'

'Today is Saturday ninth of May. All day.'

'Right, yes, of course. That means it's exactly three weeks today.'

'Right. And do you feel ready?'

I'm distracted by the piston-like action of his arms, pumping down forcefully with each step. I can't stop looking at them. It's in such contrast with my own arms, swinging gently by my sides. 'Er . . .' I drag my eyes away and make myself focus on his face. 'Ready?'

'Because with only three weeks until E-day, you should be in tip-top condition by now and ready to go.'

'E-day?'

He smiles at me kindly. 'Event day, Daisy. The day you're preparing for. What all this is about.'

'Oh, right. Yes, of course. Well, I suppose—'

'Now is not the time to slack off. But you know that of course. We athletes don't need much preparation for serious undertakings really, do we?'

'No—'

'When I ran the New York marathon in 2010, I was already covering ten miles most days, in not much more than two point five, so stepping up to the twenty-six miles was no hardship really. That's the kind of fitness you want to aim for.'

'Right . . .'

'And you'll find that as you increase your speed and distance, you'll want to do more and go further and be faster, and you'll enjoy the sensation of all your muscles tearing apart and filling with blood to make them larger and harder to propel you on, as you get leaner and more efficient with every step.'

'Jesus—'

'You know that the more exercise you do, the bigger your heart gets? Of course you do. So not only will we live longer and better and more comfortably, we will also show more heart to our fellow man. We can be more tolerant, more generous, more kind and giving, just through exercise and fitness.'

'Um, I'm not entirely sure that . . .'

'How are you feeling now, Daisy? You're doing so well, you really are. I'm very impressed and proud. You might want to just pump your arms a bit, it will help you go faster. And tone up those bis and tris too.'

'Right . . .'

'And, while we're on the subject, a little bit of fake tan on those legs wouldn't go amiss. You know, if you're going to be seen in shorts a lot.' He indicates his own deep-brown thigh, which I now notice is smoothly shaved. 'Between you, me and the ducks, I've been doing it for years. Just until I can get some proper sun on them.' Then he taps the side of his nose and winks. 'Word to the wise.'

'Oh, right. Good tip. Thanks.' Note to self: never wear shorts.

The next day, Sunday, Abby is out of bed and Lycra-ed up before me, so I have no chance to sneak off and meet Danny. We hadn't arranged to meet, but he's such a creature of habit I know he'll be on that canal path at ten every day, without fail. But today he must travel alone.

'I'm coming with you today, Daze. That OK?'

'Course.' I smile at her and do feel a little flicker of pleasure at the thought of a long walk with my bezzie. 'It'll be lovely to have you with me for a change.'

She smiles broadly. 'Good. It'll give us a chance to have a chat about . . . stuff.'

She doesn't say any more but, about ten minutes into the walk, she stops suddenly, thrusts her face into mine and very darkly says, 'Naomi.'

'What about her?'

'Have you rung her? Have you asked her if she knows what Graham's done? Have you asked her what share of your mum's half of the estate she's getting?'

I hadn't. I didn't ring her on Friday, when I opened the letter, and I haven't rung her since then either. I shake my head slowly.

'Well then,' Abs says, grabbing my shoulders and gripping them tightly. 'You should do that. Come on.'

'No, Abs . . .'

'I really think you should. She might be able to shed some light, maybe explain what's happened?' She takes hold of my arm, but I dig in my heels. Literally. The magic trainers have very good grip. She turns around to fix me with her voodoo stare when she feels resistance, but I don't look away.

'No, Abs,' I say, more forcefully. My God, I'm doing it.

Abby blinks. 'But–'

'I really don't want to ring Naomi now. I'll do it, I will, but I'm not ready right now.' We look into each other's eyes for about ten seconds, and I feel myself weakening. 'I'll pop round there and see her, OK?' Stare. 'Soon.'

She doesn't move for a second or two longer, obviously expecting me to crumble, or explain anyway, but incredibly, I do neither. Finally she drops her gaze and my arm, in that order. 'OK, well, it's up to you. It would be beneficial though, I'm sure of it.'

'I know. Thanks.'

She shrugs. 'Well I tell you something else,' she sets off again, 'whoever you've managed to rope in as your

203

walking partner isn't much cop coz you're just as bloody slow as ever.'

'No I'm not!'

'Yeah, Daze, you are. Come on, pick it up a bit. Maybe I'll take the morning off tomorrow and come with you both, speak to him – what's his name again?'

'Danny.'

'Yeah. Maybe I'll take a little look at Danny Boy, see if he's up to the job. Maybe tell him a thing or two about fitness and walking and how to complete a marathon.'

I'm literally cringing at this point. I stop walking, my eyes half closed and shudder from my shoulders. Abby, in her false-lash-effect mascara, acrylic nails and teeny tiny tight little shorts, telling someone like Danny about how to *walk* a marathon. Oh God.

Plus, if I'm completely honest, I don't really want Danny to see me like that. You know, standing next to Abby.

'Jesus, Daisy, will you please come *on*?'

'Actually, Abs,' I say, remembering with relief something from yesterday and running to catch her up, 'you won't be able to, because I'll be walking on my own for a couple of weeks from tomorrow.'

'Why? What's going on?'

'Danny's going on holiday with his brother for two weeks. Surfing.' That was the errand he'd had to sort out Friday morning – collecting his dollars from the bank. 'It's fine, I'll be fine. I'm much better than I was, and I've got used to the route now, so . . . What?'

She's stopped again and is now shaking her head with

her hands on her hips. 'Oh no, no, no, no. No you don't. I'm not having that.'

'Oh come on, Abs, I'll be fine.'

'OK, while I am now less terrified of you dying out here, I am still concerned about you getting lost, wounded, dehydrated or attacked. And I'm still a bit concerned about your pace. No, don't look at me like that. I can see that you have sped up, no question. These nine miles are now taking you under four hours, which is a giant improvement.'

'Only just over three.'

'Yeah, OK, three hours. Ish. But you should be walking at four miles an hour by now. Nine miles should be taking you no more than two and half hours, if not less.'

'You're kidding?'

'No. I'm not. That's the pace we need to set to complete the walk in the allotted time. Seriously, if you take three hours to do nine miles, how long is it going to take you to do three times that much?'

I press my lips together, squint a bit and look up at the sky. 'Wait . . .'

'Brilliant. The point is, I don't want to be still trudging round London at bloody ten o'clock in the morning . . .'

'*Nine* o'clock, Abs. Three times three is nine. Remember?'

'Yeah, I remember, but what you're forgetting is that after four or five hours, your pace is going to be considerably slower than at the beginning. Right? So even if you start off at four miles an hour, you won't finish at that rate. Which means you need to start off even faster. Which means you need to pick it up now.'

'Abs, can I ask you something?'

'What?'

I stop walking and pluck nervously at my tee shirt. 'What's going to happen to us if we don't do it in the allotted time?'

She shakes her head quickly. 'Just . . .'

'Are we going to be made to quietly disappear at the finish line? Will we ever be seen again? Will our DNA be found on a river bank somewhere in twenty years? Is our torn clothing going to turn up in the boot of a rusty old car at the dump?'

'Yes. Either that, or we'll be disappointed with ourselves.'

'Right.'

'Anyway, I think it's time you started walking with that friend of mine I organised for you before you met this Danny character.'

'He's not "this Danny character", Abs, he's a really decent bloke.'

'Sure. But . . .'

'He's kind and sensitive and so caring and sweet. Honestly, I've never met anyone like him.' Oops. I bite my lip quickly to stop myself from saying any more. Bugger.

'Really?'

I push out my lips and wave a hand. 'Yeah, well, you know . . .'

She stops at this point and grabs my arm so I am forced, against my will, to stop and talk about Danny. 'Hold on one second. Daisy May Macintyre. Have you fallen for this bloke?'

I just shrug nonchalantly and pull the most 'I'm-so-bored-with-this-conversation' expression I can summon up. Abby is my unconditional, top of the heap, A-number one best friend. She's kind, thoughtful and generous and always has my best interests at heart. She would do pretty much anything for me. I absolutely cannot let her know how I feel about Danny.

It's not that I don't trust her. No, wait. It's exactly that. I don't trust her not to immediately start trying to make things happen between me and any boy I like, as soon as she finds out about it. For all his obvious charms, I don't know Danny very well yet. He could well be into really freakish things like, I don't know, *Star Trek* or something. Maybe he dresses up as Worf at weekends and goes to conventions and pretends to use a phaser (set to stun, obviously – those venues don't have adequate insurance for anything else). Or worse, maybe he's in a macramé circle and they all get together and swap patterns and eat flapjacks. And besides all that, if I'm totally honest, I know I'm just a lump of mud at the moment. Danny is a gorgeous, toned sculpture. He would no more look at me than he would consider going on a date with a bowl of Weetabix. I couldn't bear it if Abby somehow managed to contact him and tried to set us up for a date. And then he had to look around him awkwardly and fiddle with a nearby pencil, and say something like, 'Oh, yeah, great. I'm just not sure how I'm fixed that day.' And she'd know she hadn't even given him a date yet, so she'd come home and make pity-chilli and we'd watch *Notting Hill* together on the sofa while she rubbed my hand. God no.

'He's OK,' I say to her on Sunday on the canal bank. 'Very sweet but a bit brainless, you know?'

She grins and starts walking again. 'Like, brawn, but no brain, you mean? Yeah, I totally get that.'

'Yes, that's it exactly.'

'What a shame. I bet I know someone that knows him – could have found out a bit more about him if you want . . .'

I shake my head listlessly, resisting the strong urge to grab her by the collar and shake her, screaming '*Noooooo for the love of everything holy, noooo!*'. 'Nah. Thanks, but there's no point. He's sweet but dull. Know what I mean?'

'OK. Well he's away for two weeks anyway, so let me tell you a bit about your new walking partner instead.'

When we get home, Abby settles in for a nice Sunday afternoon on the sofa with her beloved, and I settle in for a long session on my bed thinking about contacting Naomi. I've told Abs that I'll pop round there, but at the moment that feels about as likely as me popping round to a house in Notting Hill to visit Hugh Grant. Although, frankly, nothing like as pleasant. Even if Hugh took one look at me and said 'Piss off, you mad stalker', it would still be quite significantly better than this proposed visit to Naomi.

I've read somewhere that serious athletes practise visualisation techniques to help them achieve their goals, although I'm not entirely sure how that would help. Apparently if you focus all your energy on your goal, get a very clear image of it in your head and then put yourself in that picture, truly achieving it, it will happen.

I'm not convinced. Surely everyone would be visualising winning the lottery or sleeping with Matt Damon. I have, of course, been visualising that for years, but it's never happened. Anyway, I'm a serious athlete now so I close my eyes and conjure up a clear mental image of the finish line: in this case, Naomi's front door. I see the flawless black gloss paint, the brass letter box, the little ornamental tree pruned into a three-tiered pyramid in the pot next to the door. OK, good. Now I have to put myself into the picture. I start by mentally turning into Naomi's road – Laurel Avenue – and walking along the pavement towards her house. Here we are. A 1930s-style semi-detached residence complete with block-paved driveway, full double glazing and gas central heating. Must be viewed to fully appreciate the range of accommodation on offer.

I stand at the end of the path and look at the shiny black door, at the big bow windows, at the cherry blossom now covering the ground like used confetti, and my imaginary feet stall right there as the memory of the last time I was here slams into me.

I'd gone round one evening because Mum had let slip to me in a morphine-careless moment that she hadn't seen Naomi for a while. She realised by my reaction that she probably shouldn't have said it, and refused to elaborate on how long 'a while' was. Then she dropped off to sleep, so I took the opportunity to pay Naomi a visit. The cherry blossom tree in the front was almost bare and the pavement was clogged with a litter of brown and gold leaves.

'How *dare* you dictate to me when I should and

shouldn't be visiting my own mum?' she demanded at top volume. 'Who the fuck do you think you are, the visitor police?' We were still standing in her kitchen, waiting for the kettle to boil. I hadn't even taken my coat off.

'I wasn't dictating to you, Nomes, I was just worried about . . .'

'Jesus Christ, just because you live there, doesn't put you in charge.'

'I never said . . .'

'*I* will visit my own mother when *I* decide to. Have you got that?'

Tears were already filling my eyes, and then Russell joined in. 'God, Daisy, you're such an interfering witch. You've got to let Naomi do what Naomi wants to do, without sticking your oar in all the time.'

I'd rounded on him. 'Why don't you stay out of this? It's got nothing to do with you.' My mouth was starting to go out of shape as I fought to keep the tears in.

'It's got everything to do with him!' Naomi exploded. 'When he has to deal with seeing me upset every day and trying to make me feel better and help me cope with your appalling . . . dictatorship.'

'That's not . . .'

'Mum's not that bad at the moment anyway,' she went on nastily. 'She's just using her illness to get people to visit her.'

There was a horrified silence. We all just stared at each other as the kettle rumbled up to its boil crescendo and switched itself off. The click and sudden quiet seemed to snap us all out of our shock and I left soon after.

'"Let Naomi do what Naomi wants"?' Abs had said, outraged, when I told her about it. She was silent on the subject of what Naomi had said. 'What a fucking hypocrite! He tells you not to interfere, which in itself is interfering! And this is two sisters talking about their dying mum he's sticking his oar into. Ugh, horrible man.'

Now she wants me to go back there and it's almost more than I can stand to think about it, let alone actually do it. But I have to remember that Naomi wasn't always like that. We used to be close friends. When I was nineteen and Naomi was twenty-one, we went for a week self-catering to the Sol de Mar apartments in Malaga. I organised the whole thing on my own as she always seemed to be so busy, but that was OK, that was how it was. We spent two days inert by the pool, then on the third day, after lengthy discussions, she finally agreed that we needed to be a bit more adventurous. We tied on our sarongs, slid on our flip-flops and set off down the beach to check out the activities. There wasn't much – in the end it came down to a choice between pedalos – 'dear God, no' (effort) – inflatable banana – 'please God, no' (fear) or something called 'Dreamz'. It looked harmless enough – a wide, flat inflatable that we had to lie on while it was towed behind a small speedboat. As we looked at each other we glimpsed in our periphery the narrow speeding horror that is the inflatable banana going past in the background; then grinned as we focused back on our nice, wide, comfy mattress. Yes, this was going to be most relaxing and enjoyable.

It was one of the most terrifying things I have ever done. We smugly took hold of the handgrips – just canvas

211

straps at the front – propped ourselves up on our elbows and prepared for a pleasant ten-minute chat while we bobbed gently over the waves. Then the operator started the engine, opened up the throttle and flung the boat out into the open sea. Naomi and I slid instantly to the end of the float, our arms stretched to their limits, and instinctively – and lightning fast – wrapped the straps around our hands so tightly our fingers went purple. The operator seemed to feel we would get the most out of the ride if one or both of us got dumped in the drink, so he spent the entire ten minutes zig-zagging the boat through very fast, very tight, violent turns, making us bounce over the not inconsiderable wake he was leaving. He did this with one hand on the wheel, one eye on the horizon and the other gleefully fixed on our shocked, pleading faces. The float skidded across the surface of the waves in a huge arc, from the extent of the rope on one side of the boat right across to the other side.

But in true indomitable English spirit, Naomi and I clung on. The more he flung us, the tighter we gripped. Every muscle in our bodies was rigid with the effort of keeping afloat, and our arms and shoulders burned with the massive force of our entire body weight pulling on them. We were not chatting, we were not smiling, we were not enjoying it. This was an endurance test and we were determined to get through it.

After one hundred and twenty-seven hours on the thing (about four minutes), I could feel my grip and my resolve weakening, and for a moment I gazed at the deep water next to me with longing. It would be so easy just to slide into that churning blue and white void, just to let go

212

and slip away into oblivion. I risked a quick glance to my left and caught a brief view of Naomi's wild eyes before she slid out of sight as we changed direction again. Seconds later she was back, briefly airborne, then thudding back down onto the canvas with a sickening jolt. Her hair, red at that time, slapped down onto her face a nanosecond later. She was shocked, white, and bleeding from the mouth, but I could see fire in those green eyes and a grim determination on her bloody lips. She reminded me of the woman clinging to King Kong's hand as he carried her off through the jungle. The survival instinct had kicked in and Naomi had zoned out. She wasn't on that float any more, she wasn't aware of her pain and her struggle, she was just doing it.

And then I knew I couldn't – wouldn't – let her down. She was never more my hero than at that precise moment, getting through, surviving. I twisted the straps another turn around my aubergine fingers and dug in for the duration.

Finally, finally, the boat slowed. The driver, defeated, turned round in his seat to face forwards again, and Naomi blinked and found herself back on the float. We turned and looked at each other with hope. Was it over? Had we survived? Bouncing over the waves behind that little boat was like crashing repeatedly into concrete, and we looked down to assess the damage. All four of our elbows were skinned and bloody; Naomi had bitten her lip badly; one of my acrylic nails had been torn off, along with most of the nail bed; and our wrists were swollen and sore with deep, red welts from the straps that had been wrapped round them. But we were triumphant!

Breathless, wounded, shattered, but triumphant – and elated. Tentatively I released one of the straps and raised a numb, near-black hand towards Naomi for a weak, mid five, but she didn't respond. Instead, she dragged herself to the front of the float, raised herself up on her poor damaged elbows and yelled at the driver, 'Is that all you got?'

Back on my bed in Abby's spare room, I'm finding that visualisation doesn't work. Either that or I'm doing it wrong. Tears are sliding silently down my face and plopping into my lap and I'm hit yet again with the aching pain of loss. Only now I can acknowledge that it's not just my mum I miss; it's Naomi too.

Two days later, on Tuesday afternoon, here I am, in the park, waiting for my new partner to turn up. I'm pacing up and down, frowning a bit, shaking my arms, and it's not because I'm trying to warm up before we start. In truth, I'm not really sure what to make of this situation, but I know I'm not thrilled at the prospect. I'm about as far as you can get from thrilled before you start coming back again. But I also know I'm a long way away from indifferent, which has left me feeling rather mixed up and apprehensive. We've met before, more than once, but I'm still unsure whether I like him or not, so spending three or four hours a day with him for the next two weeks feels like an ordeal looming. I almost made an excuse not to come this morning, but then I reminded myself that today is May 12th, which is only just over two weeks before the MoonWalk itself. I really do need to train every day if I'm going to complete it without, I don't know, dying or something. Plus there is absolutely no doubt in my mind that Abby would find out if I didn't show up today. So here I am. This strange man, whom I can now see approaching me across the grass, has already motivated me to come out and walk today. Great.

'Well good afternoon, Miss Senior Ladder and Wheelbarrow Inspectorate Officer Lady. How are you on this glorious, God-given, sun drenched day in May? Wretched and irritable?'

I roll my eyes. 'Ha ha.'

He grins. 'Excellent. You've perked up to sarcastic. What a relief.'

'Look, Felix, I'm not really in the mood to be made fun of today – well, any day, actually – I am here simply because Abby wants me to train with you for some reason. I love Abby, and I need to train, so here we are. Do you mind if we make a start straight away?' I flash a brief smile, then turn away from him and start walking briskly towards the gap in the fence. Felix strides quickly to catch up to me.

'Certainly, my queen. But can I just say–'

'Um, I'd prefer to walk in silence, if you don't mind.'

'Oh. Right. I see. You like the silence. Well, I have to say, that doesn't surprise me. In fact I would go so far as to say that of all the sullen, morose and generally gloomy people I walk with, you're the one that I would have put money on liking the silence.'

'Uh-huh.'

'Oh yeah. It's a shame, actually, because I still think you'd be quite interesting to talk to.'

'You think so?'

'Definitely. There's an air about you. Kind of

mysterious. Like you're harbouring some terrible secret or something.' He turns completely to face me and walks sideways for a few moments. 'I know!' He sticks an index finger in the air. 'Your great grandmother was a Russian spy. That's it, isn't it? I knew it the moment I saw you wandering aimlessly around Lichfield estate that day. She was a spy, and was somehow responsible for the capture of dozens of innocent soldiers.' He wrinkles his nose. 'Actually, no, that doesn't really do it for me. Why would you still be worrying about that now, after all these years? The old lady isn't a threat to anyone any more, she's now virtually motionless in a nursing home somewhere and no one there knows about it. Your mum accepted the truth years ago and got used to living with it, so it wouldn't . . .' His voice tails off and in my periphery I see him jerk his head down a little. 'Are you OK?'

I must have flinched a bit when he started talking about my mum. But I'm not going to explain that to him. I nod. 'Mm-hmm, fine, thanks.'

'Really? Because I could have sworn I saw something then. Like something bit you. Did something bite you? You can tell me, I won't laugh.'

I close my eyes briefly. 'No, nothing bit me.'

'Oh. Well that's very odd. Perhaps I imagined it. So. Back to the evil spy.'

'Felix,' I say, stopping and turning to face him. He performs an elaborate screeching to a halt manoeuvre, windmilling his arms and throwing his head back.

'Yes?'

'Do you remember that time we were walking once, and I said I preferred to walk in silence?'

He snorts once with laughter. 'Yes, hah, because you only just said it a minute ago, so of course I remember. I get it. Very funny.' Then he rearranges his features into a serious expression and dips his chin. 'OK, point taken. I will forever more hold my peace.'

'Thank you.'

'And yours.'

'My what?'

'Your peace. If I don't talk, I'm holding both our peaces, aren't I? Because presumably you had planned never to talk anyway, which means it's all down to me.'

'I see. Well, I appreciate it.'

He nods. 'You can count on me, then.'

'Thanks.'

'No problem.'

We look at each other a moment longer, then turn and resume walking. Through the gap in the fence and onto the canal bank is the spot where Danny and I always stop to warm up a bit. We run on the spot for a few minutes, or do some star jumps, then touch our toes and stretch out all our leg muscles. 'It's absolutely vital to warm up properly every time before you exercise,' he's told me, 'to help prevent muscle stiffness. It also allows for greater economy of movement, because the viscous resistance in warmed muscles is much lower. And it prepares your body for the activity ahead as all your muscles are much more efficient when they're warm. Did you know that the haemoglobin in your blood releases its oxygen much more readily at higher temperatures?'

Of course I didn't know that. That's specialised knowledge, and absolutely fascinating to hear. I glance sideways at Felix as he blithely strolls along, not bothering with any kind of stretching or warm up. I bet he doesn't know a thing about haemoglobin or the relative viscous resistance in warmed muscles.

'Oh wow, look at that duck!' he exclaims suddenly, confirming it. 'Did you see that? Did you see the way it landed on the water? I love the way they do that.'

'Beautiful.'

He stands and grins at the canal for a few moments, while I walk on past him.

'Are you not a nature lover, Daisy?' he asks me a moment later.

'Of course I am. Just because I don't exclaim in paroxysms of joy every time a duck lands on the water doesn't mean I'm not a nature lover.'

He nods. 'Mm-hmm.' He walks annoyingly fast, for someone who's turned up in a pair of jeans and an old Cult tee shirt. He's even got his hands in his pockets and is giving the impression of someone out for a Sunday stroll, while I'm practically running to keep up with him. I'm getting a bit out of breath, actually.

'What do you mean, mm-hmm?'

He glances over at me and shrugs, which reminds me briefly of his arms holding up that wheelbarrow full of bricks. 'Mm-hmm doesn't really mean anything, does it? It's more an indication that the information given has been absorbed. Now if I'd have said "Ha", that would have been totally different. That might have suggested that either I found what you had said very funny, or, depending on the tone of the 'ha', that I didn't believe you.'

'Are you annoying on purpose, or does it just come naturally?'

'I think it comes naturally.'

I smile, in spite of my exasperation. 'Well, for your information, I am a great lover of nature. I always have been.' I glance to my right, at the canal water, and notice about five or six ducks floating around quite near me. As I walk, they swim alongside, as if they want to make friends. 'Oh look, Daisy Duck,' my mum's voice comes into my head, 'they're following you. They know you're their queen.' My eyes grow hot suddenly and I look away. 'I used to love feeding the ducks,' I mumble, more to myself than anything.

'Oh yes,' he says confidently. 'That's a staple part of growing up, like falling off your bike, or toasting marsh-mallows. Everyone should feed stale bread to ducks at least once in their lives.'

'You make it sound pathetic.'

'Do I? I didn't mean to. I actually mean it sincerely. Feeding the ducks is wonderful. Food for the soul. Like, you're linking yourself to nature in some way. Stepping out of your closeted, suburban, civilised existence for half an hour and getting right down in there, interacting.' He turns to look at me. 'Kids grow up with a greater respect for nature, feeling like they're actually part of it, instead of just observing. And it builds such strong bonds between mums and their children. A shared experience. We never forget it, do we, even decades later.'

'And does it solve world poverty and cure all known diseases?' I can't help it. I actually agree with him, but for some reason feel the need to ridicule what he's saying.

219

He snorts out a little laugh, and turns to face front again. 'No, no, it doesn't do that.' Then, more quietly, 'I don't think anything can.'

I feel bad now. God, how annoying is that? He's finally gone quiet for a few moments, which is a relief, but now I'm frantically searching for something to say to relieve the tension. 'Well, I don't know about feeling like part of nature and bonding and all that, but I know I certainly used to love it.'

He turns to me and smiles. 'Exactly. If people carried on feeding the ducks when they grew up, even if it was only once or twice a month, I think there would be a lot less stress in the world. It's such a peaceful thing to do. So relaxing.'

'Not for my mum. There was always a very high risk of me drowning in the lake or falling into nettles or wandering off or getting stuck in something.'

'Wow. And you seem so normal. You're obviously a hard-core thrill seeker using a cunning mask of indifference to hide a passionate love of danger and excitement. But every so often, the need for risk and peril bursts out of you and must be quenched. The question is, why would you hide it?'

'I wouldn't call getting stuck in ankle-deep mud a white knuckle ride exactly.'

'But it's all relative, isn't it? Being anchored indefinitely in ankle-deep sucking mud at five years old is terrifying. I mean, you don't know how long you're going to be there, if anyone knows where you are, whether a wolf might suddenly appear and try and eat you. It's the toddler equivalent of a bungee jump from a helicopter

220

for someone of . . .' He hesitates and turns to face me. I meet his eyes and find him staring intently at me as he walks sideways again. It makes my face go hot and I look away quickly.

'Someone of my age?' I suggest.

'Phew, yes, thanks. I was in the conversational equivalent of ankle-deep sucking mud for a moment there.'

'Terrifying.'

'God, it was. So you were a bit of an adrenaline junkie when you were five then?'

I smile. 'Who said I was five?'

'Christ alive! Your poor mum must be a nervous wreck. Where does she live? I'll send her some stale bread so she can reclaim some tranquillity and . . .' His voice trails off and even with my head down and my eyes blurring I can see him bending down to bring his head level with mine. 'Hey. Are you OK?'

'I'm fine. Can we just get on with the walking please?'

He jerks back suddenly, as if he's been slapped. 'Yeah, sure. Um, Daisy?'

'What?'

'Did something I said offend you somehow? Because I really didn't mean to. And if I did, then I'm sorry.'

I blink a couple of times, then look up at him. His eyebrows are pulled together and he's peering at me the way you might at someone who's just coughed blood into a hanky. 'My mum was always really cool actually. About everything.'

He nods seriously. 'I bet she was.'

We walk on in blessed silence for a few minutes, and

I start to relax again, but it's short-lived. A moment later the bridge over the motorway appears in the distance and in my chest my heart falters, mis-beats, stops all together, then after a moment's hiatus, bursts into renewed activity. Only now it's faster. Ventricles and valves open wider; blood gushes through veins and arteries; oxygen saturates my muscles; and adrenalin surges through my body. My pupils dilate but my vision tunnels so all I can see is the danger ahead; and my palms sweat, my face pales and my stomach starts to churn, ready to expel any excess weight. I am now half-blind, shaking, sweating, panting, dizzy, nauseous and desperately need the toilet. Billions of years of evolution have concluded that this is the optimum state in which to face my foe.

'You OK?' a man's voice says, apparently from inside a washing machine.

I don't answer. I open my mouth but only to get more air into me. The entrance to the bridge is mere feet away. I have to walk across it without Danny. My hands are clenched and my knuckles are as white as my face. Darkness is encroaching as we draw nearer to the bridge. I can't crawl across it in front of Felix, but I know if I try to walk on it, I will probably pass out. Or throw up. Or both. Hopefully one after the other. If they happen at the same time, I'll choke to death. Oh God, how unbelievably embarrassing would that be? Heat presses on the back of my tongue and my eyes start to water. Oh Christ. This is it now. Humiliation and death by one means or another await.

'Shall we cross that bridge another day?' the voice says. 'It's lovely along here.'

Everything inside me stops. Looks at each other. Downs tools, nods, and disperses. I practically pass out anyway. Just for fun.

THIRTEEN

Georgia Ling
Mornin all! Hope you all hav a gr8 Day!!!!!! Xxx

 Georgia Ling likes this.

Simon Stiles   Thanks gorgeous girl. C U later xxxxx
Daisy Mack   What are you so cheerful about?
Maria Jones   Morning hunni! Xxx
Lucy Pitbull   Whatcha!
Shazza Peterson   Morning! Xx
Mick Hampton   Aint it a luvly one? x

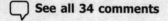 **See all 34 comments**

How come when I put something mildly entertaining on my status, like when I said I was hunting through the gear looking for something my act might like, I get three or four comments; but Georgia gets thirty-four comments just for saying good morning? Am I missing something? Maybe I'll ask.

Daisy Mack
Am I missing something?
  Suzanne Allen Loads, Daze. x
  Georgia Ling Aw hun xx
  Jenny Martin Every day, love. We all are.
  Abby Marcus Where do you want me to start?

OK, forget that. Never going to get a sensible answer on there. I don't have time for it anyway. I've got to get ready for a fun night out tonight. I've been given my instructions – be ready by six p.m. – and if I'm not I will probably be executed. Hung by the neck until I'm dead. Shot at dawn. Pulled apart by horses. Yuck. What a terrible way to go. I think I'm safe from that, though. Far as I know, Abs doesn't have access to any horses. Not vicious, bloodthirsty ones anyway.

Today is Thursday, May 14th. I walked with Felix again this afternoon, but not yesterday. He wasn't free then apparently. I have no idea why. It was quite sad yesterday trudging round the circuit on my own, remembering Danny at every point. Here's where he caught his shorts on a bramble and made a tiny little bobble ('Damn it,' he said, very Rhett Butler, 'these will have to be replaced now'); that's where he told me about helping his father get through the marathon they did together a few years ago ('If you are ever doubting the human spirit or questioning humanity, Daisy, go and watch the end of a marathon'); this is the tree he leaned against while the water he was drinking dripped onto his chest and made his shirt stick to him. I missed him at every step, and the prospect of walking with Felix the following day didn't help.

Felix and I haven't really got to the point of finding anything out about each other yet. I don't know why I said 'yet'. I'm not interested in ever finding anything out about him. Except maybe his mobile phone number. At the moment we are having to arrange our next walk at the end of the current one, which could be awkward if either of us has to change plans at the last minute for some reason. Not that I'm ever likely to have to. I have no job, virtually no family, no plans and no life. My social diary is unremittingly empty. The best I can hope for to cause a last minute change of plans is a medical emergency of some kind. Anaphylactic shock maybe. No, that's not going to work – I'm not even allergic to grass cuttings. Appendicitis then. Or a road accident. A compound fracture or a concussion. That's about it on my agenda for the foreseeable future, and none of them is even a definite. Ooh, except for tonight's fun activity. Must get ready.

The strangest thing happened after my walk today. Strange but good. Wonderful, even. Felix walked me all the way back to the flat – apparently he wanted to talk to Abs about something, but she wasn't here. I went desperately into every room looking for her, but no luck. I closed my eyes briefly while inside the coat cupboard, knowing that this meant I was going to have to spend more time alone with him. Obviously I had to offer him a coffee, seeing as he was already standing in the kitchen, and surprisingly he accepted. That wasn't the strange, wonderful thing. Strange, yes. Wonderful, not so much. He started talking about nature again. Ooh, what a lovely houseplant that is, is it a spider plant? How long have

226

you had it, has it grown much? I love plants, aren't they marvellous, so green and planty. I just smiled and nodded, waiting for him to finish his coffee, until finally out of politeness, or boredom, or to make my eyes point in a different direction, I looked at the plant he was talking about. And that's when it happened. The strange, wonderful thing. The plant he was talking about, the spider plant that's been on the windowsill in Abby's kitchen for millions of years, the one that I've seen every day but never really looked at before, is none other than the plant I gave Mum for Mothers' Day all those years ago. The plant that disappeared. The plant that I thought had died, through my own neglect. The plant that Abby – my amazing, breathtaking, stupefying best friend and best person in the whole world – has saved.

I took in a sharp breath and moved a step nearer. My hand came up to my mouth and my eyes filled with tears yet again – second time today (first one was my usual when I woke up; nothing on the walk with Felix today, thank God) – as I first recognised it, then worked out exactly how it came to be here and what had happened to it in the intervening few weeks. Last time I saw it, it was brown and shrivelled, failing badly, dropping . . . Not leaves. What are they, on a spider plant? Spiders? Let's just say leaves. It was dropping leaves and curling up and I had no drive, no impetus to do anything about it. I just sat and watched it happen, convincing myself that there was nothing I could do because I lacked the know-how. And it was clearly beyond saving anyway. But here it was now, thriving on Abby's windowsill. All the brown leaves had gone and there was a whole lot of new growth springing out of the existing leaves. I reached out a hand and touched it, tears rolling freely down my cheeks now, and I shook my head in amazed delight.

'Yeah, plants *are* great, aren't they?' Felix said beside me.

I actually laughed! I turned and looked at him with his serious, reverential expression, like he'd just seen the thirty-third Chilean miner walk out of the capsule, and it made me laugh, even though I was crying at the same time. Anyway, I didn't feel like explaining anything to him, so let him carry on thinking I was struck down in awe and wonder by the mere existence of a plant, I didn't care. He went home a few minutes later and I carried the plant like the Olympic torch into my bedroom.

There it is, on my dressing table. I can't stop staring at it. And touching it. And smiling. It's like having a little tiny piece of my mum back.

My phone quacks. Shit, I really must get ready.

Abby Marcus   On my way home now. Hope you're ready.
Daisy Mack   Yes, completely. Standing by front door, waiting for you.
Abby Marcus   Oh Christ. You haven't even started have you? You've got fifteen minutes, Daisy. Log off and get changed.

How does she always know?

Daisy Mack   Yes I have, actually.
Abby Marcus   Going into your bedroom and

228

sitting on the bed doesn't count. You've actually got to take your dirty clothes off and put some clean ones on. Preferably with a little wash in between.

Daisy Mack I know, Abs. I'm doing it, don't worry.

Abby Marcus Please hurry Daze.

There's something a little bit plaintive about that last message. It's in liquid crystal – or whatever it is that makes the computer screen work – in black and white, but I can almost see the pleading in her eyes and feel her hand squeezing my arm. Obviously I'm going to make extra special effort today, after what she's done for Mum's plant. And for me. It's the absolute least I can do.

Actually, maybe I should do a bit more than the least. Maybe I should do a lot more. Maybe I should clean the whole flat, do all the washing and make the dinner? I glance at the clock. Not feasible now. She's on her way home. Shit. She'll be here in ten minutes. The one thing she wants me to do right now is be ready by the time she gets home, so that is what I will do. The cleaning and cooking bonanza can happen tomorrow.

'No.' It's the first word Abs says after walking through the door. Her breath smells of extra strong mints.

'No?'

She shakes her head. 'No. Uh-uh. No way.'

I shrug. 'What?'

She takes hold of my arm and leads me across the hallway and into her and Tom's bedroom. I get that extremely uncomfortable feeling you get when you've been snooping around in someone's private things, and later find out that they've saved and resuscitated a very important plant for you. I feel so guilty about it I decide to confess everything to her right then and there. I open my mouth, take a breath, and then she says,

'You're not going dressed like that.'

I shut my mouth.

'You look like my grandmother,' she goes on. 'And she's been dead for eighteen years.'

'Gee, thanks Abs.'

'Don't be stroppy. You've either looked in the mirror and are silently agreeing with me, or you haven't looked in the mirror. Either way, you know I'm right.' She flings open her wardrobe doors and plunges her arms in. 'You shouldn't wear black all the time,' she mutters as she rifles through the clothes hanging there. 'You need to *mm kmmm shmmm* . . .' The final words are lost in the muffle of clothes, but I get the gist. 'Aha, here we go,' she says, pulling out a shiny turquoise top with black swirls all over it. 'Try this on.'

I take it but shake my head. 'Abs, seriously, this won't fit me. You're much smaller than me.'

'No, I'm not. Not any more. Can't you see? All that extra exercise this past few weeks has made such a difference.' She points at the mirror on the back of the wardrobe door. 'Look.'

I stare at her a moment, letting that information sink in. Is it really possible that I'm now as svelte and willowy as the gorgeous Abby? Could all this manic walking have had the side effect of turning me into Cameron Diaz?

Abs smiles at me and nods again at the mirror, lifting her eyebrows, so I start to turn tentatively towards it. I feel like one of those women in those American TV programmes where they go away for three months and have thousands of dollars of plastic surgery and liposuction and false teeth and hair extensions and everyone is so proud and impressed with what they've achieved. I hear a swell of triumphant music in my head as an unseen hand pulls the red velvet drapery away from the mirror, there's a drum roll, I gasp and . . . There I am. It's just me, in my black jeans and purple tee shirt, looking pretty much the same as I ever did. Oh, my hair is a bit longer.

I turn to Abs with a frown. 'What are you talking about? I look exactly the same.'

She's shaking her head and grinning. 'No, you don't, Daze. Seriously, when was the last time you looked in the mirror?'

'This morning, obviously.'

She's still shaking her head. 'You didn't. You haven't really looked at anything for ages, yourself included. Months. Probably not since before . . .' She trails off.

'Since before Mum died, you mean? You can say it, you know. It's not as if you're reminding me. I hadn't forgotten.'

'No, I know. I just don't want to keep shoving your face in it. Anyway, the point is that you did actually put on quite a lot of weight the past three or four months. And now most of it has gone. You probably didn't even notice, but that applies to a lot of things at the moment.' She takes a little step back behind me and looks over my shoulder to admire my reflection.

'Oh my God, Abs, that reminds me! I found the plant you saved. In the kitchen. It's alive. I can't believe it!'

She becomes very still for a second, then turns her head away from the reflected me and focuses slowly on the real me instead. 'Are you seriously telling me you've really only just noticed?'

After a second's embarrassed pause, I nod sheepishly.

'I took that from your mum's place months ago. While you were still living there.'

'I knew it had gone. I thought it died.'

She shakes her head. 'Died? And then what? Blinked out of existence? Took itself to the rubbish bin? Floated up to plant heaven in a beam of golden light?'

'No, no, I didn't think that. I don't know what I thought. Nothing, probably. All I knew was it had gone, and wasn't coming back. But now . . . It's almost as if . . .' My throat closes over and my lip starts trembling. Abs comes up and puts her arms round me and I rest my head on her shoulder a moment.

'Right,' she says, drawing away and holding me at arm's length. 'I was happy to do that for you, you know, Daisy Doo. And I'm so glad it's made you happy.'

I nod but my throat is still aching too much to speak.

'So is it safe to say that you kind of owe me one?' I nod again. 'Brilliant. So you can repay me right now. Don't wear that plain old tee shirt this evening, wear this top instead.' She flicks her eyebrows up once. 'And maybe put some make-up on.'

An hour later we're walking straight into the Dragon's Den, which is a pub just down the road from Abby's flat. I'm in the turquoise top, which amazingly does fit me. 'It's a bit big for me,' Abs added earlier, as I was pulling it over my head. 'Mum seems to think my boobs are bigger than they are.' She nodded with satisfaction. 'Looks great on you, Daze. Much better than on me. You might as well have it. Just don't ever wear it in front of my mum.'

Which, with a stab, reminds me of Mum's jewellery. After she'd given it to us, I wore some every day when I went to visit her. She loved seeing it. I won't say it made her happy – nothing could do that in those final few weeks – but it certainly made her smile.

'This colour is so beautiful on you,' she said once, looking at a diamond and aquamarine ring I was wearing. 'Graham gave me that on our tenth wedding anniversary.' I was holding her hand and she was transfixed by the contrast between her grey, transparent skin and mine, cream and solid. Well, I was, anyway. I couldn't stand looking at it for long, so I focused on her face as she lay there in the bed that had been her home for over a week. Her hair had become so thin her scalp was clearly visible through it, and her skin had a faint yellowish tinge to it. Apart from around her eyes, where it was very dark and shadowy. She felt so fragile, I was worried I would break her bones, just by holding her hand. That was the day I went straight to the hospital to visit Graham after seeing Mum in the hospice. He'd been admitted with severe breathing difficulties the day before, and Mum was desperately worried about him. I told her he was fine. I said he was being discharged that day, that it had just been an allergy to something. I told her I was going to go and pick him up now and take him home. I said he was being stroppy and demanding with the nurses. You can say anything to someone who's dying. She'd smiled.

'Ah, that sounds like him,' she said. 'Nothing wrong with him then. Just don't let him see that you're wearing the ring already,' she'd called out to me as I was leaving her room. I had to come back in and ask her to say it again. Her voice was little more than the rustle of paper.

By the time I got to the hospital, I'd forgotten all about the ring. As I approached the door to Graham's room, a plump nurse in a uniform that was clearly far too big stopped me and smiled.

'Don't be too long,' she said softly. 'He's very sleepy.'

I was horrified by the sight of him – inert on his back, grey and thin with an oxygen mask over his face. His breathing was laboured, even with the oxygen, and rattled in his chest as he strained to push the air out again. But he raised his head a little and beamed when he saw me, then lifted one bony hand off the bed and held it out towards me. I reached to take it as I sat down, then caught sight of the ring still on my finger. Quickly I slipped it off and put it in my jeans pocket, then took his hand, blinking back the heat in my eyes. I don't think he noticed what I'd done.

'How's your mum?' was his first question. It was little more than a whisper. Like the sound of the nurse's nylon-clad thighs rubbing together.

'Fantastic,' I said. 'She's doing so well today.'

'Really?'

'Oh yes. When I got there, she was standing in the

hallway having a laugh with the nurse on the front desk. She's off to her painting class now, and I think they're having a little party later to celebrate someone's birthday.'

'How did she look?'

'Um, a little pale, you know, but pretty good. She's had her hair done, so it looks all bouffant and glamorous, and she's done her make-up today.'

'Oh.' He relaxed his head back onto the pillow and closed his eyes. 'That's wonderful.' He smiled faintly and after a few minutes his breathing eased a little and I realised he'd gone to sleep. I leaned over to kiss his cheek, then stood and left, pulling my car keys out of my pocket as I went. I didn't even hear the ring hit the floor. It was only thirty seconds later I realised it had gone, but it might as well have been thirty years. It was probably already someone else's family heirloom by then. I searched my pocket in the car park with growing dread, yanking the fabric right out, then the other side, then each one again, and again, and again. Eventually I had to accept that it wasn't there, so turned and sprinted all the way back, panicky 'unh' sounds coming out of me with every breath. The plump nurse hadn't found it and it hadn't been handed in, so I conducted a fingertip search of every centimetre of lino in that hospital room, and outside the door, and along the corridor, on the stairs, on the next floor up and one down. My tears left dots on the vinyl. I never found the ring. Abby held me as I cried that evening.

'I've got an idea,' she said over my sobs. 'Claim on your insurance. Use the money to have a replica made. There are detailed photos, aren't there? Can you find them?'

I raised my head off her shoulder. It wouldn't be the same, it wouldn't be Mum's ring. It wouldn't ever have been on her finger. But I would still be able to show it to her, and she would never know what I had done. And I would have an echo of the ring that was gone. A ghost. I hugged Abby so tightly then and felt a weak beam of light pierce the clouds of my wretched despair. I knew the folder with all the jewellery photos in it was in the safe in the hallway. I could ask Mum to let me use the key again. I would take the photo to a jeweller and get them to make an exact copy. I would get a bank loan to do it if I had to, and claim the insurance money back . . . later. When I had more time. This would only take a couple of weeks. Three tops, probably. I was sure I could hide the loss for three weeks.

Mum died four days later. She never knew.

The Dragon's Den pub is a very bland, characterless place. There are tables with parasols on a terrace outside, an average menu and salad bar, magnolia walls and a ladies' darts team. Inside it will be full of families tucking into scampi and warm chicken salad while Norah Jones plays softly on a mini sound system behind the bar.

Only this time it's as if we've accidentally stumbled into a Quentin Tarantino movie. It's identical in every way, except there are no guns, knives or milkshake-drinking gangsters. And – I blink – rather more nerdy types in glasses. The room is unnaturally, disturbingly quiet, even though it's pretty crowded, and everyone is unmoving, stilled as if by some unseen sorcerer's hand. I glance around quickly, checking to see if there's someone with an automatic weapon somewhere, keeping everyone under control. There isn't, but dotted around are a number of small fold-out card tables, each with two people sitting at it, silent and motionless, both staring down intently at the table. Some of them are holding their heads in their hands. Some of them are softly drumming their fingers. One or two have leaned over and rested their foreheads despairingly on the table. The air is hot and humid, heavy with a thick zoo and fried onion body smell; but the most powerful scent in the air is the unmistakable stench of fear.

'Oh Jesus, you've brought me speed dating, haven't you?'

'No I haven't,' Abs says over her shoulder. 'Come on.' She grabs my arm and pulls me further into the room. 'We need to get a good table.'

'What for?'

But she's ahead of me now, pushing and weaving through the maze of tables and hot bodies. She finds a free table and beckons me over.

'Brilliant,' she says delightedly. 'Didn't think there'd be any left by now.' She glances around. 'God, where are the rules? Usually they leave them on the tables.'

I glance nervously at the crowd. 'Don't tell me. The first two are that we don't talk about it, right?'

She looks at me and laughs. 'It's not *Fight Club*, Daze.' She gets up. 'I'll get us some drinks. The others should be here in a minute.'

I'm not at all happy with those words 'the others'. It reminds me of *Lost*. They're obviously some nebulous and slightly menacing group, different from us in some vague way, who are all going to try and hurt me or trick me for no discernible (or ever explained) reason. Either that, or they're people from Abby's work.

As she pushes through to the bar, I take the time to peer more closely at the small tables, but my view of each one is blocked by an elbow or a shoulder. I look frustratedly around the room, and finally spot a poster on the wall next to the bar, which reads:

Here Tonight!

Excitement! Thrills! Suspense!

GAMES NIGHT

and American supper

I squint at the words, then look back at one of the square tables. As I watch, one of the three people carefully lays out some small plastic tiles in a line on the green board in front of him. 'Palmette,' he says, somewhat smugly. 'Bingo on two triple words, one hundred and fifty-eight points.' He leans back and folds his arms as his opponent's mouth drops open just a little.

Bingo? Triple word? Wait, is that . . . Scrabble? This hot, hormonally-charged, high-octane tension-fest is about *Scrabble*? I peer at the crowd, and now I can see that most of them are not wearing the drainpipe-jeans-and-hoodie combo that has become the uniform of today's troubled youth, coupled with the sunken eyes and sallow complexions of a drunken, drug-induced stupor, as I at first thought. This lot are mostly dressed in beige. I stare for a second, taking in the edgy, hostile atmosphere, and the snarling, undiluted aggression on the faces of all the nurses and primary school teachers. Weird.

'Here you go,' Abs says, putting a glass down in front of me. She's only bought two drinks.

'Is Tom coming?'

Her face doesn't screw up or look annoyed suddenly, or angry; but something alters. Some tiny muscles in the skin around her eyes contract slightly, or maybe her lips get a fraction of a millimetre thinner. I don't know; the change is not really discernible. But it's there. 'No,' she says, and slugs her wine. 'Rod and Fiona are in the car park.'

My malaise hitches up a notch or two. 'Great.' Rod and Fiona are from Abby's work. These are the two dullest driving instructors in the world. And, apart from Abs, the entire species tends towards the dull side. Trainspotters shun them at parties. Actually, no they don't, because Abby's colleagues don't go to parties. They're all too busy cross-referencing their coin collections alphabetically by country and denomination.

'Don't be like that. We need them.'

It turns out that we are participating in a pub quiz, and Rod and Fiona are our best bet at getting any science, history or parking questions right. Moments later, they appear from the car park, Rod grinning widely from his red face as usual, Fiona looking anxious in a cardigan. I'm not sure if these two are a couple or not, but every time I've been to one of Abby's work dos, they've arrived together. Maybe they just car share. It seems more likely.

'Evening all, evening all,' Rod says affably. 'Evening, Abby, long time no see. How's those forward and reverse gears going for you? Ho ho!' He says this in a suggestive tone, as if he's just made some really lewd but clever innuendo.

'Same as they were this afternoon, Rod,' Abs says, smilingly. 'Come and sit down next to Daisy. All right, Fee?'

Fiona smiles as she's addressed and moves to sit down beside Abs. 'Oh, I'm fine Abby, thank you. I don't know what use I'm going to be, it's a long time since I was at school you know.'

'Bloody long time!' Rod bursts out, then looks at me pointedly. 'Eh? Eh?'

I glance at him quickly and smile, then turn towards Abby with a look designed to kill. She's reading the rules and it bounces uselessly off the top of her head.

The first round is a picture quiz. Ten pictures taken ridiculously close up, and we have to guess what they are. It's like looking at a picture of the edge of a table, only really close up. Fun.

'That one's definitely an onion.'

'No it isn't. It looks more like an aeroplane propeller.'

'No, Roderick, no, I really don't think so, actually. That's no more an aeroplane propeller than I am.'

'Well it's not a bloody onion.'

'It's either an onion or an open wound.'

I have a stealthy rummage in my bag for my phone and click onto Facebook. I so need to leave a status update about this, but when I look up I find Abby glaring at me with exactly the expression I was giving her earlier. I raise my eyebrows in a 'What?' face, but she just narrows her eyes and flicks them down at my phone. I return it to my bag.

Round two. Entertainment. How ironic. Rod's talking about films.

'Now, you see, the first Land Rover was not produced until 1949 . . .'

'Oh dear God, not this tedious story again.'

'. . . but the film makers of *Ice Cold in Alex* made a bit of a faux pas . . .'

'No one cares, Roderick.'

'It was set in 1941, right? So just what exactly was that Land Rover doing there? Answer me that one, eh?'

'It's not clever to Google famous film mistakes you know.'

'Abby.' I say it a bit too loudly and all three faces look round at me.

'What?'

'Where are the toilets?'

She frowns at me. 'You can't go right now, we're in the middle of a round.'

'I really don't think my input will be missed for one and a half minutes. Or at all, frankly. Seriously, how many questions have I answered?'

'Now, now, come on,' Fee says, leaning over the table at me. 'Doing a quiz isn't about getting the answers right, you know.'

I squint at her. 'It isn't?'

'Sshhh,' Rod butts in aggressively.

We all look at him and Fiona pulls her cardigan more tightly round her with a sigh.

'Sorry, Rod,' Abby says, then looks at me meaningfully. I'm not entirely sure what the meaning is. 'Just wait until the interval please,' she stage-whispers.

Something's off here. Abby's acting odd, not looking at me, fiddling with a strand of hair, turning her face interestedly towards Rod, as if she's actually listening to what he's saying. I narrow my eyes at her, willing her to look at me, but she doesn't.

'What's going on?' I say eventually.

She looks up at me and smiles sweetly. 'What?'

'Something's clearly up. I want to know what it is.'

'It's Shirley Bassey!' Fiona shouts out suddenly, and I notice one or two heads at nearby tables turning in our direction, then excitedly going back to their answer sheets.

'Keep your bloody voice down, woman,' Rod hisses at her; then raises his head and announces to the room in a booming voice, 'No it isn't, it's Sandie Shaw.'

'No, Rod,' Fee declares patiently, 'I know for a fact it was Shirley Bassey. Sandie Shaw did "Puppet on a String".'

Rod rolls his eyes, and moves on to the next question.

'Well?' I ask Abby. 'What have you got planned? Please tell me you haven't set me up with someone?'

She inhales and lets all the breath out slowly. 'No. Well, kind of. In a way. There is someone I want you to meet . . .'

'Oh Christ.'

'Just wait until the end of round three. Please? Then I'll explain everything.'

Round three is The Monarchy. How long can it last? 'OK.'

'Brilliant.'

Round two ends. Round three. Rod makes jokes about queens that are borderline inappropriate. Fee rolls her eyes and angles her body away from him to disassociate herself.

'What legendary King Arthur of England was reputedly killed by his own son?' says the disembodied voice through the speaker above our head.

Rod's head snaps up and he frowns towards the bar. 'For crying out loud . . .'

'Ooh, no, oops, sorry,' the voice says. 'Given that one away there. No points for anyone for that one.'

'Well that's hardly fair,' Rod says loudly. 'I knew the answer but now have no advantage over everyone that didn't.'

'Not her fault, Rod. Anyone could make that mistake.'

'Yes, well, that's a matter of opinion, isn't it? When I was in the army, we did quizzes all the time and no one ever . . .'

'Right,' the voice announces thirty years later, 'that's the end of round three. Round four will begin in fifteen minutes, to give you a chance to refill your glasses. But no swotting up on Legendary Quotes during the break.'

I stand up. 'OK, Abs, can you please show me where the toilets are?' I can pump her for answers away from Rod's far too interested gaze.

She frowns up at me from her resolutely seated position. 'Come on, Daze. You know very well where they are.'

I widen my eyes. 'Abby. Toilets. Now.'

'Oh. Right. OK.' Incredibly, she gets up and walks away from our table, leaving me standing there, a bit dumbstruck. I think I might have just done an 'Abby'.

In the ladies, she's peering at her face in one of the mirrors, but as usual no adjustment is necessary. She turns away from her reflection to look at me as I come in.

'Before you say anything,' she says, putting a hand up, 'I have not set you up with anyone.'

'But you . . . Oh. What?' I've stalled. I wasn't expecting that. My pre-planned speech, that took me the entire journey from our table to the toilets, is apparently redundant.

'Aha, you see,' she says, grinning triumphantly. 'You shouldn't jump to conclusions.'

'I wasn't . . .'

'Yes you were. You're always assuming that I'm trying to control you, or run your life for you, but actually I'm not. I wouldn't dream of interfering in that way, and I think it's pretty unfair of you to think so.'

I lower my chin a little. 'Oh God. You're right. I'm sorry, Abs. I shouldn't have assumed that you were trying to take over my life.'

'I should think so.'

'So there's nothing going on here apart from a simple quiz? Even though Rod knows all the answers on his own so my presence here is, let's be honest, pretty pointless. You're still saying that my severely less than average general knowledge is the reason you asked me?'

She flicks her eyebrows up smugly. 'I've sorted you out a job.'

After a few minutes' mature and intelligent discussion on how she is not trying to control me or take over my life, we leave the ladies in silence, banging the door, and stomp back to our table.

'Oh dear,' Rod says loudly. 'No through road? Eh? Hahahaha!'

'Oh shut up, Rod,' Fee interjects, then reddens aggressively.

'Hi Abby,' a male voice says behind me, and I look round. It's a short bloke with sandy hair and freckles, wearing a white shirt and black waistcoat.

'Hello, Alex,' Abby says grumpily. 'I'm afraid I might have wasted your time.'

'Oh. Why's that?'

'Because the person I wanted you to interview isn't interested in the job after all.'

'Oh. Right. Well that's a bloody shame. We're really desperate.'

'I know.'

'And from what you said about her, she sounded like just the person.'

'Yeah, well, she is, she'd be brilliant. But, you know, it's not my place to arrange an interview for her, apparently. Apparently I'm a bossy, interfering control freak.'

'What, because I asked you if you knew anyone that might want to work behind the bar?'

She nods. 'Yes, apparently so. So, sorry, Alex, I know you were counting on her, but . . .'

'Hold on a minute.'

They both turn to look at me.

I pause before I say the next words because I know

that once I've said them, once they're out there in the air, there's no going back.

Abby puts her hands out to her sides, palm up. 'What?'

Deep breath. Here goes. 'I never said I wouldn't do it.'

FOURTEEN

Abby Marcus
Wondering if I might have made a huge mistake . . .
> **Daisy Mack** Yeah, you did.
> **Daisy Mack** No, don't worry, you didn't.
> **Daisy Mack** Actually, now that I think about it . . .
> **Daisy Mack** No, no, it's fine, you're fine. Everything's fine.
> **Georgia Ling** You 2 crack me up! ;) <3 <3

So now I'm a barmaid. Or will be, tonight. What an extraordinary year this is turning out to be. For me, anyway. For barmaids the length and breadth of the country, it's just another year being a barmaid. Unless they're doing a parachute jump for charity or something. That's quite extraordinary. For a barmaid. Not for someone in the paras, obviously.

When Abby had calmed down last night I went off for my interview with Alex, the bar manager. After a demanding and very probing question and answer session:

Alex: You're over 18, aren't you?

Me: Yes.

Alex: When can you start?

I finally emerged, exhausted but elated to learn that I had been successful.

I have to say, it didn't feel much like a fantastic achievement. My skills and experience weren't really gone into in any great detail. There was no psychometric profiling or IQ test. He didn't even want to watch me pull a pint. But he agreed to give me a couple of weeks' trial, starting the next night, so what could I say? Actually, Alex, I don't think I'll be very good at this? I don't know if I can commit to full-time employment right now? You're making a huge mistake? Don't wanna? Just the thought of Abby's reaction when she heard about that gave me chilly goosebumps all over.

It was fortunate, though, because my interview took place at exactly the same time as the rest of the quiz, so by the time I came back to the table, I had missed the end. Even if I did have to take rather a long detour via the beer garden.

'Ah well, never mind,' Fee was saying, doing her cardigan up. 'Maybe we'll have better luck next time.'

'You think there'll be a next time, after that appalling performance?' Rod said loudly. 'I don't suppose our Abby here will be wanting us on her team again, will she? Eh? Eh?'

Abby smiled graciously. 'Of course I will, Rod, don't be daft.'

'Right, great. Same time next week then is it?'

Even from a distance, I could see the panic in the whites of Abby's eyes. 'Oh, well, we'll have to see . . .'

248

'I'll be working this time next week,' I announced, arriving back. Abby's face spread open in a delighted grin. Which made me so glad I had agreed to undergo that strenuous interview.

'Oh Daze! You got it? That's fantastic. Well done you.'

She hugged me tightly and offered to buy me a drink to celebrate, but I really just wanted to go home. Rod and Fiona were now sitting silently in their coats, so we decided to call it a night.

'Remind me never to be forced by you to do a pub quiz with those two again,' I said on the walk home. 'Honestly, why didn't you ask someone else to come?'

'I did. Rod and Fiona were the only two who could make it at short notice.'

'I can't imagine why.'

'And I needed a reason to get you into the pub.'

I turned to stare at her. 'So the entire thing, the pub, the quiz, dragging Rod and Fiona out of their homes, pretending to care about getting the answers right – it was all just a ruse? To get me to that interview?'

She met my eyes and nodded solemnly. 'Entirely.' She grinned and slapped me on the arm. 'It worked, though, didn't it?!' She then performed a little celebratory dance on the pavement, spinning round and punching the air, while chanting 'I'm a genius, I'm such a genius.' I felt a huge surge of affection for her as I watched, and couldn't help but smile fondly.

And then I was once again stunned by her manipulative, controlling, underhand machinations.

So tonight is my first shift at the Den (as we employees like to call it) and I haven't got a thing to wear. Smart black trousers, white shirt, Alex told me yesterday, which just about rules out all my jeans and tee shirts. And I don't have anything else. But I'm too worried to worry about that. If I turn up in the wrong garb, I might get sacked. Is that possible, before you've even worked somewhere? Anyway, as reluctant or, let's be honest, terrified as I am to go tonight, I don't want to be sacked before I've even started. Abby's right, I need to get back into the world and start taking care of myself again. I also know I need to face the other things lurking on the 'TO DO' list, like call Naomi and find a place to live, but those things have always been set firmly in my future, something that will probably happen to me one day, but might not; like my retirement, or going on holiday on my own. Or, let's face it, my wedding.

The 'TO DO' list is looking a bit different though. The entry at the bottom about opening the letter from the solicitors has been crossed out (not by me, must have been the Black Marker Pen Fairy); and now I guess I can cross out the 'Get a job' entry. Although maybe I'll leave that one for now. Just in case it all goes hideously wrong tonight. It would be soul-destroying to have to write it back in again. But I am feeling quite proud of myself right now, and of what I have achieved. All I've got to do now is find a flat and ring Naomi. (Plus of course 'Look to the future', 'Focus on being positive' and 'Smile once a day, every day'). Wow, that was very easy to say. But actually doing it, actually finding and moving into a new place, on my own, and being completely alone for the first time in my entire life with no one to rely on or take care of or help me or talk to will be like finding cash on the pavement compared to talking to Nomes after all this time, with everything that's happened. Of course she knows about what Graham has done with his will and everything, and about the 'generous legacy' he's left me. What I don't know, and ought to know but am not sure whether I want to know, is what she thinks of that. I haven't heard from her, so I'm assuming she's not outraged on my behalf and hasn't stormed round to see Darren and demand he settles things differently. Of course she hasn't. Why would she? She knows as well as I do that I didn't really deserve anything anyway. But I need to speak to her, to understand, or to make her understand. Or just to say sorry. It's going to be so hard.

'Let's cross that bridge when we come to it, shall we?'

A man's voice breaks into my thoughts and I look round. It's Felix, of course, seeing as we're currently walking along the canal bank in the sunshine. It's a week since Danny went off on holiday and I'm counting the days until he comes back. Walking along here together, we would probably be talking about the Olympics, or the best way to increase stamina or build muscle definition or something. A really interesting, valid conversation. He'd be pumping his arms alongside me, breathing properly, in through the nose, blowing out through the mouth. As usual Felix has his hands in his pockets and looks like he should be whistling. He hasn't said much so far this morning – I've heard his voice but haven't really paid attention to the words. No doubt it will have been something about grass. Gripping.

'Pardon?'

'I said, let's cross that bridge when we come to it.' He

raises his eyebrows and jerks his head slightly forwards, to indicate something along the path ahead of us. It's the bridge over the motorway, of course. My nemesis. I let out a held breath. For a second there I thought he was somehow tapping into my thoughts, and was talking about my phone call to Naomi.

'The bridge, you mean?' I say, starting to feel anxiety closing its fist around my insides.

'Yes. That's why I said "bridge".'

'Oh. Right. OK. Yes. Sure.' How can I tell him that I can't possibly cross that bridge? He already thinks I'm pathetic, he won't be supportive and kind, like Danny. He won't hold my hand and put his other arm round my waist and hold me tightly with his lips so close to my face I can feel his soft breath on my cheek while I gibber and claw at the moon. I'm going to have to do it on my own. Beads of sweat break out on my lip and mild nausea starts to churn through me.

'There's a good walk on the other side that'll take us past a couple of farms. It'll make a nice change, I thought. Bit of different scenery to keep us interested. What do you think?'

I nod silently in terror, but as far as I'm concerned, there is no other side. I might as well try and think about what will happen to me after I'm dead.

When we arrive at the bridge, I'm feeling a little bit dizzy from breathing too fast and then holding my breath, but I'm determined not to stop. I know Felix has been watching me carefully during the approach, but I'm pretending not to have noticed. I'm not going to humiliate myself in front of this infuriating person,

252

so I round the corner onto the concrete almost confidently. I say almost confidently: what I mean is I almost manage to look confident. One step into thin air, though, and I freeze.

'Are you OK, Daisy?' I hear him ask, but it sounds like he's a long way off. Probably on the other side by now, holding his sides and trying not to laugh. I nod. At least, I think I do. I've shut my eyes and everything is swaying quite badly already.

'Do you need help?'

I shake my head and try to say, 'No thank you', but no sound comes out. Fortunately at this point my phone quacks in my pocket and I step backwards away from the entrance to the bridge, pulling it out as I do so.

Abby Marcus Hi!. What are you doing?
Daisy Mack Passing out. What are you doing?
Abby Marcus Passing out???
Daisy Mack Bridge. Never mind. Did you want something?
Abby Marcus Oh, charming. Well I just wanted to say that I've got a little surprise for you, but maybe I won't bloody bother now.

I read the words through, then again, and then a third time, but they make no more sense on the third reading than on the first. Anyone would think, reading them, that I'd burned a hole in her brand new Gucci jacket, or taped over her wedding video. I read through my own comment again but can't see anything in it to provoke that reaction.

Daisy Mack   What's up with you, moody Mary?

Felix is swinging one of his legs, listlessly kicking the ground while he waits for me. As I meet his eyes, he grins at me pleasantly. 'Critical incident?'

'What?'

He jerks his chin towards the phone in my hand. 'I'm guessing you're dealing with a life or death situation?' He's still smiling as he speaks and his tone is light and cheery, as if he's asking me if everything is all right with my meal. 'Some kind of catastrophic emergency is unfolding, no doubt? A tragic disaster? Fire, earthquake, tornado, something like that?'

I stare at him for a few moments, then jerk as if suddenly understanding what he's saying. 'Ohhh, right, I get it. You're being sarcastic. Of course. Very entertaining.' I turn my back to him and focus again on my phone. Abby hasn't replied. Which means she's either suddenly lost the signal, run out of battery power, dropped her phone in the toilet, or is seriously annoyed. The first three aren't likely, but what on earth could I have done to annoy her so much?

Felix is looking at his watch now. I roll my eyes and click my phone off. 'OK, OK, you've made your point,' I say, dropping my phone back into my bag. 'Shall we go?'

His smile falters a little, but only for a second. 'I wasn't trying to rush you, my queen,' he says, bowing his head. 'I merely wanted to know what time it is.'

'Sure.' I've turned back to the bridge and am now right at the entrance, trying not to see the traffic streaming past a million feet below. 'Whatever.' Infuriatingly there's a slight tremor in my voice and when I reach out to take hold of the handrail, I misjudge the distance totally and stumble slightly to my right as I grasp thin air.

'Hey, what's going on?' Felix is at my side in an instant, his hand on my elbow. 'Are you dizzy?'

Unfortunately, as I lost my balance then, I accidentally looked directly over the edge at the road, and all the air was driven out of me in a whoosh. I shut my eyes and nod silently.

'Do you need to sit down for a minute?'

Over the rushing noise in my head, I am quite surprised to spot a note of genuine concern in his voice. I wasn't expecting that. Derision was more the note I was expecting. 'Not sure . . .'

'Well, look, sit here on the grass for a minute, until you feel better.'

I open my eyes and glance at him quickly. 'No, I mean I'm not sure if there's any point. It won't make any difference.'

'Why?'

I close my eyes for a moment and sigh. Might as well just say it. He already thinks I'm an absolute loser. 'Because as soon as I get close to the bridge again, I'll start to feel dizzy again.'

He looks quickly at the bridge, then widens his eyes and brings his face nearer to mine. 'Are you saying . . . that it's the bridge making you dizzy? Then you must think . . . You can't mean . . . that this bridge is *haunted*?'

A loud laugh escapes me, in spite of my tremulous state. 'No, it's not inhabited by some malevolent, undead

255

spirit that has come to this realm from the depths of hell to terrorise all potential bridge-goers to the brink of madness or death. I wish it were that simple.'

He chuckles; a rich, mellow sound. 'Well then, why is it making you dizzy? Is it to do with magnetic forces? Or, no, wait, are there naturally occurring gases in this area that you're particularly sensitive to? No, no, I know, you're allergic to . . .' He looks around for a second, then his eyes land on some random plants sprouting at the bridge's entrance, and he points at them triumphantly. 'You're allergic to these weeds!'

I'm smiling now. 'No, nothing like that. I honestly wish it were though. I think all of those things could be overcome, or dealt with somehow, so that I could get across. As it is, I think I'm probably going to have to live here.'

'You can't overcome magnetic forces, you know,' he says darkly.

'How about gravity?'

'No, you can't . . . Actually, you can, can't you? Birds and aeroplanes overcome gravity all the time. Why?'

I press my lips together resignedly. 'It's gravity I'm sensitive to. Not weeds or magnetism or strange smells. Just gravity. The most important, powerful, universal force in the . . . universe. I expect.'

He's frowning and rubbing his chin exaggeratedly, almost like a cartoon, while looking at me sideways. It's quite funny, actually. 'You're allergic to *gravity*? Christ alive, that's absolutely terrible. There's *nowhere* you can go to get away from it.' He squints and looks up for a few seconds. 'Unless . . . every birthday, your parents take you on one of those anti-gravity flights, where the plane dives towards the earth every so often and you experience relief from your symptoms for a few exquisite seconds.' He follows the descent of the imaginary plane with his eyes. 'But they can only afford it once a year, and they scrimp and save assiduously for twelve months to pay for it.' He looks back at me, grinning. 'Is that right?'

I nod seriously. 'I look forward to those precious seventeen seconds all year. Even the wild nausea and copious vomiting afterwards are worth it. You have no idea.'

He nods, pulling a very sympathetic face. 'What torture. Have you considered living on the moon?'

'Wouldn't work. They got all the brochures a few years ago. Gravity still exists there, although it's less, so I'd still suffer. And they thought they might have to sell the house to get the fourteen billion dollars together for the ticket. It probably wouldn't be worth it.'

He grins again, nodding approvingly, then quickly composes a serious face. 'No, no, I see what you mean. Well,' he says, pushing his fingers through his hair, 'looks like you're just going to have to live with it.'

'That's pretty much what Mum and Dad said.'

'Your parents are awesome.'

'Yeah. They were.'

He jerks his head a little when I say this, but I said it very softly so I'm not entirely sure he heard me. Probably best if he didn't, really. Although I have astonished myself by participating in a joke conversation involving my parents. I even said 'Mum' without feeling stones in my throat. In fact, I was smiling. I actually enjoyed it.

He turns to glance across to the other side of the bridge. 'So how do you want to tackle this then?' He looks back at me. 'We are going across it, Daisy. Don't suggest a different route. That's not happening.'

I had opened my mouth to speak, so I close it again. 'OK.'

'How do you normally get across?'

'Well, my usual tactic is complete avoidance. When that doesn't work, I hold onto Danny very tightly, keep my eyes shut, and he kind of drags me over.'

Felix's eyes widen. 'Danny?'

'He's the bloke I normally walk with. He's away on holiday at the moment, which is why . . .'

'Oh, yeah, yeah, I remember, Abs did explain all that.' He nods, thinking. 'OK. So Danny Boy pretty much just uses brute force to get you over, right?'

'Nothing wrong with brute force. It bloody well works.'

'But it doesn't really help you in the long run, does it?'

'There is no long run.'

He frowns. 'What do you mean?'

'I mean, I avoid bridges as a rule, so I don't need to think about a long run.'

'You avoid bridges?'

I nod. 'Bridges, high buildings, balconies, lifts, stairwells . . .'

'*Lifts?*'

'Yep.'

'And stairwells?'

'Uh-huh.'

'Well, how do you get up anywhere?'

I smile, ever so patiently. 'You're not getting it, are

you? I don't go up anywhere. Because I avoid all those things. See?'

He's nodding even before I've finished speaking. 'Yes, I do understand. It was just a joke. Obviously it's the going up you're avoiding by avoiding those things, right? You're not scared of bridges and lifts per se?'

And now I feel stupid. Which is annoying because I wanted him to. 'Well, no. Obviously.'

'I get it, Daisy. But you can't avoid stairs and high places and bridges your entire life. Can you? It's so limiting.'

'I don't see why not. My mum did.'

He widens his eyes and looks astonished. '*Did* she?'

'Yeah, she did, and she got by very well, thank you. No one absolutely *has* to cross a bridge if they don't want to. No one should feel forced, or under pressure to do it, if they're not comfortable.'

'But this is all in your head, Daisy. Can't you see that? Obviously you've picked up on your mum's fear since you were born and have learned that bridges and high places are dangerous things and need to be avoided. But that's not correct. Your mum's fear is incorrect.' He folds his arms and scrutinises me for a moment. 'Has she ever had therapy for it?'

'No, and can we not talk about it, please.'

'Maybe she should think about that. Ooh, why don't the two of you go together? It would be so good for both of you to overcome your fear together. And then you could go shopping and have lunch after the sessions . . . What's up? Hey, what's the matter?'

I'm crying, obviously. Not sobbing loudly or anything,

I managed to hold onto that; but nothing would stop the water leaking from my eyes and running down my face.

'All right, look,' he says kindly, 'we don't have to go over the bridge if you feel that bad about it. Not today anyway.' He reaches out a hand and touches my arm very briefly.

'That would be good,' I manage to mumble. 'Thank you.'

'Hey, no problem. Shall we carry straight on for now?' As he turns away from me to look up the path, I notice for the first time that he's wearing a single shark tooth round his neck on a leather thong. It's such a surprise to see it there, although I don't know why. I'm surprised at being surprised, I suppose, seeing as I barely know him. He could have a flick knife in his sock for all I know. Too late I realise that he's turned back to look at me again and I'm rather embarrassingly staring at his throat. 'What do you think?' he says.

'Well I have to say I'm a bit surprised to see it, but actually it does look kind of sexy.' No. It's all right. I don't say that. I almost, almost, *almost* say it, then realise in the last possible nanosecond that he may not have meant that. I just shrug instead.

'Come on then,' he says, punching me lightly on the arm. 'Let's get going before Abby gets Mountain Rescue out.' I experience the weak heaviness of relief flooding through me.

Incredibly, he doesn't mention the bridge episode once during the rest of the walk and, after several minutes, I find myself relaxing and my muscles loosening.

'Wow, you're smiling,' Felix says at one point. 'You should do it more. It suits you.'

'Once a day, every day?'

'Uh . . . What?'

'Nothing.'

When I get back to the flat, I practically float in through the door, warm and serene from the beautiful sunshine and the pleasing ache in my hips and thighs. I stretch luxuriously in the hallway, enjoying the feeling of tautness in my legs and remembering lying face down on the floor after my first long walk, unable to move. How could I have found it so unpleasant and difficult? 'See you tomorrow?' Felix said as he left me, and I'd nodded. I'm looking forward to that already.

I glide into my room, still faintly smiling, still floaty and light with the relief of not being ridiculed, and the first thing I see is a pair of black trousers. Ah fuck it.

FIFTEEN

Daisy Mack

has discovered that I definitely do not like surprises. Thought I did; was wrong. They are bad, bad things, and no good can ever come of them.

> **Abby Marcus** Oh, that's great Daze. And there I was thinking I was doing something nice for you. What an idiot.
>
> **Daisy Mack** I wasn't talking about that Abs.
>
> **Abby Marcus** Sure you weren't.
>
> **Daisy Mack** I wasn't. I was actually talking about you springing that quiz on me last night.
>
> **Abby Marcus** Fine. Whatever.
>
> **Suzanne Allen** You two do realise that everyone can see this argument?
>
> **Jenny Martin** Shut up Suzanne, this is better than Corrie!

Actually, I *was* talking about the black trousers and white shirt which she very sweetly left on my bed as a lovely surprise, but I realised just too late that I probably

262

shouldn't have put that on my wall. Abby's been in a foul mood all day, for no apparent reason, so I'm trying not to provoke her. Telling seventy-three 'friends' how much I hate the fact that she's manoeuvred me into this horrendous and unbearable position (getting a job and becoming independent) by going out and thoughtfully picking out the necessary work clothes for me was probably not the best way to avoid provocation.

'Bieber's bollocks, Daisy, put your fucking shoes away,' is her opener when she comes in from work that evening.

'Sorry, sorry, sorry.' I scuttle out of my room to the hallway and scoop up the trainers. 'Hiya,' I say with a smile as we meet each other by the door. 'Good day?'

'Yeah, fucking marvellous,' she says. I'm not convinced.

'Oh. Bad students?'

'Look, Daze, I'm shattered, OK? I just wanna stuff my face then veg out in front of *Come Dine with Me*. Do you mind if we save the inquisition for another time?'

I put my hands up. 'No, no, of course, that's fine.'

'Great.' She moves away towards the living room, then turns back suddenly and comes up to me. 'I'm sorry,' she says, much more softly, and gives me a quick hug. When she pulls away, I'm stunned to see her eyes are filling up.

'Hey,' I say, taking a step towards her, 'whassup?' The mysterious hallway woman flashes into my mind and I feel a cold plunge of dread. I convinced myself at the time that it was nothing more than a discussion about sweat bands, but that seems ridiculous now. What was it Tom was saying? Did sweat bands even feature in the conversation? Oh God, I wish I could remember. I'm such a terrible friend. Here is my best pal in the entire world almost in tears, probably about her faithless boyfriend having conversations with strange women all over the place, I actually witness one of them, and I can't bloody remember it. I hate myself.

'Nothing, just feeling bad for snapping at you,' she says now, rubbing my arm with a smile. Then she walks off leaving me mystified in the hallway.

The only possible explanation for this strange behaviour is that it's her time of the month. Although we do usually synchronise, and it's not time for me yet. Plus I've never noticed her getting as moody and volatile as this before. I stand there and wonder about it for one more second, then hurry back to my room to get ready for work.

It's been over three years since I last went to work. I hope I remember how to do it. I won't say I'm looking forward to it, but the atmosphere in the living room is so chilly tonight, Tom's eyelashes have frost on the ends of them. It's actually a bit of a relief to have a reason to leave the flat for the evening; I just wish it wasn't *this* reason.

My first shift doesn't go particularly well. It's a Friday night, so the place is pretty packed out by half past eight, mostly with kids staying up late because there's no school in the morning. The whole place is alive with the sound of voices breaking. Standing there behind the bar, the eyes of the whole world on me – or at least, the eyes of my just-turned-eighteen audience – I feel like I'm starring in some kind of performance, and I keep forgetting my lines and dropping the props. It doesn't take long for these sharp youths to suss me out and I quickly spot a kind of 'Mexican nudge' travelling around the pub. Heads turn; grinning, expectant faces are revealed, staring at me hungrily. But what are they waiting for? What are they *longing* for? I realise the answer the first time a glass slips from my useless fingers and smashes on the tiles. There's a split second's hiatus, then the room explodes into noise, everyone cheering and stomping, high fiving each other and clapping each other jovially on the back. I think some money even changes hands. I try to curl up into a tiny black dot and blink out of existence, but it doesn't work. I have no choice other than to carry on failing at life, in full view of this hostile crowd of onlookers. It brings to mind the time I fell over on the stage during the school play when I was thirteen, and Mum stood up in the audience and asked if I was all right. She even said 'Daisy Duck'. I could have died. I longed for death, actually. Lying prone on that stage, with my wig falling off and my ankle throbbing, I would have been more than happy if someone had secretly replaced the fake gun with a real one and shot me once in the back of the head. I was known as Lame Duck for months after that. Actually I think I still am, in certain circles.

But the sarcastic cheers and foot stomping and Alex's oh-so-patient smile are almost as bad. Once the first glass goes and Alex says, 'Doesn't matter, love, it happens', my hand shakes every time I make a drink. Which I also can't do. I don't know where anything is or what quantities of things to use or how to do it, and have to keep on asking Millie, the other girl working here, or Barry, the barman.

'He's called Barry,' Millie shouts to me over the din,

giggling. 'Can you believe it? Barry the barman! It's hilarious! Like Mr Bun the baker!'

It isn't anything like Mr Bun the baker but I nod and grin anyway. I need her on my side. 'Ha ha, yeah, fantastic!' I call back, then turn back to the throng at the bar and wonder if any of these tee-shirt-clad kids did their GCSE coursework before coming out. 'What can I get you?' I ask the least spotty one.

'Four Malibu and Cokes please, darling,' he says, exaggeratedly nodding and trying very hard to look like he's on the electoral roll.

I tilt my head. 'Really?'

'Yeah, if it's not too much trouble, babe.'

'Um, well, only slightly. How old are you?'

'I'm eighteen, innit.'

'Right. Of course you are. So you've got some ID?'

'Course I 'ave.' He reaches behind him and pulls a wallet out of his jeans pocket, then opens it and a condom falls out onto the bar. 'Oops!' he says, picking it up. 'How embarrassing.' I don't look at it. He waves it around a bit to make sure I've seen it, but I'm staring blankly at his face. 'Probably shouldn't keep it in there, should I? Awkward!' My face is immobile. 'Better keep it safe, eh? Might need it later.'

'Excuse me!' a voice cuts in from the side and I turn slightly to look. 'Can I have two pints of lager please?'

'All right, mate,' Condom says, turning to him. 'I was first.'

'Yeah,' says Lager, 'but I'm not waiting another eighteen months for you to get yours.'

* * *

266

At quarter to one we're all done and I drag my coat down from its peg by the crisp boxes. My feet are hurting, my face is still red and my new work clothes are soaked in alcohol. At least they'll last. Ha ha. I pull my coat on and trudge to the door.

'Oh, Daisy,' Alex says, coming up behind me. Here we go. He's going to tell me not to bother coming back. And frankly, who can blame him? No doubt I won't even get paid for tonight as I wasted so much booze. I turn and face him with a tired smile.

'I'm so sorry about that, Alex,' I start. 'I was completely useless, I know. And mental arithmetic was never my strong point. Who knew that stuff was ever going to be useful in real life? If they'd only told me I'd need it one day, I might have paid more attention.'

He puts his hand on my arm. 'You were fine, love. Honestly. You coped very well, seeing it was your first night, and a Friday. Can you come back tomorrow at six?'

I jolt backwards, as if someone has just let off a party popper in my face. 'Seriously?'

He nods. 'Yeah, you did well. Better than a lot of newbies I've seen.'

'Wow.' I don't speak for a moment, not quite able to believe what he's saying. My hand fingers my phone in my coat pocket. Must update my status: I want to celebrate! Eventually I nod. 'Yes, I will. Thanks, Alex. See you tomorrow.'

In the car park, I tap it in quickly, eager to get some virtual pats on the back for my achievement.

Daisy Mack

has got a situation here.

Stupid really. No one will be up at this time.

> **Abby Marcus** You got it then? Brilliant. Where are you now? Waiting up for you. Need to know how it went.
>
> **Nat 'Wiggy' Nicholson** Does that mean you've got a job, Daze? Thrilled for you ☺
>
> **Suzanne Allen** At last! This can only be a good thing, Daze. Well done you, really pleased xx
>
> **Rachel Pimms** Excellent! xoxoxo
>
> **Georgia Ling** Omg what r u on about pmsl xx
>
> **Jenny Martin** Houston we have a problem.
>
> **Daisy Mack** On way, Abs. Discuss at home. x
>
> 👍 Jenny Martin likes this.

Apparently lots of people are up at this time. And their responses are exactly what I wanted. Although the fact that they're up at this time and sat staring into Facebook kind of calls their judgement into question a bit.

God knows why Abby is waiting up for me. If she was that bothered about finding out how it went, why didn't she come into the pub and see me? And why is she asking me about it on my wall like that? I never discuss private things on my wall. That's what private messaging is for. Or texting. Not that she ever texts me though. She really needs to sort out her mobile contract. Or read the instruction manual.

As I come up to the front door of the flat, it's yanked

open from inside before I manage to get my key in, and there stands Abs, in her PJs, glaring at me. 'Come on, come on, get inside,' she says, stage-whispery, then grabs my coat and pulls me over the threshold. She even does a furtive glance behind me, as if she's checking to make sure I wasn't followed, before quietly closing the door.

'What's the matter?' I ask her, as I go through the internal door into her hallway.

'Nothing. Come and tell me all about it.'

She scuttles ahead of me off towards the living room where she tucks herself under a blanket that's lying on the sofa. The flat is freezing, as it would be at . . . I glance at my watch. Half past one in the morning.

'Sit,' Abby commands. I sit. 'So what happened? Tell me everything. In great detail. Leave nothing out.'

'Do we have to do this now?' I venture in a quite frankly death-defying move. 'I'm shattered to be honest . . .'

She stares at me a moment, then opens her mouth to say something, but doesn't say it. Then does. 'But I want to know,' she says. Not petulantly. Not sulkily. More . . . furtively. If that's even possible. I narrow my eyes. She's in her PJs, ostensibly ready for bed, but there's something odd about her appearance, something that doesn't quite add up. As I peer, I realise eventually what it is. She's still wearing a full face of make-up. Why would she get her pyjamas on, but not take her make-up off?

'Is something wrong, Abs?' Not that wearing make-up with PJs is particularly odd, but added to the other oddities it does seem a bit . . . well, odd.

'What do you mean?'

I pause. My bed is calling to me. I can hear its voice, floating on the frigid air. It's telling me what the temperature difference is between it, and the air around it. It's not Winnipeg, but it's close. 'Nothing. No. Just . . . could we leave this 'til tomorrow?'

'Of course I wasn't,' she says. Stops. Gives a tiny shake of her head. Then continues. 'Of course there's nothing wrong, why do you think that? Just because I've been waiting up for you all this time automatically means something must be wrong? Can't I just take an interest in what you've been doing? Can't I just care about you, and how you're doing in your life? Is that such a big problem for you?'

I shake my head. 'No, no, of course not. I didn't mean that. I was just thinking that . . . Never mind. It's OK. I'll tell you.' So I tell her quickly about Millie, and Alex, and Barry the barman, and the smashed glasses; I tell her about the banter, and the cheers, and the sarcastic stomping, and the children smoking just outside the door and Millie chasing them away; and I know as I'm saying it all that I had a fantastic time and talking about it all now is making me grin. Abs is hunched over on the sofa, nodding and saying 'Mm-hmm' and 'Right' a lot. She glances at her watch a few times too, and rocks a bit in her seat. She so wants to go to bed.

'So, all in all, a pretty successful night, then?' she says, when I finally stop talking.

'Yes, I suppose it was. I mean, it certainly didn't feel like it at the time, but now, looking back . . .' There's a sudden soft click from the hallway, and I stop talking. Abby flinches when she hears it; it sounds like someone in sports socks trying to close the door really, really quietly. Abs glances quickly towards the door, then back at me. Her expression is unreadable. It's as unreadable as a blank page. She has apparently erased every hint of expression from her face. Nothing wrinkles, twitches or moves, up or down. She looks like a doll.

'Abs . . .?' I start to say, but there's no time as in that second, Tom's head comes into the room.

'Oh,' he says, freezing as soon as he sees us. 'Abby. I thought you said you were going to your mum's tonight?'

I jerk my head. Last I heard she was going to veg out in front of the telly.

'Changed my mind,' Abby says dully. 'Wanted to see how Daisy was getting on at work.'

The head nods, then moves forward a bit and the rest of Tom follows it into the room. Abs is staring at him with her smooth doll face and, as I look from her to him, I notice that his expression is different from usual too. His usual expression is expressionless, and he now definitely has one. It's difficult to tell because not much has changed, but his eyes are fractionally wider and there's a tiny crease in the skin between his eyebrows. Good God. He's panicking. The man's so panicked, he's practically hyperventilating.

'Oh, great,' he says, nodding slowly. 'So, er, what time did you get in?'

I'm not sure whether this is directed at me or Abs, but she resolves my dilemma by answering in a flat monotone. 'About fifteen minutes ago. We've just been talking about it. Haven't we, Daze?'

I start in horror. Why have I been brought into this?

271

Both heads swivel on their necks and two sets of eyes turn on me expectantly. Well, no, more imploringly, in fact. It's the weirdest feeling, as if both people are silently pleading with me to say . . . What? I don't know.

'Yeah,' I say eventually, with a little nod. Abs and Tom both release a long breath and sag a little when I say it.

'Great,' says Tom.

'Uh-huh,' says the doll sitting where Abs used to be, in a 'told you so' tone. 'So where have you been?'

Tom's face, already alabaster pale, turns a whiter shade, as whatever blood usually trickles round it drains rapidly away. He looks down at the floor, fidgets with his trousers, looks up again, rubs his head, then says, 'I, um, went to the pictures.'

'Right,' Abs says without hesitating, then rapidly stands up and strides over to him at the door. 'Well, I'm off to bed. Night, Daze.' And she leaves the room. Tom presses his lips together at me, says, 'Nnurr', and follows her.

I think about this very uncomfortable and seemingly meaningless conversation for a few minutes while I get ready for bed, then exhaustion takes over and I fall asleep almost as soon as I put my head on my pillow. It's a deep satisfied sleep, the sort that gets earned by a hard day's work, and for the first time in months I sleep uninterrupted the whole night.

When I wake up in the morning the first thing I see is Abby's giant 'TO DO' list. It leaps into the frame like an accusation, and I reseal my eyelids quickly. If I'm going to sleep as deeply as that again, I'll have to stop going off staring at The List. A huge inventory of my failings is not the best thing to see first on waking up, before I've even had a chance to acknowledge that yet again I am continuing to be alive.

Then my eyes fly open. Wide open. Oh my God. Oh my God oh my God oh my God. I leap out of bed towards The List and stand and stare at it properly for the first time in ages. Or, let's face it, *ever*. My eyes actually feel a bit weird, staying looking at it, and they try to look away a few times to start with, like a hesitant lover. But this time it's easy to keep looking. It's great to keep looking. I feel myself start to smile as I'm looking, and then I'm grinning and moving towards the dressing table where I know my handbag is. I don't take my eyes off the list the whole time as I rummage blindly around in my bag, right to the bottom, until I find what I'm looking for, produce it, then stare at it in glee. It's a pen. It's a beautiful, glorious, perfect black pen, designed at this moment for one fabulous thing only. I stride back over to the 'TO DO' list, holding the pen up above my shoulder like a javelin, and bend slightly at the middle to find the item I'm looking for.

'So long, sssssucker,' I say out loud. I don't know why I did that. Then slowly and carefully I draw a single straight line through the words 'Get a job'. I have officially crossed something off The List, and it feels fantastic. It feels better than fantastic. I stare at the words a few moments, now with a thin black line through them, and I cross them out again. Then again; and then a fourth time. Then I re-cross out the 'Open the envelope' entry at the bottom that Abs has already crossed out for me. Oh yes, crossing things out on here feels good.

A few minutes later I've wolfed down a bowl of

Shreddies standing tapping a foot in the kitchen, and am hurrying to the hallway to get my trainers on. This crossing items off The List activity is addictive. I want more. But I can't keep re-crossing out the same two things: it wasn't nearly satisfying enough. So I have decided to tackle a couple of others as soon as I get back from my walk today. The sooner I get the walking done, the sooner I can crack on with them. Felix isn't meeting me until ten but I can easily text him and get him to be there earlier. Or if he won't or can't I will simply wander around on my own for a while until he is ready.

'Bye, Daisy,' says a voice and I stall in the hall. Glancing sideways, I notice for the first time that Tom is sitting bent over on the armchair by the door in the living room. He's still in his dressing gown, although it's gone nine o'clock, and something about his demeanour is suggesting he hasn't shaved yet. I think it's the hunchedness of him.

'Bye!' I call out, leaving my laces undone in my rush to get outside. I'll tie them later, when there's no threat of listless lovers looming up.

I set myself a new personal best getting to the canal bank and quickly fire off a text to Felix. While I wait for him to answer I walk briskly up and down with my hands on my hips, picturing myself at the starting line of the women's hundred metres final. I jog a little bit on the spot and roll my shoulders back a few times, then tip my head energetically from side to side, blowing breaths out of my puffed cheeks. Something makes a loud cracking noise in one of my ears so I stop doing that. Instead I spend some time stretching. Not really sure how to do this properly but I saw them do it on the telly once years ago. One leg straight out in front, toes up, then bend the standing leg as I lower my bottom towards the ground. Then swap legs. Very good. Now thighs.

'Daisy Duck, are you prevaricating?'

It's my mum's voice, coming back to me from the time, years ago, when I really ought to have been hunting for a job – my first job – and didn't want to. Well no, not just didn't want to – was determined not to. Was actively finding a multitude of other things to do to avoid it. Suddenly my room needed a thorough clean out; my clothes needed sorting and donating to charity; there were some books I desperately wanted to read. But what I'm doing now is nothing like that situation. In fact it's the absolute opposite. I am right in the middle of preparing myself for a major challenge, there's nothing to avoid, and even if there were, I'm not. I stop stretching while I think about this, then shake my head and do a few lunges. At least, I hope I do.

'Only, you seem to be doing a lot of things other than the thing you ought really to be doing.'

'No, Mum,' I reply in my head. Still not sure what she's on about. I'm training hard and I've crossed two things off The List already. And am doing a third later.

'Are you sure you haven't overlooked something?'

Well that's one thing I am absolutely sure of. I know I have definitely overlooked lots of things these past few months, but how can I possibly identify what I haven't noticed?

'Well you could go back over it and look again,' says a third voice suddenly. Or more accurately, a second.

Actually, let's face it, it's the first voice, seeing as neither of the other two in this conversation has actually spoken up to now.

'Pardon?' I say, realising as I look up that Felix has arrived, and it was him who spoke. Which means he has no doubt been wryly observing me warming up like a medal winner as he approached along the canal bank. Great.

'To identify what you haven't noticed,' he says in a matter-of-fact tone. 'You would have to go back over what you have noticed, and think about it all again.'

I gawp at him open mouthed for a few seconds as the startling realisation of what he's just said ignites in my mind. It seems that apparently I was answering all my mum's questions out loud, and Felix saw and heard the whole thing. Oh hell.

'Right,' I say, wondering frantically how mad I must have looked. 'Thanks.'

'Glad to help. Shall we go?' He turns and strides off along the canal bank. I hesitate only a second or two and in that time he seems to cover half a mile. I trot to catch up with him.

'You didn't help actually,' I say quickly. 'I mean, I wasn't really . . . I wasn't . . . It's not as if . . .'

He puts up a hand. 'Hey, it's fine. I'm not freaked out, don't worry.'

I eye him sceptically. 'Why would you be freaked out?'

'No reason, because I wasn't. It's perfectly normal.'

'What is?'

He turns and faces me as he continues striding forwards. 'Reasoning things out aloud. I do it all the time. Helps get things a bit clearer in my head.'

I glance at him quickly, eyes narrowed, sure that he's mocking me; but he's smiling at me frankly and nods a little as we make eye contact. His eyes, I realise, are a deep, shiny brown. Never noticed that before. And that shark tooth is there, lying in the hollow of his throat. My foot snags suddenly on a tree root and I stumble, flailing my arms. Felix's hand shoots out towards me and grabs my elbow as my body gracefully lurches forward and my legs take three giant ungainly steps to try and catch up with it.

'Whoa, you all right?'

His arm feels like iron as it takes my weight and I almost stumble again, although there are no tree roots at my feet this time. I shake him off. 'Yes, yes, fine thanks.' I close my eyes briefly, feeling very gauche. 'Right. OK. So I'm not a fruit loop, then. According to you, anyway.'

He grins. 'Yeah, well that's not saying much, to be honest.' He looks down at the ground a few moments and fiddles with the bottom of his tee shirt. 'So, from one fruit loop to another, you're perfectly fine.'

'Now I feel much better. Thanks.'

He shrugs. 'I aim to please. So what's going on today? Why the sudden rush?'

'What rush?'

He jerks his head and squints ahead. 'You. Unable to wait. Texting me at nine twenty-three. Demanding to meet up thirty-seven minutes early. Remember that? It was only forty-eight minutes ago.' He shakes his head. 'I dunno, I may have to rethink the whole "you're not a fruit loop" theory.'

I smile. 'I wasn't demanding that we meet up early.

I merely suggested it. As a possibility. If it was convenient.'

'All right, so no actual demands were made. Fine. Let's just say you suggested very strongly, shall we? And before you say anything, it was convenient, it always is, so don't start worrying that you've put me out in some way. More than happy to start early. Means we can either finish early, or go for a bit longer. But you haven't answered me. What's the rush? Why the sudden urgency?'

I think about this for a few moments. I can't explain about wanting to cross more things off The List. Apart from the fact that it would mean explaining why The List exists in the first place, which would involve telling him about Mum, and Graham, and my shattered life, which I don't want to do, he would also conclude at the end of the story that I really am completely bonkers. What, rushing out to get my training done early so that I can get home more quickly and draw a line through some probably very simple tasks that I have so far found to be entirely beyond me? I don't think so. But what can I say instead?

'I've got an appointment,' I resort to. No need for him to know it's with a biro.

He nods slowly. 'Sounds intriguing. What is it? Hair? Nails? Feet?' He bends down so his lips are at ear level, then whispers, 'Proctologist?'

'None of the above.'

'Ooh, curiouser and curiouser. None of the above. Anyone would think you don't want to tell me.'

'Well . . .'

'But of course I know better than that. What could

you possibly want to keep a secret from your oldest walking partner?'

In spite of his rudeness, I find myself smiling again. 'Well, if you must know . . .' I search my brain frantically for something funny '. . . Jedward are coming round later to watch *Othello*.' Not funny at all. I try to suck the words back in but they can't be unsaid.

He grins. 'Really?' He bows his head as he looks at me, as if in some kind of acknowledgement. Recognition of my razor-sharp wit, no doubt.

'Yes. The Olivier version.'

'I understand completely. We'd best get cracking – don't want to keep those two waiting.'

'You're right. Especially not after last time.'

He snorts this time, giggling like a girl. 'They do love their Shakespeare.'

'Yes they do.'

'So,' he says after a moment's pause, 'do you want to talk about your prevarication?'

I look at him. 'What prevarication?'

He shrugs. 'Might help you work out how to deal with whatever it is you're avoiding.'

'Who says I'm avoiding something?'

'Well, you do, for a start. And, if I heard correctly, your mum is also worried about it.'

'No, she's not, she was talking about something else.'

'Oh yeah?' He makes a 'pfft' sound with his lips. 'You've really got this whole avoidance gig down, haven't you?'

I glance sideways at him but he's not looking at me, he's just walking along, smiling to himself, as if I'm some foolish child being ridiculous.

'Don't judge me,' I say, maybe a bit more defensively than I meant to. 'You don't even know me.'

He stops and turns towards me, putting his hands out. 'Hey, no, I'm not judging you. I'm not, honestly. Please don't think that. I'm just making conversation.'

'Well stick to the weather, then, please.'

We resume walking. 'Plus,' he goes on, as if I haven't spoken, 'it might even help you to talk about it.'

'It won't.'

'Well have you tried?'

A wall goes up in my head. It's the wall that always goes up whenever anyone mentions my mum. Not that he has, but he's talking about talking about her. Or at least, he's talking about getting me to talk about whatever it is that Mum seems to think I'm avoiding talking about. 'I don't want to talk about it.'

'I reckon it's something to do with . . . whatever your appointment is really about today. And as much as I'd love to think so, I don't think it's John and Edward.' He taps his lip with his index finger. 'And something to do with prevarication, although you're refusing to admit that.' He turns and looks directly at me.

'No, I'm not refusing, I just don't know what it is.'

'Aha!' He points a finger at me. 'I knew it!'

I shake my head. 'No, no you didn't. You didn't know. Because I don't even know, so how could you?'

'Elementary, my dear Daisy. I put it to you that you do, in fact, know. Because when I came upon you a few moments ago, you were clearly having a conversation about it with someone who wasn't even there.'

'No, I wasn't . . .'

'And of course everyone knows what that means, right?'

'No . . .'

'Good grief, haven't you ever watched a . . . well, any genre of film? OK, I'll explain. If the protagonist is having a conversation with him- or herself, it's really a conversation with their subconscious. Which means that whatever's being said is the absolute truth, even if the protagonist doesn't realise it. This is basic stuff, Daisy. Rom Com for Dummies.'

'No, it wasn't . . .'

'So whoever you were chewing the fat with not so long ago – i.e. your subconscious – is telling you that you've overlooked something. Something important, I'm guessing, otherwise why would your subconscious have bothered to bring it up?'

Part of me is angry and upset and devastated that he's telling me the voice in my head that's been a continuing presence in my life, guiding and advising me and keeping me from falling apart these past few months, isn't my mum; but part of me is dying to know what it is that I've overlooked. I go through a split second spectrum of emotions, struggling for a moment to contain the furious outburst that seethes up inside me; then the drain of sadness that pulls me down; the quick prick of curiosity; and finally the overwhelming longing, the desire, the *need* to know what's going on in my life and what I might have missed. I turn back to Felix, keen to know if he thinks he can help me delve into my psyche, root out what's happened, and solve the mystery. He's staring at me unblinking.

'Christ alive, what the hell was that?'

'What?'

He stares at me and rubs the back of his neck. 'That. What just happened. Right there.' He jabs a finger at me. 'On your face.'

Oh no. Oh God. I've drooled or my nose has bubbled or something. I rub my hand over my face self-consciously, praying that if some vile secret product from my interior workings has somehow made it out in public, then maybe Felix didn't see it. I close my eyes. Of course he saw it: he's just referred to it.

'No, no, there's nothing there,' he says, watching me wiping away at myself. 'It was just a little bit weird for a couple of seconds.' He bends at the waist and examines me more closely. My face gets all embarrassed again and goes hot, just to let me know that it's gone bright red while he's staring at it. 'I thought you might be having a stroke.' He turns his head a little and looks at me sideways. 'But I see you're actually fine.'

'Oh, right, I see. Well yes, I'm OK.' Apart from a severe case of palpitations and a hot flush. Maybe I'm menopausal. 'Just, um, thinking about what you said. About my subconscious and everything.'

'Aha. Makes sense, doesn't it?'

I shrug, trying to look like I'm only partially interested in what he's saying. 'Yes, I suppose so. I was just thinking, you know, how I would . . . how would I, you know, find out this thing? This thing that I don't know. How would I find out what it is? Do you think?'

'Well that's the beauty of the situation, Miss Daisy. You already know.'

I frown. 'No, that's not what you said just now . . .'

'No, what I said just now is that your subconscious is telling you something important. The fact that it's in your subconscious means that you definitely do know what it is. You just haven't noticed it yet.' He looks around himself and spreads out his arms. 'You can be a tad distractible, you know.'

As I look at him he raises his eyebrows meaningfully and flicks his eyes from left to right. What on earth is the matter with him? I'm frowning – maybe he's the one having a stroke? There's a mnemonic about spotting a stroke – what is it? I've seen it on the telly enough times. In fact I think the last time was only a couple of days ago, after *Homes Under the Hammer*. The one where they had bitten off more than they could chew with that ghastly cottage in Fareham. Oh come on, focus. Why can't I remember it? Something about the face. Face, face, what was it? His face is smiling at me – could that charming and very infectious expression have been caused by a bleed in his brain? No, that's ridiculous, what am I thinking of? Maybe not a stroke then. I glance away to try and work out what he's indicating and in that moment am absolutely stunned to discover that somehow, by teleportation or alien abduction or space wormhole or time-machine, we have seemingly already crossed the bridge over the motorway and are now safely tucked up in the run-down housing estate on the other side. I glance around at my surroundings, open-mouthed, feeling exactly like Lucy emerging from the wardrobe for the first time and staring around me at the enchanting wonders of Narnia – a black bin bag, ripped open by

283

foxes probably, spewing take-away food onto the street; a few empty beer cans; cigarette butts and chewing gum; and most importantly, wondrous grey tarmac under my feet, stretching reassuringly, solidly, gloriously away towards the gleaming Vauxhall Cavalier parked next to the kerb ahead.

'See what I mean, Daisy my dozy friend?' Felix murmurs by my side. 'You really are missing so much.'

SIXTEEN

Daisy Mack

is quite frankly speechless. Dumbstruck. Without words. All that I thought I knew is gone. Is it irrevocably changed? Or the same as it always was? Was I wrong then, or am I wrong now? Could I be right, now? Is anything what it seems? Why are we here?

> **Abby Marcus** For someone claiming to be unable to make coherent vocal sounds, you sure do talk a load of rubbish.
>
> **Daisy Mack** Your support means so much.
>
> **Abby Marcus** Glad to help, of course. Now what in a cat's chance in hell are you wittering on about?
>
> **Daisy Mack** A breakthrough. A weird one. Tell you later.
>
> **Suzanne Allen** What kind of breakthrough? Have you discovered the meaning of life? Have you stumbled on a crashed alien vessel? Are you ready to find Jesus?
>
> **Jenny Martin** You guys are great!
>
> **Nat 'Wiggy' Nicholson** Whateva it is, you enjoy it babe. Xxxx
>
> **Georgia Ling** Amayyyzziiiiing! Loooool! <3<3<3

Abby Marcus Are you finally coming back into the world my darling friend? ☺

When you're sitting in the beige, nondescript office of an oncology consultant, words coming from him in a low, unobtrusive monotone as he explains calmly that the world has just ended, everything takes on a peculiar, underwater sense of unreality. Dust particles caught in a shaft of September sunshine glisten like gold dust, suspended like us in that terrible moment, no longer affected by gravity. Strange words like 'secondary' and 'palliative' float in insubstantial speech bubbles above my head, not having sufficient power to penetrate fully the wall of my conscious mind. A close up photograph of a poppy – the single thing of colour to break up the beige banality of the walls – becomes first a screaming mouth, then a blood stain, seeping through the paintwork from some unseen violence on the other side. The world, the universe I now find myself in, is a cold, alien place, with nothing familiar, nothing predictable. The world I was born into, the only world I have ever known – the one with my mum in it – is coming to an end.

'Looks like I've had it then,' Mum said, as the difficult words and complicated vocabulary simplified themselves into a single, cogent fact. She turned to me but how could I meet her eyes? How could I look into that face, knowing what I'd done, what I was responsible for? I was looking down at our hands, linked together, and felt a distance opening up between us, me already pulling away, receding. Or was it her, starting to drift? That was the first day of the rest of her life.

So now I've made it over the bridge without even noticing. A sense of unreality is upon me again, changing the universe, altering what I know – what I *knew* – to be fact. Things have massively changed. Again. Am I not afraid of heights after all? And if not, what on earth has been making me feel that I am? Or is it possible that I am so easily and completely distracted that I can encounter my phobia, my terror, my nemesis, the thing that's caused me such acute stress and fear my entire life that I have spent massive amounts of time and energy going out of my way to avoid it, and not even notice?

I look at Felix again, still smiling warmly at me. 'This isn't . . . I mean, I don't . . . Did we . . . did we actually cross the bridge?'

'Oh yes, we most certainly did.' He glances behind him. 'Look, there it is.'

'But . . . I don't get . . .'

He touches my arm lightly. 'Come on, Daisy. I'm sure you already know that most phobias are in the mind?'

'Yes, but it doesn't make the fear any less real.'

'No, it doesn't, but you know it's irrational. You know deep down that in fact you're not in any real danger. You know this. If you really thought there was a realistic chance of plunging to your death from that bridge, you wouldn't ever go across it, would you? Hands and knees, commando, or otherwise. But you know it's actually safe. You've crossed it. So the fear is in your mind and all your mind had to do was think about something else and not the fear. Bingo.' He grins. 'Shall we carry on?'

'Was that your plan then? You did that on purpose? Distracted me with chat and just walked me over?'

He's grinning so broadly, he's obviously feeling it as a personal victory. 'Well, kinda. No, I haven't been plotting it for ages, but I did think that your friend's brute force strategy wouldn't always work. You needed to have a way of doing it when you're not with anyone. The only thing to do was conquer it.' He rubs his chin a moment and I hear the faint rasping of his stubble against his hand. 'Have you ever heard the story of the wind fighting with the sun?'

'Um . . .'

'They're arguing about which one is more powerful, so they decide that whoever can get this lone traveller's cloak off him is the winner. So the wind blows and blows as hard as he can, but the harder he blows, the more tightly the traveller pulls his cloak round him. So he gives up and the sun has a go. He comes out and beams down and straight away the traveller takes his cloak off himself, no brute force required.'

'Ah, I get it. You're the sun, right?'

'Well, you know, I have been told that.'

We share a laugh and fall silent for a few moments. As we walk, I'm absorbed with it, amazed that my life-long fear could simply be wiped out like that, so easily. And as I reflect on it, suddenly I'm startled by the real-isation that it's not a lifelong fear at all. How could I have forgotten this? There was a time when I wasn't scared, *before* I was scared, and now I've remembered that, I'm amazed that I could ever have forgotten.

When I was about fourteen, I went to visit my dad in New York, all on my own. Obviously I haven't forgotten that fact, it just doesn't feature in any thoughts I have about my life at the moment. It's almost as if it happened to a different person, a different version of me. Dad's firm had only sent him out there about six months earlier and we hadn't visited him there before, so I was very excited. But Naomi had her exams so she couldn't go. Dad originally said that I couldn't go either, not if it meant travelling on my own, but Mum spoke to him and convinced him I would be fine.

'You're a strong, independent woman,' she said to me at the security check. 'This journey will be a piece of cake for someone like you.'

'I know, Mum. I'm not scared.' I was already starting to glance around me, excitedly taking in my surroundings, noticing what was going on. A tiny wizened old woman was trying to walk round the outside of the electronic portal, and the fierce-looking guard kept telling her to do it again. She was getting very flustered, flapping her hands and looking back over her shoulder towards a shrivelled old man, presumably her ancient husband. He couldn't help her though, he was completely occupied by trying to keep his trousers up after taking his belt off.

'Good,' Mum said. She hugged me tightly. 'Remember, don't talk to any strangers, don't even make eye contact.'

'I won't.' The tiny old woman seemed to think that she should at all costs avoid going through the portal. Meanwhile the old man was emptying his pockets and tossing the items into the plastic tray that had already been through the x-ray machine. The woman operating the conveyor belt rolled her eyes and moved the tray back to the starting line.

Mum was holding my arms, gazing at me with wet

eyes. I was only going for a week. She stroked my cheek. 'Enjoy yourself, sweetheart. I'll miss you so much. But don't worry about me, I'll be OK.'

'OK.' I hadn't been intending to worry about her, but when she said that, I started to wonder whether I should.

'Have fun,' Naomi said grumpily. 'Don't get stabbed or anything will you.'

I grinned. 'Thanks, Nomes.' With a final tight hug, Mum let me go and I walked away from them both (Graham had stayed in the car park for a smoke) without looking back once. When I got through the security check, the craggy couple were face down on the floor with their hands behind their backs.

I couldn't imagine why anyone would find this sort of thing daunting. I followed the signs to the correct departure gate, waited for the call to board, identified myself as the lone minor to the woman at the entrance to the plane and found my seat. While I was putting my bag into the overhead locker, I took a moment to have a quick look round. I was at the front of the cabin in a special seat for lone minors apparently, so I had a perfect view of the strange phenomenon that is the travelling public. There was a middle-aged woman with a laptop sitting in the seat next to me, so I smiled and said hello as I sat down. She looked up briefly in my direction, made a verbal noise that sounded a bit like 'hello' then went back to Candy Crush Saga, or whatever she was doing. The stewardess who had directed me to my seat was standing at the open door, checking boarding cards and telling people which aisle to go down, depending on the location of their seat. But it made no difference, they all just wanted to follow each other.

'Seat 12A, straight down here; 12B, follow straight down; 26F, use the far aisle, please; 32G, far aisle. Oh, no, Madam, not this aisle, you need to use the far aisle for 26F; 13H, far aisle. No, sorry, *that's* the far aisle.' On and on it went, no one listening, the poor stewardess repeating herself over and over, people bumbling down the wrong aisle then snarling everything up by trying to come back. I smiled the first few times it happened, then started giggling, and eventually Karen the stewardess and I wound up playing a little game with each other, guessing whether or not the person would be listening. She kept completely calm the entire time, which was so impressive in the face of being blatantly ignored while trying to help people. But she didn't give up and she didn't get cross.

'How do you stay so calm?' I asked her. 'They're all such idiots.'

She smiled. 'They're not, Daisy, they're just preoccupied.'

The take-off was the most exciting thing I had ever done at that point in my life. Just when you thought the plane was already whizzing along the runway as fast as it could go, it sped up even more and flattened you into the back of your seat. I watched the entire thing out of the window, amazed to feel the rumbly, bumpy road surface suddenly give way to floaty air. The fields and traffic shrank away below us so very fast and I was higher than I'd ever been before in about fifteen seconds. I was exhilarated, thrilled, impressed and shocked. But I was not scared.

During the flight I read my book; watched *Toy Story 2* and *The Haunting*; enjoyed a delicious coq au vin with duchesse potatoes and green beans followed by chocolate orange pudding, crackers and cheese; and snoozed on and off for a couple of hours. A baby further towards the back screamed virtually the entire time and the woman next to me sighed and squirmed and spent a considerable amount of time and energy looking back over the top of her seat. I went for a stroll up and down the plane a few times, rotated my ankles, wore the eye mask. It was fantastic.

When the plane landed, I watched in amazement as countless so-called mature adults refused to obey the rules. What was an innocent, impressionable child like me supposed to learn from that? The seatbelt sign was on throughout the descent and landing, but as soon as the plane's wheels touched the tarmac, the cabin was peppered with the clacking sound of seatbelts being undone. Some of these idiots even stood up and started getting their bags out of the overhead lockers, obviously thinking that the seatbelt rule didn't apply to them. My new friend Karen went on the intercom and reminded us all ever so sweetly that the seatbelt sign was still on and could everyone therefore please remain in their seats with their seatbelts done up until the captain deemed it safe enough for it to be turned off. As one, the passengers remained standing and continued to collect up their bags. Karen said it again a few minutes later, but it wasn't working.

'The problem is,' I said to the almost silent lady in the next seat, 'that they're not allowed to use an angry voice.'

'Mmm.'

'Maybe if they shouted into the mic "SIT THE FUCK DOWN!" they might get a better response.'

Dad was really pleased I was there and excitedly showed me a timetable of activities and sight-seeing, complete with drawings, that he'd clearly spent hours preparing. We rode bikes in Central Park, shopped on Fifth Avenue, did a walking tour round Greenwich and went on a 'Food on Foot' tour, a mammoth American eating extravaganza that started off better than it ended. But most significantly, we went up to the Empire State Building Observation Deck. I knew what to expect – I'd seen sets of it plenty of times in films – but even knowing that, I remember that I felt no fear, no anxiety, no stress. In the lift on the way up I was not dizzy, I was not shaking, I did not feel an almost overwhelming sense of imminent death. I was just excited and happy, looking forward to peering out at the incredible view. It was an amazing experience and a fantastic trip, marred by no stress, no worrying, no fear and only one lot of vomiting.

'You OK?' Felix says now, after a few minutes of silence.

'Mm-hmm.'

'So Miss Daisy Queen of Ducks, now that you've conquered your fear of heights, what are you going to do next?' He's using an abrasive American accent and thrusts an imaginary microphone in front of me with a massive toothy grin.

I glance at him with a smile, then lean down into the imaginary mic. 'I think I might take up flying.'

He puts his hands up. 'Whoa, that's a big leap! Wait a minute, do you believe you can– ?'

'No of course I don't, fool. But yeah, OK, you're right, maybe not flying. But I feel . . . unfettered for the first time in ages. Like I could almost float off the pavement and start swooping around.' I just stop myself from spreading my arms out into wings and sprinting along the pavement going 'nnneeeeeeeeeeoooowwwwwww'. My fingers twitch, but propriety stops me.

As we approach the Lovely Lawn some time later, the pavement is a little too narrow to walk shoulder to shoulder, so I go in front, automatically pushing aside the overhanging plants, then holding them back for Felix to follow.

'Wow,' he says as he takes hold of the branches. 'Look at that.'

I stare at the plants. 'What about them?'

In response, Felix takes a firm grip of one of the stems and I wait for him to do everyone a favour and break it off. But instead he brings it up to his nose, pushes his face into it and breathes in deeply. 'Wow,' he says again. 'Have you smelled these? They're gorgeous.'

He holds out the blooms to me and I hesitate a moment before leaning forward to take a tentative sniff. My nose fills with a heavy, luxurious, floral scent and I'm instantly transported back to my childhood. I breathe in more deeply and close my eyes. It's not a specific memory, not an immediate apparition of a smiling Mum holding up a huge bouquet, or a blissful summer's evening in a garden somewhere; but a feeling, a strong sensation of what it felt like to be a child, how the world fitted around me. How comfortable and right everything was. There's no fear in that place, no anxiety, no misery. The worst

294

thing about it seems to be a deep, subconscious under-standing that I'm not in charge, but that's no bad thing. I want to stay there in that moment, inside the scent, feeling warm and safe again, loved and protected. But then I realise that I'm standing on a pavement with my face stuck in some flowers being held by a virtual stranger, and it's getting a bit weird. I withdraw and look up at Felix. He's grinning at me like a nan at a nativity.

'Wow,' I say inadequately.

'I noticed you enjoyed them. Did they take you back?'

I stare at him. 'What?'

He moves the branch gently back to its original posi-tion and releases it, then jerks his chin towards the pave-ment ahead of us. 'Shall we?' He sets off but I'm still looking at the blossoms, wondering why I've never stopped to smell them before.

'What did you mean, take me back?' I say, jogging to catch up.

He shrugs. 'Nothing. Just the way smells do that, don't they? Kind of recreate an entire life you used to have, in your head.'

I'm speechless.

'Hey,' he says suddenly, as if he's only just noticing, 'I only live round the corner. Fancy a drink? I'm gasping.' And he strides off ahead of me, over the road.

This is by far the weirdest walk I have ever been on, including the one with the remote control car and the Malteser. Long story. But while I'm dithering on the pavement not knowing whether to follow him (could our tentative friendship withstand a non-walking encounter?) or try to find my own way home (unlikely, let's face it

– got lost in one turn, remember?) Felix has rounded the corner ahead and disappeared. A small panic grips me and once again I'm back in that maze with nothing but identical fences on every side. I cross the road quickly in Felix's direction, not wanting him to have to come back to get me, only to find me crying on the pavement. I spot him standing by a garden gate a few houses up and walk quickly to join him.

Daisy Mack
is wandering yet again into unknown territory. Literally, and figuratively. Physically, and metaphorically. Bodily, and mentally. Wish me luck.

> **Suzanne Allen** This sounds exciting. I'm not wishing you luck, you don't need it. Just enjoy yourself. xx
>
> **Georgia Ling** Wot r u on about loooolz <3
>
> **Nat 'Wiggy' Nicholson** Your be fine hunni take care xx

As he opens the front door I hear a phone ringing somewhere in the background and he breaks into a sprint up the hallway towards the sound.

'Come on through,' he calls back over his shoulder. 'Be right with you.'

I follow at a more moderate pace down the cream-painted hallway, past a couple of closed doors, into a very elegantly simple living room at the end: black leather sofas, hardwood flooring, large flat screen telly. Very modern, very masculine. Very attractive. I wander around, taking a good look at the photos on the walls and cabinets, absorbing information about my host. There are plenty of pictures of him with various people – smiling and shaking hands with another man in identical black morning suits and buttonholes; standing by a barbecue with three other people; cheek to cheek with an old lady, both in woollen hats and scarves; wearing a Santa beard and holding a little girl of about three on his lap. It's definitely him – I can easily recognise those dark eyes. There is also a single large frame with a collage of pictures of Felix in it, mostly in a wetsuit and sometimes just in shorts and flippers. I linger over these particularly, because the scenery behind him is so exotic.

'Sorry about that,' he says, suddenly coming into the room. I jump quickly away from the pictures.

''S'OK, people get phone calls all the time, it's the curse of modern existence.'

He grins and walks over to me. 'No, I mean the photographs of me with hardly any clothes on.'

I raise my eyebrows. 'Wha— ? You . . .? Oh, you mean . . .?' I want to pretend I hadn't noticed, but it seems a bit pointless as I practically had a magnifying glass held up against them.

'It's my great aunt Winnie's fault,' he says.

'Ah, she likes taking photos, does she?'

'No, she just loves Instagram.'

I blink. 'Instagram? Did you say your *great* aunt?'

'Yeah, she's got loads of apps. Shall we have a drink? Lemonade? I'll get them. Walk this way.' He turns dramatically round and strides off like a giant across the land towards the hallway, so I scuttle behind him.

The kitchen is ultra-modern, with high gloss black doors, a dark glittery floor and state-of-the-art appliances strewn across the marble work tops. Coffee maker, water purifier, designer microwave, chrome juicer, they're all there, gleaming and apparently untouched. Felix is pouring out two pale green drinks from a jug which he replaces in the stripey Smeg fridge.

'Wow. Gorgeous kitchen,' I remark, taking it all in.

'Oh thanks but I can't take any credit. It's all Aunt Winnie.'

'Oh, right.' I'm slightly curious but starting not to be surprised. This room is *so* Aunt Winnie. 'What's this all about?' I incline my head towards a series of about six photographs in heavy wood frames on the wall by the door, mostly of people doing various dangerous things. There's a hand reaching out over a gaping shark's mouth; a group of people in life jackets and helmets sitting in a dinghy; someone swinging on a rope across a ravine; someone else – or maybe the same person, it's difficult to see properly – standing on a rocky path with a bicycle over his shoulder. I lean in closer. They all look like Felix.

'Wow. Are these all you?'

He comes to stand at my side, our shoulders just touching. 'Yeah. My year of living dangerously.'

I'm standing very, very still. 'Good God. Are you actually feeding your hand to that shark?'

He laughs. 'Actually, great whites have had a bit of bad press. They're nothing like as vicious as they're made out to be.'

I stare at the rows of enormous, razor-sharp teeth, exposed to view as the flesh around them is skinned back in a giant snarl. 'You know what, I can see that now. He just wants to be loved.'

He laughs deeply, looking at me the whole time. Eventually I find myself grinning, in spite of myself. And deep down, in a place that I thought no longer existed, I feel something else. It takes a moment for me to identify it but finally I realise with a start that I'm enjoying myself. I'm enjoying being in Felix's company. More than that, I like him.

'Aha,' he says, ruining it, 'she smiles. It's a miracle!'

I return instantly to scowling.

'Look,' he says, pointing at a different picture, 'that's Aunt Winnie. Love her.' Aunt Winnie is a tiny, frail-looking, very *very* old lady. In the picture she's sitting under a blanket in an armchair smiling weakly, her feet up on something in front of her. Her eyes are watery and red and her skin reminds me of talcum powder. Sticking out of the bottom of the blanket are two huge, hairy black gorilla feet. Felix peers at the picture for a while, a smile on his face. 'She's hiking round Australia with her grand-daughter at the moment.'

I blink, struggling to resolve the two images. This tiny, fragile woman with candy floss hair, waving at the camera with transparent skin, striding briskly across the outback, kicking rattlesnakes out of the way.

'Here we are then,' Felix says, holding out one of the lemonades.

'Thanks.' I take a large gulp, suddenly realising how thirsty I am. The lemonade is absolutely delicious. Sweet, with a strong tartness, making the glands in my jaw throb. Which feels incredibly familiar. I hold up the glass and peer at the liquid, as if it might hold some answers.

'You'll never find any answers at the bottom of a glass,

you know,' Felix says darkly. 'Many have tried; none succeeded.'

'This is delicious.' I look up at him. 'And familiar somehow. I'm sure I've had it before, but it's not the sort of thing I usually buy.' (No need to tell him that I don't usually buy anything right now.) 'Where do you get it from?'

'Have you?' He looks puzzled for a second, then beams. 'Oh, I know, I gave a batch to Abby a while ago. Is that where you had it?'

'A batch?' I frown. 'Why did you give her lemonade? Most people give wine or chocolates.'

'I know but she asked me specifically. It's my own recipe so it's kind of exclusive. You like it then?'

Felix made it? *Felix* made it? I nod enthusiastically. 'I love it. I can't believe you made it. It's extraordinary.'

He seems to swell just a little bit, and grins. 'Just one of my many talents. Are you hungry?'

'Um . . .' I examine my innards and notice that there's a growling sensation there that I haven't felt much for months. Even after eating a few decent meals with Abby my appetite hasn't come back properly. But now, after months of eating mostly rubbish, it's like my insides are waking up after a whole season of hibernation and are storming around my internal cave roaring and clawing at the air. I smile and look up at Felix in a kind of wonder. 'Yes, I find that I am.'

He spins dramatically and strides over to the fridge. 'Piri-piri chicken wrap, tomato salad, warm pitta bread and roasted red pepper houmous?'

'Wow. Sounds lovely.'

'Yeah, it's Aunt Winnie's favourite.' He starts pulling things out and bringing them over to where I'm sitting. Flour tortillas, tomatoes, salsa in a jar.

'Really?'

He looks at me. 'No, Dozy, not really. She's eighty-one. Piri-piri sauce would probably finish her off.' He's standing on the other side of the counter top and now puts his elbows on it, and his chin on his hands. 'She's more of a shepherd's pie girl, to be honest.'

'Of course she is.' I sip the lemonade as he turns back to the fridge. 'So why are you here, in her house?'

There's a long silence, during which I start thinking 'Shit, shit, shit.'

'I'm just house-sitting while she's away,' he says eventually, and although I can't see his face properly, I know he's hiding something.

'Oh, right. Nice for her, knowing that you're here, looking after things.'

He nods. 'Yes. I suppose it is.'

'So who's house-sitting for you? While you're here?' I ask this in a soft voice, to try and convey the message 'you don't have to answer if you don't want to' at the same time. But he does.

'No one.'

'Oh.' God, this is frustrating. Who leaves their own home empty to go and house-sit in someone else's? There's so much more to this than he's giving me, but he's not volunteering information, and I can't keep asking. 'That works out nicely for both of you then,' I say in the end, so that he can either say more, or let that be the end of it.

'Absolutely,' he says with a distinct air of finality. 'Now, help me find a lime-zester will you?'

Winnie is obviously one organised lady as we find the zester very quickly on a shelf with a garlic press, pestle and mortar, and apple corer. We also find a drawer containing a torch and spare batteries, bandages, a full first-aid kit, a variety of medications and ointments and, inexplicably, flares.

'I found walkie talkies in the next one along,' Felix says reverentially, as we both stare down into the drawer.

'Christ, what the hell is she expecting?'

'Probably just likes to be prepared.'

'Do you think she's got a gun somewhere?' We're both whispering.

'She probably took it to Oz.'

'Bloody hell.'

Felix raises his eyes and looks at me steadily, so I grab my glass and raise it. 'Here's to Winnie, for being the most together, battle-ready, fully tooled up, frail little old lady I know.'

'Hear hear,' he joins in, raising his own glass. 'Ah Daisy, you're so . . .' He stops there, as if interrupted by something.

'What?'

He doesn't reply, just puts his glass down on the counter and looks at me earnestly. 'Seriously, I really think you should answer that now.'

'Answer what?'

His eyes flick down to my pocket. 'That duck in your pocket. You can't ignore it forever, and it's pretty insistent.'

'What? What duck . . .?' I put my hand in my pocket and find my phone, and realise then what he means. But he must be mistaken. My phone has not made a sound the entire time. I look at the screen. Six alerts from Facebook, and a text message from Abby. 'Oh . . .' I quickly click onto the site. They're all from Abby too.

Abby Marcus Where are you?

That one was about an hour ago. Then ten minutes later:

Abby Marcus Daze, please answer. Where are you?

And five minutes after that:

Abby Marcus Seriously Daisy, I need to know how long you are going to be.

The final two are two minutes and three minutes later.

Abby Marcus DAISY MACINTYRE ANSWER ME, I'm getting desperate.

and

Abby Marcus OK, you're either deliberately ignoring me for some reason or you can't hear me. I'll have to text you.

The text is a revelation. Two in one year.

> I rly need yu 2 get bak 2 th flt as sn as
> yu can. Smthngs com up Pls hurry.

When I've finished reading I let my phone hand drop and look up at Felix.

'Everything OK?' he says, pausing in his tomato-slicing activity.

'I've got to go,' I say quietly. 'I'm sorry.'

He lays the knife down on the chopping board. 'Oh. That's a shame.'

I nod. I'm floundering again. How did these messages arrive and me not notice? The Facebook alert sound has become like the sound of a crying baby to me. I am tuned in to it, alert to it, poised waiting for it at all times. How else could I keep up to date with all the goings on in the outside world? It's my link to normality, my window to other, ordinary lives still carrying on. People going shopping, seeing films, having lunch, kissing . . .

'I'll walk back with you,' Felix is saying in the background as I start to make my way zombie-like to the hallway.

'Thanks,' I reply automatically. My hand is gripping my phone so tightly it's starting to hurt, but suddenly I'm worried about missing something important. What if Abby tries to contact me again and I don't hear? What if one of my friends buys something new and exciting and reports on it? What if one of their friends makes a witty comment about it? I could miss it all. This strange new world I've entered is unpredictable and I feel a need to get back to my own world. Back to the flat, to my room, to normality. As soon as possible.

As Felix and I walk briskly back along the pavement, presumably in the direction of Abby's flat, I quickly send a text to her to say I'm on my way. Felix and I don't speak at all on the journey. He walks next to me and I'm aware of him there, but only as a guide at this moment. Finally now I'm starting to feel tendrils of panic snaking their way into my bewilderment and my hand on my phone grips more tightly as the other hand clenches. What has happened to Abby? Why is she so anxious to talk to me? Is she hurt or in danger? Have I failed her in some way? God, I need to get to her and try to put this right.

Finally we round the corner at the end of the road and there in front of us is Abby's building. I scan the front of it quickly for plumes of black smoke or flames stroking the outside of the windows, but there are none. The roof is still intact, as are the walls. All is quiet calm. Birds fly past silently in the sunshine. A quick glance along the road outside the entrance confirms that no ambulance is parked there, and no police car. There is only one car, a large black saloon with no blue light on top and no hi-vis stripes. As we draw nearer and all seems to be well, my thudding heart starts to relax a little and I begin to feel more composed. But then I notice something that stops my heart all together.

The car parked outside the flat is Naomi's.

SEVENTEEN

Georgia Ling

boo sooo bored sittin in dentist ☹

> **Jill Grayson** dey r k a guess lol sme tymes it can b borin a hate dentist lol#
>
> **Simon Stiles** you gonna get falsees like my nan lmao xxxx
>
> **Steve Seagull** chin up babes, iss all gooooood ;)
>
> **Karen Fleet** soon be da weekend tho yay! partayyyyyyy
>
> **Kev Owen** Get on with some work then lol
>
> **Dawn Mitchell** why you in dentist hunni? Hope your ok???
>
> **Georgia Ling** jus chek up chicky xx

Sarah Baker

had a fab time meeting some great people last night, wish I hadn't had so much samboucca tho, now got to get ready for work, not feeling to great lol

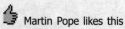 Martin Pope likes this

> **Martin Pope** Ha ha! Serves you right.

306

Julie Burrett Wouldn't wanna be you today!

David Robinson Did you remember to sky plus homeland?

Stacey Macey me too hun. Hard day for me to day, gotta get train back to Farnborough later

Paula Freeman shoulda come with me to the concert. It was amayyyzing.

Abby Marcus

is not very impressed. Got things to do, places to go, sat here wasting my time waiting. Some people are so bloody inconsiderate, thoughtless and downright selfish.

Suzanne Allen What's happening? Who's peed you off today? Pm me? x

Abby Marcus I have a feeling you'll be finding out everything before too long!

Suzanne Allen Ooh that's intriguing. Give me a clue?

Abby Marcus You can guess Suze. What usually pees me off?

Suzanne Allen Don't you mean 'who'??!

Abby Marcus Yeah, you're on the right lines. Although it's not quite as straightforward as that. It's related to that, if you get me. I won't go into detail on here but watch this space. Or your phone. Coz it won't be on this actual space.

Suzanne Allen OK. Just remember what we talked about. That 'thing' that usually pees you off – it's not entirely to blame. Go easy, yeah?

Abby Marcus Yeah, I know Suze, I haven't forgotten. But it's not what you think this time. I'll fill you in later.

Ellie Harley I know a few people like that Abs. Don't even give 'em the time of day. xx

I close down the screen, none the wiser. Abby is clearly pissed off with me, but that's nothing new. I had been hoping to find something out about why Naomi is here before actually going inside and facing her, but of course there's nothing there. There wouldn't be. None of the people who are indiscreet enough to put deeply personal stuff like that on Facebook know anything about what's happened, because they're so bloody indiscreet and are always putting deeply personal stuff like that on Facebook. Abby and Suze are far too sensible to do anything like that, which is why they're the ones who know more.

Even they don't know everything, though. I'm hoping to keep it that way.

I twist and look over my shoulder one last time to watch Felix's tall frame strolling away behind me. My sense of unreality, of being in a new world, of brighter, heightened perception, fades further and further into the background as he does. Somehow the world seems more stable, more ordinary now. The colour is draining away with the tide that is Felix, leaving behind a monochrome monotony that can be predicted, and is reassuringly dependable.

I walk up the path to the external door to Abby's building and as I reach out to the handle I notice that my hand is shaking. Knots of anxiety are tying themselves up inside me. What on earth is the matter with me? This is just Naomi, my sister. I'm going to talk to my sister, why should that make me anxious?

I know why.

I hesitate outside Abby's door. I could simply turn and walk out again, not see her today. I know I've got to see her, we need to talk, discuss everything that's happened, but that doesn't have to be today, does it? I stare down at my feet, remembering tying up my shoe lace here earlier today in a bid to get away from Tom quickly. Something vague stirs in my memory again, about my discussion with Felix, but it's as insubstantial as mist and I can't quite grasp it. But one thing I do remember. I was crossing things off Abby's list this morning, and talking to Naomi is definitely on it. I decided this morning that I was going to sort out some of the other things on it as soon as I got back from my walk, and now here I am and here she is. It's a gift.

I go in slowly, trying to walk normally but somehow automatically going into 'stealth mode'. I can hear the sound of an awkward silence coming from the living room, so at the very least I should go and rescue Abs. A small spark of irritation flares up in me that Naomi has just arrived unannounced, expecting us all to be available, or alternatively to drop everything we're doing for her convenience. But it dies in me before it takes proper hold. Of course she would expect me to be available. What else have I got in my life at the moment? Nothing, and she knows it.

Abby's voice reaches me from the sofa, saying, 'Oh, I think that's her now. I'll just . . .' and seconds later her face appears in the hallway, scowling into mine.

'Where the fuck have you been?' she hisses.

'Walking. With Felix,' I add unnecessarily, although somehow it makes a difference.

'Well I've been trying to entertain your sister for about a decade, waiting for you to come back. I thought you'd only be a couple of hours. Will you just go in there and see her?' She turns me round and pushes me towards the living room door. 'And make sure you bloody ask her if she knows you were left out of the will.' I nod and take a step but she seizes me and turns me back to her. 'And ask her if she knows why he did it.' I nod again, and turn back, but she stops me again. 'And ask her how much she got.' Nod. 'And see if she'll share hers with you.'

Naomi is wearing knee-length white shorts, silver Fit-Flops and a pink tee shirt with a picture of a ribbon in a loop on it. Her hair is shiny and mobile, her make-up is on, her nails are polished. She looks very together. The sight of her after all these weeks makes a surge of love rush up inside me and I step quickly towards her, smiling. She glances up at me as I approach and gives me a smile and I find I'm suddenly wondering if I have twigs in my hair or dirty knees. 'Hello, Daisy,' she says, standing up, and to me it sounds like the greeting you give someone when they get out of prison.

'Hi,' I rejoin, and we hug each other. I want to cling on longer, give and receive comfort with someone who feels the way I do, but she pulls back and regards me.

'How have you been?' she asks sadly. 'All right?'

I nod, even though it's the opposite of what I mean. 'I've been better. You?'

She sighs deeply and nods. 'It's been hard, hasn't it? Russell was very fond of Graham too. But we're getting there. It's a long road, that's all.'

'Yes.' We lock eyes for a few moments, then she looks away and sits back down. I move to the sofa and sit opposite her.

'So you're doing a walk for breast cancer,' she says conversationally, as if it's just something I'm doing.

'Yeah, I am. That's where I was, actually. Out training.'

'Oh, wow, well done you. But . . . didn't Abby say it was just a walk? You don't need much training for that, surely?'

I bristle a bit at 'just a walk', but I manage to stay calm. 'Well, you know, it's a pretty long walk.'

'Oh, right.' She pauses, thinks about it for a moment, then smiles broadly. 'I'm doing my bit. I got this tee shirt. All the proceeds go towards the research.'

'Yeah, they're great. Looks nice.'

There's a moment's silence and I start thinking about all the questions Abby wants me to ask – what Naomi knew of Graham's will, did she know why he did it, whether he did the same for her or did she get her full entitlement. But I can't ask them. Naomi knows as well as I do why he did it. It doesn't really matter whether she was aware of his plans or not.

'I've had a letter,' I begin, letting her off the hook. 'From the solicitors.'

She looks relieved that she hasn't had to be the one to bring it up. 'Oh, yes, yes, of course. Darren told me about it.'

'He . . . *told* you?' This statement settles on me like a cool, soothing balm on a scald. It changes everything, in an instant. I sit forward. 'Weren't you there, then, when the will was read? In the room?' I'd always assumed I was the only one not invited to the will-reading, but if Naomi was also excluded then maybe it wasn't a personal slight, not another consequence of my actions all those

311

years ago; it's simply down to the fact that we aren't – weren't – Graham's actual children, not blood relatives. And then maybe I *was* forgiven for what happened. I feel as if a dark shell that has been sealed over me for years is starting to crack and a shaft of bright light is breaking through.

'Oh no, I was there,' Naomi says, and the darkness slams shut again with a clang. 'But I didn't see that personal letter to you. Darren told me what was in it.'

'Oh. So . . . What did you think?'

She frowns a little. 'What did I think? You mean about Graham's will? About your share?' I nod. 'Well, it's not as if we weren't expecting it, is it? The thing is, Mum left everything to him, so he was free to do what he wanted, wasn't he?'

'Yeah, I know he was, but . . .' I'm not sure what I'm trying to ask her. 'Naomi, did you think it was right? Or fair? I mean, you know what Mum wanted, you heard her talking about you and me being well off. Don't you think Graham kind of let her down when he went against her wishes?'

She shrugs. 'Maybe he did, but there's not much we can do about it now, is there? The will was signed, he died, and now everything's in the process of being divided.'

'But does the will *have* to be abided by? I mean, who's the executor? Don't you think Mum's wishes should have been . . .?'

'You'll have to speak to Darren about it, Daze. I really don't have anything to do with it. I'm as much in the dark as you are.'

'Well, not exactly. Darren and Lee still talk to you, don't they?'

'Not every day.' She jerks suddenly. 'That reminds me.' She reaches down and now I notice a carrier bag at her feet with what looks like a heavy vase in it. Something from the house, maybe? She lifts it onto her lap and takes it out of the bag. When I see what it is I get a cold feeling in my belly. 'Darren and I agreed that we would scatter Graham's ashes beneath that tree in the park where Mum's are,' she says, holding the vase in both hands. 'And as it was his birthday last week, we thought that was a good time to do it.'

His birthday. I missed it. How could I have forgotten? And yet I am not surprised at myself. It's exactly the sort of thing someone like me *would* do.

'This is his urn,' Naomi goes on. 'The three of us went down there and had a little ceremony, said goodbye. As you weren't there, we kept these back for you so you can go and do it in your own time.' She holds the urn up a couple of inches, just in case I hadn't seen it, then lowers it back down and puts it on the floor.

'Why didn't you tell me?' I ask her.

She looks mildly surprised. 'Oh, Daisy, would you have wanted to come? We just assumed you wouldn't. And you know, Darren and Lee really wanted to get it done on that particular day – there just wasn't time for any messing around.'

'Messing around? What do you mean?'

She shakes her head, movements too tiny to indicate a negative. This was more like shaking off an irritant. 'Well I don't know but it's nothing to do with me, you'll have to take it up with Darren and Lee. He was their dad so it was all up to them.'

'But you could have said someth—'

'Seriously, Daisy, speak to them about it.'

She knows I won't. She knows they won't answer me even if I do ask. And anyway what's the point in asking? It's done, it can't ever be undone. 'Right.'

Naomi glances at her watch now, and stands up. 'I'm sorry, Daze, I've really got to get going. I wanted to see you but you weren't here and now I'm in a bit of a rush.'

'Oh, OK.' We both stand up. 'Thanks for coming.'

'No problem.' She swings her bag onto her shoulder. 'Have fun on your walk.' She opens the door to the hallway. 'Oh, Abby. Hello there.'

'Oh, hi, I was just coming in to, er, see if you wanted a cup of tea?'

'No thanks, I've got to get off. Russ and I are getting coving. Nice to see you again.' She turns and speaks over her shoulder. 'Take care, Daze.' And she's gone.

The second the front door closes Abby comes running back in to see me. 'Bloody hell, Daisy! I can't believe she knew about the will but didn't say anything! Didn't argue for you! Why wouldn't she do that? But the executor of the will can choose not to go along with it, you know that right? Do you know who the executor is? Is that the urn there? How weird was that?' She inspects the urn closely, then turns to me. 'Daisy? What did she . . .' She stops. 'Daze? You OK? Oh, Daisy.' She comes to where I am and enfolds me in a tight hug.

Tears are streaming down my face and I put my head on Abs's shoulder.

'What is it?' Abby asks. 'Because she knew about the will? And didn't do anything?'

I shake my head. 'No, no.' My breath is coming in gasps. 'How could they, Abby? Why would they?' I'm sobbing but I also know the answer.

'Ah Daisy, I know it's disappointing. But money isn't everything. You can still get a place with what you've got, and now that you're earning . . .' She stops because I'm shaking my head against her shoulder. 'What?'

I lift my head to look at her, and wipe my eyes. 'It's not the money, Abs. Yes, it would have been lovely to get it, to be able to buy somewhere, even if it was just a deposit on a place.' I wipe my nose with my hand. 'The money's upsetting. Mostly because I know Mum wanted me to have it. You know, she was almost happy at the prospect of us both getting it. She knew it would set us both up. But it's only money, isn't it? Doing the ashes without me . . .' I shake my head. 'That's something else altogether.'

She nods slowly. 'Ah. Yes. You're right. That is incredibly hurtful. Spiteful, even.'

'And irreversible. It can't ever be undone. I'll never get that back.'

She rubs my arms. 'But, Daze, why would you want to do it with them anyway? You've never liked Darren and Lee much, wouldn't it be better to do it this way, on your own, rather than with . . .'

'My sister? My own flesh and blood?' I shake my head. 'I don't care a bit about those two. I don't care if I never see either of them again. But Naomi . . . We grew up together. We should be close now, shouldn't we? We

315

should be looking out for each other more than we used to before. She's the one other person in the world who knew our mum like I did, who loved her like I did. Who misses her like I do. Isn't she?'

'Yes . . .'

'But she's let me down. She went with Darren and Lee to do the ashes ceremony and grieved for Graham and Mum with them instead of with me. How could she do that? How could she let me down like that? How could she not tell me?'

Abby is shaking her head. 'I don't know . . .' She pulls away from me and looks closely at my face. 'She did say something about how you must have been expecting Graham to disinherit you, so I'm guessing everyone knows why he did . . . Could that be anything to do with it? Do *you* know why he did it?'

I shake my head. 'Don't . . .' I close my eyes. That's the one part of this that I can't bear for my wonderful friend to know about. I look at her. 'I'm going to have a lie down, Abs. Do you mind? I'm shattered and I've got work in a few hours.'

She shakes her head. 'No, no, of course I don't mind. Good idea. It's probably what you need right now.'

In my room the first thing I see is the bloody 'TO DO' list. I walk towards it and stare for a few moments at the frenzied crossings out from this morning. Hard to believe that was only a few hours ago. I can see by the repeated pen strikes and the crinkling, even slight tearing in some places, of the paper around them that when I made those marks I was energised, animated, active. Looking back now, I see that I was facing forward then, finally moving towards the future instead of away from the past. I wanted to get out, get the walk done and get back as quickly as I could so that I could cross some more things off the list, move my life on a bit more. And then I rushed out like a white rabbit and experienced the most mystical walk of my life. Everything took on a surreal, dreamlike quality, and nothing was as it had been. It was as if my head had opened up and life could get back in. I wasn't scared of heights in that universe. I noticed things there. Flowers smelled good and Felix and I were friends. We even flirted a little and had lunch together. Or nearly did.

But now I just want to lie down and stare at the ceiling. This ceiling is greatly in need of a really good stare. It hasn't had one for a couple of weeks and it's very overdue. So that's what I do. I'm not going to sleep before my shift in the pub. I'm probably not going to sleep ever again. My world has not changed back to what it was before this morning. My world has been taken away all together.

Daisy Mack
Is the saying 'what goes around comes around' good or bad news?

 Suzanne Allen likes this

Georgia Ling   Aw hunni ☺
Nat 'Wiggy' Nicholson   Its good Daze. Unless you got some skeletons in your cupboard lol
Abby Marcus   It's always good. It means people get what they deserve. You gotta want that, right? They'll get theirs one day. You mark my words.

317

I stare at those words from my bed and know that Abby must never, ever understand that it's me who has got what I deserve.

I also resolve never to let her say 'mark my words' again.

As I'm lying here, a large part of me is thinking about not going to work later. Or ever. I very much don't want to move. I could just lie here for the rest of the evening, and the night, and all the days to come. That sounds lovely. Nothing to think about, nothing to do. Abby could bring me food to keep me going. Or not. Actually she probably won't as I can't see her supporting this new direction my life's taking. But never mind, I'll just exist here as long as I can. Descend slowly into blissful oblivion and not think about anything or anyone. Should only take about three or four days before dehydration gets the better of me. And being on a soft comfy bed is a hell of a lot better than in a canyon somewhere with my arm trapped under a heavy boulder. I'll just drift off to sleep and simply not bother to wake up again. Sink right down deep into the dark that's been pressing in at the periphery, give in to it finally after all these months of resisting. Let go at last and fall for eternity into the cool, soothing blackness of . . .

'Right, come on, you lamo, you're not going to lie here wallowing for the rest of the evening, you've got work to go to.'

OK, maybe not.

Once I'm at work aching from the knees down, bleeding from the fingers thanks to two broken glasses and soaked from wrist to belly button in lager, things start to look up. Being a Saturday night the place is even more packed than last night so I'm dishing out drinks at the intense rate of two a minute, which is a steep learning curve – more of a learning line really – but I'm picking it up. Millie is telling me in forty-five second bursts about the film she watched this afternoon and Barry is chatting up anyone in the room that has, or appears to have, a pair of breasts.

My current customer gives me a ten-pound note and I go and meet up with Millie at the till.

'So then,' she says immediately, as we ring up our orders, 'he signs the covenant thingy that binds him to say yes to every opportunity that comes his way, and the first thing that happens is . . .'

We both turn back to the throng at the bar and there in front of me is Danny. Sexy Danny with the fair hair and Lycra shorts and shapely thighs. He beams at me.

'Hey, Daisy! Wow, I didn't know you were working in here.'

'Danny!' I smile back, trying to look immaculate and sophisticated. The toilet paper wrapped round my cut fingers uncurls itself and falls onto the bar. We both eye it uneasily for a second, then I grab it and drop it on the floor. 'Great to see you. Did you have a good holiday?'

He looks edgy for a second, then nods. 'Yes, fantastic, thanks. Um, can I get three pints of lager please?'

'Sure.' I reach below the bar for the glasses and start pulling the pints. I want to speak to him more; to lean my elbows on the bar (after giving it a thorough wipe, obviously) and gaze into his eyes; to tuck ourselves up in a corner somewhere and talk about the world while a lone jazz trombone plays sad songs until morning; but a tall, wide man with an orange face is crushing in over his shoulder, his arm out with a twenty-pound note on the end of it.

I put the drinks on the bar. 'Here you go. Eight pounds seventy please.'

Danny hands me a tenner. 'Have a drink on me,' he says. Then he gathers the three drinks together, winks at me and is immediately absorbed back into the mêlée. I turn reluctantly back to the till.

'. . . so he drops the homeless dude off in the woods somewhere, and you really think he's going to get murdered or something, but then he meets this beautiful girl on a moped . . .'

'Malibu and Coke and a Bulmer's please, love.'

Oh God. I deal with the next customer and the next and the next without really paying proper attention, constantly searching the crowd and the room beyond for a glimpse of that beautiful blond head. Once or twice I thought I saw the top of it, but then it was gone again. Millie and I meet at the till and she tells me the rest of the story, but I lost interest ages ago. Eventually, after about two hours, there's a moment's lull at the bar and Millie and I take a step back and lean against the wall for a few seconds.

'Bloody hell, I can't believe–'

'Oh my fucking God,' Millie cuts me off. 'Fucking fucking fucking fucking hell.' Her voice starts to crack.

'Jesus, what is it?'

She's covered her mouth with her hands, then quickly turns her back. 'There's a dude over there, don't look now, over there, by the quiz machine, no don't look now, leather jacket, black jeans, see him? I said *don't look*. Fuck!'

I try to glance surreptitiously over to the machine and just catch a very quick flash of black leather. 'OK, yeah, got him. What about him?'

Millie has picked up a prop – it's a damp cloth, so she starts furiously cleaning the optics. 'Who's he with? Can you see? Don't let him see you looking. Fuck, did he see you? Just try and look without looking like you're looking.'

'I'll go and collect the glasses,' I venture. She nods so off I go over to the quiz machine, and check out the dude in the black leather. He looks nice enough, probably about nineteen or twenty, same sort of age as Millie, trying to grow some stubble to look older, crease down the front of his jeans where his mum's ironed them. He's leaning against the *Who Wants to Be a Millionaire* game, chatting to a deeply tanned blondie in a vest top with more lip liner than actual lip. Her boobs look suspiciously round too. I pick up a couple of glasses at the nearest table, then call back loudly to Millie, 'So, what's Harry Styles like, Mills, you lucky bitch?'

She looks round at me quizzically, so I give her a meaningful stare, flicking my eyes to Leather Jacket and back. She cottons on.

'Aw, Harry was totally gorgeous. Really good company and dead sexy too, you know?'

We are rewarded by Jacket looking up suddenly from Boobs and glaring over towards Millie.

'You seeing him again?' I go on, walking back towards her. She shakes her head, thank goodness. The story would have lost any faint credibility it had if she'd come up with a white picket fence and two point four kids.

'Nah. I'd love to, but it's Harry fucking Styles. You know? It was massive fun and so exciting at the time, but I'm not kidding myself. I was lucky he picked me at all.'

I suppress a smile as I walk back to her carrying the empties.

'Well?' she hisses as soon as I arrive. I start stacking the glasses in the dishwasher.

'Looks like a complete tramp,' I whisper. 'Fake tan, fake hair, fake boobs. Not a patch on you.'

Millie turns and looks at me as if I've just saved her cat from a burning building. 'Really?'

I nod decisively. 'Without a doubt. And she laughs like a lawnmower.'

She sniggers out loud and gives me a quick hug. 'Thanks, Daisy.' Then she's back at the bar taking orders with renewed energy, chatting to the punters, flicking her hair, enjoying the attention. Her cheer rubs off on me and I start to smile too, feeling the warmth of doing something nice for someone. It's been a long time since I've felt that.

Next time I glance at the quiz machine, Leather Jacket has gone, but in his place is a beautiful blond head, one arm raised and holding the edge of the screen, two darker heads holding pint glasses flanking him. I feel a swoop of excitement and quickly wash my hands.

'See the blond dude over by the quiz machine now?' I whisper to Millie when she comes near enough. She looks over blatantly, peering so hard at his back I'm sure he'll feel it and turn round.

322

'Fuck yeah!' She nods at me approvingly and raises her hand for a high five. Sadly I don't realise that was what she was doing, so she picks up my hand and bangs it against her own. 'Lucky bitch, Daze. He's well fit.'

I put my hands up in a shushing gesture. 'No, no, nothing's happened yet.'

'Ah. I see. But you'd like it to, am I right?'

I nod. 'Well, yeah. Duh.' Although right now, as much as anything, I'm thinking about how great it will be to walk with him again. Calm, clever Danny with his fixed route and set warm-up routine. He took me by surprise one morning, actually, when he turned right on the canal bank instead of left. 'Oh, are we doing a different route today?' I'd asked.

He smiled as he did his lunges. 'No, same route. Only today we are walking away from the sun.'

'Right.' I was imagining this was essential to maintain good fitness, something about the rotation of the earth or its magnetic field or some other scientific reason.

'We need sun on the backs of our legs today,' he'd explained.

Yes, well. It was still going to be more beneficial than walking with Felix, wasn't it? Felix knew nothing about training or fitness or muscle development. He just wanted to admire the wildlife or smell the flowers.

'Well then you go, girl,' Millie says now. 'I can manage here.'

'OK.' I look over at Danny's head. 'Do you think I could borrow your lip gloss please?'

It's Peachy Passion, which feels somehow appropriate as I think about Danny's tight Lycra shorts. I sashay over

323

to the quiz machine to collect more glasses, then suddenly notice him there.

'Oh, hi again. You winning?'

He frowns. I flick my eyes at the quiz machine, which is currently flashing as it waits for a response. 'Oh, right, yeah, doing well. So how long have you been working in here?'

'Not long. You're back from your holiday then?'

He performs a sweeping gesture down the length of his body. 'It would appear so.'

'So when are you free for another training session? The walk's coming up really quickly now so I need to get as many miles in as possible . . .'

He turns back and says over his shoulder, 'Just put Beethoven, it's bound to be that.' Then he looks back at me. 'No one ever knows those classical music ones, do they?'

'Ha ha, no. So, about walking . . .?'

'Oh, look, sorry, Daisy, I can't . . . I've got . . .' He shakes his head and downs the last of his pint. 'I gotta go. Sorry.'

I frown as he starts to turn away. 'What's going on?'

'It's . . . I'm not supposed to . . . Look, speak to your friend. Abby. She knows everything. I'm sorry, Daisy.' And he pushes back into the crowd.

EIGHTEEN

Daisy Mack
Feeling like I've missed something. More than one thing. Lots of things. Again. Over and over. Anyone know what's going on??

> **Jenny Martin** Well first the earth cooled, and then an amoeba sprouted legs and crawled out of the slime and became a maths teacher ha ha!
>
> Jane Miller and 2 others like this
>
> **Mike Green** What you got against maths teachers, Jen??!
>
> **Suzanne Allen** Sounds to me like you need to do some investigating Daze! Xx
>
> **Georgia Ling** Hope u wrk it out hunni xxxx

Abby's not waiting up for me when I get home from work tonight, which is a shame because I really want to ask her a couple of questions about Danny, and then rip her face off. It'll have to wait until tomorrow, after my walk with Felix. I get a little flutter of – what is that? Pleasure? Excitement? No, anticipation, that's all – at the prospect of meeting him again tomorrow. He's a cheerful bloke and interesting to talk to. There are definitely worse ways of spending my time. I climb into bed, hesitating as I always do before turning off the light. As soon as the darkness wraps around me again I'll have nothing to do except lie motionless and think. Tonight it will be about Naomi, and Graham's ashes. Or possibly Danny's defection. But as I close my eyes I find myself thinking about tomorrow's walk instead. Felix's brown eyes and impish grin flash into my mind. I open my eyes again straight away and now it's daylight. For a brief moment I am pinned to the bed, utterly convinced I'm either dead or have been abducted by aliens, held captive for forty years and then deposited back on earth six hours after I went to bed. But then I realise I've just been asleep. I check the time and find I've been lying in my bed unconscious for over six hours. My God! It's almost harder to accept than the alien story.

There on the wall is the 'TO DO' list and looking at it reminds me suddenly that I haven't crossed off 'Call Naomi'. I get out of bed and go over there to do it, arming myself with a pen on the way. I know I didn't technically call her, but I've spoken to her and that counts. As I approach the list, my eyes flick down to the 'Call Naomi' entry and I ready myself with the pen, but when I'm nearer I notice that someone has scrawled something else in biro alongside the thick black marker pen entry. It now says 'Call Naomi a selfish bitch'. It actually makes me laugh out loud, even though I don't get to cross it out after all. Yet. And maybe there'll be slightly less ripping off of faces when I speak to Abby later.

Felix is already waiting for me on the canal bank and breaks out into a broad smile when he sees me. I grin back spontaneously, without even thinking about it, and speed up a little. He takes a couple of steps towards me as I draw nearer, swinging his arms.

'Good morning, Miss Daisy,' he says cheerfully as I reach him. We turn and start out along the canal bank. 'I'm very glad to see you looking so . . . what's the word? Jolly. After yesterday and your reaction when you saw that car outside Abby's, I did wonder whether you would show up today. Was everything all right? Did she have a visitor?'

I look up at his face, wondering if I can trust him. Well, no, it's not exactly trust I'm wondering about. It's whether or not he's really interested, or just making conversation. I can't bear the thought of confiding in him – or in anyone – just because they were hunting for something to talk about. I am certainly not going to tell him about Mum and Graham and the will and the ashes – there would no doubt be endless questions like 'Why would your sister have done that?' and 'Why would your stepfather have done that?' and I'm not answering those kind of questions. Ever. But I am starting to feel as if Felix and I are actual friends, not just exercise associates, so he kind of deserves a little bit of information.

'It wasn't Abby's visitor actually. It was my sister. Naomi. She had come to see me.'

He doesn't say anything for a while and I'm tortured wondering what he's thinking about that. My tone of voice must have given the impression that I was not thrilled at the prospect of a visit from my sister, so he's worked out things aren't good between us.

'I'm guessing she came with some bad news?' he says gently. 'We can talk about something else if you want. I've got loads of very interesting facts about sharks at my disposal. Just say the word.'

I huff out one short laugh. 'No, it's OK. She did bring bad news, but it was only bad for me. Bit tricky to explain without going into the whole . . .' I pause for a moment.

He turns to look at me. 'We have to go into a *hole*?'

'What?'

He's shaking his head when I look at him. 'Nothing. Sorry. Go on.'

'Well, she just wanted to tell me about something . . . that was really horrible to hear about. For me. But it doesn't affect anyone else, so not the kind of devastating news you might be thinking. Not that I have any idea what sort of news you might have been thinking about. But it was completely devastating for me.' Finally I stop talking. I'm surprised to see that Felix is still walking next to me and not heading back the way we've just come as fast as he can.

'She stitched you up. Didn't she?'

He's turned to face me full on and is pretty much walking sideways again. Hearing him sum up in those few words and in that quiet, gentle tone exactly what Naomi did seems to relieve some of the massive weight on my shoulders, and I sigh deeply. 'Yes. She did. In the most terrible way you can imagine.'

He shakes his head slowly. 'I'm really sorry to hear that, Daisy. Unfortunately there are people in the world who barge through life – theirs and everyone else's – doing exactly what they want whenever they feel like it with absolutely no thought to the damage they're doing. Selfish, inconsiderate and unaware. I can't bear people like that.' He falls silent for a moment and I get the very strong feeling that he's speaking from personal experience. He turns to me again. 'A . . . friend of mine . . . went through a difficult time a couple of years ago. Really tough. And I remember his father, at the time, acted incredibly selfishly. Making demands, having unrealistic expectations, that kind of thing. Completely oblivious to what my friend was going through.' He releases a long breath. 'Your sister sounds like one of those people.'

It's weird. I've only known Felix for a short time, but I don't feel defensive when he criticises my family. Normally, no matter how vile Naomi was to me, I would not allow anyone to criticise her. But Felix seems so genuine and has so obviously been affected by behaviour like this himself that I find myself feeling allied to him and not to her. I nod. 'You're right, she is. Always has been, although in the past it was mostly about being inconsiderate and not seeing anything from anyone else's point of view. Nothing she's done before comes even close to this one . . .'

He nods and breathes in deeply, releasing it slowly. 'Daisy,' he says seriously, and I feel instantly anxious in case he's going to point out to me where I'm going wrong, 'I'm sure you already know that great white sharks can smell blood in the water from a great distance away?'

I laugh out a breath, realising at that moment that I had been holding it. 'Yes.' I feel my shoulders and neck relaxing.

'Well, did you also know that they have these incredible sensory receptors, electroreceptors, in their noses, called the ampullae of Lorenzini, which mean they can detect changes in temperature and electro-magnetic fields in the water? It's unbelievable. And when you see them swimming, close up, it's the most beautiful, graceful thing you've ever seen.'

We don't touch on Naomi or selfish people in general again at all during the walk, and it passes very pleasantly. The bridge over the motorway causes me some very minor trepidation this time, apparently because I'm more aware of it, but I get over it, and get over it.

'You see,' Felix says, touching my arm, 'your main fear was a fear of fear. Now you're no longer scared of being scared, you're not scared.'

By the time we get all the way round and back to the Lovely Lawn, I'm absolutely starving. Until yesterday I hadn't felt a real desire for anything, even food, for some considerable time, so actually wanting something is still quite a novel and pleasant sensation.

'Well, Miss Daisy, that was very enjoyable,' Felix says as we approach the corner of his street. 'Here's my road, so . . . Are you exhausted now? You probably are. Probably anxious to get home and relax. Aren't you?'

'No, not really. Actually managed to sleep last night, so not tired at all.'

He nods. 'Oh, right. Good. Well, er, in that case, would

you like . . . Do you fancy coming in for that lunch? Today. Now?'

I had so been hoping he was going to ask me that. I smile. 'Yes please.'

He releases a long breath. 'Excellent. Come on then. I'm starving.'

He makes the chicken piri-piri and houmous that he promised yesterday and we eat it in companionable silence in Aunt Winnie's marble-floored conservatory. She's got remote control windows in the roof and electric blinds that go up and down at the touch of a button.

'Wow, she's got all mod cons, hasn't she?' I'm gazing up at the magic.

'Yeah,' he says fondly. 'Great Aunt Winnie loves her gadgets.'

After we've loaded the plates into the sleek Bosch dishwasher, Felix puts a couple of little plastic pods into the Tassimo machine and it converts them into hot frothy cappuccinos. I curl my fingers round the mug and inhale the aromatic steam. Absent Aunt Winnie is one super-stylish feeble old crone. We go back to the living room and settle down into the soft leather chairs.

'So,' says Felix, eyeing me as I sip the delicious drink, 'have you worked out what the thing in your subconscious was? Or rather, is. 'Cause you can bet your life it's still there, niggling away, planting dreams, unsettling you, making you think that there's something you're missing, giving you a sense of unfinished business, loading you up with guilt—'

I put my hands up. 'Yes yes yes, all right, I get it. God, do you ever shut up?'

He grins. 'Hardly ever, actually. You know, I can help you find out what the thing is if you want? I can ease your mind.'

I narrow my eyes. 'Are you quoting Paul Simon or Paul McKenna?'

He looks blank. 'Who are they? Friends of Abby's?'

I gape. 'Are you serious? And if you are, why do you assume they're friends of Abby's, by the way? Why couldn't they be friends of mine?'

He looks suitably discomfited. 'Well, just because, um, they're both called Paul and if anyone is going to have a multitude of friends with the same name, it's Abby. *And*, before you leap to your feet and shout "I object!" can I just say in my defence that Abby did tell me you weren't working or getting out much. Or at all.'

He looks so panicked with his hands flapping around, and he talks so quickly to defend himself, I find myself laughing. It's a very odd feeling, one that I didn't expect to be experiencing again for quite a few years – if ever, in fact. I've been so muffled, so rigid with grief for such a long time, I'd forgotten that other feelings even existed, let alone that they could be felt. Now there's a lightening, a lifting and a brightening, from my head and my life, and this lessening of the heaviness I've been carrying for so long makes me feel almost as if I'm floating out of my chair. Since Mum died . . .

Abruptly I stop laughing and drop my expression. What am I doing? How could I behave like that, only six months later? I crash back into the chair with a heavy thump. It's abhorrent. It's despicable. It's disgusting. It's almost as if I don't even care, that it means nothing . . .

332

I look up, briefly registering Felix's face morphing from laughing to horror as he moves forward, about to leap to his feet, but it's no good, I can't stop, I can't carry on. My eyes feel hot and, unbearably, start to fill with tears.

'My God, Daisy, what's up?' Felix says, shuffling forward in his chair, bringing his face close to mine. I dip my head so he can't see the tears and start trying to get up, but he puts out an arm. 'Jesus, talk to me, please? Are you feeling ill? Is everything OK?'

I nod blindly. 'I'm fine, seriously, I just . . .' I look up and find his deep brown eyes searching my face. It's a good feeling, a welcome, safe feeling and I relax a little. I breathe a few moments, feeling myself calm down. 'I'm OK. Really.'

'I'm not sure I'm convinced. Actually, I'll rearrange that: I'm sure I'm *not* convinced. You looked petrified for a moment.' He glances over his shoulder, then back at me. 'Just checking no zombies have appeared at the window.'

I let out a small laugh. 'No, no, it wasn't the *un*dead that upset me.'

He peers into my eyes and my tummy feels squirmy. He picks my hand up in my lap and gently rubs his thumb over the back. 'Then what?' His voice is so soft, so kind, I feel like I could live there.

And here it is. The moment when I decide: do I tell him, or do I not? Are we real friends, or nothing more than walking partners? I'm here, in his house – well, his Great Aunt Winnie's house – and he's made me lunch. I enjoy his company. He seems to enjoy mine. He's exasperating, funny, irritating, gentle, insensitive and generous. A single tear makes its way onto my cheek and I wipe it away quickly, then focus back resolutely into his eyes. 'My mum died.'

'Oh,' he says softly. 'I'm so sorry, Daisy. That's terrible.'

I'm nodding already, but I don't want to talk about it, I don't want to go over it again, hear all the platitudes again, reassure anyone that I'm OK again. 'Yes, it was terrible. Awful. But anyway, so tell me about your year of living dangerously.'

'Abby!' I call out as I erupt through the door half an hour later. It bangs on the wall behind it and almost hits me in the face. 'Abby? Where the hell are you? I need to talk to you. Abby! ABBY!'

'All right, all right, keep your freak on, I'm here,' she says, coming into the hallway. 'What's the matter? You OK?'

'What did you say to Danny?' I begin. I was expecting to feel undiluted rage at her interference, but I'm actually feeling pretty relaxed now. In fact, I discovered when I got into bed last night that I wasn't even all that furious then; but now, after my very enjoyable lunch with Felix, I feel better than I have done for . . . about three years. I try to sound angry though, just so she doesn't get the impression I'm OK with it. Because I'm not. I'm absolutely cross.

'What have you been saying to my friends?'

'What are you talking about, Daze? I haven't been saying anything to anyone, let alone any of your friends.' She frowns briefly. 'Wait a minute – what friends? You haven't got any friends.'

I stall. She's right there. I shake my head to clear it. 'No, no, I don't mean . . . I mean someone, one person, just *one* friend that I made recently, the only one. Now he won't walk with me any more, barely even talks to me, and he says it's because of you. What did you say to him, Abby?'

'Daisy–' she says, the word catching in her throat. But I don't allow her to start making excuses.

'I can't believe you would do that to me, Abby. You're supposed to be my friend. My only one.'

'I *am*–'

'I don't need your help, I don't need anything from you. Just go away and leave me alone.' With a final angry stare into her face, I turn and go into my room, slamming the door.

It opens almost immediately and Abby's crying face appears. 'Daisy, what's happened? What's going on? Please talk to me.'

Oh God, now I feel absolutely awful, making her feel like that when I wasn't even all that angry. I certainly didn't expect her to cry. I stride over to her in the doorway and enfold her in a tight hug. 'Oh Abby, I'm so sorry. I didn't mean it. I'm so vile, I don't know why you put up with me.'

She sniffs and I hear a smile in her voice. 'Because I love you, you dolt. And you do need me, you need me plenty and don't you forget it.'

'I know.'

'It's OK though. I like that you need me. I like that I can help you. I like that I'm looking after you and sorting you out. It makes me feel good about myself.'

335

We both smile at that. 'Oh, so not entirely altruistic, then?'

'God no. This,' and she gestures vaguely around my room, which is of course, *her* room, 'this is all about me and making myself happy. Don't you go thinking this has got anything to do with you.'

'OK then. Well in that case, you're welcome.'

She laughs a little and squeezes my hand. 'So what on earth brought that on? Wanna talk about it?'

I sit back a little and look into her face. 'I saw Danny in the pub last night. Remember him? My walking partner, the friend that I made all on my own, without any help from anyone?'

'Ah.' She drops her gaze. 'Right.'

'You know what I'm going to say, don't you?'

She looks up. 'Let's put it this way: your comment about me talking to all your friends kind of makes sense now.'

'So you did talk to him?'

'Well yeah, but you knew that, didn't you? I'm guessing he told you that I had?'

'No. He said I needed to talk to you. That you knew what was going on. So here I am, talking to you. What's going on?'

She looks down at her lap again and fiddles with her fingers, then takes a deep breath. It's clearly costing her a lot to admit this to me. 'I . . . OK. Maybe I was wrong, maybe I shouldn't have, but . . . I asked Danny . . . to make up an excuse not to walk with you any more.'

'What? Why did you do that?'

She closes her eyes. It must sound bad, even to her. 'Because I wanted you to train with Felix.'

I search her face, frowning. 'Why?'

'Isn't it obvious? I mean, you've met Felix. You've spent time with him. He's lovely.'

I consider this a few moments. 'Well, I wouldn't say lovely, exactly. He's very cheerful, definitely. Obviously completely carefree. Which has been quite refreshing, I suppose. A little beam of light in an otherwise very murky and depressing tunnel.'

'Well that's one way of putting it. Either way, he's better company than one-dimensional Danny.'

'He is not!' I feel a surge of defensive annoyance at her criticism of my vague acquaintance. 'He's gorgeous.'

'Oh come on, he's an idiot. A gym bunny. All he talks about is exercising and fitness. It's so tedious.'

'Not true. And anyway he has got a lovely bottom.'

'OK, granted, he's very easy on the eye. But so is Felix, right?'

I'm pouting. I know I am, I can feel it, but I can't stop. 'No he is not. Actually he's a very irritating person.'

She laughs. 'I knew he would annoy you. That's why I wanted you to spend time with him.'

I stare at her. 'Jesus, Abby, what are you, some kind of sick sadist? Haven't I had enough to deal with lately without you sitting in the wings clapping your hands with glee every time he pisses me off or upsets me? Christ.'

'No, no, that's not it at all, softhead. I knew he would irritate you, challenge you, wind you up, stimulate you. Wake you up. Get you going.' She presses her lips together. 'Danny is like popcorn, isn't he? He's light and sweet and insubstantial. And, let's face it, a bit reminiscent of

337

polystyrene packaging. But Felix is more like . . .' She raises her hands, palm up, in a gesture of defeat. 'What? What is he like?'

I conjure Felix's face in my head, then split the screen and put Danny in the other half. Danny, in shimmering yellow Lycra, is fair, tanned, toned and solemn, touching his toes and jogging on the spot. Next to him, Felix is in an old grey Mickey Mouse tee shirt and frayed jeans; big, cheerful and relaxed, hands in pockets, grinning playfully. Danny is clearly a serious athlete, dedicated to the training he was helping me with, single-minded and committed. Very commendable. Felix is . . . I stare at the image of him in my mind and my gaze lands on the shark tooth at his throat.

'He's interesting, I'll give you that.'

Abby nods. 'Yeah.'

'And he's pretty funny. Now and then.'

More nodding. 'True.'

'And he has a pretty incredible great aunt.'

'What?'

'Oh, she's got all these gadgets in her house, you know, like the designer fridge and the plasma telly and stuff. And right now she's backpacking across Australia with her grand-daughter or something. But, Abs, when you see her, she's this tiny little old lady with transparent skin and wispy hair. You can't imagine in a million years that she would be . . . What? Why are you looking at me like that?'

Abby's eyes are widening the longer I go on talking about Aunt Winnie. 'Have you been to Felix's house?'

I nod. 'Yeah. Couple of times. Why?'

She doesn't speak for a few seconds, just stares at me. Then says, 'Fuck me.'

'What? What's so amazing about being at his house? Actually, it's not really his, it's Aunt Winnie's, he's just staying there for a while. Which reminds me, do you know what that's all about? I mean, why is he house-sitting for her, leaving his own place empty? Or is it empty?' Something occurs to me suddenly. 'Oh my God, he's married, isn't he? His wife is in their house on her own, while Felix sits in Winnie's. That's it, isn't it? They've had some kind of bust-up or something, and he's fucked off to the elderly relative's place to put some space between them. Or maybe he's caught the wife out shagging someone else. Or, no, no, she caught him out! Yes! That's it, isn't it, she's caught him out and then kicked him out, hasn't she?'

Abby is just shaking her head, a bit sadly actually. 'No, Daisy, you're completely wrong. Completely.'

'Oh. Well what then? Why's he there?'

'It's not for me to tell you, it has to come from him.'

'What?'

She shakes her head. 'Not telling you. I'm sure he'll fill you in in his own time. Especially now you've been round to his place already.' She smiles broadly and rubs my arm. 'He obviously likes you a lot. Nice work, Daisy Duck.'

The way she says it reminds me of someone talking about their pet when it won't stop harassing you. Usually it just means that they want food, or that they find your lower leg sexually irresistible. But Felix has given up so much of his time for my benefit over the past couple of weeks, walking with me, putting up with my moods, always cheerful, never grumpy or mean. And now today, making me lunch. I've always assumed he was doing it as a favour to Abby. Look at her, what sane, red-blooded man wouldn't want to do a favour for her? But suddenly now, when I think back to his awkward invitation to lunch today, his warm brown eyes gazing at me with concern, his big hand gently holding mine, it finally hits me that it seems he does like me, not just for my legs. And what's more, I'm absolutely sure that I like him too.

'Abs, I think I need to go out again.'

Felix's house is just up the road and round a corner from Abby's, which presumably is why they're friends, but even though only about twenty minutes have elapsed since I left here earlier, the house is deserted. After ringing the doorbell three times (it plays the chorus of 'Barbra Streisand' by Duck Sauce) I peer in through the front window but there's no sign of him. He could of course be out the back in the conservatory reading Stephen King on Winnie's Kindle, or lifting some weights in the state-of-the-art gym, but the place feels empty.

I turn round and go back to the pavement feeling anxious and fidgety. I need to find him, now. This won't wait.

My phone quacks in my pocket. I start walking as I pull it out of my pocket distractedly, not really interested in what Facebook might want to tell me.

Wait, what?

I actually stop on the pavement and think about that for a few moments, but incredibly find that it's true. In fact the quack alerting me to a message is more of an irritating interruption in the day's proceedings than anything

340

else and I only open up the app and read the message because I have no idea what to do next to find Felix.

Abby Marcus Go to the church.

I stare at the message for a few moments. It feels like a clue. If I do as she says and go to the church, I'll find an arrow carved into a tree or a grid reference on a tombstone or something. And I'll follow it and find the next clue, and then the next. Maybe it's Abby's round-about way of getting me to walk some more. Not her usual style, I have to say. Usually, she just instructs me to do it and I do. But she's obviously trying to keep me interested after all this time, so I'll humour her and go to the church. It reminds me of a treasure hunt Mum set up for my thirteenth birthday. I was expecting a few clues round the house and garden, but she'd spent the entire previous day tramping across the countryside tying different coloured string to tree branches and laying out stones in the shape of arrows. The clues she had written to take us to each subsequent clue were so cryptic that a helicopter pilot looking down that day would have seen the countryside dotted with stationary children, scratching their heads over scraps of paper. I was paired with Caroline Watson and we went wrong so many times we must have covered over ten miles by the end of the day. Darren and Lee's team, the blue team, was the only team to complete the course. Caroline and I eventually made a detour to a phone box after four and half hours of searching fruitlessly for a 'red cow' and Graham had come to pick us up. 'Red cow?' he'd said in the car,

341

'you've just used the phone box that stands in front of it, you pair of numbskulls. It's that pub right there!' He'd laughed hard, wiping his eyes and coughing so hard he couldn't catch his breath and had to pull the car over and spit out of the window. The blue team had won the prize, and fortune and glory and pudding had been lavished on them for the rest of the day. 'The treasure hunt winners get to pick where they want to sit; the treasure hunt winners get to go first; the treasure hunt winners can have the last walnut whip.' It was, of course, *my* birthday.

At the church I enter through the graveyard and wander among the graves for a few minutes in the sunshine, waiting for Abby's next clue. It always strikes me as odd that the sun can still shine in a graveyard. There should be some kind of dome over each one to stop the brightness from penetrating. There are a few people here visiting their loved ones, placing flowers or toys or little knitted bootees. My throat starts aching as I see them and my eyes feel hot, and I am hit once again by how absolutely final death is. How bizarre it is, how incomprehensible that someone alive, moving, breathing, speaking, loving, can just stop. For ever.

Over to my right is a figure squatting down, removing some wilting blooms from a little white vase at the headstone. I hear a voice talking, low and murmuring, and can tell from the pitch that it's a man, although I can't make out the words. I don't want to make out the words. He shifts and moves to stand so I start to turn away, but in that last moment before I turn I realise that I recognise him. It's Felix.

NINETEEN

Georgia Ling
Soooo hate waking up wiv an awful headache wen I hav'nt even had a drink the night before lolzzzz

    Simon Stiles Aw hunni you feeling rough ☹

    Mike Green you better start drinking then!!!

    Karen Fleet you going in tomoz? I got that jacket for you xx

    Georgia Ling yeh hunni im ok thanx xxxx

    Sarah McCarthy what you been doing?

    Georgia Ling Dunno hun, getting cold maybe. You ok? How's things? How long you got to go now? xxxx

    Sarah McCarthy All good thanks. Only 4 weeks left. Jake's so excited. When you coming to see us?

    Michelle West Poor you. Feel better sn. Xxx

    Georgia Ling Will come next month, hun. Difficult to get tym of work. How's Glenn?

    💬 **View all 67 comments**

Mum's not in this graveyard. She was cremated and her ashes sprinkled in the park. But it doesn't make any difference really; all these places remind me of her. Well, not so much of her. Of her death.

Naomi wasn't there in the final minutes. Neither was Graham. Graham was in hospital and Nomes and I had been sitting at Mum's bedside for four days, round the clock. Russell brought food and drinks in every day, and we went outside in the hospice grounds every so often for fifteen minutes of fresh air. We slept sitting up or resting our heads on her bed, and when she was awake we tried to make conversation, or read to her. Nurses came and went, changing her bed, changing her water, changing the dressings on her sores. Shifts ended, new people started, then they got relieved and the first lot were back again.

'Still here?' they asked kindly. It was such a loaded question. We nodded, dreading it ending; longing for it to.

On the fourth day, Naomi and I got the giggles. It was nervous energy or exhaustion or a combination of the two probably. Or perhaps our attempt to cover up the full horror of the situation we were in. Mum was dozing and, in spite of the fact that her body was systematically shutting down, organ by organ, and her frame had shrivelled away to bone, her empty stomach still demanded nourishment, still set off the audible alarm to alert us to the fact that she needed sustenance to survive. She grumbled and growled and bubbled and squeaked and Naomi and I looked at each other in surprise. It was such a pathetic but valiant final effort

344

being made by what was left of her survival functions, it seemed like little David fighting against the Goliath of cancer. And it was so *loud*.

'Good God,' Naomi said. 'Did you hear that?'

I nodded. 'Yeah. I thought it was thunder for a minute.'

She smiled. 'I thought it was a lorry going past outside.'

'Well I thought it was a plane going overhead.'

'I thought it was a plane landing in the car park.'

'I thought it was a plane crashing in the car park.'

'I thought a whale had fallen out of a tree.'

'I thought a horse had fallen down the stairs.'

By the end of it, we were doubled over laughing, wiping away tears, trying to keep it silent and not disturb either Mum or anyone else. It was the most we'd spoken to each other throughout the whole ordeal.

'Look,' Naomi said, once we'd got our breath back, 'there's been no change for such a long time, do you think it would be safe to risk one of us popping home for a wash and change of clothes, then coming back so the other one can go?'

I looked at the tiny form under the blanket. Her chest was completely still. Then after about ten seconds it rose slowly with a breath in, and lowered with the breath out. Then was still again for another ten seconds. I willed it to keep on going. I willed it to stop.

'OK Nomes, if you want. But be quick, OK?'

'Oh, shall I go first then?' She was already standing up. 'OK, if you want me to. I'll be as quick as I can. See you later.'

About ten minutes later, Mum opened her eyes and looked at me properly for the first time in days. I leaped up off my chair to her side, and she smiled as I leaned over her.

'Hello, love,' she said softly. 'You're here.'

'Course I am, Mum. Where else would I be?'

'What day is it?' So odd, the things she felt she needed to know.

'Thursday.' I didn't really know, but I figured it didn't matter if I got it wrong.

'Oh. Thursday.' She just looked at me for a long time, and I took her hand and stroked it. She glanced to the other side of the bed, then back at me. 'Where's Nomes?'

Oh shit. The first time she'd been aware of anything for ages and Naomi happened not to be here. 'She's just popped home for a minute. She wanted to have a shower and see Russell for a bit. She'll be back soon.'

'Oh, Russell. Right. Russell.' He voice trailed away and she closed her eyes.

'Mum?'

'Mmm?' She didn't open them.

'Do you want anything? Something to drink maybe?'

'No, no, love . . . s'fine . . .' She drifted off again. Fifteen minutes later, she was gone.

I rang Naomi's mobile. 'Nomes, can you come back now? Please come back.'

'Why? What's happened? Oh God, she hasn't . . .?'

'She's gone, Nomes. She's gone. Please come back. Please. Please come back.'

I'm not sure Naomi ever forgave me. Especially as I was the one responsible for her death.

*　*　*

346

Suddenly I feel as though I'm intruding on something for some inexplicable reason. Maybe because I'm watching a man lovingly tending to a grave without knowing I'm here. I glance around quickly, madly looking for a place to hide, but it's too late, he turns and sees me. A strange expression flits across his face but almost immediately gives way to smiling surprise. He glances once more over his shoulder at the grave, then walks over to where I am.

'Hey there,' he says, a little bit uncertainly. 'Nice to see you again.' He pauses. 'So soon.'

'You too.'

He raises his eyebrows. 'Really? 'Cause the way you rushed off home so suddenly earlier, you know, right after telling me such a devastating piece of news, I kind of felt that you wanted to be in a different place to me.'

'You're very perceptive.'

'Yeah I know. It comes from years of living around other humans. You start to pick up subtle nuances in behaviour.'

'Oh, yes. I see.' We stand awkwardly for a few moments while we both wait for me to apologise. 'Look, Felix, I'm sorry I rushed off so suddenly like that. It was such a lovely lunch and it was very . . .'

'Ungrateful?'

I look up at him sharply, but his face isn't angry. He looks very peaceful, actually. 'Yes, yes, you're right, I was a bit ungrateful. I am grateful to you, I really am, and not just for the food. You've been so kind, giving up your time to help me out with my training, keeping me going . . . And as well as rushing off rudely after lunch

347

today, sometimes I've been a bit moody and stroppy with you. You didn't deserve that.'

'It doesn't matter.' He looks at me long and steady and I feel my face starting to go hot. 'We rarely get what we deserve, little Daisy,' he says solemnly, and I immediately think it has something to do with the grave he was just visiting. And just where exactly *is* Aunt Winnie? Because the story about her going walkabout simply doesn't ring true. She must be about a hundred and two, don't they stop you flying when you get to a certain age, in case you die on the plane? Has Felix been lying to me? Is he hiding some terrible secret about his great aunt, pretending to the world that she's in Oz, but really she's . . . I glance nervously over at the grave but I can't investigate further because he's looking at me still and starting to move towards the gate leading back to the road.

'Coming?' he says.

So I have to follow.

'I want to explain,' I start, as we walk together back towards Abby's.

He shrugs. 'You really don't need to. It doesn't matter.'

'No, no, I do. I want to. Or at least, I want to give you the edited version of events. I'm sure you're not interested in going into the whole . . .'

'You know, I actually am interested in the hole,' he says, and at last I can hear a smile in his voice. I find myself relaxing with relief. 'It sounds like a cool place.'

'What hole?'

He grins at me and it's like the sun coming out. 'Doesn't matter, Queen Duck. None of it. Really. I totally get it.'

'You do?'

He nods. 'Yeah. Sometimes people can just be . . . unhappy. It happens. Especially if there's something . . . Especially if they're angry at the world. But you can't be angry at the world. It's not possible. So you direct your anger at one person.' He turns and looks at me frankly. 'Even if that person is really,' he pauses for dramatic effect, '*really* nice.'

'Right.'

'So, are you angry at the whole world, Daisy Duck?' His voice is very low and soft and I feel a slight tingle somewhere.

'Am I . . .? I . . . don't know. I have been . . . I am very upset. I have been very upset. For a long time. I've been a bit . . . stuck.'

He nods, as if he understands exactly what I'm talking about. 'Are you still stuck?' We've stopped on the pavement and he's standing very close to me, bending his head down, looking into my face.

I stare back up at him and can almost feel the warmth radiating from the nearness of his body. Am I still stuck? Tentatively, I feel around the area where Mum and Graham are resting in my mind, thinking back to the apocalypse that happened to me five months ago; and the second, slightly less destructive one, three months after that. Because a second cataclysm can't do much damage when there's nothing left to destroy. I zoom in on myself, a tiny white speck curled on its side with its arms over its head while violent hurricanes and tempests raged on around it. But it wasn't tempests; it was life continuing, events happening, people doing things. I was

349

shielding myself from harm by shielding myself from life.

I give Felix a weak smile, and shake my head. 'I don't think I am.'

He raises his hand and very gently strokes my cheek with his thumb. 'Then, Daisy, Queen of Ducks, I am happy.'

He smiles at me, turns, and strides very briskly away.

'Abby!' I call out as I erupt through the door. It bangs on the wall behind it and almost hits me in the face. 'Abby? Where the hell are you? I need to talk to you. Abby! ABBY!' I've made it back to the flat – must stop calling it 'home' – in under five minutes and have only one thing on my mind.

Abby puts her head gingerly round the living room door. In the background I hear Tom Hanks quoting from *The Godfather*.

'I'm here,' she says quietly, with wide, anxious eyes. 'What can I do?'

I seize her by her arms and pull her fully into the hallway. 'Oh, Abby, you wonderful, gorgeous, beautiful friend.' I'm bouncing while holding her hands, and she relaxes and grins delightedly, while she starts bouncing with me. 'Please tell me about Felix.'

Her expression takes on a kind of wise old lady appearance. She stops us bouncing, then nods slowly, smiles knowingly and leads me by the hand into the kitchen. 'What do you want to know?'

'Everything. Everything!' A grin bursts out of me, I clasp my hands together and start bouncing again. 'Anything you know about him. Right now, please.'

She nods. 'So I'm guessing that you know about his wife?'

I stop. Stop grinning. Stop jumping. Stop breathing.

'Fuck,' Abby says, and pulls out a chair. I sink into it, and put my forehead on the table. 'So I'm guessing that you *don't* know about his wife? I'm sorry, Daze, I thought, from the way you were, that he'd told you all that already. Although he doesn't talk about it much. They got married about four years ago, I think. Gorgeous wedding – I've seen the photos. And she – Alice – looks very pretty. Although most people do look pretty on their wedding day, don't they? Anyway, I think they were only married for about two or three years . . .'

I raise my head. *Were* married? 'What happened?'

Abs shrugs. 'I don't really know. He's never gone into detail, and it's not really the sort of thing you ask, is it? As far as I know, one minute she's at the doctor's with double vision, three weeks later she's dead.'

It hits me like a spade to the head. I literally sway in my seat and have to grip the table to steady myself. 'What?' It's barely more than a whisper.

Abby just nods. 'I guess that's why he's not really working, and still living at his great aunt's place. After she died, he went on a year-long round the world trip, I think. Did all sorts of things. Wrestled alligators, bungee jumped into potholes, swam with sharks, that kind of thing.' She presses her lips together, and when she speaks again her voice is very soft. 'Maybe on some level he was trying to die.'

A succession of images flash across my mind: Felix feeding his hand to a shark; Felix in a helicopter;

Felix on a bungee rope. Felix, kneeling by a graveside, talking softly. Each one suddenly makes sense. I close my eyes. Then open them again. I shake my head, understanding something about him absolutely. 'He wasn't trying to die,' I say, with certainty. 'He was making sure he was still alive.'

We don't have time to discuss it further because at this point Taj Mahal Tom heaves into sight in the hallway, his face smooth and immobile. One corner of his mouth is marginally out of alignment and I stare at that part, longing to straighten it like a crooked picture.

'Abby?' he says, coming through into the kitchen. His tone as he speaks varies slightly, a half a semi-tone each way. He seems absolutely furious. 'Are you ever coming back?' He spots me. 'Oh, hi, Daisy. How are you?'

'Hi, Tom. Fine thanks. You?'

He nods stiffly. 'Yes, fine, thank you. We're . . . er . . .' He breaks off, unable to continue apparently. And in that second the thing in my subconscious that's been troubling me for so long fizzes to the surface and breaks out in an explosion of fireworks. *Bang!* Tom and the kitchen conversation with unknown woman! *Fizz!* Abby smoking! *Wheeee!* Tom's mysterious repeated absences and late night returns! *Pop!* Tom's blind panic at finding Abby at home the other night. *Crackle!* (I'm running out of firework noises.) And then sitting uncomfortably in the living room first thing the next morning, looking wretched. Oh my God, it's so obvious now. Tom is having an affair!

Other things start to fall into place. I remember now, when I overheard that conversation between Tom and the other woman in the kitchen, I was very uncomfortable

352

about it and ran off to have a shower rather than deal with Tom and whatever lame explanation he was going to try and give. And now I realise I have subconsciously been avoiding him ever since. I just know that as soon as he gets me on my own he's going to ask me to keep my mouth shut about it. It'll just be our little secret. Yeah, sure, like I would ever side with him against my best friend – my only friend. Especially something as important and *betrayal-ish* as this. No doubt he would say that if I told her, I would be the one hurting her and it would be needless because the whole thing was nothing, meant nothing, had ended. And I would be left standing there – or sitting most likely; he would definitely have made me a cup of coffee and asked me to sit down, fed me biscuits, told me how fantastic I look, blah blah blah, all to weaken my defences before launching his attack on my conscience, the troglodyte. So I'd be sitting there in a terrible quandary, not knowing what to do. Because although it's obvious that Tom's in the wrong and is trying to get away with it, I could still end up the bad guy here.

But I immediately wiped it from my conscious mind to avoid having to do anything. What a coward. Suddenly I despise myself as much as I despise Tom. Well, almost as much. She who sees wrongdoing and does nothing is just as much in the wrong as the wrongdoer. Or something. The only reason this entire thing has gone so completely over my head is because I ducked low enough to avoid it. I rotate my head slowly towards Tom and narrow my eyes.

'You're what?' I ask him, perhaps a little snappishly.

He and Abby both flinch a little, then glance briefly at each other. 'We're . . . watching a film,' he finishes haltingly, flicking his eyes at me, then away. Guilty conscience, obviously.

'And I've got a surprise for you,' Abby says, eyes wide. 'Ooh, I'd forgotten about it. Come in the living room.'

So we all go through into the living room and sit down and Abby's telling me something about a spa day she's booked for the two of us for Wednesday, the day after we do our final big practice twenty-mile walk on Tuesday, and we'll have pedicures and leg muscle massages and sit in the steam room and have a lush lunch and the whole time I can barely hear her because I'm so distracted by the presence of the granite-faced gargoyle that's lurking on the armchair. He's tapping his fingers lightly against the television remote control and the noise it makes is very soft and quiet, as if he's so insipid he can't even be irritating properly. My mind is seething, furiously processing information and trying to come up with the best course of action – should I tell Abby and cause enormous upset for her (and for Tom, although, you know, tough shit), feel destroyed by guilt when she has to move out, find somewhere else to live, separate her share of the furniture and all her belongings, and start her life all over again; or not? If I don't tell her, he carries on carrying on and she continues to live a false life. But if I tell her, she gets very hurt and everything ends. I can't begin to know what to think.

'What do you think, Daze?'

'Hmm?' I look up at Abby's face, grinning at me

expectantly. 'Oh, yes, that looks lovely, Abby. Thank you. Can't wait.'

She flicks her eyebrows up once. 'Oh, right. Well, great. Good.' She drops the brochure on the sofa next to her and turns back to two-timing Tom. 'Well go on, press play then.'

Tom looks from her to me, then down at the remote in his hand. 'Right.' They both focus back on the screen and I'm dismissed.

TWENTY

Lesley Jones
Where does food deliverys this early im hungry but cant face the world yet ??????
> **Mike Green** Nowere you loser get up make sum toast
> **Georgia Ling** Lmfao pmsl! Les your such a lazeee bonez!!! Xxx

Walking twenty miles is no mean feat. It's a complex and difficult undertaking. We need a route worked out in advance to make sure we will have access to a toilet every five or six miles; ideally mostly flat terrain; away from traffic; and not too many roads to cross because that will slow us down. This requires in-depth and serious research and map consultation, not to mention prior preparation of refreshments, but luckily for me I know that I can totally rely on the exceptional organisational skills and attention to detail of the control freak that is Abby Marcus. She will have this all sorted out.

'We'll walk for ten, then turn round and come back.'

Oh. Apparently not.

'What? Is that your plan?'

She looks at me and shrugs. 'Yeah. You got a better one?'

I haven't, of course. I could have spent the past three days poring over Google maps, plotting a route, checking the contour lines for hills, finding out what pubs or cafés would feature along the way, working out the distance using the scale thing at the bottom. I didn't do that. I have been doing other things. And to be honest, I thought Abby was doing it all. I've hardly seen her for three days so I assumed she was elbow-deep in walking plans. But now that I think about it, why would she be absent from the flat because of that? I realise that I've had an idiotic image in my head of her standing at a desk somewhere in a bunker, pushing little plastic people around on a map, sticking pins in charts, answering an old green telephone and barking instructions to a nebulous team of helpers in the background. She's amazing at organising things. She's always in control. I can absolutely count on her to plan everything with military precision.

'Have you sorted out food?'

She waves her hand. 'Meh. We'll find a café.'

Today she has decided to wing it.

Actually she has not been quite herself the past few days. Even though it's only eight o'clock in the morning so I've literally only been in her company for fifteen minutes, I can tell that she is not as excited about this expedition as I thought she would be. She's less excited about it than I am, and I have got a very bad case of reluctance syndrome this morning. It's a genuine, recognised condition that makes everything difficult and slow

357

and accompanied by sighs and grunts. Abby has looked at me witheringly with every sigh, but has said nothing to encourage me, which is a very strange state of affairs that has hardly ever happened in our entire friendship, let alone since . . . well, since Mum died.

As we set off now along the surprisingly crowded pavement towards the end of the first ten miles, wherever that may turn out to be, I'm starting to feel an anxious churning in my tummy and am very worried she's worked things out herself about two-faced Tom. And if that's the case, should I tell her that I've known all along, or should I act surprised and horrified? Well, I won't need to act horrified. I *am* horrified. I am also disgustified and shockified, but not enough, apparently, to break the news myself to my best friend in the whole world.

I need to examine why I decided not to tell her, but I don't want to do that now. A large part of me is very worried that I didn't want her to be angry with me, but I will think about that later, when I don't have twenty miles stretching out ahead of me to be walked. With her at my side.

'How long do you reckon this will take us?' I ask, more to break the silence than anything else.

She shrugs. 'Gosh, I have no idea, Daisy. Twenty miles at four miles an hour . . .' She does an elaborate mime of thinking hard for a few moments, tapping her chin with an index finger, squinting up at the sky, shaking her head. 'I'm afraid it's just beyond me.'

'Are you OK, Abs? Only you seem a bit . . .'

She looks at me properly, frowning hard, then forcibly smiles. 'Oh Daze, I'm sorry. I've been a right cow, haven't

I?' She gives me an awkward hug as we walk. 'I don't know, I'm a bit down but I'll try to perk up. This will not be fun at all otherwise, will it?'

'Well, I'm not really expecting it to be that anyway, to be honest.'

'Oh. Great.'

'I mean, you know, because of the massive distance we've got to cover, and the prospect of blisters, and aching hips, and sore backs.'

'Uh-huh.'

'But we could also have a bit of a laugh.'

She nods. 'We could.'

'And then we've got the spa tomorrow to take all our pains away.'

She smiles at last. 'We have indeed.'

'And then in ten days' time we can do the whole thing again.'

'Shut up, Daisy.' She glares at me a moment, and then we laugh and our shoulders knock together.

At the end of her road, the opposite end to Felix's house I note, we don't go towards the park or the canal but carry straight on over the crossroads. I'm immediately in unknown territory. Again.

'Daisy,' Abby says, her tone serious. My stomach clenches. Is she going to tell me about Tom? That she's found something out about him, how he's let her down so badly and hurt her more than she can stand? How her heart is broken in two places and she'll never trust another man with it as long as she lives? Oh God, please don't let this be the end of Abby's happiness.

'What?' In that one syllable I try to make her

understand that I will always be there for her, will help her with anything she needs, and had absolutely no idea about Tom's appalling behaviour beforehand.

She looks at the ground for a moment, then meets my eyes. 'I need to tell you something.'

I can barely speak. 'Uh-huh?'

'Yeah. The thing is, Daze, I just want you to know . . . that I'm so, so proud of you. You know, for stepping up for this MoonWalk, and throwing yourself into all the training the way you have. I don't want to sound patronising, I really don't, but you've . . . Oomph! What's that for?'

I've stopped walking abruptly and seized her to pull her in for a smothering hug. 'Oh, Abby!'

She laughs lightly into my hair then holds me back at arm's length. 'Well of course I'm proud. You've had a horrible few months, but here you are, out on the street, doing the training, marching your little heart out. You've come so far, you really have. Literally and figuratively.'

'Abs, d'you remember that time you said you didn't want to sound patronising . . .?'

She punches me on the arm. 'Ah, there you go. That's what I'm talking about. You're back in the world again, aren't you? You're still alive! It's great to see.'

'Of course I'm alive. I always have been.'

She's already shaking her head. 'No, no, you haven't. Not really. Not *properly*. You weren't living; you were existing, and doing a pretty bad job at that, too. It was like you went somewhere else for a while, and I've been trying to drag you back this whole time. And in the end it was Felix that did it.' She beams at me and clasps her

360

hands together under her chin. 'You're like Dozing Beauty, and he's your handsome handyman, come to wake you up. It's a real life fairy tale!'

When she says his name, I get a strange twisty feeling in my middle. Not that she's suddenly called him into my mind – he's there the whole time now. But just hearing his name makes me feel . . . something.

I didn't arrange another walk with him after being rude and ungrateful on Sunday – I left in such a rush – so we haven't met up since the grave site. His wife's grave. I'm trying to come to terms with the fact that I'll never see him again, but it's so hard, mostly because I fully intend to see him again. As soon as I can. In the three days since I last saw him, I deliberately haven't been marching for miles all round Abby's neighbourhood hoping to come across him holding a heavy wheelbarrow somewhere. I couldn't have even if I'd wanted to – and actually I very much did want to – because I've been busy crossing a few more things off Abby's 'TO DO' list. Also, all the MoonWalk paperwork says not to do too much in the days leading up to the twenty-mile training walk, so my hands were tied.

I've been doing some subtle investigative work though. This has mostly consisted of me asking Abby to tell me stuff about him. I've found out that he's not strictly employed at the moment but is filling his time by doing favours for his – or rather Aunt Winnie's – neighbours. When I first saw him he was laying block paving near the park for an elderly couple who had been ripped off by some cowboys. The builders had taken a few thousand quid off the old couple, then ripped up the tarmac on their drive, undermined the foundations of the wall separating them from next door, and promptly buggered off. The couple had been utterly distraught and not financially able to hire anyone else. Enter shirtless Felix clutching his famous wheelbarrow. He didn't even ask for payment apparently, they just had to supply the materials and the Hobnobs (he loves them, she says; eats them by the boxload). I found quite quickly that I enjoyed hearing stories about him, and longed for more.

'You *are* interested in our Felix, aren't you?' Abby said to me yesterday in the kitchen when I'd unwittingly been hounding her for snippets. 'Want me to do a bit of digging? Find out if he reciprocates? I taught his neighbour's boy about six months ago, I'm sure I could ask him to ask his mum to find out what's what . . .'

I made myself hold my breath for a count of five. Then another three. Then said, very casually, 'Mm, yeah, good idea. How long is it since his wife died? No, no, forget that, doesn't really matter, not if they were only married for two years. I'm sure he's fine by now. Probably won't be awkward at all. Go for it.'

I held my breath. There was a brief but paralysing hiatus while she thought about it, then she wrinkled her nose as she looked at me. 'You know what? I actually think it's a terrible idea. Pestering a man who's clearly not ready to be pestered. I think we should leave it for a while – a few months at least. Do you mind?'

I released my long held breath very quietly and slowly. 'Oh. Well, OK, maybe you're right. I suppose he doesn't really want some neighbour making clumsily unsubtle attempts to interrogate him discreetly. Maybe he's hiding his grief really well and isn't as chipper as he seems?'

We both knew that I knew all about grief and what it can do. Abby nodded slowly. 'Yeah. You're right. Maybe in another six months, eh, Daze? Think you can wait 'til then?'

I smiled, almost collapsing with relief. 'Who knows?'

On Monday, during a short walk I did on my own (definitely not wandering around the neighbourhood looking for wheelbarrow-wielding widowers), I spotted an opportunity to cross something else off Abby's – or rather, my – giant 'TO DO' list. (I have created my own list in my head and the only thing on it is 'Felix'. Crossing things off Abby's list has become a kind of stepping stone towards crossing something off *my* list.) To complete my own list, I need Felix to think of me as less a pathetic lamo and more an irresistible siren, and in my limited experience I feel that I would have better credentials in the siren department if I wasn't freeloading off my friends and kipping in their spare room. So when I spotted a 'To Let' sign a couple of streets away from Abby's, I made enquiries. It was a very sweet little one-bedroom flat, freshly painted throughout with recently refurbished kitchen and bathroom, and I fell in love with it as soon as I walked in. The rent was only six hundred pounds per month, which included council tax and all utilities, so very reasonable and twice what I could afford. At which point it became obvious that I was staying at Abby's. For now anyway. It seems a barmaid's wages won't stretch to suitable siren accommodation, so I've given up scouring the local paper, shop windows and

363

notice boards for places to rent; and have instead been scouring the local paper, shop windows and notice boards for job vacancies. It's a stepping stone towards a stepping stone towards full siren status. And a teensy start towards the rest of my life.

Ahead of us, an old lady is blocking the pavement. She's right in the middle so one or both of us will have to step into the road to get past her. She's standing with her back to us, slightly hunched over, motionless. As we get nearer, I notice that she is actually moving, but not forwards or backwards, just rocking. Or swaying, really. When we reach her, she looks up at us and her lips start moving but no sound comes out. She reaches out a hand and touches Abby's arm. Abs glances at me.

'What are we going to do?' she whispers urgently. 'We can't leave her.'

I shake my head. 'No, of course not.' I face the old dear. 'Hi, are you OK? Do you need some help?'

She looks at me beseechingly, opening and closing her mouth. Her eyes are red and watery and there's a sheen of sweat on her top lip. She looks a bit grey; a few strands of hair are clinging damply to her forehead. 'Is it the heat?' She nods gingerly. 'Do you feel faint?' Again she nods, and closes her eyes. Her hand closes on my arm. She might do better in the summer heat if she wasn't wearing a winter coat, scarf and gloves. 'OK, my name's Daisy, this is my friend Abby. You need to sit down in the shade somewhere for a few minutes.' I glance around quickly.

'How about that wall?' Abby says, directing my attention ahead to a low wall surrounding a garden, with a very leafy tree of some sort shadowing it. She bends so that her face is level with the old lady's. 'Can you make it over there, if we help you?'

She moves her head slightly. 'I'm eighty-seven.' It's a whisper.

'Right.' Abs and I exchange a glance, neither of us sure whether that means she can or can't. We decide that, either way, she needs to be moved, so we each take an arm and start to propel her gently towards the low wall.

Two weeks later, we finally get there. Another three days after that, our elderly friend says, 'What's your name, dear?'

'I'm Abby,' says Abby. 'You met us just over there, a few minutes ago, remember?'

'Of course I remember, it was five minutes ago. I'm eighty-seven, not senile.'

'Oh, sorry.'

'What's yours?' I ask quickly, before Abby goes into total strop mode.

'I'm Evelyn Waterstone.'

'Hi, Evelyn. Are you feeling any better?'

'I was feeling quite dizzy,' she says, which we both take to mean that she is.

'Would you like some water?' I've got four unopened bottles in my backpack, so I slide it off and take the lid off one. I put it into Evelyn's hand. 'Have some water, Evelyn. It's brand new, we haven't drunk any of it.'

She takes a tentative sip as if not entirely sure it isn't Rohypnol. I know *that* feeling.

'Where are you from?' she says, looking somewhere between me and Abby.

'Oh, not far from here,' Abs says. 'We're both local. How about you? Are you far from home?'

She swings her head round to face Abby, as if she's suddenly become aware that she's there. 'Am I what, dear?'

'Where are you from?' Abby asks again. 'Do you need us to help you get home?'

Evelyn smiles. 'Oh, no, bless you. No, this is my home right here.'

For one hideous moment I imagine that this frail eighty-seven-year-old is homeless, sleeping rough on the streets, getting moved on by the PCSOs and scoring smack in the bus station. But then I see that Abby is looking up at the building behind the low wall and I turn and realise it's Fernfield Nursing Home. Oh, thank God.

After a few more decades of recuperation, Evelyn is good to go, so we link arms again and walk her slowly up the three steps to the front door of Fernfield.

'When I was your age, there was a war on, you know,' she says, as if we've never heard of World War Two.

I'm not as good as I should be at mental arithmetic, but Abby has evidently done a quick calculation. 'We're a bit older than you think we are, Evelyn.'

'What, dear?'

'Never mind.'

The door to Fernfield is opened and a woman is standing staring at us. 'Evelyn?' she says. 'What are you doing out?' I really want Evelyn to say she's been hanging around down the arcades.

'I went for a walk,' Evelyn says, too tired for irony. 'I like going out. Nothing to stop me going out, is there?'

'No, no, my love, of course there isn't.' The woman reaches out a hand and we pass Evelyn over to her.

'These two little girls have helped me get home,' Evelyn says, moving into the cool hallway. 'Thank you, girls, that was very kind of you.'

'Yes, thank you,' the woman agrees. Then turns to Evelyn's retreating form. As the door closes we hear her say, 'Now then, my love, how about a nice cup of tea and a biscuit?' I really want Evelyn to say, 'Screw that, get me a whisky.' But she doesn't. She doesn't say anything.

Back on the pavement we walk very slowly in silence for a few moments, while Abby repeatedly glances fondly over at me.

'What?' I ask her, stopping and turning to face her.

She smiles and shakes her head. 'I'm sorry, Daze. I suppose I'm still underestimating you. Not very long ago, you'd have run a mile – or, well, shuffled across the hallway – at the thought of interacting with a stranger, or dealing with a difficult situation or, you know, washing your hair. So I feel a bit protective of you still, like I need to be a buffer between you and the world. But after that,' she jerks her head roughly in the direction of Evelyn, 'I can see that I don't have to. You were so good with her. You're so much better.'

'Well, if I'm honest, I did want to leg it in the other direction as soon as I saw her,' I say conspiratorially. 'She looked so dangerous and volatile. But I gritted my teeth and got on with it. And it was all fine in the end.'

She laughs. 'Bravo you. I'm so proud.'

'Cheers. Shall we have an ice cream?'

When Abby's phone's GPS tells us we're at nine and

a half miles, we find a lovely little café next to the canal, and sit outside in the sunshine and eat paninis.

'Whoever decided to put avocado and brie together was a genius,' she says enthusiastically around a mouthful of bread.

'Mm.' I've got the all-day-breakfast – sliced egg with bacon, sausage and tomato. While I chew, I'm watching the trees lining the canal bank, their branches waving slowly in the breeze, making the leaves turn different colours of green, lime and yellow in the sunlight. They make dappled shadows on the golden path below, all in perpetual motion, swaying and rocking, bright and bursting with life. And in that moment I realise finally the absolute truth in the statement 'Life goes on'.

My phone dings suddenly: it's a text from Naomi. A shadow falls across the sun and the silky breeze stroking my bare arms develops teeth and brings out goosebumps all over me.

'Who's that?' Abby says. Somehow it's OK for her to ask me who's texting me. I never ask her.

'Naomi.' I read through the text quickly. 'She wants to come round this afternoon and see me again.'

'Oh, that's nice of her, isn't it?'

'I doubt it.'

'Why?'

I shrug. 'She's probably not coming for a social visit, you know, for a cuppa and a cosy chat. You can bet your life she's got a reason for coming.' My goosebumps develop goosebumps of their own, and I rub my arms distractedly.

We chew in silence for a few moments. 'Daze,' Abby says tentatively.

'Hmm?'

She studies the end of the panini in her hand. 'This thing with Naomi . . . I mean, you don't have to talk about it if you don't want to, I totally understand if you'd rather not . . . But I've been wondering . . . I mean, you've never said much about how you and Graham got on. And you lived with him all that time and looked after him . . . It just seems totally incredible to me that he would leave you out of his will like that . . .'

'He didn't leave me out. I got a very generous legacy.'

She widens her eyes. 'Five grand? You're kidding. How much was that house worth? Four bedrooms detached, lovely garden, in that area? Must be at least three hundred and fifty grand, right?'

I nod. I knew this was going to be asked sooner or later. Abby wouldn't simply accept it. I swallow a few times but my throat's gone a bit dry. Suddenly my delicious all-day-breakfast panini looks desiccated and indigestible.

'So even if he had no savings whatsoever . . .'

'There were savings too. Mum told me.'

She's silent a moment. 'Do you know how much?'

I shake my head. 'Not really. But Mum told me repeatedly that she thought Nomes and I would both be quite wealthy after her death. Well, after whichever out of the two of them died last. She mentioned a hundred thousand each once or twice.'

'A hundred thousand! Oh my God, Daisy! You could get yourself a flat outright with that, and have a bit over!'

I shrug. I haven't thought about the money really. 'I suppose so.'

'So why didn't she leave it in trust for you?'

'Why would she? Graham was her husband, she had no reason to suspect he'd leave one of us out. They each left everything to the other. If Graham had died first, Darren, Lee, Naomi and I would all have inherited a quarter of the estate each when Mum went. She would have made sure of that. But simply because my parent was the one that went first . . .' I don't need to finish.

'Did you suspect it? That Graham would do that, I mean.'

I don't answer straight away. This is the moment I've been dreading for years. Or at least, since Abby and I have been friends. I was terrified of it to begin with, like it was an infection that would spread into our friendship and destroy it, bit by bit. But as the months and years passed and nothing had come out, I worried less and actually began to feel that maybe it never would. But then Mum got ill again, and this time it was final, and all those long-buried feelings started to bubble up.

When Mum was diagnosed the first time round, I wasn't with her. Graham had been going with her to all her appointments: he wasn't ill himself then. When the doctor had given the terrible diagnosis, Graham had got angry, stood up, stomped around the room, shouted. He'd demanded an explanation.

'No one knows why, Mr Chalkwell.' The consultant stayed so calm, Mum said. Even though Graham's behaviour was borderline inappropriate. 'If they knew that, they'd use the information to find a cure.'

'Could stress be a cause? I've read somewhere that stress could cause it.'

The consultant had nodded slowly. 'It's one theory. If it was severe stress, over a prolonged period. But it's just a theory.'

Graham had told me about this, much later. Mum never did. But I knew Graham blamed me. Of course I'd suspected what he might do. Naomi and I had predicted it years before, just because of Graham's *un*predictability. In spite of that, I never completely believed that he would actually do it.

I look at Abby. At this moment, now, here on this bench in the sunshine, she still loves me. We're still friends and we always will be. At least, that's what she believes. When she's heard what I'm about to tell her, everything will change. She will be shocked and will turn away from me in cold disgust. I stare at her a few more moments, making a clear picture of her face in my mind. Then I nod.

'Yes, I suspected.'

'You *did*?'

'Yes. At least, it was always at the back of my mind. A possibility. Naomi and I talked about it. We made a pact.'

'A pact? What about?'

'Graham was always favouring one or the other of us; he took it in turns. And the one out of favour got roasted for even minor things. Naomi and I made a pact that if one of us got left out of the will one day, the other one would share fifty-fifty whatever they got with the other one.'

'Oh my God. That's so sad.'

'Well, I don't think either of us ever really thought it

would happen. Whatever his feelings were towards me, he did love my mum, I knew that. And I thought that would be his priority – making sure he did what his wife wanted. But it seems he cared less about that than I gave him credit for.'

She's staring at me now, eyes wide, mouth slightly open, the panini in her hand completely forgotten. 'What do you mean, his feelings towards you? What were his feelings towards you?'

I think back to the day of Mum's funeral. All of us watching as the cortege arrived at the house. Graham's venom as he spat vitriol at me. Darren and Lee telling me I couldn't live there forever. Then the next three months of nursing a dying man who had nothing but abuse and poison for me. My eyes fill with water and I close them, spilling tears down my face.

'He hated me, Abs.'

TWENTY-ONE

Abby Marcus
Out casually walking 20 miles with my bezzie **Daisy Mack.**
Sun's out, avocado and brie panini for lunch, and saved the
life of a little old lady. Life is good.

> **Suzanne Allen** Wow, you sound happy. Glad things are
> going well. xx
>
> **Sandie Hines** Sounds like the perfect [Wednesday] to
> me. Gorgeous. Have fun. ☺
>
> **Sue Harding** Saints on speed, 20 miles?! Take the car
> you mad woman!!
>
> **Lynne Sheridan** Casually? Lol! Good luck xx
>
> **Ellie Harley** What's all this about going round, saving
> lives?? Tell all Abster!! xx
>
> **Tracey Owen** Am well jel – chucking it down here. Wish
> I was there ☹
>
> **Manda Fear** Aw, how is poor Daisy? Bless her. Give her
> my love.
>
> **Annika Dann** Can't believe no one else has asked about
> the little ol' lady!! What happened??? Xx

Abby's staring at me in horror. 'He *hated* you? Since when? Why? Why didn't you tell me? Did your mum know?'

I shake my head. 'I don't think so. She never acted as if she did, anyway. It really only came out after she was diagnosed the first time, and she was pretty preoccupied with everything else.' I consider a moment. 'He tried to hide it from her after that.'

Abby rubs her forehead. 'But . . . I don't understand. Did he always hate you? And why did he? There's absolutely nothing about you to hate. What reason could he possibly have?'

I put the remains of my panini down on the plate and look frankly into her eyes. Here it comes. The years we have known each other and been friends, all the things we have done together, the times we've shared, they all flash before my eyes like a life. This is where our friendship reaches its end. 'Because it was my fault she died.'

Abby doesn't leap upwards in an explosion of fury, shouting and accusing and pointing. She doesn't even stand up. She barely even moves. She simply draws her eyebrows together a bit. That's all she does. She obviously hasn't quite grasped what I've said yet. The outrage will no doubt come later.

'What do you mean, your fault? How could it be? She died of cancer, didn't she?'

'Well, OK, no, it wasn't my fault she got it. But what I did when she had it, while she was having the therapy, while she was fighting for her life . . . *interfered* with the treatment. Probably caused it not to go away completely. It came back, and then she died.'

'No, no, no, Daze, that's not right.' She's shaking her head the whole time she's talking. 'Cancer isn't an infection or anything like that. You can't get it because of someone else. Why . . . what . . . What do you mean?'

'Well, you probably know about the bad effects of stress? I mean really severe stress, for a long time?'

'Hey, I'm a driving instructor, I know all about stress.' I give her a look. 'Sorry. Go on.'

'Thanks. So you know the damage it can do in an otherwise healthy person – migraines, blood pressure, random aches and pains, skin problems, immune system repression, the list goes on. I bet there's loads of stuff it does to us that we don't even know about.'

'Yeah, I've heard that.'

'But did you know what effect chronic stress can have on someone with cancer? Or more specifically, what effect it has on the cancer cells themselves?'

Abby is staring at me, her mouth slightly open. She starts shaking her head. 'Oh no. No no no. I see where this is going, and it's nonsense. You surely can't believe that–'

'Just hear me out, Abs. OK? The thing is, I don't know whether you knew but Mum had breast cancer twice. The first time was about nine years before the second time, and she recovered from it. Completely.'

'I didn't know that.'

'Well, she did. Got the all clear. I can't describe what it felt like hearing that. Like a last minute reprieve from the guillotine or something. Massive party, family holiday, the lot. It was fantastic.' I pause, thinking back to that happy time, and the dark times that came after. 'The thing was, she wasn't clear. She can't have been because it came back. As of course you already know. And the second time around, she didn't survive. It took hold the second time. They couldn't stop it.' My voice catches in my throat and Abs leans over the table and covers my hand with hers. But she doesn't say anything, just lets me get it out. 'During her diagnosis and treatment the first time round, she was subjected to massive and prolonged stress. That is, on top of the giant stress being diagnosed with cancer gives you anyway. If you want details, they now think that stress biochemically *feeds* the cancer cells. Not only that, but it also inhibits the effectiveness of the cancer drugs. So not a great thing to do, expose your loved one to stress when they're under-going cancer treatment.'

I pause. Abby is motionless, waiting for me to go on.

'No prizes for guessing who was the cause of the massive stress my wonderful mum was under, in addition to the unbearable stress of having a life-threatening illness.'

Abby shakes her head, but I nod and tap my own chest.

'It was me, Abby. *I* was the cause. And everyone in the family knew it. That's why Graham did what he did. He used to give me furious glares every time we saw each other. Like evil eyes. He absolutely despised me for it. And it's why Nomes hates me and why Darren and Lee hate me.' I hesitate again and think about that. 'Actually no, they hate me just because they're horrible people. They probably hate Naomi as well. And fluffy bunnies. But the fact remains that because of the stress I caused her, her treatment failed. The cancer came back and killed her.'

Abby is stunned into silence and I can see behind her eyes that she's working it out, changing her opinion, starting to distance herself from me, just like Mum did in that oncologist's office. What's happened to me is no less than I deserve, and I'm just thankful I have had these few years of friendship with someone as wonderful as Abby. The whole friendship has felt like it was on borrowed time anyway.

She shakes her head in disbelief. No doubt she's wondering how someone like her could ever have got mixed up with someone like me in the first place.

'No,' she says. 'Oh, Daisy, that's not right at all.'

I nod. 'I'm sorry, Abs. I should have told you before but I couldn't bear the idea of you thinking badly of me.'

'Think badly of you? Of course I don't think badly of you, why would I do that?'

'Because of what I've just told you. I'm not worthy of being your friend and I feel like I've . . . I don't know, duped you a bit by not being honest with you. I'm so sorry.'

She stares at me wide eyed for a few moments and then, suddenly, bursts out laughing. 'Oh, Daisy, you silly sausage!' She gets up and walks round the table to me then bends down and wraps her arms round me. 'Not worthy! *Duped!* You are such a dolt. Of course I don't think badly of you.'

'Well you haven't heard the whole story yet.'

'There's more? Oh, yes, please, tell me everything.' She goes back to her seat and sits down. 'And please don't leave out the part where Graham or Darren or Naomi made you think it was your fault.'

'No, it wasn't them, Abs. Honestly. I've read loads of articles in health magazines and stuff on the internet. Any cells in the body can be altered by stress, we've all seen it when someone breaks out in spots or, I don't know, gets eczema or asthma or hives. Cancer cells are no different. It's something to do with the raised adrenaline levels in someone under stress. It interferes with the process that leads to cell death.'

She nods slowly. 'OK, so you caused your mum stress. I believe that. In fact if you'd tried to tell me you'd been a perfect teenager and never brought your mum anything but joy and sunshine and bouquets of roses, I might have been a bit sceptical. Anyway, go on. You caused your mum stress. I'm all ears.'

'This wasn't the normal sort of teenage stress though. This wasn't about tidying my room or doing my homework or not giving her so much lip or whatever. This was serious.

'Did I ever tell you about my first boyfriend, Dougie?' She shakes her head. Of course I haven't told her – Dougie is so much a part of this story, I have done everything I could to keep Abby from finding out about him. 'I met Dougie when I was fifteen. Only two or three months away from sixteen, but even so. He was eighteen, nearly nineteen I think. Worked in Tesco. I mean, he had finished his education, he was out there, working full time, a proper adult. He had a dream to move away from this town and go and do something somewhere else, somewhere exciting and vibrant and alive like . . .'

'Vegas?'

'Brighton. He was a bass guitarist with this band called

Too Many Kooks. Oh my God, Abby, they were fantastic. And Dougie was so . . . gorgeous. So different from the fifteen-year-old boys I usually hung out with. He had stubble, and thick arms and a deep, man's voice, and no Game Boy in his blazer pocket. I fell completely and utterly in love with him.'

'Right. I imagine your mum was a bit worried . . .'

'Worried? I haven't even started yet. I was in the run-up to my GCSEs. Remember that time of your life, when everything you do, everything you say, everything you think, is about GCSEs? Revision and grades and options and coursework. At the dinner table, last thing at night, first thing in the morning. You can't plan a holiday 'cause of Daisy's exams. You can't book theatre tickets 'cause of Daisy's exams. You can't go to the effing toilet 'cause of Daisy's exams. There's no let-up, it's relentless.'

'Yes, I remember.'

'Well, Dougie was a very cute and very interesting distraction from all that. I drove Mum mad, going out all the time, drinking alcohol, staying up late. I started bunking off school.'

'Mm-hmm.'

I'm watching her face while I'm telling her this and she doesn't seem to be disgusted with me. But I haven't got to the worst part yet.

'I started having sex with him.'

'Dear God,' she says in a monotone. 'Teenagers having sex with each other. Whatever next?'

'You're not horrified? I was fifteen and he was nearly nineteen. Don't you think that's disgusting?'

She considers. 'Well, yeah, OK, not one of your best

decisions, but it was obviously going to happen, and it's not you that I'm disgusted with. Technically, he raped you.'

'It wasn't rape.'

'No, I know, but in the eyes of the law, you weren't old enough to give your consent, so it's statutory rape.' She raises her eyebrows. 'This Dougie committed an offence, and you were a child. You were not to blame, Daisy.'

'Well, OK, I kind of knew that, but it didn't help my mum when she found out.'

'Shit. How did she find out?'

'Read my diary.'

She widens her eyes. 'Daze, seriously? You're not telling me that you were having underage sex with an adult, drinking alcohol, probably illegally?' I nod. 'Smoking? Taking drugs?' I nod again. 'And you wrote all this stuff down in your *diary*? Where anyone could see it? Barlow's bum, Daisy, what were you thinking?'

'I guess I wasn't thinking that anyone would go snooping in my room, least of all my mum. I trusted her.'

'But did you trust everyone else? Naomi? Darren and Lee? Graham?'

I shrug. 'Yeah, I did. Back then I still didn't know what they were really like.'

'Do you think one of them could have gone snooping and found the diary? Then showed your mum?'

It's something I've wondered for years. 'I don't know. I'll probably never know. I suppose so. Anyway, Mum found out about everything. Went spare. You can imagine. Tears, tantrums, slammed doors and sobbing. And that was just her. She grounded me for a hundred and fifty years. Banned me from seeing him. Threatened to go to the police about him if I did. Timed me from the moment I left school to the moment I got home, and if it took me as much as five minutes longer than it should, she wanted to know why. It was hell.'

'No less than you deserved, though, wouldn't you say?'

'Yeah, I can see that now. Back then I was straining at the lead to get away. I hated being confined, always had. I used to say I wanted to be a discoverer when I grew up. Until I did grow up and discovered there was nothing left to discover.'

'So that was your mum's massive and prolonged stress?'

I shake my head. 'No no, the worst is yet to come.'

'Hit me,' she says gamely. 'I can take it.'

I'm sure she can. The question is, can I?

'Obviously I carried on seeing him.'

'Ah. Didn't see that coming.' She smiles knowingly.

'Yeah. Sneaking around, lying. It was like I was having an affair. I suppose I was.' When I say those words, she jerks a bit and pain flashes across her face briefly. Or did I just imagine that, because I know what I know? But what *do* I know? I don't even know whether what I think I know is what Abby knows. I carry on. 'I stopped going to school pretty much. It was the only chance I got to see him as all my other time was monitored so closely. I was in a complete daze.' She smiles fondly at me, as if to say, 'Yes, I know all about that.' 'Eventually, he decided the time was right to branch out into the world and make his big move to Brighton. And I went with him.'

'No!'

'Oh yeah. I didn't tell anyone what I was planning, we just left one evening. I had a couple of changes of clothes in a rucksack, and a few weeks' pocket money saved up, and we just got on a train and went.'

'Fuck.'

'Yeah. We got a room in a house pretty easily. It's all very bohemian and studenty down there, so there are loads of house shares advertised all over the place. Ours was pretty basic but clean at least. One double bedroom, furnished . . .'

'Ugh.'

'Yeah. But it had a sink in the room, which was a bonus. Dougie got a job in a bar, I eventually got a job part time in a café.'

'Eventually? Jesus, Daze, how long were you there for?'

I look at her looking at me, then drop my gaze. 'About five months in the end. Four of them were miserable.' I pause. 'No, four and a half. I turned sixteen while we were there.'

'Fuck. Five months? Fuck. So why didn't you go home?'

'Exactly! That's exactly what I've been wondering all this time. Why didn't I just go home? But . . .'

'You couldn't, could you? Didn't want to lose face, admit you were wrong, that your mum and family were right?'

'Yeah, that was part of it. But also I was totally in love with Dougie. It was like an addiction. Even though I suspected he didn't really feel the same. Even though I found evidence that he didn't. But I didn't want to leave him and go back to being a school child. Obviously I knew that Mum and Graham would be beside themselves with worry, but I couldn't see it so it didn't bother me. Not much, anyway. I didn't tell them where I was, but I did let them know I was OK so at least they didn't think I'd been abducted or killed or something. I thought that was enough to make them feel better. I was wrong about that, but I didn't know that until much later, after I'd gone back.'

'So you did go back?'

'Well yes, Abs. I'm not still in Brighton to this day. I came back.'

She grins. 'Oh, yeah, course. There you are. I was so caught up for a minute, it was like it was happening to someone else. Not you.' She narrows her eyes, as if just remembering that it is me, I am the one, it is down to me that my mum suffered that stress. 'I can't believe it was you.' She shakes her head, a look of wonderment on her face. 'So you came back. How did that come about?'

I think back to that hideous day when I was sitting on the bed in our room, crying. Dougie was either at work or lying, and yet again I was stuck 'at home' on my own with nothing but Channel 4 for company (none of the other channels worked). Then someone knocked on the door. Really hard. I should have known who it was from those strident tones.

'Naomi found me. It seemed incredible at the time, like she was some kind of super sleuth. But in the end it turned out that Dougie had kept in touch with a few of his friends from round here, and one of them knew the brother of Naomi's boyfriend at the time. Very mundane. They went to the same school, I think. Anyway, as soon as she realised the person her boyfriend's brother was talking about was her own sister, she got on a train to Brighton to get me. I was horrified to see her, but . . . Well, it gave me the excuse I needed to go home.'

'Right.'

'And when I got home, I found . . .' My throat starts aching again and I swallow the tears. For a few moments I can't speak, but Abby's worked it out.

'Ohhhh. I get it. When you got home, you found that your mum had been diagnosed with cancer and started undergoing treatment while you were away.'

I nod.

'And this is after, what, a year or so of you being unbelievably difficult and selfish?'

Nod, eyes closed.

'So she does the treatment, goes to hell and back, and then eventually gets the all clear, right? But because it comes back nine years later, naturally Graham or Naomi or probably everyone around you all turn round and look at you? In their desperate need to find someone to blame and make some sense out of it all, they put two and two together and decide that because the doctor or Wikipedia or someone on a bus once said that stress could *possibly* be a factor or affect the drugs or make it worse or something, it must be your fault that she was ill again. Right?'

I nod again, tears now running down my cheeks. 'It *is* my fault, Abs. Everything that's happened, with Mum and Graham, his will, Naomi, everything. It's all down to me. I deserve it all. If I'd never run away to Brighton, she would never have . . .' My throat closes up and I can't finish the sentence.

Abby gets up from her seat and comes round the table to sit next to me. She takes hold of my arms and makes me look her in the eye. 'Listen to me. I totally get why you would feel guilty that you were away being a vile, selfish teenager while your mum had that news and started horrific treatment. It's awful and you will regret that forever. But it's not your fault. No, don't interrupt. Your huge guilt does not mean you're to blame. Cancer is cancer. It's like a spotlight on an audience that lands on a random person. It's got nothing to do with the fact that you ran away to Brighton when you were sixteen. Christ, we were all stupid at that age. That's why you have to go through your teenage years immediately before adulthood – to make you ready. It's a massive learning experience. We screw up so that we can grow up.'

'But–'

'Plus there's the very simple fact you've apparently completely overlooked, that the stress you caused her was during her *first* illness. Which she recovered from. So if she got the all clear when she was under that stress, the stress didn't damage her.'

'It doesn't–'

'You know what I think? I think that your immature sixteen-year-old brain mistook the guilt at being away while she was diagnosed for guilt for making it come back. I bet that's what happened. You felt horrifically guilty for those years between her getting the all clear and the cancer coming back because you weren't there for her when she was diagnosed the first time. But if

385

you'd thought about it clearly for a bit, you'd have realised that you can't *affect* cancer by being a selfish bitch.'

'No, it was–'

'No, it wasn't. Whatever you're going to say. Whatever the doctor said about stress and all that. The two things – you running away and your mum getting ill – happened at the same time, so your brain has made a connection. But they weren't connected, it was just coincidence. And it wasn't your fault.'

I've wanted so much to believe this over the years, but my guilt has always won. The paralysing horror I felt at the sight of her when I came back from Brighton – pale, thin and hairless – has never left me, and I've always felt like I'd caused it. She was fine when I left; something had happened while I was gone. The fact that she recovered didn't really do much to assuage that guilt. And then when she got ill again, it was obvious that the cancer had never really left her.

I shake my head. 'Even if that were the case, it doesn't explain why everyone else thinks it was my fault, does it? It's not as if they were overwhelmed by guilt by me not being there.'

She looks at me steadily. 'Like I said, everyone needs someone to blame when something bad happens, don't they? Think about it. Sickness and death are so senseless, everyone always looks for a reason, an explanation. So one minute your mum's doing her nut at the way you're behaving; next minute she's in hospital having chemotherapy.' She shrugs. 'Bingo. Light blue touchpaper and stand well back.'

I'm still shaking my head, but more slowly. 'I don't know, Abs. It's been so long . . .'

'Yes, that's exactly why it has become ingrained in you that it was your fault. It's like one of those massive lies in history that's been around for so long that everyone believes it now. Like Santa Claus.' She pauses. 'All right, bad example. But you know what I mean. Either way, your guilt is faulty. People don't die from cancer just because their teenage kids misbehave. Christ, I shagged my teacher when I was at school.'

'What?!'

'Oh yeah. Mr Martin. Science.'

'Oh my God, Abby.'

'Got pregnant, Daisy. Yes. It happened. In the science lab. My head next to a Bunsen burner. His wife left him. He lost his job. I was sixteen so no criminal proceedings but . . . I had my picture in the paper and an abortion, all in the same week.'

'Shit.'

'Did my mum get cancer because of it? No she did not. Did Mrs Martin get cancer? Did her mum? No. Even Mr Martin himself didn't get it. Alcoholism, last I heard, but not cancer.'

'But–'

She puts a hand up. 'My friend Scarlet got pregnant by her dad's oldest friend. The wife kicked him out, blamed Scarlet's parents, ended the friendship and never spoke to either of them again. Got her mum kicked out of their badminton club. Scarlet kept the baby and is now living with this forty-eight year old dude. Her mum – alive and well. If a little bit pissed off.'

'That's—'

'Wait, wait. I've got more.' She thinks for a moment. 'Another friend of mine from school. We're not friends any more, I just want to point that out. He did a ram raid of a Pets at Home when he was seventeen. Drove a car through the front window one night. Loaded it up with tins of dog food, cat beds, flea treatment, whatever he could get his hands on. Stupid fuck, didn't even think about grabbing the tills. CCTV saw the whole thing, including his licence plate. Got time inside for it. His mum? Living it up with her boyfriend in Spain somewhere.'

I start smiling, and rub the wetness off my cheeks.

'Girl I used to go to Guides with. Yes, I used to be a Girl Guide, don't laugh. She starts writing to someone in prison. Armed robbery, I think it was. Eventually gets persuaded to go and meet him, on a visit. Doesn't tell her mum. Shags him somehow under the table. Christ alone knows how they achieved that. Now she's pregnant with the baby of a violent offender. That man will be in their lives forever. *Forever*. Her mum? Changed her name and wearing a fake moustache everywhere, but no cancer.'

I start grinning broadly while Abby gently rubs my arms. I feel a huge rush of affection for her as she does this, and something else, difficult to identify. It's a surging feeling inside me, like the sun coming out, or Christmas morning when you're eight, and I feel fidgety, restless and suddenly very bouncy. My body leaps to its feet almost without me realising it as suddenly I feel a kind of euphoria. Abby knows everything, and it doesn't matter. I want to jump up and down where I'm standing, and it's such a strong feeling I just have to go with it. Sod it, who cares what the people at the next table will think? It doesn't matter, nothing matters. I'm grinning widely as I start to bounce and before I know it Abs is up and bouncing with me and we're laughing and hugging and the sun is shining inside and out and I feel fantastic.

'Wow,' she says, as eventually we calm down, 'if only I'd known such depressing tales of woe would make you so happy.'

The second ten miles go by in a flash. I feel so light-headed and almost delirious, the best I've felt for years, that I practically float home. The monstrous thing I've been hiding from Abby for our entire friendship is now out, and she's still my friend. Still my best, *the* best, friend in the entire world. I remember an old film where someone defines love as when that person knows the worst thing about you, and it's OK. I guess Abby must really love me. Unless this isn't the worst thing about me. Maybe my mum dying of cancer was just that: she died of cancer. Maybe it had nothing to do with me at all. I need to think about that properly, later, when I'm on my own.

When we come back along Abby's road to her house, it's quarter to four in the afternoon. It's taken us seven and a half hours, including stopping for Evelyn and lunch, but we've done it. My hips are aching a bit and the soles of my feet are hot, but I have no blisters or sore areas anywhere. I'm bursting with energy and feel like I could slay dragons.

'We've just walked twenty miles, Abs.'

She nods, grinning. 'I know! It wasn't even that hard. I reckon we could run a marathon, you know.'

389

'Ooh, bloody hell, we'd better start preparing straight away.'

'Yes. Quick, buy shorts.' I look at her and she's pulling a very straight and serious face, but I start giggling and before long we're holding each other on the pavement, laughing so hard our sides hurt and our eyes are watering.

Then I see Naomi's car.

'Oh shit. I'd forgotten she was coming.'

Abby touches my arm. 'Doesn't matter. Remember, you are definitely not responsible for your mum's death. It was a random disease. That's all.'

I nod. 'OK.'

'You know what I think? Graham was a miserable, bitter old man by the time he died. He got revenge on you for something that happened over ten years ago, completely ignoring the wishes of the wife he claimed to love. That was wrong, he shouldn't have done it. All the other children had the chance to put that right by asking the executor to divide the estate four ways equally. They chose not to. Your sister could have argued on your behalf to persuade the others to do the right thing. Or she could have honoured the pact you made and given you half of what she got. She chose not to. All of these ghastly people have justified keeping your share of your mum's half of the estate by convincing themselves that Graham was right, you don't deserve it. Because you did something stupid when you were a teenager. And the worst thing is, they made you believe it too. It's absolutely disgusting.'

I nod slowly. It's a good feeling, starting to accept it. 'Maybe you're right.'

'Too right I'm right. Now you go in there and tell her that.'

We link arms and go into the house together, and as I walk into the living room and Naomi stands up to greet me, I remember suddenly the 'TO DO' list on my bedroom wall.

'Oh, Daisy, there you are. I've been waiting ages. Abby's boyfriend let me in.'

'Hi, Naomi.' We hug, but I don't feel like clinging this time. 'Sorry, I was training again. How are you?'

'Getting there,' she says. 'Slowly but surely. Distracting myself with other things, you know. Like you and your walking.'

'Well it's not really a distraction, to be honest. It is in aid of breast cancer.'

'Yes, yes, I know. You said. How's it going?'

I nod. 'Yeah, good, thanks. Just walked twenty miles.'

'Wow. Very impressive. You look well on it. Have you lost weight?'

'Don't think so. Maybe.' We both sit down in the same seats we were in last time. The image of the ashes comes into my head but I push down the molten magma rising inside me. No point getting angry about that. 'So how have you been distracting yourself, Nomes?'

She grins and scoots forward on her seat a little. 'Well, about a couple of months ago, Russell met this guy at a work do, and he's . . . Doesn't matter. Long story short, the guy knows someone who's set up a little business. And we've invested.'

'Oh. Right.' I was expecting her to say Sudoku or am-dram.

391

'Yes, I know, not usually the sort of thing we would do but it's such a great opportunity – almost too good to be true, really. We're expecting something like forty percent profit on our initial investment.'

'Wow. That sounds good.' That's not what I'm really thinking. 'Actually, Nomes, isn't that a bit risky?'

She shrugs. 'Maybe. But you know, you've got to take risks if you want to make a decent return. And seeing as we've just . . .' She hesitates at this point and glances away. I'm confused for a nanosecond, then realise with a flash of clarity that she was about to mention how they've just come into some money. Of course they have. She's just had quite a substantial inheritance.

'You've what?' I ask in a very Abby-like way. I feel much more like my old self these days.

She fidgets a bit, fiddling with the edge of her jacket, and it's interesting to note that she does still have a moral or two in there. Not enough to make her behave any differently unfortunately; just enough to make her a tad uncomfortable with her behaviour. 'Oh, we've just, erm, had some plans drawn up for a new conservatory,' she says now, nodding off-handedly. 'But we might not get it done after all. Haven't decided yet.'

'Oh. Right.' I want to press it, make her say it, the way that Abby would. I glance at the door, wishing Abby would burst in suddenly on some pretext, and say something cutting and Columbo-esque, but she doesn't. Of course she doesn't. Although no doubt she's out there listening to every word.

'Anyway,' Naomi says into the awkward silence. 'I've got something for you. Thought it would be safest to bring it to you in person.' She opens her handbag and fishes out a smooth, white envelope, which she hands to me. When I open it, I see it's a cheque made out to me for five thousand pounds, signed by Darren; and another envelope that says '*Daisy Duck*' on the front. It's my mum's handwriting, but scruffy and badly formed. My throat clenches and I look up again.

'Thanks.'

'You're welcome. What will you do with it, do you think?'

I ignore the question. 'Naomi, how much did you get?'

She raises her eyebrows. 'Why do you want to know that?'

'Out of interest. Don't pretend you don't understand how I'm feeling. I presume you, Darren and Lee awarded yourselves a third each?'

'We didn't award ourselves, Daisy, it was in Graham's will.'

'Yes, yes, I'm aware of the will, thank you.' Naomi flinches a little at my cold tone. She's not used to this from me, particularly recently. 'But you know as well as I do that, as executor, Darren could have altered the will. Done the right thing and made sure I got what Mum wanted me to have. By following Graham's wishes unswervingly, you've pretty much awarded it to yourselves.'

She uncrosses her legs. 'Well, you think what you want to think.' She crosses them again. 'We all know what's been going on.' She picks up the hem of her jacket again, examining it closely.

I watch her carefully as she fidgets. '"What's been going on"? What does that mean? What *has* been going on?'

'I'm not prepared to talk about it. I just don't see why I should suffer as a result of your actions.'

'Suffer? What do you mean? Suffer how? What actions? Why don't you explain it to me?'

She doesn't answer, just sighs and looks away. And then it suddenly hits me like a windfall. 'Oh, no, wait a minute. I *do* understand. You mean you don't think you should get less money, by some of it coming to me. That's it, isn't it? You like the sound of a third much more than you like a quarter, so why should you be made to give any of that up? Right?'

'Daisy, don't pretend. I know all about what you've been saying.'

'What I've been *saying*? What have I been saying?'

Again, she doesn't answer, just shakes her head and looks away, opening her handbag and peering inside, rummaging. I'm frowning to myself, thinking back, trying to remember what I've been saying, if anything, and to whom. But the only people I've spoken to in the past three months are Abby, Tom, Danny and Felix. Apart from the odd person in a shop, or a few comments on Facebook. And I haven't said anything even remotely controversial to them. I haven't even *thought* anything controversial. Well, apart from wishing I could take some of the photos and things out of Mum and Graham's house before I left it. And secretly sniggering about Darren and Lee's pudding-bowl haircuts. But surely she can't mean that? I remember when she and I used to snigger about that together. So what on earth is she talking about?

And then Abby's words come back to me from outside just now. '*All of these ghastly people have justified keeping*

394

your share of your mum's half of the estate by convincing
themselves that Graham was right, you don't deserve it.'
I stare at Naomi's face, flawlessly made up, while she
fidgets and fiddles with her handbag, and I understand
completely. They want to keep my share; they also want
to sleep at night. So they've cooked up some spurious
misconduct of mine, apparently something I've been
saying about something to someone, to justify sticking
to Graham's instructions in the will. His original decision
was flawed because it was for revenge, for something
that happened years ago, and they could have put it right.
But they got pound signs spinning in their eyes when
they realised how much more a third of four hundred
thousand is than a quarter. It suits them very nicely to
keep me out of things. And if I'm the evil party, they can
all sleep and Naomi can eventually stop fidgeting.

'So are you going to tell me what I've been saying,
Naomi?' I know she won't. She can't. 'What heinous
thing means I don't deserve to have what Mum wanted
me to have?'

'Ugh.' She stands up briskly. 'I knew you would be
like this. It's too hurtful, Daisy. I don't want to talk about
it.' She brushes herself off, as if she's got covered in dust
or something just by being there. 'I need to leave.'

'There's nothing, is there? You haven't actually got a
single thing on me. There is absolutely no justification
for sticking to Graham's will, and you know it. In fact
there is no real justification for Graham doing what he
did in the first place.'

She starts shaking her head. 'No, now come on, we
both know, we *all* know, that what you did back then–'

395

'What I did back then was bad, yes. But nothing worse than thousands of teenagers put their parents through all the time. And certainly not the reason for Mum dying.' There's a moment's hiatus at this point while we both wait for me to be struck by lightning, but nothing happens. Except I'm sure I hear a voice outside the door saying, 'Fuck yeah!'

'You're wrong,' Naomi says, but offers no more explanation. 'And I'm leaving.'

She looks at me defiantly, while I stand in front of her, sweaty and dusty and aching. I have no money, no home, a low-paid job and no husband. But I'd still rather be me, a hundred times over.

'You know what else you are, Naomi,' I say, moving a little closer to her so she can smell my sweat. 'You're a selfish bitch.'

She smiles. 'Careful, Daisy. Your envy is showing.'

'You can tell yourself that, if it makes you feel better. We both know that this is wrong, and you do actually feel bad about it. Not enough to give up the money, but enough to invent something bad that I'm supposed to have done, to justify it. And you can tell yourselves I'm bitter about the money but I'm really not. It's upsetting because it was the one thing that gave Mum some peace in her final days, and it was the last little bit of her love and protection she could give, to keep us safe. But you keep it. I'll be fine, my conscience is spotless. You and the others go ahead and spend what you all know my mum wanted me to have. Good luck to you, I hope it makes you happy. It probably will, actually, because quite clearly money is the one thing you value above everything.'

'You might want to consider being–'

'Good luck with your get-rich-quick scheme.'

'Daisy, you think you know–'

'Or rather, your *next* get-rich-quick scheme.'

'You can't even–'

'Bye, Naomi.'

She widens her eyes at me, then glances critically around Abby's cosy little living room. 'Don't worry, I'm going.'

'Excellent.'

Her mouth opens but incredibly she doesn't say anything else, just walks past me and back through the door to the hallway. Through the open door I see Abby standing there, grinning. She doesn't bother to show Naomi out, and a second later we hear the front door slam.

Abby rushes in. 'Oh my God, Daisy, you did it! I'm so proud of you!' We hug briefly but I push her away.

'I need to do something,' I say, and walk quickly back to the hallway and over to my bedroom door. Abby follows me and stands in the doorway while I head straight to the 'TO DO' list, collecting a pen from the dressing table on the way. At the list I bend down and delightedly score a thick line through 'Call Naomi a bitch'. Then I turn back to a grinning Abby in the doorway and hold the pen in the air like a trophy.

'Done it!'

TWENTY-TWO

Daisy Mack
has suddenly got nothing TO DO
   Georgia Ling no need to shout lol xoxox
   Abby Marcus Not entirely true, Daisy, but I'm not quibbling. Proud of you ☺
   Jenny Martin lucky thing, wish I didn't
   Rachel Pimms Read a book, its good for the sole xxx

It's Thursday, the day after our twenty-mile walk and I've woken up this morning to a blank wall. It looks very bare and desolate over there, now that the 'TO DO' list has gone. No, not desolate; more, I don't know, *waiting*, maybe. Primed, like a canvas. After I crossed off 'Call Naomi a bitch' yesterday, I also scored through the things about smiling and the future, much to both Abby's and my hysterical delight, which left only 'Find a flat' on there, and that's already a work in progress so I took it down. It's in a crumpled heap on the floor now – I suppose I should throw it away but I'm not quite ready for that yet. I'm not looking at the map any more, but at least I know it's there in case I get lost again.

On my dressing table, where the unopened letter from Owen and Stiles used to stand, is the letter from Mum that Naomi gave me yesterday. I haven't opened it. I'm definitely not ready for that yet either. I pick it up and hold it to my face, breathing in deeply. It smells of her somehow. Or is that my imagination? I stroke the surface of the envelope, knowing that traces of her must linger there still, feeling as if I'm almost touching her. The spidery, uneven scrawl on the front makes my throat ache when I picture her trying to form letters and sentences with a body and mind filled up with morphine. A single tear drops onto the paper so quickly I blot it dry and put it safely back on the dressing table, out of danger.

Right. Must get ready. It's Spa Day today.

Two hours later, Abby and I are neck-deep in hot bubbling water. I feel like a boiled potato. Actually I look a bit like one too, bobbing around, but Abs of course looks amazing, even with damp hair plastered to her head and no make-up on. She's wearing an ice blue bikini and two percent body fat. I'm . . . not. I'm more of a fifteen percent kind of girl, and have got on an ancient navy blue one-piece with a scoop neck and various strategic transparent areas where the fabric has rotted a bit. But it doesn't matter because there is no one else here at eleven o'clock on a weekday morning so we've got the whole place to ourselves.

After Naomi left yesterday, Abs and I decided to glad-rag ourselves up and hit the town for a slap-up meal and a night of fun. I'd never felt more like going out and celebrating, big time. I wanted to dance and sing and jump around. We started out with a fantastic meal in a place called Bella Donna's, and after our seven-hour exercise session earlier, we really carb-ed it up. Pasta, garlic bread, tiramisu and lots of wine. Not a carb but still an indulgence. We staggered out of there at nine thirty, clutching our tummies. My legs had started to stiffen up by this time, but I certainly wasn't going to let that spoil our evening. After about twenty-five thousand reps earlier in the day, my calf muscles in particular were now screaming with the effort of keeping me upright in heels when my whole body wanted to tip forward.

'Right,' Abs said, 'where now? Hit a club? Casino? Bowling alley?'

I paused. 'Dance the night away?'

Her eyes flinched a bit when I said it, then she nodded slowly. 'Could do, could do.'

'Get a taxi down to Basicz? Hit the shots?'

'Good idea. Jägermeister?'

'Defo. Sours?'

'Doubtless. Shall we go then?'

'What are we waiting for?'

'Nothing. Let's go.'

'Can't wait.'

We immediately made absolutely no move to find a taxi. Abby looked at me.

'Your feet hurting?'

I nodded. 'Like fuck.'

She flicked her eyebrows up. 'Home?'

'Oh God yes.'

So that was our big night out. On the sofa in our PJs by ten, watching a bit of Hugh and Julia. Tom was conspicuous by his absence, but I didn't ask where he was. Didn't want to draw attention to his non-appearance. Well, that's not strictly true. In actual fact I didn't want to *talk* about his non-appearance, and if I mentioned it, we would undoubtedly talk about it. So we sat there, both pretending there was a giant elephant in the room that we weren't talking about.

'Isn't this amazing?' Abby yells to me now.

'Wonderful,' I shout back. It's an effort to be heard above the loud rumble of the water jets and the resultant furious bubbling and churning. The water is extremely active, whirling and thrashing around, moving past us and around us and under us, working incredibly hard and giving us its all to make our visit there as relaxing and tranquil as possible. Abby is standing stiffly in the middle staring down at the writhing bubbles around her, her arms rigid at her sides.

'Are you relaxed?' I shout.

'*What?*'

'I said, are you relaxed?'

She nods enthusiastically. 'Oh yeah,' she yells, 'very much so.'

'Me too!'

We give up trying to converse and wait for it to end. Eventually the timer runs out and abruptly the water drops and flattens out, stilling to a smooth calm within seconds. The room is suddenly very quiet. There's a sense of the water flopping down onto a seat, closing its eyes

401

for five minutes and breathing hard before it has to resume its frenetic activity.

'Shall we get out?' Abs says, making for the steps. I follow her without answering.

In the steam room the atmosphere has been laced with aromatic eucalyptus oil, which immediately starts me off coughing.

'Ah, isn't this lovely?' Abby says, inhaling deeply. 'Really clears out your sinuses.'

I'm coughing so hard my eyes are watering, but I manage to make one of my coughs sound like 'yeah'. I wonder randomly if it's possible to drown in steam. Whoever put the eucalyptus oil in there clearly had murder in mind.

Eventually my windpipe accepts that this is as good as it's going to get for a while, and I sit down with a squelch on the tiled bench. Abby sniggers at the sound, as if hers hadn't made a sound at all.

'Yeah, you get up and sit down again,' I croak.

She does. No sound. Rats.

I lean back against the hard, scalding tiles and close my eyes. My throat tickles but I won't let it start again. The atmosphere stills and the holes in the steam made by our entrance silently fill up again. Abby's shape disappears into the mist.

'Are you ready then?' her muffled voice says from somewhere.

'You want to leave already?'

'No, no, I mean for the walk next Saturday.'

'Oh, right.' I think about that for a moment. We did twenty miles yesterday, which, while not effortless, was certainly not massively strenuous. I did have some pain afterwards, mostly in my hip joints, but it wasn't severe and didn't impede my walking at all or prevent me from finishing. Looking back, I'm absolutely positive I could have walked for an hour and a half more to do another six miles at the end. I turn to her. No, wait, that's not her, that's a big chimney or brazier-type thing. I think. I look around blindly so I can turn to her, but it's hopeless. Doesn't matter.

I nod, but of course she can't see me either. 'Yes, I think I am. I mean, I know I am. I'm sure I could've done six more miles yesterday, so yeah. No worries. How about you?'

There's no answer. I wish I could see her expression but there's nothing but mist, swirling mist. Eventually there's a faint noise, like a strangled sob and a sniff, then a small cough.

'Abs? You OK?'

There's still no sound, but I get the distinct impression she's shaking her head.

'Are you shaking your head?'

Now I feel like she's nodding. But she could easily have been nodding the first time and shaking her head now. Oh, this is ridiculous. I stand up, put my hands out in front of me and step gingerly forward, towards the place where Abs was last seen.

'I'm here,' she says, but her voice is wet and nasal, as if she's got a streaming cold.

I make my way towards the voice and at last discover her in the mist, like a gorilla. I sit down next to her. A bit more like a gorilla. 'You all right?'

Now I'm nearer I can see that she is, in fact, shaking her head. 'Not really,' she says, confirming it. 'Oh Daze . . .'

She collapses into me, wrapping her arms round my back, and sobs onto my shoulder. In spite of the suffocating and relentless heat, I feel a chill start to uncoil in my belly. She must have guessed or found out about two-timing Tom. At least in this smothering steam she won't be able to see the look on my face when she tells me.

'What? What is it? What's going on?'

'Oh, God, Daisy, I don't know what to do. Everything's gone wrong, it's all terrible. It's Tom.'

I'm rubbing her back, which is not easy on damp sticky skin, and I can feel the hard bumps of her spine and her shoulder blades beneath the surface. She's so thin, poor thing. Probably hasn't been eating properly, or just burns it all off in nervous energy, with the stress of it all. Oh God, I wish more than anything I could take this away, make everything go back to how it was. 'I think I know, Abby,' I say quietly. 'He's having an affair, isn't he?'

She pulls back from me abruptly, holds me at arm's length, and looks as near to my eyes as she can find in the steam. 'No, Daisy,' she says, then drops her gaze and looks down at her lap. 'I am.'

It hits me like a slap. I stare at her, not able for a few seconds to absorb this new information.

'*You* are?'

She nods.

'Oh my God! Who with?'

404

She hesitates, then sighs. 'One of my clients. An idiot called Sean.'

'Oh my God! Have I heard of him? Do I know him? How long has it been going on?'

She's shaking her head, making the steam swirl around her like vapour from aeroplane wings. She doesn't want to answer, but I need to understand. 'Not all that long. Couple of months.'

'Oh my God! Not just a one-off then.'

She shakes her head no.

'Oh my God.'

'I know.'

'So . . . Tom?'

She shakes her head. 'Isn't. I'm absolutely sure of that.'

My mind starts buzzing. There are things I need to know, puzzles to solve, scenarios to think about and re-evaluate with this new factor. 'Well . . . Fuck. When? I mean, how long? How did you . . .? Christ. Does Tom . . .?' Thousands of questions flood my brain at once, all clamouring for answers, but there's one that shouts more loudly than the rest. 'Why didn't you tell me?'

She doesn't answer straight away. After a few seconds' pause, she says, very quietly, 'I didn't want you to think badly of me.'

'Why would I think badly of you? You're my best friend.'

She nods. 'I know, I know, but I couldn't bear the thought of you having a bad opinion of me. I couldn't bear to . . . disappoint you.'

'Did you think I would judge you, Abby? Seriously?'

'Yes. No. Oh, I don't know. I know you're not judgemental; you get that from your mum. But what I'm doing, what I've been doing . . . It's so terrible, how could you not hate me for it? *I* do.'

'Oh, Abby. Of course I don't hate you. I never will. You should know that.'

'Thank you, Daze.' She leans into me for a second, then meets my eye frankly. 'Now you know the worst thing about me. Is it OK?'

I'm reminded again of that old definition of love, and nod. 'Of course it is, Abs.' She breathes in deeply and releases it. 'So. Tell me. Why are you seeing someone else? Are things bad with Tom?'

'Oh God, I don't know, I don't even know, it's pathetic. Things aren't bad, exactly. Tom is . . . Well, you know what he's like. He's lovely. He's so lovely, Daisy. He rings me from work to see if I need anything while he's on his lunch. He sorts out the oil and the tyre pressure. He makes carbonara. Why would anyone do anything like this?'

I shake my head. 'I don't know. How can I know, if you don't? But there obviously is a reason, and I doubt it's all down to you.'

She looks at me sharply. 'What? How can you say that? I'm the one doing it, Daisy. I'm the one being unfaithful, cheating, betraying my boyfriend. Potentially hurting him. Devastating him, his life. How can it not be my fault?'

'Oh, Abby, I don't know. I don't understand. But I do know that no one person is ever to blame for a situation.' I pause and rub her arm. 'You told me that.'

406

She smiles weakly. 'OK, fair enough, I get that. But I still can't justify it, can I? So he's obsessively tidy, or mad about sport, or moans if I leave a single saucepan on the hob, so that makes it OK for me to sleep with someone else? I don't think so.'

'I'm not talking about those kinds of things. Housework and stuff. I mean the important things. I'm saying maybe he doesn't make you feel loved all the time. Or maybe he takes you for granted. Or . . . God, I have no idea. But if he'd been paying proper attention, he'd have noticed this. Except if he'd been paying proper attention, maybe you wouldn't have done it in the first place.'

'I don't know. Maybe. Oh God, I don't know.'

'Does he know?'

She shakes her head. 'God no.'

'You gonna tell him?'

She widens her eyes. 'Why would I do that?'

I shrug. 'I don't know. Because . . . I don't know. Depends what you want to happen, I suppose.'

'What do you mean?'

'Well, do you want to split from Tom? Do you want to be with the other bloke? Or do you want to stick and make a go of it with Tom?'

She's staring at me wide eyed. 'Split from Tom? No. I love Tom.'

'Well, I'm no expert but as far as I can see that means one of two things has to happen. You either tell him; or you don't.'

She blinks. 'That's it? That's your advice? Either tell him, or don't tell him?'

'I did say I wasn't an expert.'

'Terrific. That's incredible, Daisy. Thank you, thank you so much for helping me out of a terrible situation.'

'You're welcome.'

She shakes her head and plonks it down on my shoulder.

'Ow!'

'God, yeah, that really hurt. Boneyhead.'

We laugh, then hug. 'Oh God, Daisy, what am I going to do?'

It's rhetorical so I don't answer. I was only going to say 'I don't know' anyway.

After the steam room we sit and stare at each other in the sauna for a while. It's a hard, dry heat that judders off the wooden seats like a physical presence and makes us feel like we're going to implode.

'This is the most unrelaxing spa I've ever been to,' Abby says. 'I'm so tense.'

'I feel like I'm going to die.'

'Swim?'

'OK.'

Two-thirds of the pool are cordoned off for aqua-aerobics, so we're confined to a narrow strip down one side. We try resolutely ploughing up and down a couple of times but the water's so rough and choppy from the bodies jumping up and down in time to Olivia Newton-John, we keep getting washed into the side. I struggle back to the shallow end to find Abby waiting for me.

'Shall we go?' she shouts. I nod wearily and we head for the changing rooms.

'Thank you for that, Abs, it was lovely,' I say as we're getting dressed. 'Such a treat.'

She pauses in the towelling of her toes, raises her head and looks at me the way that teachers look at people who claim their dog ate their homework.

When we get back to the flat, we hear the television on in the living room as soon as we open the front door. We both freeze in the doorway, then Abby looks at me meaningfully.

'So you know what you said earlier about either buying the boots, or not buying the boots. Remember? You said either do it, or don't do it?'

I think wildly for a moment. Boots? *Boots?* I don't remember any . . . Ohhhhh. 'Mm-hmm.'

'Well. I was just thinking. I think I'm going to buy them.'

'Shit. Are you sure?'

She nods solemnly. 'Yeah. I think so. Because they're . . . well, they're perfect for me. And that other pair, that plastic pair . . . they looked nice but they were inferior quality. You know what I mean?'

'Um, I think so.'

'And really, something of quality may cost you a bit more initially, but then if it's quality it's more worth having. I mean, a good quality pair of boots can last you years, can't they?'

'I suppose so. Although I've never had a really decent pair. The best I've ever been able to get my hands on is those fake Uggs from the market. You know the ones that look like the genuine article, and you put them on and they feel perfect and you feel great in them, and you think you've got a bargain.' I'm getting into it now. 'But after only a couple of weeks, or a month or so, they start to come apart at the seams or sag over onto one side when you walk and let you down and then you realise you've been conned and all you've got is a fake imitation and you've spent all that time and money for something that you just need to throw in the bin.'

Abby's staring at me. 'Shut up, Daisy.'

She moves towards the living room door, gives me one last worried glance, bites her lip, then goes through it into Narnia. No, not Narnia. Narnia was quite nice in places. This is not so good. Maybe more like . . . Jurassic Park. After the dinosaurs have escaped. Only here the rampaging, bloodthirsty carnivores are cold and detached and more inclined to give you a stern frown than rip flesh from your bones.

I'm guessing there might well be a scene involving Tom being devastated shortly. While no windows will be blown out, plates smashed or doors splintered off their hinges, there is likely to be an uncomfortable atmosphere, so I decide to make myself scarce. I change into my magic trainers and hit the streets. Or more precisely, Felix's street, if I'm brutally honest. The sun is out, there's a soft breeze and I can hear music playing somewhere through an open window. It's 'Biology', by Girls Aloud, and I time my steps to the beat, swinging my arms and bouncing along energetically. It's at times like these that I wish I knew how to dance.

'What's up, Queen Duck?'

I start, and stop. I know that voice, and hearing it makes my heart beat faster and heat start to creep up my cheeks. It came from behind me somewhere but, when I turn, I don't see him. I glance quickly from left to right and back again, feeling more and more foolish, but he's nowhere to be seen. Oh God. Did I imagine it?

'Up here, Dozy.'

Too late I realise there's a ladder leaning against the wall of the house nearest to me. And by 'too late' I mean I spot it long after any opportunity to appear cool and seductive has passed. When I see it, I instantly realise that he has been observing me from above while I repeat-edly, and probably frantically, scanned the landscape for any sign of him, swivelling one-eighty degrees back and forth like a wind-up ballerina, culminating with a gasp of frustration and putting both hands on my head. I drop them to my sides quickly, but I fear the damage may already have been done.

'Oh hi, Felix.' I flick my eyes towards the ladder. 'I hope you have a permit to put that ladder there?'

He grins at me and starts to come down. 'OK, lady, I've got all the necessary paperwork. Just give me a minute.'

As he backs down the ladder, I do everything I can not to stare up adoringly at his large shape, but fail. He jumps the last two rungs and lands in front of me.

'How are you doing?' he says. 'You look . . . lovely.'

I touch the place where my hair used to be and find a hideous frizzy sauna-induced bird's nest. Lovely.

'Thanks, but I know you're lying. No doubt you're lying about that ladder permit too.'

He smiles. 'Ah, you got me. You probably need to issue me with some kind of fine now.'

I wave my hand über-casually and shrug. 'I could probably waive it.'

'You could? Hmm, not what I was expecting from you, Miss Senior Ladder Inspectorate lady. You've gone soft. What's changed?'

I shake my head. 'Ah nothing, no, I'm the same, see, I'm still the Head Ladder Inspector person.' It's very strange how finding out someone's suffered a devastating bereavement suddenly makes any conversation or interaction with them very difficult. I try to smile but the difficulty apparently extends to non-verbal communication and my lips move outwards in an awkward spreading motion. Felix's eyebrows flicker together for a nanosecond as he smiles at me, as if he experienced a fleeting terror. I know I need to bring the subject up, acknowledge that I know about it, express my sympathy, be normal about it; but what is normal, when you're talking about the sudden non-existence of someone you love? It's unthinkable.

I think back to how my friends reacted to me when they heard about Mum. Number one in the charts tended to be 'Oh, I'm really sorry', followed by 'the look' (brows up and together, head on one side); then loss of eye contact; and finally a hasty retreat out of there. Also very popular was 'Was she ill for long?' which always seemed irrelevant to me, although it did affect how they reacted subsequently. 'No, she was killed under a tree' usually shocks people into terrible silence. The sudden, unexpected cutting off of a life is

412

so horrifying that there is absolutely nothing to say after that. Of course, that wasn't my reply. I had to say, 'Yes, ill for years, breast cancer, second time round, spread this time, been in hospital for months', or anything from that selection. And the effect on the faces and voices of the listeners was immediate. They relaxed, they nodded, there was a definite appearance of relief there, and they became much more comfortable with the whole situation. 'Years, you say? Oh, well, that's all right then.' Well, they didn't say, that's all right, but you could still hear it. And I wanted to scream, 'How is it all right? Her end was drawn out, her suffering was gigantic, her agony was enduring. Her death was not a relief.'

Felix is still looking at me. OK, I've got to say something. I arrange my features to make absolutely sure I'm not doing 'the look', then put my hand on his arm. 'Abby told me about your wife. Felix, I was gutted to hear it. I'm so sorry. But at the same time, I'm massively impressed.'

He looks startled to begin with and flinches a little. From his expression, I'm not sure that he's all together happy with Abby for telling me his most private and painful secret. If he'd wanted me to know, of course, he would have told me himself. And frankly, should have done, right after I told him about Mum. But then he visibly relaxes when I don't do 'the look' and one side of his mouth turns up.

'Impressed? That my wife has died? That's a bit creepy.'

'No, no, God, no, sorry, I didn't mean . . .' Stop. Deep breath. Start again. 'I'm not impressed by that. Although,

413

I suppose yes, in a way I am. I mean, it certainly left an impression on me. But no, what I'm trying – not very well – to say is, I'm impressed with you. How happy you are, in spite of this horrific tragedy happening to you. I'm . . . in awe of you, Felix. How do you do that?'

He takes a step closer to me, and my belly starts to churn like the frenzied water in the spa earlier. He looks at my face for a long time then blinks rapidly and jerks his head. 'It's . . .' He looks down. 'Every day is like . . . It's like a battle of wills. I have to decide, every day, that I won't be crushed by it. I . . . *will* myself to keep moving and not curl up in the dark somewhere on my own and let myself be sucked down to the depths. I make my head focus on things, good things, like the sunshine, or cake, or other people. As long as I'm thinking about something, as long as I'm busy, then I . . . get by.'

I stare at him until my eyeballs dry out.

'Oh, God,' he says, breaking out into a grin and putting his palms out towards me, shaking his head. 'You look . . .' He moves his hands briefly towards my arms, as if to touch me, then drops them. 'Shit.' He rubs the back of his head distractedly. 'No, it's not really like that any more. I mean, I'm a lot better. Honestly. I'm sorry, I didn't mean to . . .'

My eyes have lost all power to revolve away.

'I'm . . . *really* sorry, Daisy.' He takes a couple of deep breaths and inches still nearer to me. 'It's awkward enough trying to talk to someone about their bereavement, and I just carved three more notches on the awkward stick.'

There's a brief silence. 'You . . . have an awkward stick?'

He huffs out a laugh. 'I do.'

'Can I see it?'

He shakes his head solemnly. 'I don't carry it round with me any more. Too . . . awkward.'

'Of course.' He smiles at me and I'm pinned to the spot. 'Felix, I really didn't mean to intrude . . .'

'No, no, you didn't. I'm serious. In fact it's better – for me anyway – if people actually acknowledge that it's happened. Don't you find that? It's hard, but not talking about it doesn't make it easier. Even my family avoid the subject completely and act as if I've never even been married. Or that no one has. In fact women in general don't exist. They get all uncomfortable if ever they accidentally refer to their own wife in a disparaging way. They cut themselves off mid-moan, bite their lips and look as if they want to apologise for even daring to be annoyed that she forgot to Sky Plus *House*, or whatever.' He shakes his head. 'How on earth could their little spat have any bearing on what happened to Louise and me . . .?' He breaks off and blinks rapidly, then jerks his head. 'Oh, Daisy, God, I'm sorry, I don't usually . . .'

'No, I know what you mean. Just after Mum died, just about everyone that knew about it stopped referring to their own mums. I mean, ever. A few of them were still living with their parents, but where they used to complain about the restrictions that puts on your social life, they just stopped. Never spoke about their mums at all. I found it kind of . . . offensive. Insulting, even.' I

415

consider that a second. Yes, that's it. 'Mm, insulting. Can't explain why.'

He's nodding too. 'You're right. It's as if they think you're going to have a complete mental breakdown right there in front of them if they so much as mention their own wife. Or mum.'

'Or that they're reminding you, by bringing mums – or wives – into the conversation. Like, I don't know, maybe you'd forgotten that she was dead, and then they say the thing, whatever, which reminds you of your loss and makes you start feeling sad again.'

He nods, smiling. 'So. You lost your mum. When?'

'November.'

'That's not very long.'

'No. Six months.'

'I'm sorry, Daisy. I didn't really get the chance to talk to you about it the other day. It's very tough, losing a parent. How are you doing?'

'I think . . . I'm over the worst.'

He nods. 'The first year is the hardest, I think.' He reaches out a hand and gently touches my cheek. 'You know, I always thought there was something a little bit sad about you.' His fingers on my cheek feel like they're made of white hot metal and blaze a burning trail across my skin. 'A little bit sad.' I feel his breath on my face. 'And very, very special.' He pushes his hand into my hair and round the back of my head, gently pulling me towards him. 'Daisy, I think . . . I think that . . . you . . .'

'You do?' I breathe, moving closer to him until our bodies are touching. His other hand creeps around my waist and seals us together, then he bends his head down and, not grabbing and shoving tongues in all over the place, but very gently and tenderly, he kisses me. And finally I know for sure: movie love really does exist.

TWENTY-THREE

Abby Marcus
Picture the builder who pointed a blow torch at a pressurized can of insulating foam to see what would happen, and then multiply by one million. That's how stupid I am.
    Wendy Harber   What you bin up to Abs? xx
    Suzanne Allen   Everything ok???
    Tracey Owen   Lol, surely you're not quite *that* stupid?!

Minutes later I'm sprinting away from him. Stretching my legs, pumping my arms, expanding my lungs, running like the devil is behind me; not a charming, funny, kind and sensitive man. Running is not something I'm good at, but I am definitely a lot fitter than I used to be and it's a good thirty or even forty seconds before I have to stop, bend over and gasp hoarsely with my hands on my knees. Felix cannot see this, fortunately. Actually, no, it's not fortunate at all. It is precise and careful planning. I walked serenely away from him just now, after nonchalantly agreeing to have dinner with him in one hour, while he walked away from me in the opposite direction.

Then as soon as he couldn't see me any more, I legged it like I was being chased by demons. For forty whole seconds.

Doesn't matter, I'm nearly back at the flat now, and I can walk very fast the rest of the way. I need to be back at Felix's in about fifty-five minutes, which will give me time for a lightning shower and panicked change of clothes. As I walk, I plan what to wear, but my mental clothes rail is pretty empty, mostly because all my clothes are littered around the room in untidy heaps, and I don't have much anyway. I meant to do my ironing a few nights ago, on my last night off work, that was the plan, but I didn't do it, oh God, why didn't I? (Oh, yes, I wanted to watch that thing about the woman who was pregnant for forty-five years. Most disappointing that she didn't then give birth to a slightly overweight, balding accountant.) So I now have twenty minutes to find something, iron it, change into it, and transform myself into an irresistible siren. I picture my dirty, sweaty tracksuit and steam-frizzed hair. I might just do it.

The front door ricochets off the wall behind it as I slam into the flat and I fling it quickly shut behind me with a bang. Immediately I notice the preternatural quietness blanketing the entire flat, which stills me where I stand. Too late, I remember that I'm making myself scarce while two-timing Tom – oops, gotta stop calling him that – knocks a lamp over in his distress at being told the bad news by Abby. I creep up to the living room door and listen for a few moments but there's no sound of sobbing or a magazine being put down in anguish, so I push it open.

419

Abby's there, on the edge of the sofa, her hands clasped together against her forehead, head bowed, elbows on her knees. It's a human sculpture of misery and my heart contracts at the sight.

'Abs?' I walk over and sit down next to her.

She looks round at me. 'He's gone, Daze. He's left me.'

'Oh, Abby . . .'

'I told him about . . . everything, and he just stared at the floor the whole time, not moving. Like he was . . . I don't know . . .'

'A marble statue?'

'Hm? Yeah, yeah, I suppose. He went so pale, like, in shock, which, you know, he probably was of course, then he looked at me, stared at me for a second, and left.'

'He didn't say anything at all?'

She doesn't respond for a few moments, only holds her head with both hands as if shielding it from the danger of a world without Tom. Then she frowns fleetingly and blinks.

'No, no, he did say something. He said . . .' She chews her lip, and looks suddenly very distressed. 'He said . . . "Thank God." Or something. As if . . .' She looks right at me, stricken. 'As if he was . . . *glad*.'

I take hold of one of her hands and rub it gently. 'He's not glad, Abs. Of course he's not.'

'How do you know?'

'Because I know you. I . . . kind of know him. A bit. He adores you, and rightly so. Who wouldn't? There's absolutely no way anybody would be glad about this.'

She shakes her head worriedly. 'I don't know . . .'

420

'Abby. Believe me. That man is devastated beyond reason and has probably gone somewhere to contemplate death.'

She looks up at me. 'Do you really think so?'

'Undoubtedly.'

She smiles weakly and sniffs. 'Thanks, Daze.'

'I didn't do anything, softhead. But don't give up on him. He'll think about it, probably with a beer or two, then he'll grasp what he'd be losing and realise that it's not worth it.'

She nods sadly. 'At least I've been honest with him. Now. I gave him that much.'

'Absolutely.' I risk a furtive glance at my watch. It's getting dangerously close to the time I need to leave. My transformation will be breath-taking, exquisite, stunning, and will need at least fifteen minutes. I stand up and walk to the door, then turn back and look at Abby as a tear rolls slowly down her cheek. Nah, I can transform in five minutes. Easy. 'Come on,' I say, going back and putting the telly on, 'let's watch *About a Boy*.'

'You hate that film.'

'No I do not, what are you talking about? Now budge over.'

She's right, I do hate it. Hugh is not a hero in that film. He's selfish and thoughtless and lazy. All the things I hate.

Thirty minutes later, I leave Abby dozing on the sofa and creep to my room to scrabble around for an irresistible siren costume. For the second time this year I've forgotten to invest in siren clothes. My wardrobe is short of exactly one sexy black dress and a make-up professional. I plump for skinny jeans and my best black tee shirt (the one that's still the blackest), coupled with some smoky purple eye shadow, a hint of mascara and some pink lip-gloss. There's no time now to shampoo, treat, dry, style and straighten my hair, so I smooth the front down as best I can and pull the rest up into a knot at the back. My hands are shaking so much most of the hair is back to a frizzy ball by the time I've finished fiddling with it, but there's no more time.

Only twenty minutes later than I planned, I'm tiptoeing silently across the hallway the best I can with every muscle shaking and my stomach twisting and churning in knots.

'Can you make a bit more noise please?' Abby says, coming suddenly into the hallway. 'I'm still half asleep.'

'I was being quiet!'

'No you were not, Queen Elephant. I thought the house was falling down!' She stops and stares at me. 'Where are you off to? What's that on your . . . Holy hand cream, it isn't . . . are you wearing . . . *make-up?*' She sounds like a dad speaking to his teenage son. 'You can't go out wearing that. Come with me.' She grabs my hand and leads me into her and Tom's room, where she sits me on the bed and flings open the wardrobe. She inserts one hand into the clothes there, then turns to me. 'OK, so where are you going and what do you want to happen there?'

I roll my eyes. 'Abs . . .'

'I'm serious. The outcome you want is dependent on what you wear. Where are you going?'

So I tell her about Felix and the dinner, determinedly continuing over her squeals of excitement, but I leave out the part about what I want to happen there. I would tell her if I knew the answer.

'Right,' she says, rubbing her hands together. 'You need fresh, chic and feminine. Let's see what we've got.' And she plunges her hands in.

I sit on the bed and watch, and while she's umm-ing and ahh-ing I'm brought back to a time not too long ago when I was rummaging through her wardrobe without her knowledge. Shame burns my face from the inside out.

'Abs,' I say quietly. 'I have a confession to make.'

She turns with one hand still on something tiny and transparent. 'Mm-hm?'

'I found your cigarettes.'

Her eyes flick automatically to the floor under the bed. 'Ah.'

I nod. 'I'm so sorry. I thought you were smoking, I recognised the signs. The breath mints, the sneaking out after meals. It reminded me of Graham. So I came in here a couple of weeks ago and had a root around.' I hang my head. 'I'm really sorry.'

'Oh.' She looks away. 'Well, I guess you were proved right, weren't you?'

'Yeah, but so what? What does it matter if you're smoking? It's none of my business what you do. If you want to smoke, you go right ahead, do it openly, you don't have to hide it. It's not as if it's illegal or something.'

'But, Daze,' she says, taking her hands out of the

423

wardrobe and turning to me properly, 'how could I do that, knowing about Graham, and your mum? It's so monumentally insensitive. They lost their lives and I'm blithely playing Russian roulette with mine. It's appalling.'

'Oh my God. Is that why you were doing it secretly?'

She nods without looking at me.

'I thought you were hiding it from Tom. Not me.'

'Why would Tom care if I was smoking?'

I shrug. 'I suppose I thought it was to do with the . . . affair. I mean, when I thought he was having one. You'd found out about it and were dealing with the stress by smoking. You know what, Abby, I don't even know what I thought. I wasn't thinking about it at all really. Only that I wanted to find out one way or another. Maybe it's got something to do with Graham, letting my mum down when he started again. I don't know.'

She smiles. 'Well, you're right about the stress. Keeping it quiet from you has been terrible!'

Eventually she comes up with a pretty little flowery skirt and matching powder blue top, then quickly and expertly restyles my hair with steady hands. When I check the mirror, I look fresh and chic and feminine, completely different to my usual straggly, butch, track-suited self. I look like a proper woman. I look like I used to look.

'You look gorgeous,' Abby says, smiling at me in the mirror.

'I know, right?!'

'Oh shut up!'

We go to the hallway together. 'Abs,' I say, turning by the door, 'are you going to be OK?'

'I think I'll cope without you for a couple of hours, Daze. Just don't make it any longer than that, I'll be a wreck.'

'I'm talking about—'

'I know what you're talking about, dunderhead. I'll be fine. I'm going to watch the rest of that film and go to bed.'

'Are you sure?'

She looks at me earnestly, thinking about it. 'Actually, no, I'm not really.'

'Well, look, it's fine, I'll stay . . .'

'I might watch *Mickey Blue Eyes* instead.'

I stare at her. 'No.'

'Yes,' she says laughing. She takes my arm and propels me towards the door. 'So you'd better leave before you accidentally see some of it.'

Mickey Blue Eyes is a travesty of a Hugh film. Poor concept, no plot, bad dialogue. Mediocre acting. Yes, even Hugh. Although he does better than most in it. I've only been able to watch it seven times.

'Well if you're absolutely sure . . .'

'Just go, you dolt.'

By the time I get to Felix's I'm shaking so much, I'm practically a blur. Felix probably thinks I'm standing behind opaque glass. He stares at me a while when he opens the door, as if trying to get his eyes to focus properly.

'Wow,' he says eventually. 'You look absolutely . . . different.'

I blink. 'Absolutely different?'

He's shaking his head as he invites me inside. 'No, no, that's not . . . Oh God, sorry. I was a bit – *am* a

425

bit . . .' He stops talking at last and watches me as I walk past him into the hallway. 'I'm just . . . glad you're here.'

'Me too.'

I don't know how I could ever have thought of him as rude and irritating. He's wonderful company, and the meal is superb. He claims to have cooked it all himself, but I have a sneaking suspicion there might be some empty Marks & Spencer's cartons hiding at the bottom of the bin in the kitchen. But I don't care because it is delicious, and he is increasingly lovely. As we eat I focus hard on not thinking about the little shark tooth lying in the hollow of this throat, which is pretty much the only thing I can see at this proximity. He's across the table from me, and we're both leaning over our plates, so the damn thing is practically bashing me on the nose. When I look up at him and see it there, the little island of caramel skin and the pulse beating away below, I have to quickly look down at my food again, or over at the other end of the room, or at my hands, or at anything that's not his throat.

'Everything all right?' he says, noticing me trying not to look at it.

'Oh God yes.'

He tells me all about his time working with the sharks in South Africa – how incredible the great whites are as hunters, the power of their sense of smell, their solitary lifestyle.

'Killer whales are classed as the top predator in the world,' he says intensely, 'but they hunt in groups. Great whites hunt alone, which is so much more skilful.' By

426

the time he's cleared away the dessert plates (home-made chocolate orange mousse) and topped up my wine glass for the third time, I've got a real hankering to leave everything and go to South Africa to work with sharks for three months.

At the end of the evening he insists on walking me back to Abby's, even though it's only five minutes' walk. But when we get there, I'm disappointed. I wanted it to go on longer.

'Well that was the shortest walk we've ever done together,' he says by Abby's door.

'Yes. It was short.'

'Yes it was.' He moves closer. 'But no less enjoyable.'

I giggle nervously feeling sixteen again, then he leans in and surrounds me with his warmth and his smell and, hesitating only briefly, kisses me lightly on the lips. 'Thanks for a lovely evening, Daisy.'

'Oh, you're more than welcome. I mean, thank you, too. It was wonderful.'

He takes a small step away but gently touches my face. 'So are we walking this week?'

'Well, I will be. I think I have to. But not very long ones. No more than three miles a day. Will you be . . .?'

'Yes I will. Um, that is, if you want me, of course?'

I reach up and take hold of his hand, then press the palm to my lips. 'I do. Most definitely.'

Inside the flat, it's still quiet, but better somehow. It's a more wholesome silence, softer; unlike the brittle, splintery silence from before. The television is still on so I go straight into the living room and find Abby lying on the sofa eating Doritos.

'Daze!' she says immediately, looking up at me with a smile. 'How was your evening? Did you . . . you know?'

'No I don't know and no we didn't. How could you even think that?'

She shrugs and reaches into the Doritos bag. ''Cause he's stupidly sexy and one hundred percent into you.'

A flame of pleasure ignites inside me and quickly takes hold of my insides. 'Did he say that? When did you speak to him? What were his exact words?' I sit down next to her and shove my hand into the bag.

She grins. 'Not telling you. It's nothing to do with me anyway.' She punches me lightly on the arm. 'I knew you two would be good together. I bloody knew it, and I was right.'

'Oh come on, Abs, you can't tell me something like that and then not tell me what he said. It's not fair.'

She flaps a hand. 'Tough luck, Queen Duck. Ha ha!' She gazes at me fondly. 'I bloody knew you would be good for him.'

'What? You . . . Hang on. You thought *I* would be good for *him*? I thought it was the other way round.'

She pushes her lips out. 'Hmm. Well, yes, I suppose it does work both ways. And yes, it's true, I am excellent at picking a good man.' She turns her head slightly so that she can regard me sideways through narrowed eyes.

I raise my eyebrows. 'And to which good man in particular are you referring, Madame?'

She smiles. 'Do I need to tell you? I know your head is all full of our Mr Happy right now, but there is only one other good man who is relevant here.'

'Tom, you mean?'

'Yes, Tom I mean, of course Tom I mean. Who else would I mean?'

'Well, there was another man in your life recently . . .'

'Ugh, please don't bring that up. That idiot doesn't class as a good man.'

I frown. 'Then why did you . . .?'

She stops me by putting a hand up. 'Daze, I really don't want to think about it right now. I have no idea why I did what I did, other than that the guy looked a bit like Jake Gyllenhaal . . .'

'Seriously?'

'Only a bit. But turns out there was nothing else to him.' She shrugs. 'Not my finest moment.'

I regard her a few moments. 'Abby, I'm so, so sorry.'

'What now? Why?'

'I've been a terrible friend to you recently. You've been going through your own personal hell and I've been so selfish, only thinking about my own problems . . .'

'Oh God not this again.' She turns to face me full on. 'Daisy May Macintyre will you please, please, for the love of lingerie take off that hideous hair shirt. I won't put up with this. You're a great friend, and if you weren't then a great friend like me would not put up with you.'

'You just said you won't put up with me . . .'

'Shut up.'

'OK.'

'You must be a decent person because you have decent friends. Well, friend. Me. Decent people have decent friends because if they weren't decent people then other decent people would not hang out with them.' She frowns. 'Well, maybe they would, actually, because they're so decent.' She squints at me. 'Anyway, I don't call what you've been going through selfish. You've been grieving. And no one should ever, *ever*, feel bad about that. Including you.'

'OK, I know. But I just think that –'

'Nope.' She puts her hands over her ears and raises the volume of her own voice by a couple of decibels. 'Not listening. It's moot now anyway because I'm not going through my own personal hell, so you have nothing to worry about.'

'You're not? How come?'

She keeps her hands over her ears. 'Promise you're not going to self-flagellate again?'

'Bloody hell, Abs! No way!'

She lowers her hands. 'You do know what self-flagellation is?'

'Well, yeah, course I do.'

She squints at me again. 'Hmm. Well, OK then.' She grins and shifts a bit nearer to me. 'Tom came back about half an hour after you left. We've had a really good chat. And guess what, Daze? He knew.'

'Knew what?'

She rolls her eyes. 'That the Piltdown Man was a hoax, you dimwit. I mean about me. What I was doing. He knew the whole time.'

'Fuck!'

'I know!'

I frown. 'Hold on. Knew the whole time? And didn't say anything? Just let it – *you* – carry on. While he was still living here?'

430

She nods solemnly. 'Yeah, I know. It really had an effect on him, I can't believe I didn't spot it.'

'What effect?'

'Oh come on, don't tell me you didn't notice how quiet and moody he's been all this time?'

I blink. 'Moody? You mean, he's not . . .?'

'Not what?'

I hesitate. Ah. This is a bit tricky. How to ask your best friend if her boyfriend really isn't a silent monument to monotony after all? I shrug. 'Well . . .'

She stares at me uncomprehending a moment, then her eyes widen dramatically. 'What, you think he's really like that? Bloody hell, Daze, of course he isn't!' She stares at me incredulously, then jams her hand into her pocket and brings out her phone. 'Look at these,' she says, head bent over the screen as she selects the 'Photos' icon. After some scrolling she thrusts the phone in front of my face and I focus on the tiny images. The first one shows a man dancing in what looks like a giant orange wig, a tartan kilt and a huge plastic red nose; next is what could be the same guy running a marathon dressed as a hot dog; the man pulling a goofy face at the camera; grinning with his arm round Abby; slow dancing with someone, looks like Abby; sitting astride a motorcycle, helmet under his arm. I scroll quickly down and find more and more photos of what is now obviously Tom – animated, grinning, full of joy and having fun. To me, it looks like some alien life force is inhabiting the cold, marble monolith that used to be Tom. Or maybe the cold alien life that was there is now gone. I know as well as anyone how misery can make you withdraw from life, from having fun.

I look up at Abby, who's nodding away to herself. 'That's the real Tom,' she says quietly. 'That's the man I'm in love with.'

My eyes fall on a picture of him crossing his eyes and sticking out his tongue. 'I can see why.'

She takes the phone back from me, gazes at the home screen for a second, then flaps a hand. 'Well anyway. Apparently some colleague of his came round here a few weeks ago and told him all about it. Saw me with Sean somewhere, apparently. Couldn't wait to shoot straight round here and fill him in.'

The conversation between Tom and the unknown – slightly older – woman in the kitchen weeks ago comes into my head now, and I try to examine it a little more closely now that I know what was going on. But it's a blurry image, more like a half-remembered dream than a clear memory, and I can't seem to get it straight. A little heat comes into my face as I realise that I paid almost no attention to it, even though it should have been obvious that it was highly significant in my friend's life. I frown a little. 'Unbelievable. Why would anyone do that?'

Abby shrugs. 'Don't know. Strong moral code? Overwhelming sense of right and wrong? Interfering busy-body? Ha, maybe she fancied the pants off Tom?'

I smile as that seems to be what she's expecting, but I'm not feeling it. 'Yeah, probably.'

'Whatever. Doesn't matter. Because she solved a big problem for me. I didn't have to tell him myself. Or rather, when I did tell him, it wasn't a massive shock. In fact, it was a massive relief! That's why he said "Thank God" or something.'

'A relief? Why would your girlfriend cheating on you be a relief?'

She shakes her head as she smiles at me, and in that moment she looks exactly like Snow White smiling at Dopey. 'He wasn't relieved I was cheating on him, Daze. He was relieved I'd told him.'

I shake my head with a frown. 'I'm still not sure . . .'

'Don't you get it? If I hadn't told him, it would have meant that it was still going on. Or that I'd chosen the other guy. Or that I didn't really care about Tom or our relationship. For him, me telling him was confirmation that I choose him, not the other guy. That I still want him. Still love him.' She's grinning broadly now and has a gorgeous flush on her flawless cheeks.

'Oh . . . I think I do get it. That's wonderful, Abs. I'm really pleased for you. So. Where is he now?'

'Just popped out to the offie to get some wine. Champagne, actually.'

'Ooh, champagne. Lovely.'

She nods and pulls her hand out from the Doritos bag. 'We're celebrating. We'd love you to join us.'

'Of course I will. Celebrating your reunion?'

'A bit more than that, Daisy Duck.' She reaches out her left hand towards me, hovering it in front of my face and I look down and see a great big beautiful diamond sparkling on her third finger. My breath catches in my throat as I look back up at her to see she has tears in her eyes. 'We're getting married.'

TWENTY-FOUR

Daisy Mack

Feels like walking 26 miles. And to give myself a challenge, I'm doing it virtually naked. Starting at midnight. Debating whether or not to tie my feet together, but that's probably ridiculous.

 18 people like this

Abby Marcus Hmm, that sounds fun. Mind if I join you?

Daisy Mack I'd be honoured, milady.

Jenny Martin Best of luck ladies. Thinking of you in your madness! Xx

Nat 'Wiggy' Nicholson Are you INSANE???!!!!!

Suzanne Allen So proud of you both. I know you can do it. You know you can do it. All you have to do is do it! Good luck xxx

Georgia Ling amayyyziin. Best of luck u 2 xxxx

So here we are on the train to London to walk a marathon by the light of the moon. All around us, the train compartment is dotted with other ladies in walking gear

434

and the distinctive pink caps that we've all been sent by the organisers to identify us at the start line. We don't need to wear them yet, but we've all donned them anyway, probably as the sense of shared adventure takes over. It's like the Fellowship of the Hats in here.

Abby and I are tense. We're sitting opposite each other, silent by the window, with an impractical little table between us holding our enormous bum bags. I mean, of course, enormous bags. Not enormous bums. Rucksacks are a no-no, apparently, because of the chafing, so instead we've brought rucksack-sized bum bags, to hold all the food, Vaseline, safety pins, spare socks, sun cream, plasters, blister dressings, gloves, money, train tickets, admission paperwork, mobile phones and sunglasses. We're worried we've forgotten something. We're worried we'll get a blister. We're worried we'll need the loo and be miles from a toilet. We're worried we'll get to twenty-two miles and won't be able to continue.

But that's not why we're tense.

'I can't believe it,' Abby says quietly, leaning forward towards me as she glances furtively around the compartment. 'There's only seven hours to go. We've actually done it.'

I shake my head urgently. 'Shut up, Abby. You've jinxed it now. Just keep quiet and with luck we'll get to midnight. Then we can relax.'

'Yes, you're right. Sorry.'

We're not tense about the hugely demanding mental and physical challenge ahead, and the immense battering our bodies and particularly feet and hips are going to

435

take, or the pain we're going to endure. We're tense because we've got through almost two months of preparation for a MoonWalk, and so far no one – *no one* – has made a joke about Michael Jackson. Not one. Not a single comment about grabbing our crotches; walking backwards; wearing one white glove; looking out for zombies and werewolves or squealing 'Ooh-hooo' as we walk. Nothing. Every time we've told someone what we were training for, we've looked at each other, waiting for the inevitable, waiting to cringe, but it hasn't come. Now, it has become sacred. No one must do it now, after fifty days of training, with only six and a half hours left until the start. We absolutely *must not* hear it now. It will feel like a spell being broken and we will be doomed. Well, maybe not doomed. But pretty disappointed. We glance around the compartment repeatedly, checking to see if anyone is approaching to ask us why all these women are wearing matching hats, but no one is moving. It will be disaster if we have to say the word 'MoonWalk' to one more person.

Abby picks up her bum bag and unzips it. Then zips it up again. Unzips it. Zips it. Unzips. Zips.

'Stop it!' I whisper harshly, putting my hand on it. 'You're drawing attention.'

'Sorry.'

Eventually after ninety-five anxious minutes it's our stop and everyone in a pink hat disembarks in a wave, like strawberry bon-bons spilling out of a bag. As I reach the doors I notice one pink hat not moving on the other side of the compartment. She must be asleep! Quickly I move against the flow to where she's sitting with her back to me and gently nudge her shoulder. 'This is it,' I say, 'we're all getting off.'

She turns immediately – ah, not asleep then – and I see that her hat says 'Universal Studios' in embossed lettering on the front. Bugger.

'What?' she says. 'What are you talking about?'

'Nothing,' I say, retreating. 'Sorry, my mistake.'

'What's going on?' she asks, turning properly to face me. 'Why is everyone wearing these hats?'

'Sorry, gotta go!' I call, backing towards the doors as fast as I can.

'It's a MoonWalk,' I hear a voice say as I reach the opening. I dive onto the platform and walk briskly away from the train just as the woman's voice starts to say, 'A MoonWalk . . .?'

'Abby!' I shout out loudly, to prevent myself from hearing any more.

'Yes?' says a voice in my left ear. 'I'm right here, dolt. No need to scream.'

We are swept along the platform in a pink tidal wave, our feet barely touching the ground, down a set of steps to the underground. Pink tributaries join the main flow at every junction, coming in from every train from every different part of the country, until there is a giant pink flood moving slowly towards the tube. I am starting to get a feel of the enormity of this event. We nod and smile at our fellow walkers, feeling safe in their numbers, united by a dread of unimaginative and obvious gags.

When the train arrives, it too is full of pink. So many people have chosen pink tracksuit tops and pink gloves and pink hair, the whole train looks like confectionery.

'I think we'll be all right,' Abby says again as we are squeezed, like fat cells into spandex, onto the train.

'Shut up,' I growl, and jerk my head at a denim jacket and an anorak looking decidedly out of place at the far end. They are glancing at the pink cloud that's arrived and chatting to each other, no doubt wondering what's going on, why is everyone wearing pink, have they missed something? A few pink hats are standing within talking distance of the denim. They could easily overhear the conversation and decide to enlighten them. Or denim could ask them outright. They will say it's a MoonWalk. It will be carnage.

'Look away,' Abby advises. 'Focus on something else. Listen to a different conversation going on.'

She's right. I turn away and occupy myself successfully with a discussion about toilets – frequency of, distance between, queuing for – that is going on to my left.

When we reach Hyde Park Corner we burst out of the train like pink toothpaste and get squirted along the platform and up the steps. Up on the street, it is a pink deluge. Pink is pouring out of every street and every tube station in every direction. Nothing but pink as far as we can see, all moving towards Hyde Park like pink lava. Now and then we catch a glimpse of a dark suit with a briefcase, trapped in the flow, panicked and struggling, but they are swept away pretty quickly.

'Wow,' I hear Abby say as we look around us at the phenomenal numbers.

'Yeah.' I feel suddenly very special and thrilled to be

a part of this magnificent effort, and inexplicably tears come into my eyes. All these women, all these people, united in the fight against breast cancer; all working together and putting in this fantastic effort to try to help save lives and stop suffering. 'For you, Mum,' I whisper. 'This is all for you.'

When we reach Hyde Park we have to pin our walker numbers to our clothing somewhere as without it we won't be allowed past the security and into the Big Pink Tent. This must be to stop all the thousands of people from breaking in who want to walk twenty-six miles in their bras tonight just for fun. We've read all about this in the literature, and I can't wait to get there.

'What do you think it looks like?' I ask Abby excitedly. 'The Big Pink Tent?'

She looks up from where she's struggling with a safety pin and regards me silently for a few seconds. 'I think the clue's in the name, Daze,' she says. 'Ow! Moses on a moped. Can you help me with this, please?'

Ten minutes later we're queuing up to get into the Big Pink Tent. It wasn't difficult to find. Firstly, there's a swarm of pink flowing constantly towards it; and secondly, it's a fuck-off mahoosive tent in the middle of Hyde Park. And it's pink. By now it's almost eight o'clock and the sun is just about gone. It's not cold – yet – but there is a slight chill in the air. We're still wearing tee shirts and hoodies, and I have no idea how I'm going to cope in just a bra at two a.m. I presume we'll be walking quite briskly and will keep warm that way.

'Can I borrow your phone a minute?' Abby asks as

we finally get inside the tent. I was hoping that with this many people here, it would be steamy and hot inside and get us all warmed up before we launch our woefully underclad selves on the chilly night air in four hours. But it isn't. The thing is like an aircraft hangar inside, with what looks like a few dozen underwear-clad people milling around on the floor.

'Course.' I rummage my phone out of my giant bum bag and hand it to her. 'Why?'

'Just wanna text Tom, make sure he's on his way.'

Of course he's on his way. In fact he was probably on the same train as us. Or the one before us. He's probably invested in a pink hat from somewhere to help him blend in. Since they got engaged he hasn't wanted to be any more than five feet away from her. And that sounds creepy, like he doesn't trust her or wants to keep an eye on her or has suddenly got massively possessive and insecure. And to be honest, under the circumstances, who could blame him? But it's not like that, not at all. It's like he feels he's been graciously granted a second chance. And now all he wants to do is make sure Abby has got everything she needs to be happy. Which is, basically, just Tom himself.

She grins as she's typing the text, her eyes sparkling with delight. Something naughty in that one, by the looks of things. I take the opportunity to check out my surroundings.

The Big Pink Tent is divided up into regions, depending on how long you anticipated you would take to complete the walk when you registered. There's a pink area, an orange area, a green area and a yellow area. Abby told me that she'd put down seven to eight hours as our time, so that puts us firmly in the pink group, which is far and away the largest. The serious athletes in here all have green or yellow walker numbers, and they will be the groups that leave first. They're planning to take between five and six hours to get round. Our walker numbers are pink, and we will be leaving bang on midnight, with the pink herd. Having not noticed the benefit of any shared bodily warmth in this cavernous tent, I'm losing hope that all the thousands of walkers that will start with us will help keep me warm either. I'm starting to wish I'd brought a hot water bottle. Or a sleeping bag. Mmm.

'Here you go,' Abby says, handing me my phone. 'He's nearly here already, silly fool. I'll text him again later, if you don't mind.'

'No probs.' I tuck my phone away. 'Why don't you ever text from your own phone?'

'I do!'

I shake my head. 'You don't. Or at least, you don't text me from it. You always contact me by Facebook message. What's wrong with your phone?'

'Nothing.' She huffs out through her nose. 'I just always run out of texts.'

'How? Haven't you got unlimited?'

'No, Dozy, it's impossible to run out of anything if it's unlimited. I only have a thousand a month.'

'A *thousand*?! How the hell do you run out then?'

She rolls her eyes. 'I use them all. Foam-head.'

'Oh, well thanks for clearing up my confusion. Except, oh, wait. I'm still confused. You always use Facebook. So how do you use them up if you don't use them?'

She studies me a moment. 'I used to use them all up texting Sean. OK? Now enough about that stupid boring stuff, please? I wish it had never happened and the sooner we can all forget about it, the happier I'll be. Please?' She raises her eyebrows at me in a pleading expression and my heart tugs with affection.

'I love you, Abs,' I say spontaneously.

Her expression changes instantly from sad and pleading to warm, wide grin. 'I love you too, Daisy Duck.' She wraps her arms round me and we hug each other tightly. Then she draws back, looks me in the eye and says, 'Get your top off.'

It's starting to warm up slightly in the tent so once we're down to our bras and have tied our tee shirts and hoodies round our waists, I actually feel OK. Better than OK, in fact. All around us are hundreds upon hundreds of people of all different shapes, sizes and colours, in nothing but bras. Tall women with tiny boobs; short women with huge ones; fat women with wobbly ones; skinny women with non-existent ones. Even a few men with tissue paper ones, sparkly bras on over hairy chests. We all grin at each other as we mill around, feeling united in our chilly embarrassment, and therefore not embarrassed at all. This is the strongest feeling of sisterhood I've ever known; a feeling of belonging, of communion with these other women, an intimacy and understanding that almost borders on actual love for them. If someone told me now to throw my arms around the next random person I meet and give them a giant hug, I wouldn't find it difficult. In fact, I would struggle to limit myself to just one. I want

442

to fling my arms around everyone in this tent and hold them tightly with my eyes closed. I want to stand on a podium and give a rousing speech about comradeship and solidarity and girl power, and finish talking with a giant fist pump while the audience starts cheering before I've quite got to the end. We are in this together; we will experience this and endure this and enjoy this together. We will triumph. Together.

'Toilet,' Abby says suddenly, and marches off.

And this moment, right here, in this fantastic inspiring place, surrounded by people willing to put themselves through quite an ordeal to stop more women going through what Mum did, is the right moment to read the letter that she left me. I have been waiting for a good time to read it because I know it will defeat me, so I've been carrying it around with me everywhere for the past week, hoping the perfect moment will arise at some point. It's been in my bum bag since this afternoon, before we left. Right now, I could ride a tsunami; fight a bear; brave an inferno; lift a car. I doubt very much I'll ever feel stronger, so I unzip my bum bag and pull the envelope out. There's my name in Mum's distorted writing, but instead of just staring at that as I have done since Naomi gave it to me, this time I turn it over, open it and pull out the letter inside. My throat clenches instantly and starts aching when I see more of Mum's handwriting, spidery and scruffy like on the envelope. I can see the effort it cost her to write this, and I have to close my eyes for a moment before I start reading.

My darling darling darling girl,
I'm so incredibly proud of you, my Daisy
Duck.

Immediately I have to stop again as everything in front of me goes blurry. I look around me at the heaving crowds and spot an area just behind me against a pillar where I can sit down. It's not far from where I'm standing so Abby should easily find me when she comes back. I untie my hoodie from my waist and bundle it up to make a cushion then sit down on it. A few more deep breaths, a couple of painful swallows, then I resume reading.

I hope you know that. You're mature and strong and independent and so much like me when I was your age. I couldn't have hoped for a better daughter. Don't you ever change, my beautiful angel.
There's something I've wanted to say to you for years now, but I've never had the strength. Or maybe it's not strength I needed. Maybe I've just been too scared to talk about it because it hurt me so much and I can't bear to go through even a small part of that pain again. But that was very wrong of me, my darling. I've seen you in pain too, I've seen you torturing yourself and I've done nothing to help you. I'm so very sorry, Daisy. When you ran away to Brighton all those years ago, I wasn't sure I

444

could carry on living. I was terrified, sad, upset, hurt, worried, anxious, unhappy. Everything I'm sure you've imagined I was feeling. I missed you so intensely, every day, every second. I hated not knowing where you were or what was happening to you. It was such an overwhelming feeling, nothing else in my life seemed to matter for that short period. I'm not blaming you, angel. You were sixteen, you were an idiot, it's expected. Especially you, with your independence and strong will. But when you came back and I was already ill, I was distracted by that and I didn't speak to you properly about it. It's my biggest regret, and I'm writing this because I think I only have a few days left and I don't want to bring this all up again now. This way, it will be afterwards, a few months afterwards, and hopefully you will be getting used to things and getting better.

What I neglected to tell you back then, darling girl, is that I forgive you. No, that sounds pathetic and doesn't even begin to convey what I feel. But I need you to know that I forgave you back then, as soon as I knew you were safe. In fact, I wasn't ever angry, not really. I knew you had a free spirit, I wanted more for you than what you could find here, so I had been expecting you to fly away sooner or later.

445

All right, maybe not when you were fifteen, but still!

I know you felt terrible when you came back and saw me like that, and that you blamed yourself for some reason because you weren't here when it all started.

I have to stop again and raise my head. Through the blur I see Abby, some distance away, her back to me, watching the crowds and the various activities going on. What an amazing and wonderful person she is. I experience a strong feeling of love and belonging when I look at her, a sensation I haven't really felt properly since Mum died. But here is my family now. I wipe my eyes to clear them and go back to reading.

Graham was certainly angry with you for not being here. I think he felt that your absence made the whole thing worse for me. I can't deny that I wished you were there with me. But at the same time I was glad, in some ways, that you weren't, that you weren't dragged down with me, that you were out there somewhere, living your life, happy. At least, that's what I thought.

But when you came back, my beautiful girl, that was when the sun came out again for me. That was when everything looked up and I finally began to feel whole again. That was when I really started out on the road to recovery. It was having my whole family round me, feeling the love that I have for you all, so deeply, that helped me get well, and gave me these extra years with you, and for that I am grateful.

So that's what I wanted to say, sweetheart. You and Naomi have been and will always be everything to me and I will miss you more than you can possibly imagine. But it gives me comfort to know you will benefit in a small way from this. I'm leaving everything to Graham to make things easier for him after I've gone, but don't worry, I know he loves you and will make sure you get your inheritance. You and Nomes will be quite comfortable for the rest of your lives. It's reassuring to know that.

It's hard for you now, sweetheart. I know that. And I know you are going to bear the brunt of looking after him in the coming months. I am so grateful to you, my darling. You are the strong one, remember. You are the selfless one. Be strong for me now, gorgeous girl. You will always be my inspiration.

I love you, love you, love you.

Mum xxx

A few people stop and ask if I'm OK as they pass, but I can't answer. I just nod through my sobs and lay the letter down on the floor beside me. Someone stops and gently presses my shoulder, and when I look up I see that it's Abby. She gets down on the floor beside me and

I wordlessly hand her the letter. She reads it quickly and when she looks back at me I see she has tears in her eyes too.

'Oh wow,' she says breathily. 'That's lovely.'

I nod and smile a little through my tears, then Abby leans forward and embraces me again and we sit and hold each other and cry together, in the middle of a Big Pink Tent.

After a few minutes, she pulls back from me and holds up the letter. 'I love the bit where she says he was angry with you for not being there.' She shakes her head as she says those last words. 'Makes it sound so . . . inconsequential.'

'I know. I guess she didn't really know just how much it affected him.'

'And she certainly didn't know he would do what he did. With the will and everything.'

'No. And I'm very glad she doesn't know about that. At least she died believing that Naomi and I would be set up for life.'

'Exactly.' She hands me back the letter and I fold it up and put it away. Then we both wipe our eyes and sniff. 'Who needs money,' she says, 'when you've got friends?'

I grin. 'Abso-bleeding-lutely.'

'Tattoo?' she says after a pause.

'You what?'

She points to a long table at the other side of the tent. 'Over there. We can have a tattoo done. What do you think?'

'Um . . .'

448

'Oh, not a real one, dough head. It's a stick-on. Christ alive, can you imagine walking twenty-six miles in the freezing cold with the searing agony of a new tattoo to deal with as well?'

So we queue up and get a stick-on tattoo – mine's a glittery pink bra on my shoulder, Abs has gone for a pair of pink footprints – then we queue up and get our free pasta meal and toffee muffin; and after that we queue up and have a lovely shoulder and back massage, courtesy of all the hundreds of volunteers who aren't walking but who are here to give up their free time too.

Then, suddenly, it's eleven o'clock and things start happening. Music plays and there's an announcement for those with yellow numbers to make their way to the start line. Everyone looks around in awe as yellow-stickered people start to thread their way through the crowd towards the exits and I wonder if I could hide myself among them and start now too. I turn to Abby to suggest it, but she's already solemnly shaking her head.

'What?' I ask her. 'You don't even know what I was going to say!'

She raises her eyebrows in an 'oh really?' expression. 'No, Daisy, we are not going to hide ourselves among these athletes and start now. OK?'

Yet again I'm defeated before I've begun. But it doesn't matter, I'm in a top mood again and nothing can diminish it. Energy is flowing through me, I'm buzzing with it, and I can't stand still. Fortunately at that moment, someone on a stage at the front of the tent announces that we're going to do a short aerobics session to warm up, and I start jumping.

At eleven twenty, the music stops and all the green starters are called to the line. The pinks and oranges step aside reverentially to allow them through; then when they've gone we go back to leaping about and clapping.

At eleven forty the oranges leave us, which is quite frankly a relief as they were starting to get a bit superior. The rest of us, all the pinkies, finally have enough room to perform the aerobics manoeuvres properly.

'Oh my God,' I say to Abby at eleven fifty.

'I know!'

Finally the pinks are called to the line and we all file out silently. We're warm now, but as the freezing night air hits us, everything shrivels.

'Remember to wear your plastic capes,' an announcer is saying. 'It may only be a thin sheet of plastic but it will provide valuable insulation.'

'Where the fuck are the plastic capes?' Abby snaps. I spot someone handing them out at the exit and grab two. As quickly as we can with shaking hands, we unfold them and put them on. Aaah, toasty.

'No fucking difference,' Abby mutters.

'Come on, let's jump up and down.'

There are so many people in the pink group, we have to shuffle along shoulder to shoulder towards the start line. Bouncing up and down as we move is proving effective, and gradually people around us start doing it too. Pink-hatted heads all around us spontaneously start bobbing up and down, like atoms vibrating in a heating liquid. It's a Mexican Bounce.

At eleven fifty-eight, my phone beeps with a text. It's from Felix.

Good luck Queen Daisy of the ducks. Remember: left, then right, then, and this is crucial, left again. Stick with that and you can't go wrong. Don't worry, you'll get the hang of it. I will be with you in spirit and I will see you for a foot massage tomorrow. Very much love, your Felix xxxx

I giggle and it buoys me up as our pink herd amasses by the gates. My phone beeps again.

PS Please avoid touching between my toes; I can't bear it. ☺ xxxx

'Who's that?' Abby asks.
'Felix.'
She smiles. 'He's coming after all?'
'I don't know, he won't say.'
'That means he is. Lend me your phone, will you?'
I hand it to her. 'Why do you still need it, now you're not texting Sean any more?'
She shrugs and grins at me. 'Used mine up texting Tom.'
I gape. 'A thousand texts?'
'Yeah.' She shrugs exaggeratedly. 'What're you gonna do? OK, he's going to meet us at the finish line. He says he'll follow our progress around the streets and will be at mile twenty-six from seven a.m. onwards. We're going

to have to get a wriggle on, Daisy Doo. Otherwise he'll be hanging around in the cold for hours.'

'God, yes. Don't want him turning into an ice man.'

'What?'

'Nothing.'

A giant digital clock above our heads flashes into life with the number 30 on it. Immediately it starts counting down. The crowd chants with it.

29! 28! 27!

'Here's your phone,' Abby says loudly over the chanting.

26! 25! 24!

'Thanks.'

23! 22! 21!

'Daisy, can you tell me something?'

20! 19! 18!

'What?'

17! 16! 15!

'Well, it's a bit odd . . .'

14! 13! 12!

'What is it, Abby?' I'm getting agitated and feel penned in by all these other women. Why are they here? They're just in the way.

11! 10! 9! 8!

'Well, it's something I noticed earlier . . .'

7! 6! 5!

'What?!'

4! 3!

'Why have you got . . .'

2!

'. . . photos of the inside of my shed on your phone?'

1! And we're off!

Air horns sound, whistles blow, a giant cheer goes up and we shuffle through the gate onto the street.

'Let's do this thing!' I shout, and we slap our hands together in a high five.

MILE ONE

'I feel OK. Are you OK? I'm OK!'
  'It's one mile, Daisy.'

MILE FIVE

'So you actually took photos of the inside of the shed to make sure you put the rake back in the right place?'
  Pause. 'Yes.'
  'You put an awful lot of time and effort into avoiding training, didn't you?'
  'I know.'

MILE TEN

'For the love of Lonsdale, will you *please* stop singing, Daisy?'
  'But I feel so fantastic, I want to sing, why would you make me stop, it's not fair.'

'Urrr, because it's awful?'
'Meh.'

MILE FIFTEEN

'Wow, look at that. Orange walkers.'

'What? Where?'

'Right here. Yeah, you snotty lot, acting all superior, like being orange makes you a bit special. Well look who's coming past you! Oh yeah! Eat our dust, ha ha ha ha ha!'

'She doesn't mean it. Sorry, so sorry. Daisy, for crying out loud.'

MILE TWENTY

'What's the matter with you, misery guts?'

'God, I have no idea. Maybe the fact that it's half seven in the morning, I've been walking all night and I've got sore toes has got something to do with it. What do you think?'

'I think you're a grumpy groo and need to spend more time smiling and enjoying yourself. Grumpy groo.'

'Grumpy groo? *Really?*'

MILE TWENTY-TWO

'Tired.'

'Unh.'

MILE TWENTY-THREE

'Second wind?'
  'Nope.'
  'Me neither.'

MILE TWENTY-FOUR

'Wow, look at that sky! Look at it! It's totally amazing, isn't it? Don't you think?'

  'Oh my God yes, yes, it's beautiful, look at those colours, the clouds all pink and orange, reflecting off everything, amazing. Kind of makes you believe in a higher power a little bit, doesn't it?'

MILE TWENTY-FIVE

'You know all the yellow walkers will be at home by now.'
  'Shut up.'

MILE TWENTY-SIX

'Woohoo! We made it! We fucking made it, Abby! We did it! Where's Tom then, where is he, can't believe he's not here and we fucking made it, we did it everyone, we did it!'

  'Um, Daisy, don't forget this is a *full* marathon.'
  'What?'

'OK, now we've actually done it. Bit of an anti-climax this time, thanks for not telling me.'

'Oh get over yourself. We've just walked twenty-six point two miles!'

'Oh my God, we have haven't we? How bloody incredible is that?!'

'It's amazing. I'm so proud of you, Daisy, you worked so hard, you trained every day (eventually), you stomped and trudged and meandered and nearly died and finally here we are and we've done it. Bloody hell what a feeling!'

'I'm on top of the world!'

'Shut up, Daisy.'

Someone puts medals over our heads and there's a photographer to capture our grey, dusty, exhaustion for ever. He gives us a card with the website address on it so we can locate our picture and buy it later.

'Oh God, Daze, we *have* to do that, that will be amazing, to have this euphoria, this amazing feeling captured forever in a photo, I gotta have it, don't you think?'

'Sure.' That photo will never see the light of day.

The urge to flop down onto the grass and doze in the sun is almost overwhelming, but all the literature and information we've had over the weeks has stressed repeatedly that, because of the danger of dehydration in the sun, muscle spasm or cramp, and rapid cooling of our bodies, we absolutely must *not* do that. The grass is, naturally, littered with prone bodies, all falling asleep in the sun.

'Don't sit down, ladies,' a voice calls out, approaching

us, and I look up to see that two-timing Tom has appeared, silent and severe as usual . . . No, wait a minute. He's grinning! Abby lights up – if that's possible, she's pretty much already glowing – and Tom jogs towards her, grabs her round the waist and picks her up, spinning her round in the air. 'You did it, you did it, you did it!' he chants happily, while she spreads out her arms and throws her head back, allowing herself complete relaxation in his arms. At exactly the same moment as I realise I'm staring at them, a deep voice says into my ear,

'That's verging on voyeurism, you know.'

I turn to find, to my absolute delight, Felix standing there, hands in pockets, grinning down at me. My exhausted heart makes a valiant effort to thud, in spite of having been hard at it all night, and a smile forms on my dry, cracked lips. 'You came.'

'Well of course I did, you dozy Daisy. Not telling you whether or not I was coming would have been very cruel if the surprise turned out to be that I wasn't.'

'True.'

'And it was very important to me to see what you look like when you look like crap.'

I frown a little. 'What?'

He closes the gap between us and puts his hands on my waist. 'And I'm very pleased but not surprised to see that even after pulling an all-nighter, when you're sweaty, exhausted, dirty, dry and unkempt . . .'

'All right!'

'. . . that you're still wearing that incredibly, breathtakingly, heart-stoppingly beautiful smile.'

458

'Oh . . .'

He brings his face very close to mine and I can feel his warmth surrounding me as his hands move across my back. 'You look happy. I love to see you looking happy.'

And as his arms close around me and he kisses me right there by the finish line, I know that finally, I am.

EPILOGUE

Local man Terence Wilson, 53, of Cleveland Avenue, Westfield, begins a two-year jail sentence today after being convicted of three counts of fraud at Westfield Crown Court.

Wilson, an unemployed father of two, admitted obtaining money by deception, after a two-year long campaign spanning two continents and involving twelve separate victims.

'It's possible there are more victims,' said Inspector Dean of Westfield police outside the court yesterday. 'This man's activities could go back decades and involve quite small sums of money. But it's only those who have lost substantial amounts that have come forward.'

Inspector Dean went on to say that Wilson's profit from the scam, involving the exporting of non-existent cars to Eastern Bloc countries, totalled in the hundreds of thousands of pounds.

'Some of his victims spent their life savings on this apparent "get-rich-quick" scheme,' Inspector Dean said.

'Like all good confidence tricksters, Wilson was very convincing,' Dean went on. 'He seemed to present a genuine idea, with genuine contacts. It wasn't just trusting old ladies who fell for it.'

Russell and Naomi Mann, of Laurel Avenue, who invested an undisclosed sum six months ago, are among the con man's younger victims. The couple first became suspicious when their contact in Belarus did not return any of their calls or emails. Mr Mann was reported as having invested sufficient funds to buy twenty old vehicles, which he was told by Wilson would make a profit of forty to fifty percent on his original investment.

'It's the classic "easy money" inducement,' Inspector Dean commented yesterday. 'All the contacts and details are done for you, all you have to do is put up the money and wait for your returns to come rolling in. It's very tempting. But my advice would be, if it looks too good to be true, it probably is."

Mr and Mrs Mann declined to comment.

Read on for an exclusive extract from Beth's new novel

CHAPTER ONE

There's a text on my husband's phone. It's lying on the counter near the kettle and I just heard it vibrate. He's put it on silent, probably thinking I wouldn't hear it – that's the only reason someone would put their phone on silent, right? – but I still can. It sounds like an automatic gun, our neighbours probably heard it. Pam and Mike next door are no doubt up off their sofa already, frantically dialling three nines before you can say *Crimewatch*.

I look over at the phone but it's face down, probably so that it doesn't light up noticeably when texts or calls arrive. Bit of a pointless precaution if you ask me, given that it sounds like a horse falling downstairs. Maybe it's also a precaution against someone – well, let's be honest, *me* – getting a glimpse of the name of anyone who might call or text.

Eventually the glasses and cutlery stop rattling from the aftershocks and I glance over at hubby to see if he's noticed. Of course he's noticed; the house shifted on its foundations. But he's not going over there to read the message, or even check to see who it's from. Why is that? I'm staring openly at his back now, boring my eyes into him, trying to force some kind of reaction, or acknowledgement at least, that someone somewhere is trying to contact him. But he doesn't move. Or at least, he doesn't alter what he's doing, which is determinedly washing up.

'I think you just got a text,' I say über-casually, then pick up a tea towel and saunter over to the draining board. 'Want me to see who it was?'

He's working on getting a particularly stubborn bit of baked cheese off the side of the lasagne dish and doesn't look up: this job apparently requires full concentration. 'Oh, did I? No, no need,' he says lightly. 'I'll have a look in a minute.'

I nod slowly. 'Oh, OK.'

Adam finishes the dish, carefully rinses the soap off under the cold tap, then places it gently upside down on the draining board. He empties the washing-up bowl, turns it over, wipes its base, then wipes the excess water from the draining board. Finally he turns and walks to where I'm listlessly drying up a wine glass. He's smiling as he reaches out towards me but I don't move. As soon as his fingers touch the tea towel in my hand, they stop approaching and intertwine themselves into the fabric, drying off.

'Great grub, Gracie,' he says, then grins and raises his head to look at me. 'And I'm pleased to announce that the Wife of the Year award goes to . . .' He performs a miniature drum roll with his index fingers on the kitchen side. 'Oh, well, no surprises there, she's been the hot favourite right from the beginning, it's last year's winner, it's Mrs Grace Littleton!' He raises his arms and makes whispery crowd cheering noises in the back of his throat, while glancing around the kitchen at his imaginary audience. I smile at him, charmed by his boyishness as usual, and, for the moment anyway, the mysterious text message goes out of my head.

'Come on,' he says, jerking his head towards the door, 'let's watch the lottery. Did you get the ticket?'

'Yep, it's in my bag.' I retrieve the ticket from my handbag on the kitchen chair and follow him into the living room.

Adam and I have been married just a year – today is our first anniversary actually. We exchanged presents over dinner. One year is paper – I know this because I Googled it a few days ago – so I bought him a book called *Keeping the Magic Alive – How to Get and Give Satisfying Lifelong Sex* by someone called Dr Cristina Markowitz. On the front there was a full-colour photo of a pair of gorgeous naked models pretending to be a satisfied married couple, and the whole thing was wrapped in clingfilm, presumably so that people couldn't sneak into Smith's when they ran into difficulties, read up on a couple of tips, then dash back home again to finish the job. There was a nasty moment when I was paying for it involving Chloe on the till holding the book up in the air and shouting at top volume down the store '*BRYONY!* HOW MUCH IS THE SEX BOOK? BAR CODE WON'T SCAN', but eventually I'd carried it home (in my fingertips, like a hot coal) and wrapped it in cool blue shiny paper, releasing a tense breath once it was finally sheathed. A small part of me half expected the steamy photo on the front to burn through the wrapping paper, like the lost Ark of the Covenant, leaving a naked body-shaped scorch mark on the outside.

I'd grinned as Adam opened it, hoping he'd get the joke. I thought it was absolutely hilarious that someone had written a book about it, and more than that, that somewhere people were actually sitting down and reading it. 'Ooh, look at this one, Steven, do you think we could manage that?' 'Oh I don't know, Barbara, I've got that presentation tomorrow. What else is there?' For crying out loud, people, stop reading books about it and do it!

Adam looked at me quizzically once he'd unwrapped it. 'Wow. Um, you trying to tell me something, Gracie?'

'No, no, of course not, but don't you think it's hysterical? I mean, imagine Steve and Barb in bed together flicking through the pages . . .'

'Who are they?'

I frowned. 'No, no one, just imaginary people, I'm just pretending.'

'Oh right.' He opened the book at a random page and read in silence for a few moments. 'Very interesting,' he concluded, then closed it and laid it on the table. It practically sizzled when it touched the surface. 'Thank you very much.'

I was disappointed. He had completely missed the joke. 'You're welcome.'

If I'm completely honest, I was also hoping he might read it.

My present was a gorgeous bunch of carnations, with guaranteed freshness for seven days. I'd put them in a vase immediately and placed them in the centre of the table. 'Lovely, thank you.'

He'd smiled, pleased with my reaction. 'No problem. Shall we eat?'

We haven't won on the lottery again. I never expect to, and would be happy to stop doing it all together – it seems so greedy when we already have so much – but Adam always wants me to buy a ticket on the way home. 'It's fun,' he says, 'something for us to enjoy together.' I'm completely in favour of that, so I oblige, week after week, stopping in at the newsagents' on the corner of our street on my walk home from town every Friday. Yesterday, it was the man with the funny eye, Larry, behind the counter. There are two men who work there but I don't remember the other dude's name.

'Lottery ticket again, Gracie?' he said, taking it from me. I smiled. Clearly he didn't need me to answer. 'Hope you get lucky.'

'Thanks, Larry,' I said, glad that I knew his name, thankful that it wasn't the other guy. 'I intend to.'

After the lottery results, we watch a cheerful film about a man whose daughter is kidnapped and sold into prostitution, and then we decide to call it a night.

I'm in the kitchen finishing off the clearing up and, as I'm wiping down the tiles behind the sink, I remember suddenly Adam's text from earlier. He hasn't been in here since then so his phone must still be over on the counter by the kettle. I could have a very quick look at the preview, just to find out who it's from. I won't actually open it and read it, I'll literally just look at the name. Of course, the first part of the message will be visible in the preview as well anyway, so it won't matter if I read that bit – anyone could see it as it's on display so it can't be that private, and I won't be able to help it. I glance up at the kitchen door, listen carefully for a few seconds and, hearing nothing, I move quickly over to the kettle and start hunting around. The phone must be here, but I discover straight away that it's not where I remember last seeing it. I look behind the kettle but of course it's not there either. I check the entire length of all three kitchen sides, in the sink, behind the microwave and have a cursory glance into all the cupboards, but it's not to be found. Where the hell is it? Adam has definitely not come back into the kitchen since we left to watch the lottery earlier, so how could it have moved? Have I moved it myself? No, I know I haven't because I wanted to look at it but Adam was there awarding me Wife of the Year, and then we both left together. So how could it . . .?

Unless. A cold dart shoots through me briefly. He did get up once during the film, to go to the loo. 'Ooh, pause it a second,' he said, 'need a wee.' I'd done it, then taken my turn against my friend Ginger on *Words With Friends* on my phone while I waited. I think back now – could he have gone into the kitchen at the same time? He didn't seem to have been gone for a particularly long period of time. But then, to go upstairs to the loo and come down again would not take very long, so the extra four or five seconds it would take him to divert via the kitchen on his way back and seize the phone would not be notice-able. I know he definitely went upstairs because I heard him running up two at a time. I remember thinking, good, he won't be very long. But then I'd taken my turn on the word game, so obviously he had been long enough for me to do that. Bloody hell, that's obviously what he's done. Now I'll never find out who it was from.

When I get upstairs, he's already in the bedroom, but no sound is coming from the room. I remember to step over the penultimate stair to avoid making it creak, then stealthily cross the landing and peep into the bedroom through the crack of the door. Sure enough, there is Adam, standing motionless at the end of the bed, staring down at the screen of his mobile phone, the light from it illuminating his face bluish white. He's not replying, not smiling, not reacting at all to what he's reading. Unless you consider his non-reaction as a reaction in itself. It's spooky actually, his complete lack of response to this message. He's utterly immobile, as if frozen. Then, as I watch, he very slowly lowers the phone hand to his side, raises his head from its bowed position and stares straight ahead, into space.

'Ooh, it's a bit chilly in here,' I say, blustering in. I'm rewarded by him jumping guiltily and slipping the phone fluidly into his trouser pocket as he turns to me with a smile. I feel a small leap of hope: he didn't get a chance to delete the message.

'Come on then,' he says, as if nothing has happened, 'let's get into bed and warm each other up.'

Everyone thinks Adam is out of my league. They don't actually say it – not to me anyway – but I can see it in their eyes when they look at us. Even my own mum, for God's sake. She kind of glances from me to him and back again, then gives a tiny uncomprehending shake of her head before turning away. She thinks I haven't noticed, but of course I have. My sister Lauren fancies him rotten and wouldn't hesitate to betray our sisterly bond if she ever got the chance. I'm not sure I'd even blame her. Adam is tall and handsome and successful and charming and everyone adores him, my family in particular. That's not to say they don't adore *me*. Of course they do. They're always 'Oh Gracie, you're so funny' and 'Isn't Gracie just fantastic?' and 'You look pretty today, Gracie.' But when I first brought Adam home to meet everyone, it was a family bucket of shock and awe all round.

'Hi, everyone,' I said proudly. 'This is Adam.'

They looked up as one from what they were doing – watching *Doctor Who*, I think – and stared open-mouthed at the golden Adonis that had dropped from Mount Olympus to stand at my side. There was a brief hiatus during which the TARDIS materialised noisily, then Mum and my brother Robbie were scrabbling for the remote – 'Pause it, pause it, quick, who's got the thing, who's got the *fucking thing*?' 'I've got it, Christ, stop pressuring me, I'm doing it!' – Lauren was standing up slowly, trying to look like Pussy Galore; and Dad leaned back in his chair with a satisfied grin, as if to say, 'finally'.

Adam was my landlord. Don't worry, no impropriety took place, a tenant dating her landlord; I've Googled it and there's nothing that says it's inappropriate. It's not as if he took advantage of me while I was renting a room in his house or anything hideous like that. No strategic holes in bathroom walls; no cameras planted in my room; no extorting sex for rent money; no sleaze; just a shop on the high street. I'd gone in there a few months earlier to enquire about a flat I'd seen advertised in the local paper. My friend Annabel Price had lived there after having her illicit baby when the rest of us were still in the sixth form, and we all used to pile round after school and pretend to be grown ups, alternately drinking coffee and smoking on the fire escape, and holding the baby; while somewhere in the background Annabel sobbed into her sterilising tank.

I knew that hideous little place, I knew its mouldy walls and its stained carpets and the latent nappy smell and when I saw it advertised I was very excited. I was twenty-four at the time, so it was aeons and aeons since I'd left school, and here was a chance to relive those heady days.

Adam was sitting at the single desk in his tiny office, which was squeezed in between the East of India and the dry cleaners. It had a plate-glass front with his name, 'Adam Littleton', etched onto it in an arc, and underneath it said 'Estate Management'. It was very impressive. It was August and the sun was shining straight through that enormous window, so inside was barbarically hot. As soon as I stepped through the door, my instinct was to run from the fire, but Adam looked at me and smiled, so I stayed. I did want that flat, after all.

'Hi, how can I help?' he asked straight away, standing up and coming around the desk, allowing no chance at all for the potential customer to change their mind and leave.

I scanned the properties displayed on the walls, hoping to see the advert for the flat that had appeared in the paper. 'Um, I saw a flat, in the paper . . .'

'OK. Which paper was it?'

I blinked. I had been expecting him to ask which flat it was. 'I think it was the *Herald*. It was a one-bedroom . . .' But in that very small space of time, like a magician, he'd produced a sheet of paper from somewhere and was holding it out to me to check.

'Is this the one?'

I moved forward and took one end of the paper. He held onto the other end. 'Yes, that's it.' I looked up at him. 'Is it still available?'

He whipped the paper away dramatically, leaving my hand in a grasping position in mid-air. 'You don't want to live there,' he said, theatrically screwing up the sheet of paper and tossing it backwards over his shoulder, 'it's a dump.'

'Oh, well, no, the thing is–'

'Now, I've got something for you that's a lot more suitable,' he said, rubbing his hands together and opening and closing his fingers. 'A much nicer place, coming on in a few days.'

'But I don't–'

'Take it from me, you won't believe your eyes when you see this.' He focused on my eyes for a split second longer than necessary, rubbed his hands together again and flexed his fingers, then delicately reached into his top jacket pocket and pulled out a small, folded piece of paper. It was approximately the size of a postage stamp.

I stared down at it in the palm of his hand, then looked up at him and pressed my lips together. 'I'm sure it's lovely, but I don't think it's big enough for me.'

There was a second's pause, then he burst out laughing, throwing his head back and guffawing fruitily, then

leaning forward and clutching his tummy. It all felt a bit
. . . exaggerated, as if he was trying to give me the
impression that he thought I was hysterically funny, rather
than actually thinking I was hysterically funny.

Eventually he stood up again and wiped his eyes,
puffing out a couple of 'whoo!'s and nodding appreciatively at me. 'Oh my God, that was hilarious!' he
proclaimed. 'You're very funny.'

'Thank you. Um, can I just find out about the– ?'

'So this property is not even being advertised yet,' he
cut in, and began unfolding the sheet in his hand. 'It's
so much more you, if you'll forgive me. Classy, attractive,
modern and stylish. I think you're going to love it.'

He was right, it did look lovely. Obviously very recently
decorated, new bathroom and kitchenette, brand new
carpets everywhere, light, spacious rooms. It was definitely
going to be far more than I could afford. 'There's no price
on here,' I pointed out, searching through the information
sheet. 'How much is the rent?'

'Same as that other place.'

I widened my eyes. 'No way!'

He nodded decisively. 'Totally way.'

I stared down at the photos. 'I don't believe it.' I looked
up at him and found his eyes on me. 'It does look
gorgeous,' I said, holding out the sheet of paper towards
him, 'but it's not really what I'm looking for.'

'In what way?'

He was so abrupt, I was a bit startled. 'Oh, um, only
that it was that flat in the paper, on Hardwick Road,
that I wanted specifically. I like it.'

'But why would you want somewhere shabby like that

when you can have this beautiful new place for the same money?' He actually scratched his head. 'It just doesn't add up.'

'Well, it does for me. So, is it available or not?'

He leaned against the edge of the desk and put his hands down either side. 'Look, um, Miss . . .?'

'Grace. Just call me Grace.'

'OK, Grace. I'm going to make an assumption about you, if you'll allow me. You're planning on moving into this flat on your own, right?'

'Well that's fairly evident, seeing as I'm here on my own.'

'Right. So you'll be living there alone. What will you do if you need to change a fuse? What if the pipes burst? What if the electrics cause a fire? Supposing you need to re-plaster somewhere, or grout something. What will you do?'

I shrugged. 'Isn't all that down to the landlord?'

He smiled smugly. 'Not everything, Grace. Not decorating. Not emergency repairs in the middle of the night. Even if he does take responsibility, he's got to get there, hasn't he? What if you've got water flooding through the ceiling at three a.m., destroying all your belongings, soaking the carpet and the plaster, putting you at risk of a ceiling collapse? What will you do then?'

I shrugged, trying to look much more offhand than I felt. I hadn't really thought about any of that, and was now gripped by panic. But I certainly didn't want him to know it. I'd have to Google what to do later. 'I'll do the simple things myself and get my dad to do the rest. Why?'

He shook his head patronisingly, as if no way in hell was I ever going to cope with anything. 'Wouldn't it just be easier if you got a place that didn't need anything doing to it? So you'd never have to worry about anything or think about anything or pay for anything?'

Fifteen minutes later, we were looking round the new place. Turned out to be his own flat, just above the shop. I wandered around the large cream rooms and compared them mentally to Annabel's woodchip and cramped kitchen. I had to admit, this place was attractive. An hour after first walking into Adam's shop, I'd signed the contract and agreed to meet for dinner the following evening. Adam told me months later that as soon as I'd walked in, he wanted me to rent it. He liked me that much, that quickly.

The next day is Sunday and we have a long lie-in then wander round to the pub for their very reasonable carvery lunch. Larry from the corner shop is in there with his wife so we stop at their table as we walk past.

'Get lucky last night then, Grace?' he asks me, trying to wink. At least, I think that's what he was doing.

I shake my head. 'No such luck.'

'Oh well, never mind. There's always next week.'

'Yeah, you're right. Hope springs eternal!'

'Never give up, never surrender!'

'You can't keep a good man down!'

'There's a light at the end of the tunnel!'

'Follow that rainbow!'

'Yes, thank you,' Adam cut in, and took my arm. 'Seeya Larry.'

When we come out after dinner, it's started raining so we run shrieking back to our house then snuggle up on the sofa to watch a romance about a woman whose husband gets killed so she slaughters everyone responsible.

The text message is on my mind all day. And all the next day, while we're both at work. All week, in fact. Repeatedly I try to get on my own in a room with the phone, but fail because the phone is always, without exception, in Adam's pocket. Then, on Thursday evening, he takes it out of his pocket to answer a call from his mum, and at the end, after clicking it off and closing it down, he distractedly places it on the kitchen table. I freeze. I am electrified, and my eyes immediately zoom in on it lying there as he walks away. It's exposed, vulnerable, and I need to attack. We move around it, preparing the dinner, back and forth across the kitchen, and I'm acutely aware of it the entire time. I can't stop thinking about it. It's permanently in my periphery, the only thing I can see. When will he leave the room? He must need the toilet eventually – surely he will leave it there when he goes? It would look very suss if he goes off upstairs for a wee and stops at the table on the way to pick up his phone. Surely he would want to avoid arousing my suspicion like that?

'Gracie?'

His voice finally breaks through my reverie. 'Hmm? Sorry?'

'Wake up, dolly daydream. I've asked you three times to put the kettle on for the gravy. You're miles away.'

'Oh, sorry, just thinking about Dad. You know his

birthday is coming up. I've got no idea what to get him. What do you think?'

'Oh, I don't know, you're good at that kind of thing, I'll leave it to you.' He turns away. 'Just popping to the loo.'

I nod, watching in horror as he moves back towards the table. 'Um, do you want a drink, Ad? How about a beer?'

He stops, turns back, looks at me. I hold my breath. 'Yeah, OK, thanks.' He turns back to the table and takes the final two steps to get there, then scoops up the phone and without breaking stride slips it into his pocket. Then he's through the door and on his way upstairs.

Friday night comes around again and I'm home first, as usual. We've already agreed we're having Chinese tonight, so I've got no dinner preparations to make. The house is stifling, so the first thing I do is unlock the sliding back door and push it open. It makes no difference; the gentle breeze on the street hasn't made it to our enclosed garden, and the heat and I move around the yard sluggishly in oppressive waves. I head back inside to wash up the breakfast things, straighten the cushions on the sofa, twitch the curtains. I know I'm just killing time, but I have literally nothing to do and I can't relax.

'You need some hobbies,' Mum is always saying. 'Why don't you take up knitting?'

Yeah, I know what that means. There's absolutely no way I'm having a baby yet. Not with Adam, anyway.

I stop, midway through a pointless wander across the hallway. What the bloody hell does that mean, 'not with Adam'? Who the fuck else will I have a baby with? He's my husband, isn't he? I know I definitely want kids some day, so what am I actually thinking? That when the time is right, I'll go off and do it with someone else? Of course not.

I resume my pointless wandering and push that thought out of my mind. Or at least far, far to the back where I can't really see it. Maybe I'll get it out and examine it properly one day.

When the phone rings in the living room a few minutes later, I'm standing in the kitchen staring into the fridge for some reason. I slam it shut and move swiftly to the living room, grateful to have a purpose at last. Just as my hand reaches out to grab the receiver, I hesitate. It'll only be PPI people after all; they're the only people who ring the landline any more. Well, pseudo-people. No actual fingers press actual keys.

The answer phone clicks on and plays its message, and after the beep I wait to hear the usual spooky silence of the PPI computer waiting to see if anyone is there and then giving up and going down the pub. But instead I'm shocked to hear the sound of a man's deep voice coming into my living room from the speaker.

'Hello *Adam*, it's *Leon*. Long time no see. Betcha didn't expect to hear from me again! Just thought I'd give you a call, let you know I'm in the area. Would be great to catch up with you soon, mate. Don't worry about calling me back, I'll be in touch. See you soon.'

The phone clicks as *Leon* replaces the receiver, and the room falls silent. In my mind I could hear the italics in his voice as he said those two names, as if just in saying them he was trying to make some kind of point. But what point could he possibly be making? And why? And, by the way, who the fuck is *Leon*? We've been married a year, how come *Adam* has never mentioned him to me before? I know everything about him, all his friends, all his old jobs, where he used to live, everything.

Ha ha ha. That's just me being sarcastic with myself. I, of course, know none of those things. A creepy phone call from a weirdo called *Leon* is not remotely surprising, considering what I do know about Adam.

I don't have any more time to consider it now as I hear Adam's car on the drive. He's home. I walk away from the phone and go into the hall to greet him, as I always do.

'Hi there,' he says as he sees me. 'Good day?'

I nod. 'Yeah, not bad. You?'

He nods too. 'Yeah, good.' He starts up the stairs and I follow behind. 'Finally sorted out that three-bed semi in Whitlow.'

'Oh good.'

'Yep. The owner can't believe it. He thinks I'm God!' He starts to change his clothes.

I sit down on the bed and watch as he folds his dirty shirt in half, then in half again, then places it carefully into the laundry basket behind the door.

'Wakey wakey!' he says, as he straightens the creases in his trousers before hanging them up.

I smile. 'Oh, sorry, just zoned out a minute.'

'Everything all right, Gracie?'

I nod, quickly. 'Oh, yes, yes, fine. Just . . .'

He stops what he's doing. 'Just what?'

'No, nothing, just there was a call for you.'

'Oh yeah?' He's dressed again now and heads back downstairs. Dutifully, I walk behind. 'Chinese or Indian?'

'Neither, actually. He sounded English, I think. Possibly London or Essex . . .'

I come into the kitchen where he's standing with the East of India's menu in one hand and the Moon Hung Lo's in the other. 'What?'

'Oh, sorry, I thought you meant . . . Um, we haven't had Chinese for a while, have we?'

He bounces the menus up and down in his hands as he looks at me with a smile. 'No, that's true, but I'm really in the mood for a good curry tonight. What do you think?'

What I *think* is that we haven't had Chinese for a while, and actually I would run through our street singing 'Don't Stop Me Now' wearing nothing but a splash of perfume and two gold tassels for the chance to eat sweet and sour chicken balls, just once. But I nod and smile nauseatingly. I despise myself sometimes. 'OK, yes, curry would be lovely.'

'Cool.' He puts the menu down on the kitchen counter and brings his phone out of his pocket. As always, I feel a stab of . . . *something* when I see it. He scans the menu, looking for the restaurant's phone number. 'Did you say there was a call for me?'

'Oh, yes, there was. Someone called . . . *Leon* . . .'

His head snaps up, the hand holding his phone frozen in mid-air. 'Who?'

I'm staring at him. His usual air of ease and nonchalance is gone abruptly, replaced by an intense stark alarm. 'What's up?'

'Who did you say called?'

I frown, hesitating before speaking to let him know I'm not pleased with how he's behaving. If I'm brutally honest, I also do it to torture him, just a teensy bit. 'It was Leon.'

He brings his face closer to mine. 'What did he say?' He's speaking slowly, his hands still not moving.

'Um, well he said something about being in the area–'

'Shit.'

'–and that he would see you soon.'

'Shit shit shitting fucking bollocks. Anything else?'

By now, the phone is back in his pocket and the take-away menu all but forgotten. My stomach notices this and gives a loud growl in protest.

'You can hear for yourself – it's on the answer phone.'

Adam bursts into life, turning and marching rapidly into the living room. Seconds later I hear the answer phone message playing, that deep gravelly voice filling our cosy living space like a poisonous gas. When it reaches the click at the end, there's the sound of a small movement, then the beep and the voice comes on again. 'Hello *Adam* . . .' At the end, Adam plays it a third time, and then a fourth, until my head is filled with that horrible raspy voice, pointedly saying my husband's name, over and over.

For what seems like an age, there's nothing but stillness and silence from the living room. Eventually I walk quietly into the hallway and look through the door. Adam is standing by the phone, arms hung loosely at his sides, head bowed. Neither of us moves.

Suddenly, Adam sucks in a deep breath over his teeth and darts into life. He spins on the spot and finds me standing there, but barely registers me. His eyes flick once to mine, there's the briefest smile, then he's striding past me up the stairs.

'Who's Leon then?' I ask pointlessly, running after him. He strides into our bedroom, but before I can catch him up, he's out again, passing me on the stairs as he runs back down.

'Oh, no one. Just someone I . . . used to work with. Years ago.'

'Oh, right. So why are you so pissed off?'

He stops in the hallway and turns to face me. I'm standing on the bottom stair still, so for once we're about the same height. He puts his hand out and gently touches my cheek. 'I'm not pissed off, Grace. Not really. I don't like the bloke, we fell out at school and I wasn't expecting ever to hear from him again. That's all.'

'I thought you said you used to work with him?'

He puts his arm back down and puts his hand into his pocket. 'Yeah, that's right, I did, we worked together for a while after we left school, but we didn't really have much to do with each other.' The hand in his pocket reappears holding the car keys, and he jingles them a bit, distractedly. 'He's a bit of a prick, to be honest.'

'Oh.'

'Yeah. World-class knobhead.' He looks at his watch then back at me, and smiles fondly. 'OK, well, I'm off to get the food.' He leans towards me, one hand round the back of my neck, and kisses me. As we break apart, he stays close, his thumb gently stroking my neck. 'Don't worry about him, Gracie. He's nothing.'

I nod. 'OK.'

He stares into my eyes for a few moments, kisses me again, then draws away and moves to the door. 'Warm the plates up, sweetheart, I'll be back in a few minutes.'

He wasn't.